THE TRIALS OF ASHMOUNT

TRAGEDY OF CEDAIN BOOK ONE

JOHN PALLADINO

THE TRIALS OF
ASHMOUNT

For Mom, without whom, this book wouldn't have been possible. Thank you for the unending support and love . . . and for putting up with me.

And for Dad, although you won't ever be able to read this, you always wanted to publish a book. Unfortunately, dementia got the best of you. You won't be forgotten.

CE
C
CYROK
The Frosted Spires
Vox
Coldridge
Timberglade
Aleki
Gyrloft
Bryn
Zemur
Anepolis
Pinecrest
Lochwall
CALRYM
Largos
Valkrynd Mountains
Kelm
Ilidros
VESSIA
Argoa
Hathoran
Valakur

AIN
Maceport
Andora
Bario
ERIA
ester
Rivane
Argate
Qelt
Warwin
OOTHE
Yordiv
Ashmount
The Ashwood
Sultiva
N
W
E
S

PEOPLE WHO MAY DIE

Alondo Sedoa – King of Remeria.

Alyst Garcovi – Nephew of King Mikas.

Anditus Roberon – Old friend of Hillion Stoole's.

Angazo Giresh – Friend of the Wintlock family.

Archmagicus – Head Magicus of Ashmount.

Arena Hyrel – Duchess under and adviser for King Mikas Garcovi.

Ashté – Magicus and Healer in Vox.

Atticus Crenshaw – King Alondo Sedoa's adviser.

Bertrand – King Mikas Garcovi's chancellor.

Blago Adavir – Cyroki captain.

Caius – Loyal friend and ally of Demri Slarn's.

Castede Varono – One of the five House Heads of Buzzard's Bowl.

Chardaine – Barrister working for Roachford and Singleton's, a law office.

The Chell – quintuplet gladiators in
Scayde Haklon's House.

Demri Slarn – Magicus criminal on the run
hunting Doram Quandis.

Doram Quandis – Magicus and Demri
Slarn's target.

Edelbrock Brendis – Minor nobleman
looking to improve his standing in
Lochwall and Jaylena's husband.

Enebrial Hubbart – Long-dead Magicus,
researcher, and author.

Everic Deywin – Lochwall's marshal.

Fezzel Wintlock – Seradal's brother.

Giant/Ko-Hkar – Candidate in
Ashmount's Trials.

Glaouse – Well-traveled Magicus who
meets Demri in Auchester.

Gordane/Gordy Brendis – Jaylena and
Edelbrock's son.

Harlem Maccaro – Jaylena's father and
duke under and adviser for King Mikas
Garcovi.

Hillion Stoole – Kelden's father and a
baker.

Ilic Strictland – Retired Falcon Knight who
volunteers his expertise to train new
soldiers.

Jaidik Wintlock – Seradal's and Fezzel's
father.

Jakci Robinius – Magicus and Enforcer
professor at Ashmount.

Jaylena Brendis – Edelbrock's wife.

Jedkah of the Splintered Manes – Leader of his Camel Clan.

Kalixa Shivalli – Magicus and Glyphist professor at Ashmount.

Kelden Stoole – Hillion's son who believes he's destined for a better life.

Kingston – Easily distracted Falcon Knight.

Lekhan Roelk – One of the five House Heads of Buzzard's Bowl.

Mikas Garcovi - King of Calrym.

Myri Celioh – Student of Ashmount from Demri's past.

Nauc Othepi – Guard in Warwin.

Old Vulture/Vecchio Rizurri – Oldest Falcon Knight.

Ollitha Oxhorn – Prominent Falcon Knight.

Porric – Demri's hired guard.

Renard – A Falcon Knight page.

Royal/Decklin Hoarst – Captain in the Cyroki military.

Savakkis – Head gladiator of the Velvet Mother's House.

Scayde Haklon – Owner of Buzzard's Bowl and wealthy nobleman.

Seradal "Sera" Wintlock – Gyrloft citizen who raises Gyrfalcons.

Sikoi of the Splintered Manes – Villic's friend.

Smugface – Blago Adavir's second-in-command

Speaker/Githandus Felimar Mydenwold – A mysterious and very old being.

Stanton Brick – Agent of the Velvet
    Mother.
Stasia Falconel – Leader of the Falcon
    Knights, and during times of warfare,
    governess of Cyrok.
Sturgeon Gothal – Duke under and adviser
    for King Mikas Garcovi.
Sungoa – Kelden's friend.
Tanibris – Head servant of Scayde Haklon.
Tikmo – Vessian student at Ashmount.
Trigg Gelbrandy – One of the five House
    Heads of Buzzard's Bowl and Edel-
    brock's lover.
Velturo Ondakka – Duke under and
    adviser for King Mikas Garcovi.
Velvet Mother –Mysterious and powerful
    figure. One of the five House Heads of
    Buzzard's Bowl.
Villic of the Splintered Manes – A nomadic
    warrior in the Camel Clans.
Vithor Bane – Prolific and gross busi-
    nessman.
Yudri Wintlock – Seradal's and Fezzel's
    mother.

ELIZER CORBÉO

Five Years Ago
Andora, Remeria

He pissed himself. Warm urine dribbled down his thighs. A familiar sensation, reminiscent of childhood memories. He tried to ignore the uncomfortable feeling. It was an embarrassing mess for a thirty-year-old.

He'd never felt this afraid in his entire life. Prickled skin, sweaty palms, and now sticky clothing. His knees wobbled as he crouched, quaking in the claustrophobic closet. Elizer Corbéo was trying his damnedest not to knock anything over. To his right, a precarious broom perched against the wall. He was afraid he'd bump it, causing enough noise to alert the intruders. On his left, an assortment of pickled goods was stacked on and below wooden shelving. In glass jars. Touching any of those could be disastrous. With the need to urinate gone, Corbéo found it much easier to prevent himself from moving.

Mother Avani, save me. He wasn't a pious man, but in

that moment, he hoped divine intervention would save him.

Corbéo had further problems developing—the closet was near a fireplace, and the innkeeper had built up the fire moments before the intruders arrived. Corbéo wiped his dripping forehead with the back of his hand. He kept his mind focused on the surrounding disasters within the small interior. He peered through a crack between the ancient wooden sheet—if one could call it a door—and the left side of the wall, his eyes passing over a pile of murdered people. Corbéo's neck ached from the constant shifting necessary to observe the room. The fingers on his left hand were numb, yet he still rested his hand on the door's hinge, an action to prevent himself from tipping over.

Drunkard's Haven, on a normal day, was an obnoxious place to be. The tavern's innkeeper was a nice enough fellow and offered Corbéo free meals whenever he played his music or sang, or both, to the patrons. The kindness of the staff was another positive. However, most of the guests were often loud and annoying, probably because a bulk of them were manual laborers and entered late in the afternoon, exhausted. Now, most of them lay in pools of blood.

Corbéo remembered when Charity Bang visited him in his rooms, offering a free lay because he attracted extra business for her and the other prostitutes. She was, as her name implied, often the one to take extra care of those who helped the inn out. From his position, he could still see her prone body. She hadn't moved in many minutes. *Pretending to be dead, I hope.* He didn't believe it though. It was a rare person who survived swimming in a lake of their own blood. And he thought he'd spotted some guts, but he'd stopped looking at her. Retching would only give away his location.

Pacing back and forth across the room was the first of two late-night invaders. Thin, cloaked, and walking with a limp, the man had murdered close to twenty people. His only other identifiable trait was his stutter. Corbéo didn't know anybody with a stutter, so the man was not a local, or if he was, he wasn't a frequenter of Drunkard's Haven. He wore a loose cloak with the hood up, and it was impossible to tell anything else about him.

The second man—a fellow Calrite judging by his beige complexion—involved in this horrendous event was bulky with thick arms and legs and didn't care if anybody recognized him. He sat in a chair to the left of the closet, almost out of view, leaning back on two of its legs with his muddy boots resting atop the oak table and crushing somebody's half-finished meal. Thin Man called him Caius. He was filing his fingernails with a knife that was dripping blood. Corbéo couldn't tell if the blood was from Caius's fingers or one of the two armed guards he'd killed. The rest of the civilians, all unarmed, Thin Man had dealt with. One at a time. Interrogating them before using his powers to kill them.

Other than Corbéo and the intruders, only one other person was still alive—the innkeeper. He was kneeling in the middle of the tavern, hands bound behind his back and tethered to his legs. He was weeping and putting up a sorry fight, not that Corbéo could blame him, but he was sure that wasn't the right strategy in this situation. When two men waltzed into a tavern full of people and dispatched them without a thought, sobbing would not help.

Thin Man stopped his pacing behind the innkeeper. The bound man tensed, shuddering and whimpering.

"W-w-where is he?" Thin Man's voice was a low dull growl. The authority he wielded was frightening.

Any other time, a stutter would've caused Corbéo a smirk of self-satisfied understanding that he was better than them. Not here, though. And if Corbéo came out of this alive, likely never again.

The innkeeper didn't answer. He shook and cried. Thin Man reiterated the question, stammering through the *W* again. The purpose of his visit was to locate somebody. Corbéo couldn't remember the name; it wasn't him, so he didn't care.

He couldn't help but admire Thin Man. He was impressive. To possess such talent and power over everyone while stuttering was awe-inspiring. Often, something as small as a misplaced freckle could reduce one's ability for others to accept them. A stutter? Unquestionable. And yet, Thin Man did it. Corbéo could only dream to have that sort of influence over others. Thin Man's mere presence was *terrifying*.

"I don't know who you're referring to! You've already killed everybody in here. Please let me live." Tears threatened to flood the innkeeper's cheeks once more.

"I was told that D-D-Doram Quandis was here. Give me his location now, and I will spare what insignificant life you have left." Thin Man walked around the front of the innkeeper. He dragged a chair over and sat in full view of the prisoner. "He's a tall, tanned man and has a small p-paunch. Might have an alias. He's obviously a c-coward, too, or he wouldn't have left these p-p-p-people to die."

Corbéo blanched. The description fit him well, but he wasn't using an alias, nor did he know who Doram Quandis was. He hoped the innkeeper had not noticed where Corbéo hid during the initial attack, or Corbéo assumed he'd inform Thin Man. Corbéo would give anyone up to save his own skin. He didn't want to die.

Thin Man reached over and used a finger to lift the innkeeper's face by the chin. Corbéo didn't see what happened next because Thin Man's body shifted in the way, but the innkeeper screamed in agony. When Thin Man moved, the innkeeper's body slumped over, his empty eyes staring in Corbéo's direction. Smoke rose from the innkeeper's chest, and a bloody mass extended from his body, ribs poking out. It was as though he exploded from the inside.

Somebody passed by the crack. Corbéo stiffened, hand falling from the hinge, and he held his breath. The closet door was wrenched open in a violent crash, hinges pulling away from the wood, splinters shooting into the air. Corbéo would've pissed himself if he had any left.

In front of him stood Caius, a toothy grin on his face. "Well, hello there, little weasel!

Fuck. Corbéo hadn't been paying attention to him. He'd become distracted by the terror caused by Thin Man.

"Why don't you come out and play with the adults?" He reached into the closet and extracted Corbéo by the collar. His flailing arms knocked over a stack of the glass jars, breaking them into shards that rebounded off the back of his booted ankles.

"W-w-well, well, well. Looks like we f-f-found you, Magicus."

A Magicus? Me? The thought escaped him just as fast as it formed because Caius threw him to the ground. Corbéo broke his fall with his elbow. Excruciating pain reverberated up his forearm, and tears gathered in his eyes. Things were only going to become worse.

"We've been traveling all over Cedain looking for you, squirt." Caius loomed above him, filing his nails again with the bloody knife.

"I don't understand who you are or why you think I'm who you're looking for. If you let me go, I have money, I come from a family of—" Corbéo stopped himself. He knew it didn't matter. They weren't looking for money.

"It's been so long, he doesn't recognize me, C-C-Caius." Thin Man limped forward, lowering his hood. Half his face was a marred, burned mess, the other half reminiscent of a Remerian, slightly tanner than a Calrite. "Yes, you remember now, d-d-don't you? *You* crippled me. And *you* will pay d-dearly."

"I don't know who you are! Leave me alone." Corbéo let the tears fall. The end was near.

Caius laughed. "Sorry, Doram. My friend's been waiting for this moment for fifteen years. This ain't gonna be fast."

Corbéo took another look at Caius. *Something's familiar about his face.*

"D-d-despite the lengthy period in which we have tracked you down and the extent of my physical ch-changes." Thin Man gestured at his scarred face and then his bent legs before returning to gaze at Corbéo with disgust and hatred. "I think you enjoyed this m-m-m-much more when our roles were reversed."

Corbéo had no clue what he was talking about. "You have the wrong person." Tears continued streaming down his face, dripping onto the wooden boards, mixing with the blood he'd scrambled into. He looked away and saw it. Leaning against the tavern bar counter was his lute.

Thin Man followed his gaze. "You're masquerading as a fucking b-b-bard?"

Caius retrieved the lute. "Not poor quality, though I'd expect somebody with your reputation to purchase something less beggarly."

That was the intention of purchasing this particular lute. His family used to be an important noble faction in Calrym, but then they lost favor. If any of their political rivals found him wandering the countryside, he'd make a great hostage. Not that purchasing an average-looking lute had helped him avoid that fate. His attempts at blending in had failed. And the Corbéo family wouldn't have been able to pay much for him. They had fallen from grace in recent times, struggling to remain relevant.

"Enough p-p-playing." Thin Man's eyes narrowed.

Corbéo's fear escalated. Things would become serious, fast. "Guards!" It was his only hope. A last chance at salvation. The gamble somebody outside was investigating and would hear him.

Thin Man and Caius laughed. He supposed he would too, in their situation. Instead, he sobbed, wishing that he could just retreat to his family. Back to the wealth he'd originated from.

Whistling, Caius strode to them, swinging the lute around the tavern like a walking stick. He looked down at Corbéo and took a deep breath, a hint of recognition flashing in his eyes, followed by surprise.

"Please," Corbéo said, raising his hands. "Don't do this."

The expression disappeared, and Caius lifted the lute above his shoulders, like a mallet. "Judging by the stories I've heard, you're quite the coward." Corbéo thought that was obvious. Then again, they weren't actually talking about Corbéo. "Too bad your friends are all dead. No help for you now." Caius brought the lute down.

Realization dawned for Corbéo on who the man was, then the lute smashed on his face. Stars blotched his vision and his face slammed onto the tavern's floor, skidding through somebody else's blood. The taste of salt on his tongue. He had no clue if it was his or any of the other victims'. His head pulsed, like dozens of explosions in his forehead. He yelled out in pain or terror, likely both. Or perhaps he didn't yell and only imagined it.

Snap. Corbéo screamed again as a boot ground into his hand, breaking digits in multiple places. A stabbing pain pressed into his waist—the knife Caius carried? Then the boot crunched down on his hand again, breaking even more bones and stirring around those that were already broken. He screamed, cried, and passed out for a moment. Consciousness returned. Was that fortunate or unfortunate?

"Careful, C-C-Caius. Don't kill him yet."

Corbéo whimpered, eyes closed tight. He shook, both in pain and in fear. He didn't want to be here anymore. *Why didn't I remain in Lochwall?*

"This was a simple task, considering his skill," Caius said.

"Sometimes you're j-j-just lucky."

Corbéo took a breath then another. He cracked his eyelids open. Stars swam in his vision, and he groaned. He looked at Caius. "I know you."

Caius knelt. "No. No, you don't." He pried open Corbéo's mouth and pulled his tongue out.

A single slice later, and Corbéo's mouth filled with blood. He screamed, then choked on blood. Caius tossed the muscle onto the tavern's floor.

Corbéo moaned, then tried to speak. "Phese, phese." He couldn't form words, his mouth full of blood. He coughed. Swallowing without a tongue was unpleasant.

"I've waited t-too long for this." Thin Man knelt beside him. "Stab him there, C-C-Caius." Thin Man pointed at Corbéo's shoulder.

Caius complied, plunging the knife deep into his flesh.

"And there." Thin Man pointed at Corbéo's thigh.

The knife bit into his leg. He screamed. Again and again. He wanted it to end. His hearing went away, his pain and yelling muting his surroundings between the different areas Caius punctured with the tip of his knife. Thin Man's laugh sometimes penetrated Corbéo's deafness.

And then, after what felt like forever, Thin Man spoke. "Let's finish this."

Thin Man opened his hand, palm facing Corbéo's chest. Bones cracked and agony exploded inside his body. A bright light took over his vision, though he'd closed his eyes. Another snap, a gigantic pain in his chest. Death washed over him.

EDELBROCK BRENDIS

1st Cycle of Autumn, 231st Reign of Garcovi
Lochwall, Calrym

The resplendent mirror rested inside a solid gold frame with plenty of embedded colorful jewels imported from foreign countries. There was a high relief of an exuberant lion chasing a spectacular doe, glass splitting them forever apart. Pretending to admire his reflection, Edelbrock Brendis put on maroon silk robes, covering his overweight naked body. He wiped away drying sweat from his graying goatee, cleared his throat, and took a long swig of chilled water from a brass pitcher. He glanced at the mirror and saw Trigg Gelbrandy lounging on rumpled satin sheets. Trigg was an important noble, one of five people in possession of a deed to one-fifth of Lord Scayde Haklon's gladiator arena, Buzzard's Bowl.

Trigg smiled, yellowing teeth shining through his thick bushy black beard, playing with Edelbrock's sanity. To Edelbrock's dismay, he hadn't found a single gray hair on Trigg's head. He'd thoroughly investigated earlier, under the pretense of gazing at the man's lips, just before planting his own on them. Distractions. That's what it took to keep Trigg Gelbrandy happy.

Trigg rolled over on the bed, spent cock flopping to one side like a wet sock. "You don't have to leave just yet." The high-pitched voice irritated Edelbrock, and the shock that it emanated from the muscular fellow would never disappear. This begging had become a routine during the more recent visits. Trigg was getting attached.

Edelbrock cleared his throat again. There was still some Trigg in it. "Now, now." He turned around and noticed a splotch on his newly purchased robes. He sighed. Whether it was grease from food they'd consumed earlier in the evening or more Trigg, the stain would likely not come out.

He took a moment to unclench his jaw and smooth out his face, putting on a mere grimace in place of his utter horror and frustration. He'd purchased the robes to appear much wealthier than he was, and it cost him. There'd be no way to pawn them off now. It was worse than that. He'd spent extra, requesting custom-made pockets inside the robes where he could hide various parchments and other necessities. Inside the sleeve of his right arm, he held a more nefarious device. If his wife ever found out how much he spent on the robes, she'd kill him. She'd kill him for being here with Trigg. Adultery was not something he expected her to brush off.

It'll all be worth it soon. He couldn't wait to rid himself of the nuisance. Trigg was becoming too clingy, too needy. And like most nobility, he complained about things Edelbrock only hoped would happen to him.

"You know I risk staying, especially this late." Edelbrock dropped his arms to his sides. His right hand retracted into the sleeve of the robe, checking to make sure everything was still where it should be. It was.

He scanned the bedroom, grander than it had any right to be. A wooden chair with a plush cushion on the seat sat in front of an expensive writing table made of pine and stained a glorious mahogany. Strewn over the lush, carpeted floor were articles of clothing that created a path from the open closet to the bed—various garments that were each worth far more than Edelbrock made in a cycle. The open window that he always entered and exited to avoid prying eyes from curious people currently allowed a cool breeze to filter through the room.

"Well, don't leave without saying goodbye." Trigg was whining again and shivering. He wrapped himself in a sheet, only covering his chest. His lower half remained visible and shrinking. He patted the bed beside him. He'd want a kiss. They'd been seeing one another for nearly two cycles now, once or twice a week. On a tough week, it could be three. This week was a tough week. "I would like it if we could just get rid of her."

Anytime Trigg brought up Edelbrock's wife, a perfect image of her likeness birthed in his mind. Which reminded him he needed to leave. If she was still awake, she'd be irate. Judging by the hour, it was unlikely she would be. But precautions.

A flash of annoyance must have flickered across his face because Trigg stood. "Is something wrong, Lordy?" A terrible nickname. Edelbrock was a minor nobleman, which didn't come with any perks other than a useless title: baron. It was a significant gift from the king to bestow this upon a simple soldier, thus the "lord." At first, Trigg called him Lord E but that'd evolved into Lordy.

The things I have to deal with just to progress in life. Married to a kook whose father was one of the king's advisers, fucking a moronic man-child, Edelbrock didn't have a guess for what was next in life. He hoped for something successful.

He realized he needed to respond. He shook his head and offered a thin smile. "No. I'm just worried Jaylena will suspect. I've been gone far too long already, and it's not common for me to be out this late. I'm running out of excuses, and 'working late' isn't going to keep . . . working. She suspects I may do something carnal." He cleared his throat again—why? He'd never experienced any difficulty with Trigg before—and wondered if his wife would taste Trigg on his lips. A fear he often went home with. "I must hurry." Edelbrock took a step toward Trigg, left hand extended to pull him in for a hug and kiss farewell. A routine he'd been using to train him.

As predicted, Trigg leaped to his feet and embraced Edelbrock. He whispered into Edelbrock's ear, "One day, we need to make this official, Lordy. Together we could—"

"It's as official as it needs to be, Trigg." The nobleman stiffened in Edelbrock's arm. He knew that would be a crushing blow to Trigg, who had fallen madly in love with Edelbrock, as planned. What an unfortunate problem for Trigg. Edelbrock slipped his right hand back into the sleeve, toying around with the device for a moment. He found the trigger and pulled.

"What was tha—" Trigg slid from Edelbrock's grasp, thumping onto the wooden floor. A small dart stuck out of his upper thigh. Drool slipped from Trigg's mouth, and a fading clarity was fast disappearing in his eyes.

"Sleep well," Edelbrock said. He bent over, removing the poisoned dart from the man's leg. Trigg would die in a matter of minutes, and the charade would finally end. He retrieved the brass pitcher and took another sip of the water, clearing away the taste of Trigg's lips. He wouldn't have to kiss him again.

He crossed the room, stepping on two of Trigg's fingers as he did so, and opened the second drawer down on the writing table. Inside were the two items he needed: an example of Trigg Gelbrandy's handwriting and the official deed listing the Gelbrandy estate as owner of one-fifth of Buzzard's Bowl, a name borrowed from previous gladiators of the arena. Fighters? Gladiators? Edelbrock didn't know what to call them. Didn't really care, truth be told. Somehow, the nobility adopted the name. And instead of giving the arena a grandiose title, they'd accepted the change.

Buzzard's Bowl's popularity spiked in recent times, after Lord Haklon invested significant funds into creating a business focused on the fights. He built five identical buildings and called them Houses, selling deeds to them. The owners could then purchase, buy, and trade warriors during the off-season, and four times a year, they'd make loads of money during the games. Not to mention the fame that came with the spectators cheering for men and women fighting under your name. Edelbrock wanted nothing more than to be one of these five families. He didn't care if his House performed well or not. Either way, he'd have a lot of power and riches. And then he discovered Trigg, and the golden opportunity showed itself.

Edelbrock pulled out the chair in front of the writing table and guided his body onto the inviting cushion. He dipped one of the fine swan quills into a pewter inkwell and left it there for a moment while he grabbed a nearby blank piece of parchment. Then he copied Trigg's handwriting. He used a letter Trigg never finished. Within a few minutes, Edelbrock felt confident he had the various quirks of Trigg's handwriting figured out. Inside one of his pockets he'd paid extra for, Edelbrock retrieved a stamped parchment—notarized by a money-hungry barrister who was apt to do these types of things regularly for anybody willing to cough up exorbitant sums— and drafted a will.

He assigned all property and monetary accounts to Trigg's half-cousin's son, as that was his closest living relative. The Gelbrandy family had been disappearing for quite some time, and with Trigg's death, his surname would extinguish. By leaving everything to Trigg's half-cousin's son, Edelbrock hoped he was establishing a sense of reality, as the next part of the will would be difficult to sell. He scribbled his own name as the beneficiary of the deed to one-fifth of Buzzard's Bowl. He finished off the document by assigning a few random riches to various friends Edelbrock knew about. Relief surged through him, knowing the time he'd spent researching was about to pay off.

Edelbrock slipped the will and the deed back into the second drawer down on the desk. He dried off the quill, replacing it in its spot, and gathered up the drafts he'd used to practice Trigg's writing. Edelbrock hid those inside his robes for fire kindling at his own home. He wouldn't leave any trace of evidence here.

He checked Trigg's body. He wet his finger with his tongue and then wiped off the small circle of blood that had formed when the poisoned dart entered Trigg's thigh. Edelbrock's goal was to make it appear as if the man had dropped dead. He thought it would work well. If he were to be caught, he'd die. Any violent crime

committed in Calrym meant a brusque hanging. A lifetime in prison if you were lucky.

Edelbrock looked at the bed where he'd acted adul-
terous. He had little regret. He didn't exactly like Trigg,
but it was fun to learn new things. Then he made his
way to the open window, grunting to heave his body
over the ledge. He face-planted on the graveled path
that circled the manor. Cursing himself for becoming
fatter as he aged, Edelbrock brushed rocks out of his
skin and pulled up the hood to his robes. He hobbled
toward his home, nursing a skinned knee and not
looking forward to his wife's questions concerning his
whereabouts. If she reported him to her father, he'd be
in a world of trouble.

E delbrock lived in Lochwall, a bustling city, and
thus, even after the moon had reached its peak,
walking home in his dirty robes drew a suspicious eye
or two. The drunks he cared little for. They certainly
didn't have room to judge. The patrolling guards were
his primary concern. Somehow, he didn't run into any
tonight. He kept to side alleys, claustrophobic paths
with buildings on either side, threatening to suffocate
him on his way through. A cool mid-autumn breeze
swept between his legs, and he pulled his robes tighter.
Something about it felt ominous.

He found his modest home not, as he expected, dark
with the quiet of the sleeping, but with several lights
aglow. Because of their financial state—Jaylena had a
habit of overspending because of the lifestyle she came
from—they could only afford rushlights. The mere sight
of the small candles burning actual fat caused immediate distress. Edelbrock recalled a time when they'd

placed half a dozen lanterns around the house. Now? Rushlights. The ominous feeling intensified.

Then his wife screamed, followed by the sound of something smashing. Narrowing his eyes in concern, he opened the door and hurried inside. He slipped his boots off and walked into the kitchen where Jaylena stood in a state of dishevelment, a broken ceramic vase on the floor and blood trickling down her hand. She wore one of her fancy full-length dresses—a memory of riches long since spent—and stood in that stiff, awkward way she often held herself, a result of her noble upbringing.

"Where have you been?" She emphasized each word through gritted teeth. Her matted hair stuck to her in sweaty clumps, and narrowed eyes stared at him over her pointed nose. She carried herself in the typical rigid-backed manner she often did. In fact, he felt much like the mouse a hawk stares down right before it swoops in and claims its prey.

"Securing our future, my darling." *Cheerfulness will fix this.* Then, avoiding the broken vase pieces on the floor, he went to kiss her. One of the king's dukes, her father agreed to let them marry, under but one condition: after they married, he didn't want to deal with them anymore. Edelbrock was never the man's choice for his daughter, but love presided. A dissipating, forgotten love. But if the duke received word Jaylena was unhappy? It would become a larger scandal than their relationship already was, and Edelbrock could find himself on the wrong end of a noose.

She sneered but allowed a peck to grace her cheek. Well enough, he didn't desire kissing her lips so soon after his night with Trigg. It just felt wrong. "I've had enough of these late nights without knowing where you are or what you've been up to, Ed." She paused a moment, seeming to consider something, "I've had half a mind to write to my father." The threat lingered a moment between them.

"Heh. Uh. Well, you don't have to do that, my love." He gave Jaylena a reassuring, though nervous, pat on her shoulder. Truth be told, if Edelbrock had the balls, he would've disposed of his wife similar to Trigg. The problem was that Jaylena's father wouldn't be dense enough to buy it, and Jaylena's proximity to Calrym's king would draw out the anger of the regent. "Now, can we please go to bed before we wake up Gordy? I've had an endless day at work." The fact that his nickname for his son rhymed with Trigg's nickname for Edelbrock wasn't lost on him. But he'd come up with his first. And he worried Jaylena would find it odd if he stopped calling his son by it. *Just being paranoid.*

"I will not!" Her shrill voice echoed throughout the house, and a cry emanated from one of the other rooms. Gordane had woken up. "And now you've woken up the baby!" She stomped out of the kitchen to console their son. If there was one thing that Jaylena did well, it was take care of Gordane. Otherwise, she was turning into more and more of a pain in the ass. Even though she took care of Gordane, something was off there. Had been for days. The first cycle or two of Gordane's life, Jaylena doted on the boy. Now? It seemed more of an obligation. Something was off.

Sighing, Edelbrock swept up the remnants of the vase with a broom. Long ago, they'd employed servants. They'd had money for fun things. Now, he'd borrowed more money than he could pay back in a lifetime. Except his scheme had worked. They'd be rich soon. Gordane stopped crying, which helped Edelbrock's sanity. After ensuring there were no more loose pieces of ceramic on the ground, he walked to their bedroom, discarded his stained robes into a chair, and dumped the rest of his attire on the floor. He collapsed onto their very average bed, naked and exhausted.

The bedroom door flew open, and his wife stood there red-faced. "You dare to sleep now?" she shrieked, stepping in and slamming the door shut. Gordane cried once more.

For the love of Mother Avani. He'd cried out to their god more than enough times to know she wouldn't help with anything small like this.

"You, who dares sleep with another person!"

Edelbrock blinked, confused. Jaylena couldn't know. It was impossible. Nobody followed him, he was sure of it. There was such a certainty in her face that he knew no matter what he said, she would believe that he was an adulterer.

"L-listen, uh, I . . ." Edelbrock might be a smooth talker and great at manipulating people when he planned for it, but surprised? He had no chance.

"I've had enough of your lies, Ed!" Gordane bawled in the background, but it didn't even phase Jaylena. "The marshal will be here soon. I'm over this." She almost sounded remorseful, but her face contorted with restraint, her sharp nose pointed slightly up, as if she were better than he.

It took a moment for Edelbrock to process that. "You what?" His mouth fell open as if he were the local drunk. Images of riches, a bedroom as glorious as Trigg's, a happy Jaylena pregnant with another baby, little Gordane standing at Edelbrock's knee, them sitting in the stands of Buzzard's Bowl, crowds cheering and jeering alike at his men and women who were fighting to their deaths, and his happiness—the power to buy and do whatever he wanted rather than live his simple life. All of it came crashing down around him. Immediate. Irresolute.

"We're having too many difficulties, Ed. We can't keep living like common hoodlums. And I know what you've been doing. With *him*." Her eyes narrowed in disgust.

A knock sounded on their front door. "Lady Brendis? It's Marshal Everic Deywin." A pause. "You all right?"

Edelbrock's face lit on fire. Everything he was conspiring for, everything he'd done—and swallowed—was for her and his son. His family. And this was the thanks he was to receive? "What the fuck did you tell them?"

"Oh, I know all about your schemes, Ed." She wouldn't stop sneering. This information, this gloating, was making her more and more intolerable. "My father wasn't too pleased to find out that you were fucking a man behind my back! Lord Haklon told my father that the only way to beat that behavior out of somebody is to kill them, though I said I didn't think you were actually into men in that way . . . I mean, are you?" She looked at him, expectant and unsure.

"What? No, no!" He was at a loss for words. And the question seemed unnecessary. Who cared if he was? Was he? There weren't any laws against it. Panicked, he didn't know what to do, what to say. She'd caught him. But everything he'd done, he'd done for her. Right? Maybe he'd gotten some pleasure out of it, but not enough for her to get the marshal. This was madness. His life was about to crash down around him. He needed to figure something out.

"Lady Brendis?" The marshal called again. The pounding on the door shook the house. Gordane's cries grew louder.

"You really fucked up, Jay. I had it. Trigg Gelbrandy,

the owner of one of the five stakes of the arena, was in my pocket—"

"And if the rumors are true, he was inside your ass too!" Tears started falling from her eyes. Edelbrock was certain they were not tears of pain, but of anger. "You betrayed me! So I've done what needed to be done, Ed."

"I just secured incredible wealth for us, you ignorant bit—" Their front door burst open with a loud bang. Heavy footsteps thundered into the household.

"Jaylena! Are you in here?" This was not the marshal's voice.

Gordane continued crying. Jaylena opened their bedroom door and called out to them. "Yes, I'm just in here." She spared a moment to shoot Edelbrock a look of disgust. A look of loathing.

What has she done? Realizing five or six men were about to burst into his bedroom while he was naked, Edelbrock threw on his maroon robes.

Appearing in the doorway, for Jaylena stepped aside to allow them entry, were several faces that Edelbrock recognized: Lochwall's marshal, two of his men, and the barrister—Chardaine of the law offices of Roachford and Singleton's—who signed the documentation that Edelbrock forged Trigg's will upon. The barrister's expression told him everything: he'd sold Edelbrock out.

Behind the four men, a fifth voice called out, "Jay, are you all right?" A caring voice. A voice that used her nickname. A nickname that only two men before ever used—Jaylena's father and Edelbrock himself. This was neither of them.

The marshal and his soldiers stepped back, in deference to the fifth man who walked in. He strode over to Jaylena, gave her a gentle kiss on the lips, and then turned to glare at Edelbrock. Edelbrock couldn't help but notice the way his wife swooned for this man.

"You, my friend, are in a lot of trouble." Lord Scayde Haklon, owner of Buzzard's Bowl, waved the forged will at Edelbrock and shook his finger at him while offering a got-you smile.

Fuck. He may have even whispered it.

VILLIC OF THE SPLINTERED MANES

1st Cycle of Autumn, 231st Reign of Garcovi
Vessia

Coarse sands. The hot, beating, unforgiving sun. A camel between his thighs. Curved scimitar blade hanging from his belt, and a spear balanced in his lap. An oasis of water in the middle of nowhere, a pause of life amid the harsh deserts of Vessia. Outsiders couldn't understand it, that was for sure. If a Calrite or Remerian came on a trip, it was to visit one of the small towns. Or Hathoran, which outsiders called the *capital*. Hathoran was nothing more than thousands of tents pitched to house whomever passed by. Such towns were neutral areas and allowed clans to trade supplies. There were permanent residents, but few. They were people who'd left or were banished from a clan or decided they didn't want to live a nomadic lifestyle, so instead, they maintained the towns. The true capital of Vessia was wherever the strongest clan was—the Sharpclaws.

The Camel Clans roamed around Vessia, in the

middle of the desert, far from the towns. Devoid of most life. It was harsh, being nomadic, always on the move. That's what gave Villic happiness.

The clans often warred with one another. Fighting for territory, which made no sense because it was just sand dunes. Fighting for women, which made no sense because they had their own women. Fighting for glory, which made no sense because you didn't earn glory by killing *for* glory. But Villic loved it. He loved it all.

Villic of the Splintered Manes gave his camel, Dunecrest, a gentle tap on the side with the butt of his spear. Dunecrest lifted his head from the muddy water and turned to give Villic a reproachful look.

"Don't look at me, Dunecrest." Villic stroked the bull's neck. "The shamans said we leave now." Dunecrest grunted. Villic tapped him with his spear again. "Let's go. The gods wait for no man. Or camel," he said, after a moment's consideration.

With a lazy gait, Dunecrest joined the Splintered Manes procession. They were heading in the direction of a well-known watering hole, a place they'd spend several weeks resting at.

Jedkah, leader of the Splintered Manes, rode at the front, flanked by his many shamans. Villic, a soldier, rode wherever he wanted. As long as there were plenty of warriors spread throughout the procession, nobody made a fuss. He often rode in the back. There was a slighter chance of being noticed by a shaman, which meant a smaller chance a god would take notice. Not that Villic was avoiding the gods. He'd never do that. Killiak, lord of lords, was one to fear, but not one you could hide from.

The sun beat on Villic's neck, his forehead, his chest. It wore down the skin on his back, his legs, and his feet. He wore the traditional loose-fitting robes, though he'd removed the cowl because he didn't like wearing it all the time, despite the protections it offered. The blanket he sat upon was damp with his sweat. He didn't sweat often, but rubbing against the blanket while riding made it impossible not to. But the blanket, the only adornment on Dunecrest, was necessary. It kept flies away from Dunecrest and gave Villic's legs a better grip. He didn't complain. Anaia, goddess of light, enjoyed the relentless torture she rained down upon her subjects. Without the sun though, the shamans claimed they wouldn't be able to survive. So Villic liked Anaia. He liked all the gods.

"Villic."

Respecting the gods was something Villic never struggled with. Same with the shamans. The problem was, in his mind, the gods and shamans didn't respect him. He always got the worse assignments.

"Villic."

Problem was, Villic didn't know how to please the gods without a shaman explaining what to do. And gods didn't enjoy explaining themselves all the time. At least, that's what the shamans said.

"Villic!"

The call startled Villic. He looked up. A woman was riding at his side on her own camel. A shaman. She wore the emerald-green necklace symbolic of her station. Nervous, he ran his hand over his shaved head. He kept his eyes downcast, not meeting the woman's eyes.

"Pay attention, Villic," she said. "Stop allowing your mind to wander. You'll earn the ire of the gods. Another clan approaches." She rode down the procession, delivering the news to other warriors.

Villic bounced his thigh, feeling the weight of the spear. *Good.* It was still there. He'd lost a spear once, when he was younger. Shamans had chastised him for weeks afterward. Villic made sure he kept track of his spear now. Though he suspected the shamans weren't worrying about the spear as much as his tendency to not pay attention.

He wondered which clan they were coming upon now. The Splintered Manes already passed two clans, which meant if they were to approach, they'd be coming from the procession's rear. A third clan was halfway across the country. Which meant it had to be Seven Signs, Masters of the Lost, or Glory Blades. Since Glory Blades were the Splintered Manes' rivals, a battle might occur. The last meeting between the two clans ended in shouting between the leaders and shamans.

What if it isn't a clan? Villic couldn't imagine that to be the case. If anybody came to Vessia, it was a small group, and even they weren't commonplace. Communication was difficult between the Camel Clans and the rest of the world; Vessians spoke a different language than the king's tongue, the common tongue everyone else used.

A whiff of camel dung breached his nostrils— nothing new to Villic but rather rancid this go-around. Twitching his nose, he tapped Dunecrest's left side with his spear. The camel veered to the right, and Villic was outside the procession, riding alongside rather than within. He narrowed his eyes, examining the horizon, trying to see the approaching clan. Too much dust and sand swirled around from their own camels, and Villic saw nothing.

A bellow of horns blared from the front of the procession. Then chaos. The children, along with a few caregivers, turned their mounts around. Everyone else, Villic included, spurred theirs forward. To battle.

Villic grabbed the spear off his lap with his right

hand. He slapped Dunecrest's rear with the butt, then gripped the weapon in his hand, fist clenched. He raised it, ready to impale somebody or to throw it. His scimitar slapped his left leg with every gallop Dunecrest took.

It would seem they'd stumbled upon Glory Blades after all. Each clan identified themselves with a different war cry and a different emblem. Several tabards bouncing in the air displayed their clan for all to see—a curved blade shattering a straight blade, symbolic of previous wars against other countries.

A second blare of horns signaled they'd engaged in battle. Villic's blood flowed faster through his body. Mutaz, god of war, called from within.

Dunecrest circled around the congestion where men and women fought with one another. The front line breached, several Splintered Manes shamans fled the battle in order to protect themselves. Jedkah was rallying a force to prevent the shamans from being killed. Shamans were too valuable. At least that's what the shamans said. Villic didn't argue with the shamans.

Dunecrest charged forward, and Villic yelled. High-pitched screams of camels, the clang of metal on metal, grunts of exertion, and cries of pain and death. *For Killiak, lord of lords!* He threw his spear at a Glory Blades woman. The spear flew true and impaled her through the gut. She fell off her camel, only to be trampled by her comrades.

Villic bared his teeth and drew his scimitar. Sand and dust kicked into the air, obstructing his view. It was difficult to see farther than a few feet in any direction.

A shouting man, uncameled, sprinted at Villic's left side. A large war axe lifted above his shoulders aimed for Dunecrest's neck. Villic shouted in anger, leaning forward and slashing at the haft of the axe. He deflected the blow enough and threw the Glory Blades man off balance. The man toppled over, and Dunecrest cantered over him, crushing his face. Villic thanked Carana, goddess of life, for preventing Dunecrest's death.

Out of the corner of his eye, Villic saw a flash of fire. *Fire arrows?* He thought it unlikely. Fire arrows were useless unless attacking a building. Not enough time for the fire to catch. Villic knew. He'd tried already. Against the shamans' commands, of course. Villic had been certain Tabashi, god of fire, had encouraged him to try. It had been, in actuality, Lurzal, god of deception, lying to make Villic appear a fool. The shamans said not to listen to the gods. That was their job. Villic sometimes felt as if they spoke to him, anyway. Even though he wasn't a shaman.

And then he saw them, several fire arrows, dropping into the Splintered Manes. When they connected with people or camels, the flames seemed to almost explode, lighting everything they touched. In several short seconds, whatever was on fire blackened and died before the fire extinguished. *What . . .*

He shook his head, refocusing on the battle. "I need to pay attention." Distracted too easily, the shamans always said. He agreed.

A huge man holding a spear spurred his camel toward Villic, death in his eyes.

Villic braced himself, scimitar ready to deflect the spear's stab. The huge man lunged forward, thrusting the point at Villic. And then something odd occurred. The spearpoint, and a good half of the haft, turned into . . . *ice?* Villic's scimitar connected with the spear. Chipped ice sprayed the air, and the huge man retracted his weapon. Villic's scimitar caught in the ice, and he had to let go of the sword, lest he be uncameled.

Villic gasped as the ice melted away as quickly as it had appeared. His sword dropped to the sands. The spearpoint ignited in flames, and the man stabbed again.

What powers have the gods given him? Killiak, lord of lords, have you taken another clan's side? The Splintered Manes were the favored clan. At least that's what the shamans said. And Villic believed them.

The flaming spear jabbed at Villic. He ducked, felt a burning sensation on his shoulder where the spear grazed him. Another horn blared, this one from Glory Blades.

The huge man snarled at Villic but turned his camel around and retreated with the rest of Glory Blades.

Villic, tired, collapsed forward on Dunecrest's neck. He patted the camel. "We made it, Dunecrest. We made it."

***

Nobody seemed to know why Glory Blades retreated from battle. They were, according to everyone Villic listened in on, winning. Jedkah, leader of the Splintered Manes, was discussing with the shamans. *They know what's happening.* Villic wouldn't know until they decided it was important that he know. The same with the rest of the clan.

Not knowing what else to do, Villic dismounted and took care of Dunecrest. He fed the animal, brushed debris out of Dunecrest's hair, checked his feet for any injuries, adjusted the blanket on his back, and then let the camel wander, though not far. If the Glory Blades returned, he'd need his mount. He also reclaimed his sword and spear from the collected stash the clan had assembled—both lost and looted. The bodies were left for scavengers after the shamans offered the last prayers. The clan would rest for the evening, wary of their close-by rival.

"Killiak's Favor upon you, Villic." Sikoi, one of the few who didn't mind talking to Villic, approached. The man had a friendly smile and a booming laugh.

"Killiak's Favor upon you, Sikoi." Villic didn't like talking to anyone, but Sikoi he felt more comfortable with than most.

"Did you see what happened?"

Villic didn't want to assume Sikoi meant the strange powers he'd seen with the weapons of Glory Blades. Making assumptions often got Villic in trouble, so he shook his head.

"You didn't see the burning arrows? The lightning swords? I swear on Killiak, I saw a tree growing out of a blade, too. All signs of the gods influencing the battle, Villic. And not in our favor. Fire? Tabashi."

Tabashi, god of fire, Villic thought. He had to recite a god's whole title to remember what they ruled over.

"Lightning? Hytrok." *Hytrok, god of storms.* "And a *tree*? Nemira." *Nemira, goddess of nature.*

"Lurzal's Lies! *Don't* discuss the gods, Sikoi!" Villic whisper-shouted. He didn't want to be overheard, but Sikoi needed to hear Villic's devotion. "Are you trying to bring their fury? It's for the shamans to decide. Not us!" Villic was certain that discussing the favor of gods could lead to punishment.

Sikoi snorted, then let out one of his heavy laughs. "Lurzal, god of deception, isn't who you should curse, Villic. Killiak, lord of—"

"Don't! Don't, don't, don't!" Villic held his hand up, open-palmed. "Don't bring the Lord of Lords into this, Sikoi. He might kill you *and me* just listening to you speak. Get out of here! Leave the thinking to the shamans. You'll get everyone killed."

Sikoi shook his head. "Be well, Villic."

"Be well, Sikoi." Villic shook his head too. *Sikoi's lost his mind.*

Seeing as the Glory Blades weren't far off, and it was getting later in the afternoon, Villic set up his camp. Most of the clan members didn't have tents and slept under the open sky. Using a flint, he started a small fire and cooked some dried antelope venison. After dark, the shamans wouldn't allow them to use fire. Not with Glory Blades nearby. That would be as close as one could get to inviting Flaytz, god of death, into their clan. Villic didn't want to die. Not yet.

The shamans called an open circle—circles were usually reserved for the important members of the clan, but everyone attended open ones—so Villic left the fire and joined the rest of the clan, who made a ring around the shamans and Jedkah. Jedkah had pulled his cowl down, his face visible for all to see. Markings were plastered all over his face, each a different symbol or meaning created by piercing the skin and rubbing ash into the wounds. Other marks were burned in. Not many of the Splintered Manes had similar markings, but the strongest members often saw it as a way to prove their strength. Villic thought it was silly.

"The shamans have communed with the gods. It's agreed upon that Glory Blades *have* become blessed," Jedkah said. Loud groans echoed around the circle. He raised a hand, and everyone quieted. His authority was the word of the gods, and nobody would wish to anger him.

Villic groaned too but was a hair late. His neighbors glanced at him in confusion. Villic made himself as small as possible.

Jedkah continued, "With this increase in power, Glory Blades will return either in the night or tomorrow.

No fires allowed after dark, and all warriors will do a round of patrols in shifts. The shamans will ask Mutaz" —*Mutaz, god of war*—"for an extra blessing in our next battle. It's apparent we've fallen out of favor with the gods and must now work to regain that favor. Killiak's Favor upon all of you."

"Killiak's Favor upon you," Villic recited back with the rest of the clan. The circle disbanded, and Villic returned to his camp.

He stood near his small fire, which had almost burned away, looking for Dunecrest. Villic wiped some nervous sweat from his brow. It didn't sound good. And if it didn't sound good coming from the shamans, that meant it was bad. A true cause for concern. Villic knew the shamans masked things for the greater population. To protect them. To prevent panic. If the Splintered Manes had fallen out of favor with the gods, who knew what could happen? The shamans. And if the people demanded answers, they might get aggressive with the shamans. Villic had seen it before.

"*Ahem.*" Villic cleared his throat. "*Ahem.*"

Villic jumped the length of a water buffalo. Or two. He didn't know measurements. Villic hadn't made that noise after all. He looked around, saw nothing. Something, or someone, was in his head.

"*I'm not out there.*"

Villic passed out.

KELDEN STOOLE

2nd Cycle of Autumn, 231st Reign of Garcovi
Warwin, Qothe

Frothy white waves crashed against broken rocks, splattering Kelden and his friends with seawater, cooling them down. Graylan spat some back into the depths.

They stood on the edge of a bank, fishing poles in hand. No one had caught anything yet, though that wasn't surprising. They hadn't any bait.

"I swear you can do it. You just need the fish to see the reflection of the metal. I've seen it happen before," Sungoa said. She was biting her lip in concentration, moving the pole upward, pulling the hook through the water.

Kelden wasn't sure about Sungoa's claim, but it was something to do, and he'd completed his chores for the day. It was better than wasting the day doing nothing. If he was born elsewhere, perhaps he would've ended up with friends that preferred to do things that required an ounce of brainpower.

He stole a glance at Sungoa but didn't want to stare. Kelden feared what would happen if she caught his gaze. He fancied Sungoa more than he used to. It was becoming apparent that perhaps women weren't the densest creatures on the planet *and* that there were pleasant things to look at on them. The trick was not to get caught. Kelden hadn't yet mastered that skill, much to his own chagrin. The fact that Sungoa enjoyed doing the same things Graylan and he did only amplified this feeling.

Graylan had always been Kelden's favorite person, so he still figured he'd prefer Graylan's company over Sungoa's. They'd grown up together and, in the poor village of Warwin, had little of value. Sungoa came to Warwin later, but until she'd arrived, Kelden and Graylan were the only two children their age that could leave the village without a chaperone. The rest of Warwin's children their age were girls, and Kelden hadn't wanted to be around them for a majority of his life. That had changed when Sungoa and her family moved in.

She seemed like one of the boys that nobody really paid any attention to, rather than a girl forced to stay near overprotective parents. Her family was rather indifferent to her whereabouts. They allowed Sungoa to leave, even encouraged her to. That was the case for each of them. Though Kelden's father, Hillion Stoole, kept a tighter eye on their group than any of his friends' parents. He suspected this was because his father cared about them, despite being busy at the bakery every day.

Sungoa's black hair caught in the wind, flowing behind her shoulders. Her tongue stuck out at an angle as she concentrated, blue eyes narrowed in focus. She had skin paler than anyone else's in the village, near ghost-like, really, compared to the brown skin of native

Qothans. Clothing tugged at curves she didn't always have. Or perhaps Kelden had never noticed them. Kelden caught himself staring and shook his head to bring himself back to reality.

He switched his gaze to Graylan, who was holding a hand over his mouth, stifling a laugh. He'd been teasing Kelden for weeks now about this very subject. Kelden's face burned, and he turned away from them, focusing on the water below him and hoping that if his face was cherry red, it would go away fast. He'd remember to reprimand Graylan later with an insult or two. The bastard.

He renewed his grip on the fishing pole and dragged the fishhook through the water, as Sungoa had explained to them earlier that morning. "Fish are attracted to shiny things. Fishhooks are shiny. Pull them through the water, and we might get one." Well, he'd been trying different tactics for half the morning and not even a nibble. Not that he believed her. It didn't take a scholar to know this would be an unlikely, if not impossible, task. *Save it for the fishermen.*

"Let's do something else," Sungoa said. Kelden couldn't agree more. He just didn't want to be the one to voice it and annoy her or Graylan. *Well,* he thought, *perhaps I don't really care if I annoy Graylan.*

Graylan hopped down off a large, craggy boulder. "You're so impatient. This was your idea! Besides, what would you propose we do?" He sneered at her in the usual way, the way that said he had an idea but wanted to hear your worst one first.

A scattering of rocks, and they quieted. Horse hooves could be heard trampling grass and connecting with rocks. Somebody was heading into Warwin. This side of the village, a new arrival would be from Qelt or Argate. Warwin was small enough that if anybody arrived, it was big news. Warwin was also small enough that if anybody left, it was even bigger news. *Thank the heavens. A distraction.*

The three of them dropped their poles and climbed up the rocky shoreline to investigate who it was. A few hundred yards away, across the wheat field, an exhausted man sat atop a sweaty horse. The traveler had long brown hair coated in sweat or grease. Perhaps both. Running a hand through the matted mess, he peered at the nearby mudbrick buildings. At his belt, a sword hung in its leather scabbard—a well-used scabbard. Attached to his horse's saddle was a quiver of arrows, though no bow was in sight.

The man turned his head toward the three of them, reached down, and held out a waterskin. "Water," he said, voice dry and raspy. If he hadn't the weapons, Kelden would assume the man was a beggar astride a stolen mount.

Graylan hurried over, tossing his own waterskin up to the man. He might've been rough around the edges at points, but Graylan had a pure heart. The traveler drank deeply until there was no water left. He tossed the empty skin back to Graylan, wiped his wet beard off with the sleeve of his dirty cloak, and nodded his thanks. "I need to find a man named Hillion. Do you know him? It's urgent."

Kelden stepped forward, the other two looking at him in surprise. "That's my father. What business does a traveler of your kind want with him?" He looked at the man's sword with concern. It wasn't uncommon for brigands or men of ill repute to show up in Warwin after being on the run. However, the village's guard would drive him away. Hopefully, they'd show up soon. The guard was small and run by volunteers wielding rusted equipment—typically retired old men or drunkards looking to redeem their reputation by pretending they had a job. Most of them wouldn't offer much of a fight if Warwin came under attack. *What does this strange man want with my father?*

The rider chuckled. "I go back with your father. No need to be nervous. I'll wait here if you don't trust me. Go fetch him, boy. Tell him that Anditus Roberon is here." Roberon reached into his cloak and produced a small piece of dried meat, chewing on it while looking out at sea. He spat. "Delightful view." It wasn't. Just a vast expanse of ocean waves on broken rocks.

Annoyed at being referred to as "boy," Kelden headed to his father.

Jogging through dirt trails separating the ramshackle mudbrick buildings of Warwin, Kelden hurried toward the local bakery where his father had been working for "twenty-three years and not a day less" as Hillion said for most of Kelden's life. As luck would have it, Hillion was outside, shaking out several aprons coated in flour. The task seemed pointless to Kelden, but who was he to argue with his father about his occupation?

"Father." Kelden stopped a few feet away and bent over to grab his knees, filling his lungs with floury air. Sweat poured down his back and dripped off his forehead. Qothe remained dry and hot, even during the autumn cycle.

"Is something wrong, Kelden?" His father's voice calmed him. The kind man was always slow to act and enjoyed thinking problems through. For a baker, the man wasn't uneducated, like many other residents. This was a source of pride for Kelden; he considered himself to be more intelligent than the rest of the villagers.

He stood back up, towering over the shorter man. Apparently he'd inherited his height from his mother's side of the family, though this gave him no disillusions about his father's authority. The man was small, skinny even, but Kelden knew his father was much stronger than he appeared. "A man just arrived. He's ugly."

Hillion watched him, eyebrow raised, awaiting further information. A trace of annoyance flickered across his face. Hillion didn't share his son's blatant honesty.

"He said that he knows you and that his name is Anditus Roberon."

Hillion's face showed an immediate concern. He folded the aprons, hanging them over a line. "Come."

"Who is he?" Kelden hurried to meet his father's pace.

"An old acquaintance." His father said nothing else. Kelden knew not to question him further. If he wanted Kelden to know, he would've said something.

A few minutes later, they returned to the outskirts of Warwin. Sungoa and Graylan talked with the man, who was still atop his steed.

Roberon looked up and grinned as Kelden returned with his father. He hopped off the stallion and approached them. "Well." He looked Hillion up and down. "If it isn't Hillion Stoole."

Kelden's father rolled his eyes. "Anditus." He gave a curt nod.

"Don't look so pleased to see me!" Roberon appeared hurt or insulted. "You wound me with your lack of respect."

"I'm just surprised," Hillion said. Kelden wondered why he was being so cold.

"I understand we didn't leave on the best of terms," Roberon said. Hillion snorted at that. "I'm here to make it up to you, my friend."

"I would never trust you to make anything up to me." Hillion turned his back on Roberon.

"Mother Avani, you are damn impossible. Turn around and face me. I'm here to repay what you're owed."

Hillion turned around and held out his hand, expectant. "Then give it over and leave."

"Look—"

"You've taken advantage of me enough. Give me some coin or get *out*."

Roberon frowned. "Hill." He swallowed, glancing over at Kelden, then his gaze moved to Graylan and Sungoa, who had joined Kelden's side. They listened, just as alert as Kelden was, just as surprised, too. "Perhaps some privacy?" Though he was a prick, he seemed timid around Hillion. *Strange, considering* he *has the weapons.*

"No. Spill it, so I can erase any illusions of grandeur you may have already imprinted upon these poor children's souls." Kelden ground his teeth together at his father's words. It was unacceptable. It was only a few days until Kelden was an adult himself.

"Ashmount has put out—" Roberon paused. He must have noticed the expression on Hillion's face. "No, not the volcano. Surely you've heard of the University of Arcanical Arts?"

"Are you *serious*?" Hillion's arms flailed in the surrounding air. "Do you think I'm *dense*? I've lived here for how many years, and you don't think I know the most important place on this godforsaken continent? Get the fuck out of here!" Hillion's face was beet red.

Kelden's mouth drooped open. He continued to watch the two men, neck craning back and forth, enraptured by the argument. It was rare when Hillion got angry and even less common when he'd cuss.

Roberon held up his hands peacefully. "Let me finish, Hill. I know you're no fool, and I apologize for insulting you. It's just that people around here often live secluded lives, is all. Give me a chance." His hands drooped down to hang by his thighs. "I owe you."

Hillion grunted, staring at Roberon. Kelden could tell his father didn't buy any of what Roberon was selling.

"The university is offering a lot of money to *anybody* they haven't examined for the Trace. *Anybody*. All you have to do is make the journey there, and they'll test you, and it doesn't even matter if you're a nobody, you'll still get the same amount. If you, or . . ." His gaze lingered on Kelden for a second. "Somebody in your family has it, you receive a *very* sizable bonus to enroll. I'm on my way, myself, because, well . . ." His voice trailed off, but his left hand closed around an empty coin purse, self-conscious. "There's a half-cycle longtime frame, or so, but we'd have to leave soon to ensure we make it." The University of Arcanical Arts held annual Trials to accept new talent around the world. Kelden never considered anyone from Warwin would ever attempt the journey. He didn't realize you could earn money traveling there though.

Kelden looked back at his father. He seemed less agitated now, and his face was only a shade of pink rather than the violent rose color it had been a moment earlier. An excited pang thumped inside of Kelden's chest. Perhaps *he* had the Trace inside of him. He'd always felt like he was a more important person than the rest of the downtrodden people inhabiting his home. Maybe this was his *chance* at the life he knew he deserved.

"I just stopped by here to let you know," Roberon said. "If you wanted to travel with me or just have me bring the boy, I would do that for you." A moment later, begrudgingly, he said, "And I would offer some of my pay to you," then, in a quiet mumble, "to cover past ill feelings and all."

"You hungry?"

Roberon's eyes widened in surprise. "Well, yeah."

"Come with me." Hillion turned his back on the man, walking toward his house. Roberon gathered his horse and led the beast in Hillion's wake.

"Wow," Kelden said. He was near speechless.

"Come on, boy!" Kelden's father was inviting him? The day was getting better and better.

Kelden gave Graylan and Sungoa a goodbye nod and jogged to catch up to the two adults. This event spoke of wild opportunity. He was even willing to forgive his father for calling him *boy*.

T he Stoole house was little more than one large circle with three dividers. There was a kitchen complete with a stone shelf housing a few plates and utensils, a stone box that held sacks of food that had long expiration dates, and a stone table with two stone chairs, both of which were lined with cracks and struggled to stay standing. A shrine held a small wooden carving of Mother Avani, Cedain's Maker—wood was exceptionally rare in Qothe as it had to be imported. The other two rooms were tiny bedrooms: Hillion's with little more than a few furs on the floor, and Kelden's with a pallet of dry straw covered in a sheet that did little to prevent his body from being stabbed. Behind their house was a small lean-to with a shitting pit and a well with a water pump attached.

Hillion and Roberon sat in the two chairs in the kitchen, while Kelden took a perch on the sill of the open window, attempting to listen to the two men reminisce about their past. He was doing a piss-poor job of that task, however, as he fantasized about the prospect of leaving Warwin to go do something. *Anything would be better than remaining here.*

He had few memories of traveling when he was younger, back when his mother was still around. But ever since they'd arrived in Warwin, they hadn't left. Kelden assumed his father didn't want to leave because he was alone and had a stable life here. Though it wasn't much, it did at least provide both Hillion and Kelden with food.

Possessing the Trace would be what elevated Kelden's status. He'd become important. The Trace was the ability to use magic. A natural ability you either were born with or weren't. The trick was that a Magicus had to unlock it for you. Which was why you went to the University of Arcanical Arts. Having the Trace didn't make you a Magicus. It just allowed you to become one and gain access to power, money, and the title. Of course, it came with a caveat: the Trace was just a fancy way of saying you could access your life force or soul. By sacrificing part of your life, you could accomplish great things.

"Kelden?" The gruff, unfamiliar voice shook Kelden out of his thoughts. Roberon was looking at him, stroking his beard in one of his gloved hands. Now that they were closer, Kelden had a tough time not staring at the man's nose—battered, broken, and bulbous.

"Yeah?"

"Just grabbing your attention," Hillion said. "And seeing as you weren't focusing, I suppose I better go over it again."

Kelden straightened, leaned forward on his perch in the window, and listened.

"I can't leave Warwin."

Kelden felt a pang inside his chest of sadness. *Condemned to stay here.*

"I have a solid life as the village's baker, I have a home, and I just don't want to. I'm getting old." Roberon guffawed at that. "Well, rather, I've been lazy in my years and don't think I want to traipse halfway across the country. However, I think it's time that you do something with your life, my boy. You go to the university. Take their test, or exam, or whatever it is you must do. Get yourself paid a handsome sum of money and then do whatever it is you wish to do.

"If you're lucky, you might even become a student of the place and earn yourself a proper education. Yes, I know you think you're smart, and you are, but you've had no official schooling. For too long, I've kept you cooped up inside of this rotten place, and it's time that you figure out what you want to do. If things don't go well, then return here. You'll have earned a decent amount of money, and we can continue as bakers. You go out and explore the world awhile though, son. Find yourself, like I found myself when I met your mother." His father finished the speech, eyes glistening with tears. Kelden thought it was less about the immediate emotions his father may face about his son leaving and was more about reminiscing about old traveling days. He wouldn't have that type of adventure again.

"You want me to go alone?" Kelden asked.

"No," Roberon said. "I'll be there. As will several others, I'm sure. It's too much money for a lot of these people to pass on, and I'm sure your friends are already spreading the news."

Kelden didn't argue with that. When there was news, it spread faster than lice in the slums. Being in the village, he hadn't experienced any of this, but it was a saying he'd picked up from his father. He wondered why Roberon thought others would travel to the University of Arcanical Arts as well. *Maybe because Roberon intends on guiding us there?* Kelden assumed the other villagers knew about the money.

"We'll be leaving the day after tomorrow," Roberon said, "so get your shit packed."

Kelden's arsenal of possessions he'd gathered over his life included two pairs of trousers, four pairs of socks, three tunics, two pairs of sandals, a leather belt, a small knife, and a bronze bracelet that had been his mother's. He'd pilfered the bracelet a few years after she died and his father sold off her belongings. Kelden held onto this, but once Hillion noticed Kelden took the bracelet, his father allowed him to keep it as long as he didn't prevent the sale of any other good. The grief-stricken widower had sold off everything that reminded him of her. In more recent years, Kelden got the feeling his father might have regretted this decision.

What Kelden wanted to do was leave the piece of jewelry under his father's thin pillow as a going away present. Unfortunately, he needed money to purchase enough traveling supplies for the journey he was about to undertake, so he traded it. *Besides, holding onto the past just reminds you of how shit it was.*

After his father gave him a hug and told him to "be smart, be good, but most of all, be alive," Kelden followed Roberon out back to retrieve his horse. His father issued one last piece of advice, yelling out the door after them, "And keep your opinions to yourself!"

Roberon finished loading up the horse with their various supplies, including a bow to replace the one he'd lost, and then they both mounted. Kelden had to hold on to Roberon—he feared falling off—and they galloped to the southern end of Warwin, Roberon muttering about how overpriced his bow was. They rode to where a small group of people stood. Several small carts, pulled by donkeys, carried a meager amount of possessions. Kelden dismounted to join the foot traffic. He didn't enjoy riding.

The entire party comprised Kelden and Roberon; eight Warwin citizens; several of the village's guards who volunteered to help escort the group to safety, led by Nauc Othepi; and, to Kelden's amazement, Sungoa, whose family refused to go. As far as Kelden knew, her family didn't know she was leaving. Graylan was remaining behind to help his parents with their business. Kelden's excitement grew at the prospect of arriving at the University of Arcanical Arts, to be told he had the Trace inside him.

Nauc passed out rusted swords he squandered from the village's stores. He handed one to Kelden. Even though it had a cracked hilt, Kelden took it, proud. "Can't be too careful," Nauc said. He showed Kelden how to hang the sword from his belt with a well-worn scabbard.

Kelden sidled over to Sungoa. "Are you supposed to be here?"

"No, but it's not like my family will notice I'm missing. Besides, I couldn't let you leave me here with Graylan. What would I do?" She put her hand to her head and mocked fainting in distress. Graylan and Sungoa got along fine, but she'd always seemed to gravitate more toward Kelden. He laughed, glad she was coming. Even if they talked little, she'd add to the local scenery. Qothe was not interesting to look at. Unless you liked rocks and boring, empty expanses.

"It'll be nice to have you along," he said.

"You hardly deserve it."

"Let's go," Roberon said. He remained atop his horse, leading the travelers into the dry heat of Qothe, up and down rocky plateaus that stretched across the continent.

The walk began—it'd take six days to reach Yordiv—and it wasn't but two hours into the trek that Kelden's feet ached. *It'll be worth it,* he chanted to himself. That phrase quickly became a tumor in his head.

DEMRI SLARN

1st Cycle of Winter, 231st Reign of Garcovi
Auchester, Remeria

Dawn came fast. It always had for Demri. Every night ended with repetitious tossing and turning because his body disallowed comfort. He had been a broken individual for quite some time now, decades, in fact. He could search out the services of a Healer but knew this would cost a lot, and most people wouldn't be willing to help even if he had the coin. His reputation had always been questionable. At worst, it had driven him out of a university, several towns, and a city or two. Had he been a regular citizen and not a Magicus, he'd advocate for the hanging of a figure identical to himself. Hard work is often dirty, and when people get a tad messy, they flock to water like a dying animal in a desert.

Rolling over in bed, Demri issued that familiar daily sigh. He yawned and attempted to stretch, wincing as his injured limbs contorted. The morning ritual was an unfortunate dilemma—either remain in bed and do nothing all day or cause agonizing pain by stretching out his limbs so he could walk. Just existing was a hardship he didn't figure he'd ever reach. Earlier in life, if somebody asked him to gamble on it, Demri would assume he'd have died years ago. *Guess it's a good thing I took my father's advice.* His father had always said, "The only way to guarantee a long life is to become the person who everyone hates, for it always seems to be that type who lives until they're old and withered." Demri couldn't argue with that. There was only one person he knew that *didn't* hate him.

Rays of sunlight drifted into the room, lighting up the meager dwelling. Demri lived on the run and owned little. Most of the coin he earned went toward food and lodging, or bribes for people to do as he commanded. Grimacing through the pain, Demri swung his legs onto the wooden floor. He limped over to his clothes and dressed himself as quickly as he could, covering up the few black tattoos, Soul Glyphs, that laced his body. The process felt like it took an entire morning to complete. The glorified hut he'd rented included a bed, table, and chair, and there wasn't really room for the chair. Sliding his way around the table, he collected his cloak— complete with the pin most Magicai wore to denote their school of training, the Enforcer's in Demri's case— and threw it over himself, pulling the hood up to hide the shiny pink flesh that adorned half of his face. His legs cracked as they were wont to do; they'd broken decades ago and never healed right.

A small jingle and a *smacking* sound bounced off the floor. Demri looked down. His coin purse had fallen from his belt. "F-f-fuck!" He patted another pouch, making sure that the pair of spectacles he'd looted off of a dead Examiner hadn't fallen as well. They hadn't.

He wanted to reach for the coins but bending over

was a treacherous puzzle to solve as of late. *No worries.* He opened the door and shambled outside. The guardsman stationed outside snapped to attention. He'd been leaning against the building, whistling.

"Magicus Demri, sir, how are—"

"Stop. Go inside and grab the m-m-m-money that fell on the floor. I f-f-feel like I slept on nails last night, and my body isn't being c-c-c-cooperative."

"Right, sir. Of course, sir." The guard entered and returned a second later, holding the purse out.

Demri took the coins, ensuring he properly hung the sack from his belt. "Where's C-C-Caius?" Always the fucking *c*'s.

"Said he had to go buy something, sir, and went into town, sir. Should be back any time now, sir." He had an annoying, perpetual habit of calling Demri *sir* four thousand more times a day than was necessary. Demri had no time for politeness with underlings. The guard sniffled, wrinkling his runny nose. His nostrils glistened with the moistness of allergies.

"What is he wasting m-m-money on now?" The lackey answered with a nonanswer by shrugging. One of Demri's pet peeves, to be sure. *At least know* something *useful.*

Demri's expression spurred the man to say something. "Not sure, sir. I didn't inquire. I'm just supposed to make sure you're safe, sir."

"Mhm." Demri hobbled over to a half-rotted bench and sat. *Beggars can't be choosers, so they say.* Though he possessed little, he still classified himself as a *chooser.*

Since all the world followed Calrym's calendar, it was winter in Remeria. Auchester, the small town they'd been resting in, never saw snow, never got that cold at all. The town rested just outside a jungle and remained warm year-round. The morning's dew already washed away from the warmth of the sun, Demri tried to get comfortable on the bench. The stone buildings—constructed with imported rock, a reward for supplying the world with rare fruits—stood out among the varying greens of the jungle landscape. The guardsman claimed that only a few decades ago Auchester was a town of sticks, but they'd made enough money from their exports that the town upgraded itself to become a more habitable place.

"Ah, here he comes now, sir." The guard gestured down the road where Caius and a stranger walked.

They seemed to get along well enough, since they were laughing. *Great, another lackey I have to pay for.* Demri sneered, though the thought was half-hearted. The more men that preferred him alive, the better he figured it was. Too many people wanted him dead, and only two he knew wanted him alive—Caius and the guard.

Demri leaned back on the bench, appraising the newcomer as he walked with Caius. They followed the road up the hill, retreating from the cluster of buildings that created the center of Auchester. Demri had secured lodging away from most of the population in a tiny rundown building, and Caius and the guard didn't mind sleeping outside. Warriors often didn't. Demri supposed that if he wasn't so crippled, it wouldn't bother him. Though if he had a choice, he wouldn't spend it on the ground. Fortunately, that was one choice he could still make. Nature wasn't something that agreed with the aging Magicus. He was in his late thirties but appeared to be in his fifties. The price paid for consuming Soul Glyphs.

The jungle nearby was renowned across the world for its exotic fruits. Auchester's citizens exported these fruits and lived off the profits. Distance didn't matter because they'd place the product in sealed crates, filled with ice created by a Magicus at whichever town or city the fruits shipped out of. Auchester was too small a town to attract an ice-conjuring Magicus. It wouldn't be worth the bother.

Droplets of water started pattering on Demri's cloak. *Fucking rain.*

"Demri," Caius said. He stood in front of him. The large man was filing his finger with that damn blade again. Demri had to admit it was a great fear tactic but knew at this point it was a subconscious habit for the big man, even with the accidental nicks it caused. Next to Caius stood the stranger. "I went into town." Caius often stated obvious facts when he was delivering bad news or when he took initiative in deciding something without consulting Demri. Judging by the figure next to Caius, Demri assumed he'd done both things.

"Quite obvious, d-d-don't you think?"

"I heard a rumor that turned out to be true," Caius said. He was brilliant at ignoring Demri's sarcasm.

"And?" Demri widened his eyes. *Get to the fucking point.*

"I was at the local pub earlier, and I overheard some-body discussing a Magicus being in town. At first, I figured they were talking about you, but when I heard them describing the person, I knew it not to be you. They said he was handsome." Caius chuckled.

If there was one person who could joke with Demri, it was Caius. Demri didn't mind a laugh, and Caius's services were worth the nagging. Demri inclined his head toward the stranger. "Him?"

"Yes. Demri"—Caius turned to the guard—"Porric." *Ah, so that's his name. I really need to remember these things.* "Meet Magicus Glaouse."

Magicus Glaouse gave a slight dip of his head. "An

honor to meet you, Magicus Demri. Your reputation is admirable."

Demri raised an eyebrow at that. This was not something people usually said when meeting him for the first time. It was strange to Demri that Glaouse was a Magicus. He appeared to be a well-traveled man that didn't hide inside reading books or writing theories all day— something even the combat-oriented Magicai often preferred. His robes were stained from the dirt and grass of long journeying, and his hair was long and unkempt. Demri was further surprised that there was a Magicus in Auchester. He'd come here to avoid them. The Magicai usually stayed in Ashmount or one of the bigger cities because that's where the money was, and the Magicai charged a decent amount for their services. The only Magicai that'd be here would be one in hiding, like himself, or a Collector on a bounty.

Magicus Glaouse continued, "Caius informed me you were searching for a man in Remeria. I know whom you're looking for."

The rain picked up, heavier but not quite a downpour. Demri loathed the rain but wouldn't show weakness. "C-c-continue." Though he struggled with *c*'s, he refused to alter various words. People would be patient. They had to be, or they'd face his wrath. Even if it was a waste of power, his spite often got the better of him. He needed to be more careful not to waste his Soul Glyphs, or spend his life, because of his emotions. Demri ran his tongue across his lips in hungry anticipation. If Doram Quandis was here in Auchester, it'd be the best day. Every lead had turned out false, though Demri never knew it until he killed the person. He didn't trust that Doram hadn't stolen resources in order to aid his elusiveness.

Funny enough, Magicus Glaouse didn't bat an eye

when Demri stuttered. Either Caius warned him, the man respected him, or Glaouse was a gifted socialite. "Maynard Piccalo. You seem to think somebody named Doram Quandis uses an alias?"

"It's p-possible." Demri cleared his throat. "I've always had a speaking impediment, b-but the rest of my issues are because of that b-b-bastard. If this man is a friend of yours, I would very much like to m-meet him. T-t-today."

Magicus Glaouse gave an encouraging smile and nodded as Demri spoke. "Caius already briefed me on your need to be discreet, and as luck would have it, Maynard Piccalo is a small, fat man who nobody wanted to marry, and thus, he lives alone when he's not selling the shoes he makes. As far as I'm aware, the man has been a shoemaker for decades, so I sincerely doubt that he's this powerful Magicus Doram Quandis that you seek. To be fair, though, I have seen stranger charades. Maynard Piccalo is no friend of mine but an annoying nuisance. I will not protect the man, but I suspect he's no Magicus in hiding."

A frightened Magicus once told Demri that Doram Quandis—with a full physical description—was hiding out in Remeria, afraid Demri was going to successfully hunt him down. Demri wasn't expecting to find him in Auchester. "Fortunately for you, Glaouse, I d-don't need your opinion. B-b-bring me to the man."

"He won't leave his house until he's done with his work, no matter the reason. Caius will be able to bring you there later." He bowed low. "It was a sincere pleasure meeting you, Magicus Demri. I do hope we can get to know each other after this ordeal is taken care of, but unless there's anything else you require of me, I have work that needs completing. Thank you for meeting with me."

Demri nodded, and Magicus Glaouse trekked back to the center of Auchester.

"I like him," Caius said.

"He's a talker," Porric, the guard, chimed in. "Seems capable, sir. Could be useful, sir." The man wasn't good at providing anything useful, aside from another sword in battle. At least, that's what Caius told Demri. There hadn't been fighting since hiring Porric two cycles ago.

"D-d-don't lecture *m-m-me*." In secret, however, he agreed with both his companions. It seemed Glaouse might be a useful asset. He didn't trust him though. But he hoped he was about to meet the man who'd broken his legs and burned his face.

If Maynard Piccalo wasn't Doram Quandis, it would still be nice to blow off some steam. *I need to stop thinking like that.*

———

Maynard Piccalo's residence was a small house planted in the fucking center of Auchester. Demri glared at Caius as they stood next to each other on the other side of the cobblestone street. Caius was busy filing his fingernails and pretending not to notice Demri's annoyance. Grumbling to himself, Demri took a seat at a local bench, set beneath an awning, to escape the setting sun.

The guardsman that traveled with them—*Porric, I think his name is*—had talked to the man that sold vegetables out of the stand and paid him some money to disappear. This allowed the three of them to rest in the shade and look across the emptying street to where the fat Maynard Piccalo already retired, without a constant line of customers nearby. They'd also seen Magicus Glaouse enter with Maynard. A curious development, to be sure. According to Caius, Magicus Glaouse wasn't intending on interacting with Maynard. *He better not be warning him.*

Demri tapped his foot on the stone, impatient, the damp smell of the earlier rain penetrating his nose. He hated it. A trio of town guards walked by, and he offered them a raised hand in greeting. They nodded in return and proceeded along their path. Demri had found long ago that one of the best disguises was to draw attention to oneself. People were often less suspicious of friendly folk and even less so to those with physical imperfections, which was why his hood was down. In fact, they often treated him better because of his marred figure. He had plenty of disabilities others noticed rather fast—his speech, his limp, his burned face covering one eye and making it appear as though he may have difficulty seeing. This wasn't the case, but the eyelid was a bitch to operate and sometimes didn't like to close.

Passersby ignored the trio, though a few cast curious glances at the closed vegetable stand. The sun shined through the leafy trees standing on the horizon, like vigilant defenders of the town, stoic in their post.

"Ah, fuck," Caius said. Demri didn't even look. He knew what had happened. The man had stabbed one of his fingers again with that damn knife. He was lucky he still had all ten digits left to feel pain with at all, he'd cut them so many times.

Maynard Piccalo's front door opened, Glaouse standing in the doorway. Demri raised his hood, and Caius ducked behind the bench. Porric stood there, oblivious and useless. The fat man embraced the Magicus with half a handshake and half a hug. Then the door closed, and Glaouse made his way down the street, away from the crime that was about to take place and without noticing them.

Demri cleared his throat. "Let's get this d-done."

"Aye." Caius slipped his bloodstained knife into its small sheath on his belt. "Porric, keep an eye out for anyone that's headed into the house and redirect them."

"Understood, sir." Porric stood straighter and surveyed the area, resting a hand on the pommel of his sword. He wiped at his leaking nose with the other, wrinkling his nose and sniffing.

"Try to look more inconspicuous, you damn f-f-fool." Standing, Demri slapped the guardsman's hand off his sword.

"Y-yes, si-sir."

Demri smiled, internally of course. It brought him great pleasure when he affected somebody so much that they turned into a bumbling fool, stuttering just like him. Shambling across the street, Demri made his way over to Maynard Piccalo's house, Caius trailing behind him as usual.

"We're going to have t-to do this quickly, C-C-Caius. Too c-crowded here."

"Uh-huh."

"I'm serious."

"Yes, sir." Caius's impersonation of Porric was perfect. He even added in a sniffling effect.

"F-f-fuck off." Demri arrived at the front door and knocked.

A moment later, the door opened, and a jovial Maynard Piccalo grinned at them. "Well, hello, friends!"

Demri stepped to the side. Caius looked down the street both ways, then walked up to the man and punched him in the face.

"Oof!"

Caius shoved him back into his house. Demri followed the pair, closing the door behind him.

Maynard, nursing his broken nose in both hands,

tears running down his cheeks, glared at the intruders. "Why?"

"Have you ever heard of Doram Quandis?" Caius unsheathed his knife and slid it across a fingertip. The nails were always gone, yet he kept filing away, breaking open skin and causing continual bleeding. It was miraculous the man never received a serious infection.

"No, why?" Maynard stared at the blade.

"Liar!" Demri was unsure why he shouted.

Maynard stepped backward and tripped over a chair leg. He crashed to the ground.

Demri walked over and, with great pain, bent over to peer at Maynard. "We've hunted you for d-d-decades!" He grabbed Maynard's arm.

Maynard trembled. "I don't understand what you're even talking about!" His eyes flicked to the counter.

Caius knelt beside Maynard, pointing his knife at the fat man. "Are you sure?" He waved the blade in the man's face.

"Enough," Demri said. He glanced at the counter and saw what appeared to be a letter. Then he held his hand up, reaching into his Well of power. One of Demri's Soul Glyphs sunk into his skin, consuming some of his life and another fraction of his Well. He felt his body advance in age. Another slight change. Another fraction closer to death.

A sharp shard of ice formed at the tips of his fingers and then shot through Maynard's throat, impaling him. Maynard gurgled, blood dribbling out of his mouth and pouring out of his neck. His eyes widened, and he grabbed at the wound with both hands. He choked on the blood clogging his airway.

Demri slapped his hands away from the wound. "D-die. Quicker." He joined Caius in kneeling beside the dying man.

Caius held Maynard's hands down, and the fat man wheezed. A minute later, he died, drowning in his own blood. Maynard Piccalo remained exactly the same in death.

"F-f-fuck!" For if it were Doram Quandis in disguise, his proper face would have appeared in death once the magic dissipated.

"Let's get out of here, Demri. And you need to stop wasting your powers when I can kill them." He waved his knife in the air.

Caius wasn't wrong. *I get too caught up in the moment.* "I'm running out of Soul G-Glyphs." He started to stand, wincing at the pain in his ruined legs.

"Then stop wasting them. We'll find a Glyphist somewhere." And without waiting for a command or cry for help, the wonderful companion Demri had traveled with for years lifted him off the ground and set him on his feet without a single demeaning or disgusting look. Caius was one of a kind.

Before they left, Demri retrieved the letter on the counter. It was from Magicus Glaouse, a Collector. *I thought I was going to like that guy. Just another fucking problem.*

SERADAL WINTLOCK

2nd Cycle of Autumn, 231st Reign of Garcovi
Gyrloft, Cyrok

Cedain consisted of five countries spread across three continents. The southernmost continent included the nations Calrym, Vessia, and Remeria. Calrym and Remeria, the two richest countries in Cedain, had lush forests, thick jungles, and grassy plains spread across their lands, providing a hospitable environment to thrive in. Being south of the river, Vessia was more unlucky and consisted of a dry desert. To the east on another continent was Qothe. Mountains, rocky shores, and plains made up the poorest nation, which contained mostly small, poor settlements. The northernmost continent was home to Cyrok and had mountains. And snow. Snow all the time.

Geography was important to every inhabitant of Gyrloft, a small town on a peninsula that stretched into the Silver Sea—a body of water that separated Cyrok from the other countries. The Silver Sea was named after the reflection of the Frosted Spires mountains. Knowing all the important geographical locations of Cedain was a falconer's duty, because people purchased the birds everywhere. Each child in Gyrloft grew up learning about geography and gyrfalcons, the two components that made up the town's livelihood.

Seradal Wintlock was once a child of Gyrloft. Now, she was a young woman who had learned how to hunt with a gyrfalcon. As was every adult's right in Gyrloft, she received her own when she matured, just a few cycles past. She was lucky to receive a gyrkin, a male gyrfalcon, since they often went to people of importance —for reasons unclear to Sera since males were smaller. The last clutch was all male, and there wasn't a choice. Some of the other Gyrloftans developed an uncomfortable level of envy. She wasn't sure why. It was a bird like any other.

She shaded her eyes against the bright sun and craned her neck, searching for Russell. Sera glimpsed the bird before sunlight blinded her again. He reappeared, diving. A flash of white-and-black feathers, then his long talons plunged into the frigid sea. He retrieved a writhing fish, scales glinting in the sky, and the gyrkin flew back to Sera. He was performing remarkably well and was still young. Hunting fish required a skill that many gyrfalcons lacked—they preferred to go for other birds or ground mammals. But Sera was persistent in bringing Russell out to sea because she wanted the bird to be an exceptional hunter. He wasn't disappointing.

She held her left arm into the air and Russell glided down, landing. She'd gotten used to the weight of the two-pound bird on her arm. A thick leather glove protected her skin from harm. Russell's talons, like those of all gyrfalcons, could tear up human flesh with ease. Sera allowed Russell a moment to consume his catch, shredding it with his beak and swallowing the contents.

When he finished, Sera covered his head with a hood and traipsed back toward Gyrloft. Dusk was fast approaching, which meant freezing temperatures.

Rocky cliffs made a natural barrier against the ocean's waves that crashed into the shoreline and prevented invasion from ships that may attack. They would have to go around cliffs thousands of feet high to reach the town, and by that time, the citizens would have ample time to flee and head to the capital, Vox. This made Gyrloft Cyrok's natural "watchtower" of the continent, though Cyrok never got attacked. It was much too cold for extended warfare, and they had little of value. Although the rest of the world considered gyrfalcons exclusive to nobility, in Gyrloft, every citizen had one.

Living in a freezing environment every day wasn't fun. They spent much of their time gathering supplies to make it through another few days, which meant making sure there was enough material for fire, there was enough food, and cracks and crevices in buildings needed constant maintenance to prevent drafts. Somebody was always in need of assistance when it came to survival, and they all pitched in. This allowed little free time, and Sera remained bored. There had to be more than just living to survive.

She needed to do something. Anything. Travel the world. Travel the country, even. The only other civilized place that Sera had visited was the capital to deliver a flock of birds with Gyrloft's most prevalent falconers. Every child attended one trade in another city or town before receiving their own bird—a ritual to adulthood. Her family was content with this arrangement, but Sera found it lacking. She wondered how well her parents would accept Sera's desire to leave Cyrok and explore the world.

The journey from the edge of the cliffs to Gyrloft took several hours. When she returned, most everyone was inside. Smoke swirled out of chimneys, and candles and lanterns lighted individual log cabins. All of Gyrloft's buildings were built from the nearby forest of massive pines.

"Did time get the best of you?"

Sera jumped, and Russell let out a series of high-pitched screeches—because she jolted her arm—then flapped his wings to regain his balance.

"Best get the bird put away and get yourself inside. Your mother was starting to panic, so I told her I'd look around for you." Her father, Jaidik, leaned against their house, a stern expression on his face and muscular arms crossed—though dotted with scars from gyrfalcon talons. He was posing because he only had one boot on. He'd just started getting ready.

"Sorry." Sera fidgeted. She didn't understand why her mother worried so much.

"Don't apologize to me. I knew what you were doing. Remember to feed everyone." He turned around and walked back into the house, shaking his head. Sera knew he wasn't mad at her. He never got mad at anyone.

She walked around their cabin to a small shed her father had built. He'd packed the wooden logs with snow as insulation, and the shed pressed against the family's log cabin. On the other side of that wall was their fireplace, which provided some extra warmth, ensuring the gyrfalcons wouldn't freeze to death.

She placed Russell in his cage, securing the lock after removing his hood. Then she took off the leather glove, hanging it on a hook. Sera reached into a small pen, pulling out a domesticated rabbit. Gyrfalcons could hunt, but her family didn't have time to bring them out every day. She snapped the neck swiftly—like her father had taught her—and portioned the rabbit out, placing some in each of the gyrfalcon cages. She paused to stroke her father's bird, Golden Royce.

Done with her chores, she entered her home. Inside, she slid her boots off, then meandered into the kitchen. A delicious-smelling meal was on the dining table, untouched.

Her father sat at the head of the table, carving a duck. To his left, her mother's empty chair. To his right was her older brother, Fezzel. She couldn't help noticing how much older Fezzel looked now that he sported a full blond beard and weathered skin. Working as a hunter had matured him fast.

Sera's mother, Yudri, walked into the kitchen and shrieked when she saw Sera. The upper corners of Yudri's mouth stretched in a wide smile, her small nose wrinkled, and dark black hair framed her face—physical traits Sera inherited. "There you are! You worried me." It was a gross overexaggeration. Jaidik would've told her as soon as he'd returned. "Come and eat. I'm sure you're famished." Her mother gestured at Sera's chair across from her father—a place she'd stolen from her mother when she was just a child. "And you damn well better pay attention to the daylight next time, Sera. The last thing you need is to get stuck out there in the pitch dark."

Sera sat. "Sorry, Mother."

"Never mind that now. Get some food. It won't stay hot forever."

The table was a royal feast: roast duck, boiled potatoes, savory gravy, warm bread with thick slabs of butter, a jar of honey, a cabbage salad doused in vinegar, and powdered strawberry tarts. They also had glasses of Cyrko, a strawberry rhubarb wine that her parents pulled out for special occasions. Foreigners often decorated the drink with a gyrfalcon feather stuck into it, but the Cyroki never bothered. Feathers didn't belong in drinks.

Sera loaded her plate up. The last time she'd eaten was well before the sun had risen that morning. "What's the occasion?"

"War rumors," her father said. "Angazo just returned from Vox. While he was there, news arrived from Calrym. They've halted international trade, so we're going to have to ration any imported supplies. Governess Falconel believes Calrym will declare war on Remeria. This"—he gestured at the spread in front of him—"is a last treat before we begin rationing. Enjoy it. A war between Calrym and Remeria could last years."

War. *What is Calrym going to do and who is it going to affect?* Contrary to her earlier thoughts, she found she was glad to live in Gyrloft and wouldn't have to worry about invading soldiers, though she wondered how Remeria would fare. Eager to enjoy the meal her mother made, she shoveled food into her mouth, ignoring the ladylike manners her parents attempted to instill upon her.

<hr>

Rumors of war continued spreading. A week later, Sera woke to yelling and hollering outside and her family gone. Early morning hours saw the typical family feeding their animals and breaking their fast, awaiting the full power of the warming sun. Today, something else was happening. She got dressed and grabbed a piece of warmed bread her mother had left for her. Sera coated the bread in butter and gooseberry jam, cramming it in her mouth while pulling on her boots and thick fur coat.

Upon exiting the house, she saw dozens of people running back and forth, carrying loads of supplies. At the edge of Gyrloft, lines of armed men sat atop horses, shivering in their furs and looking around. They weren't local. There weren't that many weapons in Gyrloft, let alone an organized military. At first, Sera thought they were under attack, but the citizens wouldn't be ignoring the attackers by loading up carts.

Her neighbor Angazo Giresh bumped into her, his vision likely skewed because of the large sack he carried on his shoulder. "Oops, sorry." He turned his body, causing the sack to swing back around, hitting her again. "Sorry, Sera. Couldn't see."

"What's going on?"

"We pack. Then go," Angazo said, carrying the sack to a nearby cart. Angazo's fragmented speech pattern made him difficult to understand sometimes. As far as Sera could tell, he'd always been smart but struggled to speak.

Her father said Angazo hadn't always been that way, but the trauma of finding Angazo's brother's body had been too much. His brother had fallen out of a tree during a hunt, and he'd broken his neck. Angazo, at seven years of age, had been first to discover him, empty eyes staring at the sky, mouth agape. He'd become reclusive and refused to speak to anyone for most of his childhood years. When his family forced him out of the house, Jaidik took pity on the man and helped him. Eventually, Angazo recovered from the trauma, though he struggled to recover his social skills. Despite his past, he became one of the town's best hunters, though he never climbed a tree to camouflage himself or to examine the surrounding area.

"Why?" Sera asked.

"We getting invaded." Her neighbor pointed his finger to his left.

She followed the hand. Her father and Fezzel were talking to a pair of soldiers, one of them wearing an enormous bear fur. Sera joined them.

Her father smiled at her. "This is my daughter, Seradal."

The one in the bear's fur licked his mustache, small icicles clinging to the hairs. He held his hand out to shake hers. "Pleasure. I'm Captain Blago Adavir." She shook his hand. He had a harsh grip.

The second soldier inclined his head in her direction, a smug expression on his face, while his eyes ran up and down Sera several times over. He smiled when he caught Sera watching.

None of this was explaining what was happening. "What are you doing here?"

"He's helping us, Sera," Fezzel said.

Captain Adavir sighed. He tucked his thumbs into his belt and launched into a well-rehearsed speech. "Several weeks ago, my scouts reported Calrite ships moored on the western border. A military force disembarked and made camp. They have yet to do anything. A week ago, my superior consulted with Governess Falconel." Governess Stasia Falconel was Cyrok's only political figurehead. Each settlement in the country ran itself until something major occurred. The elected governor living in the capital would make important decisions for Cyrok, and the individual settlements would obey. "She ordered us to evacuate all settlements west and south of the capital. We're to hold up in Vox for your safety."

Sera smiled, elated. A trip to the capital would be nice. "We'd better gather our stuff then."

"We can't. Just the birds," her father said. "Everything else is staying, Sera. We're bringing as much food as we can carry and warm clothes and blankets. There's no room for other possessions."

She frowned, the excitement waning. The idea they may lose all their belongings to an enemy army wasn't appealing. Sera knew she should be afraid, but she'd experienced no fighting nor seen any. Nobody attacked Cyrok, and the idea that somebody had now seemed farfetched. The military wouldn't evacuate them over nothing though, and it was safer at the capital. She knew this procedure was protocol—everyone did—but it didn't make sense that they'd leave so much behind.

Captain Adavir cleared his throat. "No, we wouldn't ask you to leave your birds. Anything else you need, you'll find in Vox. We'll provide temporary quarters and food should you run out. We hope to repel the invaders fast, and everyone can return to their preferred lifestyles. My men and I will be scouting the wilds, looking for threats. I'll even station a pair here to watch for the enemy's approach. You focus on preserving the lives of the gyrfalcons. If we do our job right, you won't even see a single enemy soldier." He paused, licking his mustache again. "We have more than enough men to protect everyone, but we have to leave today."

Smugface, the soldier at the captain's side leaned forward and whispered in his ear.

"Ah, yes." Captain Adavir turned to her father. "Please get your things together. My sergeant and I are going to confer with our scouts to figure out the best and safest route."

"We appreciate your aid," her father said.

Captain Adavir licked his mustache. Bubbles of spit clung to the hairs. "Anything for the Cyroki citizens of our future."

"Your mother is caging the gyrfalcons. I'll go help her carry them to a cart." Her father left her with Fezzel.

Fezzel stared at Captain Adavir and his sergeant hiking back to the army. His face was strained, and his eyes narrowed.

"Fezzel?"

He blinked and focused on her. "Sera?"

"What's wrong?"

"I'm not sure. But this"—he spread his hand out, gesturing at the soldiers—"doesn't seem right. Something's off. Their clothing looks ragged. And there aren't any Falcon Knights among them. There should be a few at least. Be wary, Sera. I don't trust this."

Sera wasn't sure what to make of that. Fezzel was no soldier. After a moment, they followed their father back home.

Once all the food, water, blankets, birds, rabbits, and other necessities had been loaded up, Captain Adavir announced their departure, and they were off. There was little room on the carts, so the Gyrloftans walked alongside and took turns on the spare horses. The soldiers set a grueling pace. It wasn't long before children and elders sat atop one another, balancing bird cages on their laps, so they wouldn't fall behind. Captain Adavir and his soldiers showed little sympathy to the citizens and constantly emphasized that they needed to put distance between Gyrloft and the caravan. The goal was to free themselves of the narrow peninsula and escape into the forest, so they'd be difficult to spot.

Sera didn't think the Calrite army could be anywhere close, but she, and the other citizens, followed orders. Nobody wanted to die. The prospect of walking into an enemy force frightened them, so they made few complaints. Whispers of confusion and suspicion wormed their way through the citizens, but most remained complacent. A couple of times, an odd remark would be slung at Captain Adavir and his guards, but he'd deflect them, noting that urgency was important.

Soldiers and citizens alike would cast continual glances over their shoulders at the shrinking town, almost expecting disaster, though it was impossible for anyone to be behind them. The only direction the army could come from was the front of the procession.

It wasn't long before the mood soured to a gloomy depression. Few remained excited, like Sera, to reach the capital. She didn't like the reason for it, but she was traveling.

Her legs burned at every step. She walked aside the cart where her family's gyrfalcons rested. Russell eyed her, then turned his neck away, offended at not being allowed to soar the skies. Many gyrfalcons joined in a cacophonous chorus of screeching as if they, too, knew something was amiss. This visibly unnerved the soldiers, though they said nothing. Smugface ordered them not to free any birds; Captain Adavir didn't want to give away their position.

Conversation between travelers was short and whispered. Nobody had much to say, and their guides were even less talkative, only discussing their current route or news from various scouts coming and going. Sera's own family kept to themselves, and she didn't intervene. They were all exhausted.

Because there was an entire regiment of soldiers and a whole town, their pace was slower than normal travel. Three days into the journey, Sera's mother started lagging. She held the back of the cart, as if hoping it would relieve the burden of walking. Fezzel watched the soldiers suspiciously. He'd done that since they'd left Gyrloft. The soldiers, in Sera's mind, were courteous and seemed protective of the group. She liked them, and they made her feel safe. The Gyrloftans had a scattering of hunting bows and daggers on their persons, but the soldiers had proper weapons of war—swords and longbows made for farther distances. Their interactions seemed professional and skillful, and they often communicated with a simple gesture or look. They must've worked together for a long time, which raised her confidence in them.

At one point, a citizen called out to Captain Adavir, "Cyr, where are the Falcon Knights? Shouldn't there be at least one?"

Captain Adavir laughed. "You think the Avian Knights have a purpose here? They're about to go to war. I'm the best you've got. Quiet yourselves and keep marching, my friend. It's going to be a cold one, so save your energy."

They stuck toward the eastern coast the entire journey, traveling northwest in the direction of Vox, but on the afternoon of the third day, they entered the forest and escaped the peninsula. The general air of suspense and fear lightened. Rather than hug the coast the entire way up, the captain suggested they retreat into the forest to mask their presence. A majority of Gyrloftans agreed.

"I don't like this," Fezzel said. "If we hugged the coast, the forest would still shield us from this supposed army. Going in the forest will only slow us down." But after proffering this information to their parents and receiving nothing in return, he quieted.

Shouts of terror crept up the line of fleeing citizens and soldiers alike. A thick, dark smoke trailed into the sky from the direction of Gyrloft. Because they were within the trees, it was impossible to tell if it was coming from the town, but everyone assumed it had. There wasn't anything between the forest and town that would generate vast smoke. The mood of the Gyrloftans plummeted further, and people thanked and praised the soldiers more and more. Sera wasn't sure how this could've happened without spotting another large army. One couldn't see from one end of the peninsula to the other, but it wasn't far enough to escape other signs of a moving army. Smoke from fires, camp remnants, and footprints were all nonexistent.

Even Fezzel's attitude changed once he glimpsed the column of smoke. "Perhaps I was wrong."

That night, the Gyrloftans made their huddles on the ground—four or five people laying their blankets together and sleeping in a tight row to preserve heat by the fires. It was the coldest night yet, and Sera found it difficult to sleep. Whispers from soldiers on watch kept her awake late, and her father's snores didn't help things either. She only made a few complete sentences out though.

"Seems like Blago wants to double-time it, tomorrow."

"Nah, I heard he wants to proceed with the plan. No more marching."

She didn't know what that meant. The words sounded good, but the constant whispering unnerved her. Sera shifted her thoughts elsewhere.

She thought of their home, gone. The destroyed town in which she grew up. This didn't concern her the same way it bothered other refugees. She was excited it meant there were unknown places to experience. Sera decided she wouldn't return to Gyrloft and help rebuild after everything was over. She'd travel and find something else that suited her desires. She didn't know what that might be though. What would her mother and father do when the invasion was over? They'd likely echo the sentiments of the other townsfolk returning to their home. *How will I tell my family I'm not coming back?* It seemed wrong to bring up now. She'd figure it out later.

She'd fallen asleep and dreamed of watching Russell flying alongside Golden Royce, her father's bird. They'd taken the gyrfalcons out to catch wild invaders, but the invaders kept shooting at the birds with arrows, and the birds refused to swoop down.

A moan next to her startled her awake. A sick noise, like a spoon stirring potato mash or her mother's noodles. Mush. A spurt.

She heard another moan closer. It sounded like when her father had stuck a pig with a butcher's knife once. She opened her eyes just as metal flashed in the firelight, a sword being drawn from her brother's chest. Blood dripped from the corners of his chin, and he looked at her with empty eyes. She screamed until her lungs were empty.

The camp awoke. The townsfolk shouted and screamed. Sounds of steel being drawn and more people dying.

The man that stabbed her brother swore, and the hilt of his sword connected with her head. Stars blossomed before her eyes, her vision went black, and she drifted off. It wasn't until later she realized Captain Adavir's second-in-command, Smugface, had done the deed. She didn't know his name, didn't care to learn it.

Sera blinked, cracking her eyes open. Sunlight shone down from an opening in the treetops above her. Despite a light snowfall, the sun warmed her face, though it didn't take away the dull throbbing in her temple. She remembered being attacked in the middle of the night and Fezzel's empty stare. Something rough rubbed her wrists—rope wrapping her hands and ankles. Sera heard plenty of footsteps and sounds of fires popping and crackling. The smell of meat cooking was prevalent.

Shifting her body, she rolled onto her side. Soldiers patrolled the campsite. Others hunched over fires, and beyond them, a great bonfire blazed. A horrified moment later, she realized the fire was consuming hundreds of bodies.

"How about this one, Captain?"

She craned her neck to look over her shoulder. A soldier held the caged Russell.

"Yeah, sure," Captain Adavir said.

The soldier reached into the cage and retrieved the bird. The man plunged a dagger into Russell's neck and sawed his head off while he was still alive. Sera's gyrfalcon screeched once.

It took a moment for realization to dawn. Then she screamed, "What are you doing?" She struggled to stand, but the tight bindings kept her down.

The soldier glanced over at her, smirked, and continued to slide the blade back and forth, severing her bird's head off. He plucked Russell. Sera looked around the encampment. Several other groups of soldiers hovered over fires, turning spits with other birds. They were having a feast.

Boots appeared in her vision, and she followed them up to see Captain Adavir standing there, holding a bowl. "I've brought you some food." He reached into his bear fur and retrieved a pouch of water. "And a drink." He set the bowl down in front of her. It contained smoked meat and hardtack. "Calm yourself. We need leverage, not more casualties, eh?"

She was ravenous but disgusted. She also didn't want to die. "You brought me a gyrfalcon to eat?"

"Sure did." He selected a piece of hardtack and began chewing on it.

"What happened?"

"Yes, yes." Captain Adavir waved his hand at her. "You'd like to know what happened, I'm sure. There's not much to say on the matter."

"You killed my brother!"

"And your mother."

"What?" Sera struggled to free her hands. What she'd do with them, she hadn't yet worked out.

"Don't bother. I'll cut them for you." Captain Adavir produced a small knife, licking his mustache. "You try to hurt anybody or run, and we do something else to hurt you."

"What else could you possibly do?" Tears filled her eyes. Her heart pounded in her chest, whether with a burning fury or an empty sadness over her mother's death, she wasn't sure.

"We could eat more of your birds. Or." He paused, licking his mustache. She hated him for this annoying habit. "We could kill your father, too."

Her heart did a small leap of joy. *Father is alive.* "Where is he?"

Captain Adavir crouched and cut through the ropes on her hands. "He's with the others."

She waited for more information.

"The ones that are conscious, we've moved. You'll go there after you eat"—he pointed at the bowl—"all of that."

She crammed food into her mouth. She was starving. The meat didn't look appealing. Overcooked and blackened. Identifying the taste was impossible because it tasted like charcoal. It was sustenance, and she was famished. She drained the water and afterward gnawed on hardtack. The captain gave her a second waterskin to replace the first.

Sera wanted to ask Captain Adavir about what happened and why, but considering they'd just killed a bunch of her people and birds, she figured she should receive the small kindness being offered in silence. She wasn't going to get herself raped or killed for insolence.

She looked up. Smugface glared at her from across a fire. A bloody streak from a gyrfalcon's talon crossed his face—she'd seen plenty of those wounds in her life—and she didn't like the hungry way he stared. She ignored the man and finished the bread.

"Good." Captain Adavir stood. He grabbed her hands and brought them behind her body, tying them again. Afterward, he slung her over his shoulder and crossed the camp.

Smugface stood and approached her, but the captain dismissed him with a wave of his hand. "Go. You will not sully the live prisoners. You already had your fun with the dead."

Smugface looked upset and pointed to his scarred face. "Her father's falcon got me. I should get—"

The captain ignored him and waved Smugface away. He passed several carts that were in the middle of a small clearing, watched over by soldiers. Or bandits? She didn't know how to label them now.

Then Sera hit the wooden cart hard as the captain dumped her in among other prisoners. "By the way," the captain said, licking his mustache, tongue dancing over miniature icicles, and smiling down at her. "You definitely have more of your mother in you." Face morphing into a sadistic smirk, Captain Blago Adavir marched away amid jeers and laughs from his men, all laughing at her expense. Realizing the charred meat was not gyrfalcon, Sera retched over the sides of the cart, hating everything about the captain and his men. And in that moment, herself.

EDELBROCK BRENDIS

1st Cycle of Autumn, 231st Reign of Garcovi
Lochwall, Calrym

Earl Scayde Haklon was one of the most powerful and richest nobles in Calrym and *the* most in the city of Lochwall. The nobleman owned a vast estate people visited every year, including Mikas Garcovi, Calrym's king. Plenty of bets were placed over the fighters of Buzzard's Bowl, and Scayde Haklon received a percentage of every transaction that took place there. He earned his arrogant sneer and snide remarks, for sure, and the pompous way he dressed in his fine silks and flowing cape. However, this didn't mean that Edelbrock had to like the man, who had his arm around Jaylena's waist.

The marshal and his men filed into Edelbrock's bedroom, one of them holding a pair of handcuffs. Another of the guards rested a palm on the hilt of his sword.

"We can do this one of two ways, Ed," Scayde said. "We can do this the hard way." He gestured to the handcuffs, his yellow cape swirling around him. "Or we can do this the easy way. Now the hard way, you'll be most familiar with. The marshal takes you into custody, and you're arrested. You have a trial, and as we both are well aware, they will convict you of murder. Along with a bunch of other charges, I am *sure*." He emphasized this last word a little too much for Edelbrock's liking.

"However, because I have become so close with this wonderful woman." Scayde pulled Jaylena closer to him, and she giggled, her stiff body melting like butter in his arms. It made Edelbrock sick. "I have invited you to come over for a late-night chat at my estate." Scayde beamed, his bristling mustache staring at Edelbrock like a fat caterpillar.

Edelbrock ignored his wife and Scayde Haklon and instead turned his attention to the marshal. "Everic, don't do this." Everic Deywin had been Lochwall's marshal for several years. While Edelbrock couldn't say they'd ever been close, he'd had several chats with him.

The marshal frowned in response, his thin mustache twitching. He shifted a clump of skachi, an addictive chewing leaf, around in his mouth. "I'm sorry, Edelbrock, but you murdered somebody in cold blood. If it were up to me, you'd already be in a cell, so you should really be thankful Lord Haklon isn't having me do just that." He spat some skachi juice out the corner of his mouth. It landed on Edelbrock's bed. "Listen, boy, this is your chance to live. Take it."

Edelbrock frowned. The glob of spittle sank into the sheets. "How dare you desecrate my house with *your* presence, Marshal."

"Don't worry about that." Scayde shrugged. "It's not like you'll be returning here anytime soon. So what's it going to be, Ed? The simple way? Or maybe the hard way?"

Edelbrock chewed on his lip. His fingernails dug into his hands. Scayde stood there, hands spread out like he was offering Edelbrock the deal of a century. All Edelbrock had to do was accept it. Jaylena leaned against Scayde and looked anywhere but at Edelbrock. He could've killed her.

"You're running out of time, Ed."

"The easy way," Edelbrock muttered. He hated himself for it.

"Probably the best option," the barrister, Chardaine, said, offering a condescending smile and raising a pointer finger in the air, as if to elaborate how intelligent he was.

Edelbrock could've killed him, too. He'd near forgotten Chardaine's presence. Another person who'd betrayed him. Scayde Haklon had both the guard and the court in his pocket. The likelihood Edelbrock would receive a fair trial was laughable. Even if he received a fair trial, it wasn't like he'd get a better deal. He'd killed somebody, he'd gotten caught, and they had plenty of evidence. And his wife would testify against him. *Fuck her. I hope they all die.*

A tug on Edelbrock's robes brought him back. Marshal Deywin was searching his sleeves. How did they know? *Jaylena.* She knew a lot. This spoke of weeks of distrust and investigation she must have undertaken. A plot to destroy her husband. *And what about Gordy?*

"There we go." The marshal removed the tiny crossbow from Edelbrock's sleeve. He spat on the floor.

Gordane's cries distracted Edelbrock from punching the marshal. Would he ever be able to hold his son again?

"I have a carriage prepared. Bring Lord Brendis outside after you finish your search, Marshal," said Scayde.

Marshal Deywin inclined his head toward Scayde, more than a nod, not quite a bow. "Yes, Lord Haklon."

"And you, my darling angel, go fetch that adorable boy you have and meet me outside."

Jaylena exited, followed by Scayde—who gave Edelbrock a nod before leaving—and then Chardaine.

Marshal Deywin stripped Edelbrock of his clothes, searching every cavity of his body. If the marshal wasn't so rough, Edelbrock may have even liked parts of it. Marshal Deywin wasn't an ugly man, though the mustache could go, and the skachi was a definite turnoff.

A guard tossed Edelbrock a new set of large rich-blue satin robes. He slipped his arms into the cooling sleeves, surprised at how comfortable the material was. Scayde Haklon ensured even his prisoners had the finest. This detail confirmed Edelbrock was really missing out on the rich lifestyle—even Scayde's prisoners lived better than Edelbrock. He'd let it slip out of his hands. All because he'd married a conniving bitch. Because when he was younger, he'd been foolish.

"Come on." Marshal Deywin pushed Edelbrock. He found himself escorted out of his own home. For the last time.

He stumbled toward the horse-drawn carriage, morose at the thought of never returning. The life he'd desired—so close—slipped away with each footstep.

"Here, you can sit with me. Up front." The marshal hopped onto a bench where a driver sat. He dragged Edelbrock after him and addressed the two soldiers who'd traded looks. "No, you don't have to come. I've got it under control. Go home and get some rest." He leaned over Edelbrock and spat some skachi juice onto the cobbled stones, then nodded to the driver.

The driver slapped the reins, and the horses took off,

trotting down the street, hooves clicking and clacking in a regular pattern.

"I've done you a service," Marshal Deywin said. "I let you sit on the end. Jump, and you'll just cause yourself more trouble, yeah?"

Edelbrock remained silent, eyes downcast. The injustice of what was taking place irritated him. *It's not injustice,* he conceded. And anywhere that followed the rule of King Mikas—anywhere other than the nomadic Camel Clans in Vessia—any serious crime would result in lifetime imprisonment or death. He'd been caught murdering somebody. The only thing worse than that was treason against the king, which Edelbrock wouldn't have considered for a mere share of Buzzard's Bowl. Maybe the entire compound though.

Voices drifted from the carriage, as did lots of giggling. Edelbrock's blood boiled at the thought of Scayde flirting with his wife, perhaps touching her in sensual places. His muscles tensed. He wanted nothing more than to jump off his seat and enter the carriage, placing his hands around Scayde's neck and squeezing with all the power he could muster. The marshal must have felt this tension because his hand was patting Edelbrock's knee. Was it a reassuring pat or a threat? Edelbrock wasn't sure. He knew escape was impossible.

It seemed like hours for the carriage to canter through the moonlit city, though the carriage never stopped. Wherever they rode, people made it a point to escape its path. When Scayde Haklon rolled through, they treated him as if he were the king himself. Twice, Edelbrock witnessed people scream in surprise, scurrying to get other people or another carriage out of the way before Lord Haklon reached them.

The city's vast population meant there were people up at all hours. The smaller amount of people didn't lessen the constant drone of noise—laughter, wheels of carts and carriages squeaking on cobblestone, the clip-clop of horse hooves, the shout of a town guard, the retching of a drunkard, and conspiratorial whispers in alleys.

After a while, they passed through the city's gates. Lochwall was an expansive city, and impenetrable gigantic stone walls surrounded it. A previous king of the Garcovi line had created the city with intentions to lock down if there was ever a military crisis. Scayde Haklon's estate was a little outside the city and had its own smaller walls. In reality, the estate was a militarized fort with enough soldiers to form a private battalion. This, Edelbrock assumed, was to prevent gladiators from escaping or raising a coup, while also providing the spectators with a sense of security and a deterrent for those who sought to take advantage of all the money changing hands.

Similar to Lochwall, a thick stone wall surrounded Scayde's compound. Guards manned several entrances and patrolled the ramparts. Many people would even argue that Haklon's estate was better guarded than the city, if comparing by size. The center of the estate was an enormous amphitheater—Buzzard's Bowl, the arena that people came from all over the world to watch. Just inside the gated entrances were barracks housing off-shift soldiers, their proximity offering further protection. A stone mansion stood on the northern end of the compound atop a small hill—Scayde Haklon's manor.

Several other buildings, made of wattle and daub, littered the grounds: servant quarters, plenty of smaller houses and buildings that homed employees, and five buildings that could only be where the five Houses had their own personal retinue of soldiers and employees. These latter structures also led to the entrances where the fighters lived. The House buildings formed a pentagon with Buzzard's Bowl in the center and roads between each structure. Underground tunnels led to each House's hypogeum, where they would be magically sealed inside—only guards on the outside of the forcefield could open it. Inside the hypogeum, the gladiators lived in a vast complex. To reach the arena where they would prepare to fight, unseen by the citizens in the stands, they had to enter Buzzard's Bowl through another sealed entrance only Magicai could open. In fact, if Edelbrock was correct, the fighters remained underground unless fighting. It sounded like prison, though in prison you didn't have to train every day in order to survive. Or maybe you did.

The carriage stopped just outside of the spectator entrance to Buzzard's Bowl. This was confusing.

"Get off." Marshal Deywin gave Edelbrock a small nudge.

Edelbrock hopped off, the marshal following. The driver was already at the carriage door, helping Lord Haklon out.

Edelbrock gathered his robes and pulled them around his body, looking around the giant estate in wonder and, if he was being frank, fear.

"I have a bit of a treat for you, Ed," Scayde said. "We're going to discuss a few things in the King's Stand."

It was the highest stand in Buzzard's Bowl, where King Mikas Garcovi watched the games when he showed up. This was also where the five House Heads and any important guests sat.

Scayde, Jaylena carrying Gordane, and Chardaine led the way. The marshal remained behind Edelbrock, prodding him along. Knowing the barrister rode over with Scayde and Jaylena calmed Edelbrock a little. He doubted they did anything too sexual with the man watching. *Perhaps that is Jaylena's new thing?* He needed to remove that thought from his mind, so he focused on looking around as he climbed an endless staircase. Behind him, the carriage driver talked to the horses.

Buzzard's Bowl was an open-roofed circular arena with seating for thousands of spectators. Massive rows of benches encased the humongous pit below. The lowest benches were at least thirty feet above the arena's plain dirt ground. Each section was cordoned off by a railing and a set of stone stairs that climbed to the highest spectator seats. It seemed as if anybody sitting in those seats were part of a massive courthouse, judging those unfortunates who fought beneath them for their favor.

If rumors were true, the arena sometimes shaped into random battlefields from a variety of terrain and set pieces to keep both the fighters on their toes and the crowd interested. Edelbrock didn't know what watching the fights was like. Jaylena had known if he'd watched when they had a bit of money, he'd have wanted to gamble it. She hadn't wanted to waste the small inheritance her father had gifted when they married. Looking back, he knew she was right.

Scayde led them up a second carpeted, and roofed, staircase with railings coated in gold. The stairs exited onto a covered platform where there was a half wall made of thick glass facing the arena, enabling viewers to see the entire arena while remaining in their chairs. Lanterns hung from the roofing, bathing the platform in a soft glow. Scayde took a spot in a large, throne-like chair, Jaylena sitting beside him in a smaller throne. On a day when the king was visiting, that'd be his spot. The barrister sat in another chair on Jaylena's left.

Marshal Deywin guided Edelbrock to a chair and

deposited him. Then the marshal took a vigilant spot behind Edelbrock, a hand resting on his shoulder. A constant reminder he was there.

"So." Scayde waved his arm out toward the elaborate arena. "What do you think, Ed?"

"It's quite, uh, fancy." He didn't know what to say. What *should* he say to this man? The person who was going to ruin Edelbrock's life.

"Yes. Yes, I suppose it is."

He was over it. Waiting to learn what would happen. He'd been impressing and entertaining men in power for most of his life, and he knew they enjoyed playing with their prey. Unless that prey called them out, in which case the supposed prey became well-respected or loathed and deemed an immediate enemy for having the gall to speak up. "Mind getting to the point?" Edelbrock asked. Perhaps he'd predicted Lord Haklon. The man was smiling at him.

"A man that likes to skip the pleasantries." Scayde's smile lingered.

A servant approached with a tray in his hands. A bottle of whiskey and some small glasses filled with ice were sitting on it. Edelbrock assumed they'd been conjured by a Magicus. Ice wasn't something Calrites had too often.

"Mmm, do you require anything else, Lord Haklon?" the servant asked in a monotonous drone.

"Thank you, Tanibris. You may leave us," Scayde said.

Tanibris bowed and whisked himself away.

Scayde poured drinks. The first he handed to Jaylena, who was balancing Gordane in her lap with one hand. She shifted the baby in her arms, and Gordy's face came into view. Edelbrock immediately saw himself in his son. Gordy's forehead, eyes, cheeks, chin—these features all came from the Brendis family.

Second, Scayde handed one to Chardaine, who accepted the drink after first refusing. "Nonsense, nonsense." Scayde said, giving the barrister a pat on the arm. "Well deserved, my friend." Third, he passed to Marshal Deywin, who received the drink while still maintaining his grasp on Edelbrock's shoulder. Edelbrock was fourth, but he raised a hand to decline.

Scayde shook his head, *tsk*ing. "That, Ed, is an incredibly rude gesture to deny your host's drink. I shall, however, forgive you." He took the drink for himself, clinking it against Jaylena's before downing the shot. He swallowed and smacked his lips. "If anybody would like some more, please help yourselves." He set the tray on a nearby end table.

Scayde turned to Edelbrock, smiling. "Now, allow me to entertain my guests. I believe it is often customary to discuss a guest's life accolades, yes?" Edelbrock hadn't heard of this custom before. The barrister assented with an eager bob of his head—he'd clearly do anything to please Scayde—and Jaylena agreed with a sneer and stiffening of her neck.

"Perfect." Scayde turned to face Edelbrock. "Then we shall begin with the guest of the hour. Edelbrock, I understand you have a very interesting history. Correct me if I'm wrong, but when you were younger, you were a prominent military officer, yes?" Edelbrock opened his mouth to answer, but the question was rhetorical because Scayde continued. "Most notably, you led a sizable number of men during the Vessian Incursion, successfully beating back nearly twice your number and routing the major force during the Battle of Leeward."

Edelbrock remembered the battle. It had taken place south of the Valkrynd Mountains, the leeward side of the range. Dust and sand had blinded them during half the battle.

"After gaining this recognition, you received a promotion and given a command, for which, if my research and understanding into your past is correct, you thrived. Oh yes, Major Edelbrock Brendis was a name many people used to speak highly of. And naturally, once the war ended, there was no need for Major Brendis anymore now, was there? So what better way to reward such a fine young gentleman, of zero reputation I remind you, by elevating him to minor nobility, granting him the coveted title of lord.

"Surely, nothing could go wrong." Scayde chuckled, and the barrister echoed his laugh. "With such a lack of action, it then seems like you gained weight and lost a decent amount of strength. For surely, if somebody of a musculature build needed to *eliminate* some competition, they wouldn't use a poisoned dart now, would they? Interestingly enough, a frightened young woman approached me recently. In her hands was a young baby."

What? Jaylena went to him? Edelbrock groaned. The marshal's hand pressed slightly harder on his shoulder in warning.

"A boy, in fact," Scayde said. "His name is Gordane. Gordy for short, I've heard. This woman pleaded with me. It was of the utmost importance, you understand. Apparently, there was a simple man who thought he deserved more. His ambitions and aspirations had no ceiling, and he neglected the family he'd just begun. Ironic, isn't it, how the ones closest to us are all too often the ones who turn on us?

"I took the woman in. Consoled her. I live life with a simple philosophy, you see, and it's 'you never know who may have information you might need.' You may have forgotten by now, otherwise you probably wouldn't have been so shocked at your wife's betrayal, that you had a quick conversation late one night with her. Half-drunk and tired, you rambled off an elaborate plan. One of increasing your personal wealth and attempting to get into this." Scayde waved his hand to encompass the arena, his house, his entire estate.

Edelbrock didn't remember the conversation, but he believed it had happened. He often discussed important matters with Jaylena in their bed before passing out for the night. Being drunk would've exasperated this.

"Your wife found a much better way, a safer way, to get what she coveted. A married woman just wants three things, Ed—happiness, financial security, and a strong cock. You provided her with none of these, and thus, you failed at the marriage game." Scayde poured himself another drink, sipped some of it, and swallowed. "Mmm, success can't taste any better.

"So with knowledge of your attempt at stealing a fifth of Buzzard's Bowl, I hatched *my* plan. I'm more adept at completing them, as you can see. You may wonder, I suppose, why I would allow you to murder Trigg Gelbrandy. And it's a sad truth: I never wanted Trigg Gelbrandy to have ownership. As I'd foreseen from the beginning, he was an absent House Head, and that is unforgiving if you ask me. There's much more competition with an active leader, one who wishes to see their gladiators *succeed* in the arena. One who wishes to increase their earnings.

"The viewers like a show. They like people to *believe* in. They like to watch people disembowel others. Most of all, they like the thrill gambling provides. That sinking pit of despair when you lose *everything*. Or, even better, that thrill of *winning*. Knowing that you're going home ten times richer than you could have possibly dreamed is any man or woman's wish. Obviously, you had the same issue. I will tell you one thing, however, Ed. You have given your wife financial stability, and for that, I suppose she should really thank you."

Edelbrock swallowed, sweat gathering on his forehead. Chardaine rose and handed a piece of parchment to Scayde. He took it, nodding in thanks to the barrister who was now inking a quill.

"It's imperative that you sign this," Scayde said. "Otherwise, I would have to come clean about your forgery attempt, and that would lead toward a lot of legal litigation we are both attempting to avoid. I wanted Trigg Gelbrandy removed. Not only because he was a terrible House Head but also because he was the last Gelbrandy. Which meant that I could then transfer ownership to somebody else. Somebody"—Scayde's eyes flicked to Jaylena—"that will do as I wish. By securing this fifth of Buzzard's Bowl under Jaylena's name, I will regain control of another fifth of the arena. This means double the profits. The arena has never been this successful before, Ed. I would enjoy more money, and I'm sure your wife would enjoy more than the meager sum you have earned during your lifespan." He handed the piece of parchment to the barrister after signing it himself. "Sign that, and I will allow you to hold your son once more."

"*Once* more?" Edelbrock's hands clenched. He wanted to stand, but the marshal's suppressing hand on his shoulder kept him sitting.

"Details, Ed, details. One thing at a time. Sign it, please."

Chardaine walked over and handed the quill to Edelbrock. "This document allows the transfer of your one-fifth share of Buzzard's Bowl and gives it to your wife." The barrister dropped the document on Edelbrock's lap. "This second document"—he produced another cream-colored sheet of parchment—"is a legal form of divorce, allowing your wife to reclaim her maiden name and to sever all ties with you. The marriage will become annulled, as if it never happened. It's important that you understand what's happening here. For legal reasons." Chardaine offered Scayde another bob of his head, a proud smile on his face. Like he'd rehearsed this and pulled it off spectacularly. Which, judging the barrister on his behavior, he probably had rehearsed this.

Edelbrock felt trapped. There was nothing he could do about this. His wife was leaving him, inheriting the very thing he'd desired most of his life—unlimited power and money. A connection to the most powerful person he knew. "Let me work for you," he blurted. As he stammered the request, he realized how foolish he came off. It was his only shot at avoiding whatever Scayde planned for him.

Scayde laughed. "You already do."

Edelbrock frowned, and the marshal's grip tightened on his shoulder. "Sign it," the marshal said.

Edelbrock signed the deed. He didn't have another choice. And by cooperating, he'd hold Gordane again. The barrister took the deed and added his own signage to the document before taking it over to Jaylena, who also signed.

"Now the annulment," Jaylena said. She perked up, staring at Edelbrock's quivering hand. He could tell she was eager. Thirsty for the wealth she was about to receive, even at the expense of him. Angry, he scrawled his name on the document. She was so quick to leave him in the dust. Why did she ever agree to marry him?

"Marvelous," Scayde said. He removed Gordane from Jaylena's arms, bouncing the baby against his chest. "Sign your ugly marriage away, Jaylena." Gordane cooed. Edelbrock wanted to vomit. Scayde walked with the baby, surveying the arena in front of him.

"Stop that." Hatred bubbled up inside of him. "Give him here." Edelbrock tried to stand, but Marshal Deywin's hand pushed him back into his seat.

"I normally don't take demands, Ed," Scayde said, turning to glare at him. "However, in this circumstance, I understand we are all stressed and close to our breaking points." He handed Gordane to Edelbrock. "Cute child though, Ed."

Edelbrock rocked Gordane in his arms, ignoring Scayde. He feared what may come next. A lengthy prison sentence? Perhaps some demeaning work for Scayde himself. He'd said Edelbrock worked for him now.

Several minutes passed. Edelbrock clung to his son. He didn't want to let him go. He regretted he hadn't been around more. These moments didn't last forever, and his son was nearing a year old. It's true what they said. They really grew up so fast . . . something he didn't understand until he was a parent. His own parents had expressed a similar sentiment. *If I ever get out of this, I'll be around* every *damn day.*

Scayde, Jaylena, and the barrister all drank another celebratory glass of whiskey—the barrister offering a loud "ah" and smacking his lips. Edelbrock ignored them, watching his son fall asleep. The moonlight bounced off Gordane's small nose and warmed Edelbrock's heart.

"Well, I think that's about enough celebrating," Scayde said. He approached Edelbrock, reaching for Gordane.

"Not yet. Please."

"I'm sorry, Ed, but it's time we go over some further details. Unless you truly want to rot away in prison forever."

"I don't." He shook his head and allowed Scayde to take Gordane from his arms.

For a moment, Scayde looked down at the child. "Ah, they're always so peaceful while they rest, are they not?" He walked toward the glass half wall, cape flowing in the cool nighttime air. "I have figured out a way to prevent you from going to prison, Ed." He leaned against one of the half wall's supporting pillars, staring at the arena.

Edelbrock felt a nervousness any parent would, afraid of the pillar snapping, the glass shattering, and his son plummeting off the stand.

"I'm not sure how much you're going to enjoy this, Ed, but you are going to be joining in the games. You'll train awhile, and then you'll fight. For your life."

"Excuse me?" He'd left his fighting days behind. He wasn't a warrior anymore.

"You're going to be a fighter in Buzzard's Bowl. I'm giving you an opportunity to make a name for yourself. Give you a taste of that fame you were looking for."

"N-no. I'd go to prison before I'd do that." The chances of living through a single season in the arena's games couldn't be good. Going to prison for a decade would devastate him but would be tolerable. Dying wasn't something he wanted.

"Too late, Ed, I've already arranged it. The barrister's paid off. The marshal's paid off. Your wife's paid off. You want me to retract all my agreements and either ask for the money back or let them keep it? That'd be a terrible business, Ed. Betrayal isn't a good look unless you put them in the ground forever. Perhaps you're not as savvy as you may think you are." Scayde's voice dripped with a malice that wasn't there before.

"You can't expect me to go along with this." Edelbrock struggled to stand again. The marshal's hand pushed him back into the seat.

"Oh, believe me, I expect you to. In fact, you have little choice in the matter." He traded compassionate looks with Jaylena. "I apologize to you for having to put up with him for so long, Jaylena."

"It's over now," she said, hatred on her face. Edelbrock felt like a maggot to her, something she was scraping off the bottom of her boot.

"To new beginnings then, my friends!" And Scayde tossed Gordane over his shoulder. Gordy hung in midair for a split second, then plunged a couple hundred feet toward the arena's dirt floor. An audible thud followed. Edelbrock's fears came true.

Gordane was dead.

"No!" Edelbrock screamed, forcing his way out from the marshal's hand. Marshal Deywin put two hands on him, forcing him back down into the chair, restraining him. "You bastard!" He squirmed against the firm grip, trying to free himself. It was futile.

"You know where to put him, Marshal. And you, Ed. I'll be seeing you at the next Draft. Oh, how exciting this will be. Never forget that I gave you that last moment with your son." He drained another glass of whiskey, then looked at Edelbrock one last time. "I'm sorry for your loss, Lord Brendis." Then he left. The barrister followed him, silent but with a pained expression written on his face.

Jaylena hesitated before leaving. "Best of luck to you, Edelbrock. I hope you die a warrior's death."

"You'll regret this! I'll make sure you regret this! I

hope you die a miserable death, you insufferable bitch! How could you do that to our son?"

She opened her mouth like she was about to start yelling, thought better of it, and talked in a calm, serene, but biting voice. "You ruined my life. I don't want any connection to you, Ed. *Any* connection. Lord Haklon decided to help me sever those connections and bring me back up to the quality of life I deserve. With his guidance, I'm sure to return to my proper station." She paused, then said, "And any further children will come from a *proper* bloodline." She frowned, grasped her stomach, then shook her head and followed Scayde.

Handcuffs slammed shut on Edelbrock's wrists.

He was lost in grief and tears. But mostly tears.

KELDEN STOOLE

2nd Cycle of Autumn, 231st Reign of Garcovi
Qothe

It would be a slow walk to Yordiv, a city about three-fourths of the way to the University of Arcanical Arts. Old, unused trails wound back and forth between mountains and across grassy plains. Because of the poverty level of the continent, travel wasn't a common occurrence, except the odd merchant or down-on-their-luck villager looking for new life.

The journey south started uneventful—unless hunger, muscle spasms, endless walking, and constant exhaustion counted. Anditus Roberon was the only one not exhausted. He rode his horse and complained frequently of knee pain, thus he was "unable" to offer his horse up to anyone else. Kelden thought this selfish, which, as Roberon later proved, he was nothing but. Roberon also crossed words with some of the citizens who complained about their aching legs. They threatened to fight Roberon over the horse so weaker travelers could relax. However, they never followed through on these threats, and Kelden suspected this was because Roberon had experience sword fighting, whereas they did not.

Much of the time, Kelden spent with Sungoa. When he wasn't joking or complaining with her, he received basic sword training by the guard Nauc. Nauc offered to train them in the art of defending themselves. After they'd eaten their soybeans, apples, and smoked meat of the day—either brought on the journey or hunted down by Roberon with his bow—Nauc trained Kelden, Sungoa, and several of the other citizens on how to swing a blade and parry attacks.

On the third night, after they completed training but before turning in, a group of men invaded the camp, demanding money and food. They had many weapons and outnumbered the travelers. When the bandits left with everyone's money and most of the group's food, the Warwin citizens regrouped and noticed that somewhere in the commotion, Anditus Roberon had disappeared with his horse. The coward.

"I just can't believe that he would've done that after promising my father he'd escort us," Kelden said. He was shocked Roberon had gone back on his word to his father already. That he ran away at the slightest sign of danger surprised Kelden, though he wasn't sure why. All along, he'd expected Roberon to prove he was a nefarious person.

"We always knew he was a shady individual," Sungoa said.

It didn't change Kelden's surprise. He'd thought Roberon's vow to his father meant something.

"Get some sleep. We want to get as far from here as we can tomorrow," Nauc said. He was right. They needed to flee the bandits.

From then on, they set a rotating guard, though

whenever Kelden woke in the middle of the night, he always saw Nauc walking around the fire, alert.

Kelden's day of birth had come and gone unannounced; he'd become an adult and never realized it.

The next night, a smaller group of the same bandits returned. The brigands commanded they offer a woman as tribute for passing through their territory. Nauc denied this, and they drew blades. A small skirmish broke out, leaving two of the bandits dead. Unfortunately, one of the guards died in battle and another took a nasty wound in the stomach.

Kelden was lucky and only had to draw his sword and appear menacing. The fighting never reached him.

Nursing a bad morale, the group continued their march to Yordiv. The nights were quiet as the guards watched the darkness in vigilance, and all conversation was held in hushed voices.

With Roberon gone, one of the guards dead, and another wounded, Nauc became more vigilant, explaining how to fight inexperienced bandits. "Fight hard and fast, as you may surprise them. These bandits aren't used to proper resistance and won't be able to defend themselves. They won't be expecting it."

Practicing with swords wrapped in clothing helped because they could tap each other without wounding, though it was rare when a practice session ended without somebody developing a nasty welt. The bandits never returned, for which Kelden was thankful.

Kelden couldn't sleep during the fifth night. He went to relieve his bladder, then returned and found Nauc pacing.

"Don't you think you should probably get some rest?"

Nauc shook his head. "We're nearly to Yordiv. Once we get there, I'll be able to sleep easier. I'm trying to figure out how we're going to afford supplies. We're barely making it as it is." The group survived on small scraps every day, and hunger was a familiar bitch pawing at their stomachs. With Roberon gone, they'd lost a good portion of their food supplies and his hunting prowess.

One of the Warwin citizens was well-versed in edible plants and often found a root to stew up. Vegetable stew was becoming the norm, and Kelden wasn't a fan. The muck was revolting, but he hadn't the heart to tell them. Sometimes Kelden would spot a goat, further aggravating his roaring stomach. Without Roberon or his bow, he knew they couldn't catch one, though. Because of the lack of a reliable food source, they abandoned the bare roads and hiked closer to the shoreline. There, they collected mussels, oysters, crabs, snails, and, to Kelden's amazement, starfish, which Nauc cooked by boiling them. It wasn't Kelden's favorite dish, but it was better than vegetable stew.

The guard's wounded stomach festered and became infected. The closer the group drew to Yordiv, the worse he became. The night of their sixth day of walking, they arrived at the city. The wounded guard was turning yellow and complained about agonizing pain.

The group dispersed, looking for lodging and a Healer. They found both, but they also found they didn't have enough money to afford much, even after selling most of their belongings. They could secure a few poultices and bandages, along with more food for their stay in the city and the brief journey to the University of Arcanical Arts.

Nauc decided they would rest in the city until the guard's wound stabilized or he died. Kelden spent his time examining the limestone buildings—so much different than his home—and fencing with Nauc.

During their second day there, the injured man slipped into unconsciousness. The local Healer explained it was only a matter of days before he died. The group decided to press on without him, as they couldn't help him.

The southeastern journey from Yordiv to the university was much shorter and on a well-traveled road. Banditry would be uncommon, especially during this period of increased travel.

A few hours after departing, the group reached the base of the mountain range where the active volcano, Ashmount, stood. Beside the volcano resided the University of Arcanical Arts, a name given to the school by ordinary citizens to differentiate the place from "normal" universities. Hiking up steep trails, they wound their way back and forth around boulders and ascended the beginning of the mountain range.

By dusk of the second day, they reached the university grounds, though their thighs—or at least Kelden's—burned from the climb.

Kelden stared in awe at the towering volcano that eclipsed the university. Ashmount spewed bright orange lava into the air. The lava spattered onto an invisible shield, cascading down the bubble and landing in a moat that surrounded the campus. Something like unseen funnels ensured the several arched stone bridges crossing the lava river remained untouched. The lava drifted in a lazy flow until it dropped off the eastern side of the mountain range. A strong stench of old eggs greeted him. Gas from the volcano called *sulfur*, Nauc had explained.

The University of Arcanical Arts was a colossal building that didn't resemble any other construct Kelden had ever seen. The mudbrick buildings of Warwin and the limestone buildings of Yordiv couldn't compare. Spires climbed to unthinkable heights, framed against the ever-looming volcano. Hundreds, if not thousands, of windows peppered the building, and a pair of gigantic doors rested at the end of a wide stone staircase leading up to the massive school. Kelden was sure the building could have fit the entire population of Warwin and many more.

Several small tents rested outside the university and outside the protective shield, just before a bridge. As they got closer, Kelden could tell that though they were outside the protective shield, the lava wouldn't be able to rain down upon them. The height of the barrier prevented lava from landing on this side of the university, and the lava seemed to cascade down in predetermined places.

A table, several chairs, a ledger, and a huge glass cauldron holding bucketfuls of money blocked half of the bridge entrance. A Magicus sorted coin into leather pouches, setting them on the table, while another Magicus wrote something in the ledger and directed people.

A queue of weary travelers lined up in front of the ledger-writing Magicus. A couple people, smiling as they weighed their leather bags full of coin, passed Kelden, discussing what they were going to do with it.

One of them noticed him looking their way. "Just arrive here? It'll be a long wait. Good luck."

"Let's join the line then," Nauc said. So they did.

The stranger was correct. The line moved. Slow. So slowly, in fact, that after a couple hours of standing in line, they moved only a dozen paces.

A Magicus shouted in an enhanced voice, "That's it for tonight! Sorry for everyone who's been patiently waiting. Proper accommodations are available for you to use. We have many tents ready for any who wish to use them. Soon we will distribute food and drink. We will resume tomorrow. Make sure you line up in the same order as you originally arrived. We will know if you try to cut and will turn you away without payment. Thank you for arriving and rest up!"

The Magicai retreated across the stone bridge, and then it flipped itself over, making a loud grinding noise. The upside-down bridge prevented anyone from crossing it. It looked like a horseshoe made of rock, both ends stretching too far high with nothing to grip to climb it.

The group claimed a pair of tents, but Sungoa remained outside with Kelden. They had spent little time alone since leaving Warwin, and Kelden had motioned for his friend to stay.

"This could be the last time we see each other," Kelden said.

"You think so?" Sungoa asked. She raised an eyebrow like she didn't believe him, one hand on her hip.

"Well, yeah. If one of us has the Trace, then I assume they'd join the university, right?"

"If it were up to me"—Sungoa lowered her voice—"I'd stay and never go back."

"Me too." Why would he go back? His father? The bakery? He didn't need that. If he was a Magicus, he wouldn't need anything. Sure, he'd set his father up with more money, but Kelden didn't want to return to Warwin. Village life was not for him. Too small, too quiet. Maybe his father would leave Warwin too?

"Even if we don't get in, at least we get money," Sungoa said.

A man walked by the corner of Kelden's eye. He turned, seeing something familiar about the figure. Greasy hair. Luck be damned, it was Anditus Roberon.

"Hey!" Kelden shouted at the man's back. "Come back here, you coward!"

Roberon turned, chuckling when he saw Kelden. "You made it here. Alive! Good job. Guess I can tell your father I completed my promise."

"What's wrong with you?"

Roberon shrugged. "I'm not in this life for anybody but myself. My apologies. It seems I don't have the Taint. Or the Trace. Whatever they call it. Here." He handed a few coins he retrieved from his pocket to Kelden. "For your disappointment. Now, I have some money to spend. I bid you farewell."

Sungoa glared at Roberon's back. "The nerve of that prick."

"Yeah. Let's go get some food. I'm hungry." Kelden wanted to punch Roberon or do worse, but he wasn't willing to jeopardize this visit. He followed Sungoa into the tent and noticed the pleasant aroma of food.

<hr>

Kelden woke to Sungoa shaking him, and not for a short time judging by the annoyed curl in her lip. Everyone else was outside of the tent.

"It's time." She pulled her black hair into a bundle and tied it. She arched her back, and Kelden turned away. He didn't want her to think he was staring.

He cleared his throat, wanting to say something to fill the void of silence. Before he spoke, she exited.

"Hurry," she called to him as the tent flap closed behind her.

Kelden gathered his meager possessions and exited the tent, rejoining his companions in the queue and thinking about how to broach the subject with Sungoa about how he was starting to like her. He remembered why they were there in the first place and how it wouldn't matter even if she liked him back. They'd become separated if one of them became enrolled.

Yesterday, Kelden hadn't noticed the substantial variation in visitors lined up. People from all over Cedain stood in front of him. A clear majority were citizens of Qothe; Kelden recognized them easy enough. There were a couple pale people, reminiscent of Sungoa. It surprised him to learn Sungoa wasn't that pale compared to other regions of the world. He knew the palest were Cyroki who lived a much colder life than Qothe, but he didn't realize you could be whiter than Sungoa. A few travelers were a much richer black than Kelden, leading him to suspect they were Vessians from nomadic tribes he'd heard about once. The Camel Clans of Vessia.

The line moved once again. Another single step forward. It took ages for the line to progress. And why? People crossed the bridge, and they either stayed over there or returned a few moments later, rejected but happily carrying a pouch of coin.

"Did you hear? Calrym's gone to war with Cyrok," a woman standing farther up the line said.

"Yeah, I heard. Filthy business, attacking like that. What'd Cyrok do?" her companion asked.

The woman laughed. "Are you kidding? The Cyroki are exploiting good Remerian coin by hoarding those birds they sell. Won't even let my pappy open a bird eatery. They say the birds aren't meant for eating. Well, we bought one and ate it anyway. Shows what they know."

"Everyone has their own beliefs, dear."

"Yes, yes. Don't even get me started on the Camel Clans."

They spent a full day standing there, legs aching,

minds devoid of any meaningful thought. The boredom emphasized the wait. The beating sun on their necks did little to lighten the mood. When dusk approached, a man farther up the line seemed to lose it.

"Faster, damn it!" he shouted at the nearest Magicus.

A Magicus hurried over to the man, grabbed him by the arm, and whispered something in his ear. He tried pulling away.

"No! I will not! Give me my fucking money! I've been standing in line for nearly a week!" His face reddened. It was difficult to tell if the man was over-heating, furious, or frustrated. Maybe all three.

Another robed figure ran over. He touched the screaming man and a spark of light—or was that light-ning?—flared out, then the man collapsed, silent. Kelden couldn't tell if he was dead or unconscious, but either way, the two Magicai lifted the body and hauled him away. The line proceeded as normal after that. They never saw the man again.

The Warwin travelers spent another night in one of the offered tents. Sungoa consoled a sobbing woman who'd broken down over the loss of her husband, the guard who'd died when Roberon had run off. Kelden didn't blame her for being a decent person and trying to help the woman, but he couldn't help but also feel resentful of Sungoa. This could be one of their last days together.

He wasn't sure why he cared. Emotions were never his strong suit. Sure, he could like an attractive girl. And he could recognize when he *should* feel bad or sad about something. He often didn't though. His lack of response to those in distress was one of his weaknesses. Kelden didn't know what to do in those circumstances to provide comfort.

That night, he spent thinking about the money he'd

earn. He could help his father. More exciting was imagining a Magicus telling him they'd identified the Trace within him and accepting him into the school. All the power and wealth that went along with it.

———

It was now their third day of waiting in the queue. When the sun reached its peak in the sky and Kelden yawned with boredom, Sungoa approached, having left the widow's side.

"I wonder how Graylan is doing."

"Yeah. Me too." Kelden didn't give two shits about how he was doing. This was the first time in his life something *good* could happen to *him*. He knew he was being selfish. He knew he was lacking empathy for anyone else around him, such as the widow. And he was sure being an ass. He couldn't help it. He could *feel* that his life was about to change. Or at least, he hoped it was. He knew he hadn't been born a farmer. Or a baker. Or any other monotonous manual labor job. He was born for something greater. And he believed it was to become a student of the Magicai.

He stepped forward in the queue. The line never moved faster than a snail. His boredom increased, and he didn't know what to say to Sungoa. She didn't seem to have anything either, and after some awkward, stiff conversations, she left him to his thoughts.

Sungoa spent more of her time with the grieving widow, and that night was no different. Kelden was alone and unsure of what to do.

Nauc and a few of the others were having a laugh, playing cards in the corner. Kelden didn't want to learn the rules of whatever game they were playing or be forced into false laughter.

Once again, Kelden struggled to sleep. His mind wandered until he passed out. He dreamed about how the group would have to make the long journey back to Warwin. And many of them dying.

———

A boot connected with Kelden's ribs. "Up."

He stirred, groaned, and sat up. He opened his eyes as Nauc exited the tent. Mumbling threats at the man, Kelden stood and, as his normal ritual entailed, gathered his belongings and joined the procession. They were closer to the Magicai now, though considering the last few days, they wouldn't reach the table today. Kelden sighed at another day stuck in line.

"What are you thinking about?" Sungoa poked him in the back.

He jumped in surprise, turning to greet her. "Hey."

"Well?"

"I was just thinking about how much today's going to suck."

"Yeah. On the bright side, it looks like we'll reach the table tomorrow. At least we'll finally get the money we came here for."

"True. I've been thinking about something else though."

"Which is?"

"If we get this money and we don't have the Trace in us, that means we have to go back to Warwin."

"And?"

"I'm worried that more of you could die," Kelden said. He never considered *he* would have to make the journey. "What if those bandits are waiting for people who just got paid?"

Sungoa frowned. "*You* could die."

Kelden didn't think so. He was too young for death. There was still more he wanted to accomplish.

"Not to worry," Nauc said. "We'll have enough money where we can either purchase some horses for faster transportation or hire some more guards. We'll be better off than we were."

The rest of the day passed, hot and boring and full of a sulfurous stench.

<hr>

The following morning, Kelden woke up before anybody else. He'd found it difficult to sleep knowing today was when he may end up getting the chance of a lifetime. It was also the last day he'd see the group he'd traveled with.

Kelden thought of Sungoa, the pretty girl who had a family that ignored and neglected her. He thought about Graylan, his best friend for most of his life and how he'd regret not making the journey. Kelden thought of Anditus Roberon and how he was a piece of shit, and yet, Kelden enjoyed his company. He thought of the grieving widow and how her life changed. He thought of the guard Nauc and the training he'd received. Most of all, though, Kelden thought of his father, Hillion, and what would happen if the university admitted Kelden. *Will I ever see him again?* Perhaps not. The thought didn't bother him, though he felt bad for his father.

As dawn light appeared, a few others were getting up and preparing for the day. Not feeling like talking, he pretended to sleep.

"Do I always have to wake you up?" Sungoa asked.

Kelden groaned, feigning just waking up by wiping sleep from his eyes.

Sungoa stood over him once again. "We should

reach the table today," she said with obvious relief. Kelden was eager too.

"It'll be nice to get paid . . . and to know what's going to end up happening with us." He immediately recognized his lack of tact.

Sungoa's face scrunched up, almost like she'd become sick. "We're friends, Kelden, not married. You'll be fine, I hope."

Kelden blanched. He'd meant the entire group. "I . . . n-no, I meant that . . ."

"It's fine. Let's go."

It might be all right if they split us up.

The line progressed. At midday, there were only six other people ahead of their group.

"All right, so you'll all go first," Nauc said. "I don't want to leave anyone else alone."

They all agreed.

A few hours later, a very bored-looking Magicus waved one of them forward. "Next."

The widow approached the table and proceeded across the bridge. Several minutes later, the Magicus called the next person, and another of their party went forward.

Kelden sweat. His hands trembled, and his heart pounded inside his chest. An empty pit formed in his stomach. He wasn't sure what would happen, but things were changing for some of them. Or perhaps none. *A group this large is going to have somebody with the Trace though. Right? What if I don't have the Trace? What would I possibly do with my life then?*

"Next," the Magicus said after what felt like an hour. One of Warwin's guards approached the table.

Kelden was next. His palms moistened, and his mouth dried up. He drank from his waterskin, but that didn't help much.

After what felt like another entire day, the Magicus beckoned him forward. "Next."

"Good luck," Sungoa said, squeezing his hand.

"You, too. I hope I see you again." Perhaps that was too forward, but he was beyond caring. He approached the table.

The Magicus dipped his quill into an ink bottle and unfurled more parchment. A chart was inked on the page. "Name?"

"K-Kelden."

The Magicus arched a brow. "That it?"

"Kelden Stoole."

The Magicus recorded Kelden's information in the chart. "Current residence?"

"What?"

"Where do you live?"

"Warwin."

"And how old are you, Kelden?"

Sweat dripped down his forehead, and he wiped it up with his forearm. "Seventeen."

"All right, go across the bridge. They'll have further instructions for you there. Good luck." The Magicus dipped his quill into the ink bottle. He switched to another parchment and started drawing random shapes in a pattern that made little sense. Kelden wanted to inquire but decided against it.

He crossed the bridge and walked toward the university. He breached the protective bubble encasing the school grounds, and a wave of coolness passed through him. The sulfurous smell vanished within.

"This way, this way," called a hunched Magicus standing near several small tents.

He hurried over to the old man. Liver spots spread across his skin like raindrops.

"Pleasure to meet you. This way, please." The Magicus led him into a small tent.

Kelden entered and took a seat on a small wooden stool the Magicus gestured toward.

The Magicus put on spectacles before sitting behind a table. "I am an Examiner, of course."

"I don't know what that means."

"You'll learn soon." He peered into Kelden's eyes. Soon afterward, he scanned the rest of Kelden's body. After several minutes, Kelden became uncomfortable.

"It's important that you stay as still as possible, please," the Magicus said.

Kelden attempted to do just that.

A while longer passed.

"Sir, uh, mind if I ask a question?"

"Go ahead."

"What, uh, what are you doing?"

"You have the Trace. I'm trying to figure out which strain you have, though it's often difficult at such a young age."

"I . . . I have the Trace?"

"Why else do you think you've been sitting here for so long? Please keep still."

Kelden complied. He was going to be a student at the University of Arcanical Arts. *I knew it.*

After several more minutes, the Magicus sighed and set his spectacles on the table in front of him. "All right, we're done. Congratulations on having the Trace. You will now proceed to the university. We will deliver your financial compensation later, but as of now, you will join the other potential candidates for further testing. Follow the road until you reach another Magicus. She will direct you. I need your name to add to the list of confirmed prospects." He tapped a nearby list.

"Thank you. Kelden Stoole." He'd made it. He

wondered about the others though. "Can I go say goodbye to my friends? Or can you tell me if you've allowed them through?"

"No, I'm sorry. You're not allowed to leave Ashmount until all the recruits have gathered. People with the Trace are anonymous until we recruit them. If you wish to make the mistake of declining further testing, you may go. We will not allow you to reenter. If we accepted any of your companions, you'll see them soon."

Kelden would never see them again. He wished it bothered him the way it should have. Actually, he didn't. That would lead to an amalgamation of negative feelings, and nobody wanted that.

Curious, he followed the stone path leading to the University of Arcanical Arts. For the first time, Kelden noticed how strange the university's grounds were. Did the protective bubble mask the appearance of life from outsiders? There was no rocky terrain underneath the protected area. Instead, an array of brilliant greens and other colors transfixed his gaze. There were things he'd never seen in his entire life, such as lush, big trees that stretched toward the sun. He'd seen small saplings and other small bushes before, but never anything as glorious as these large, full trees. Flowers spread across the dark green lawns—the blues, reds, yellows, and a variety of other colors creating a living painting. Colorful buzzing and fluttering insects glided around the plants. A cobblestone path twisted its way through the greenery and toward a huge, double-door entryway.

A gigantic statue stood in the middle of the grounds. It was an angel, a symbol of Mother Avani, but the rest of the statue made little sense. The angel held a steel sword in her right hand and a quill in her left. She wore a pair of spectacles similar to the pair used to examine him. A small vial hung from a necklace. Kelden wondered what they meant and then noticed a dainty female Magicus standing in the huge archway of the school.

"Welcome to Ashmount!"

He grinned and quickened his pace. "Hello."

"Welcome to Ashmount," she said again, and bowed, her white robes cascading around her arms. A small metal angel was pinned to her clothes above her left breast. "I am the Healer professor here."

"Kelden Stoole." How many more times would he have to introduce himself today?

"Pleasure. I'll bring you in."

He followed her. "What's an Examiner?" he asked, thinking about the Magicus who identified the Trace within him.

"They'll explain it soon, and if I had to explain it to every new student, I'd kill myself." She sounded serious. Then she sighed. "Perhaps not. Too many people rely on me."

The Magicus led him into the building. Stunned, Kelden looked around the magnificent building. The marbled floors were all carpeted in brilliant hues of red, purple, and maroon. Golden sconces in the hallways held burning torches, though they didn't seem to give off any heat. In the more open rooms, stained glass windows hung several dozen feet high, the light from large chandeliers illuminating their various colors.

Awed, he couldn't stop looking around. Men and women wore varying robes—dull browns, crisp blacks, a couple white.

She stopped before a closed door. "You're to wait inside here until you're told otherwise, all right?"

"Okay."

"Meals will be delivered. Until the line depletes, you

will receive a bedroll to spend the night. Several doors across the hallway lead to bathrooms. We insist you don't wander off."

She turned the shining brass doorknob, and the heavy wooden door creaked as it opened. The words WAITING HALL 1B stenciled into a brass plate hung in the center of the door. Inside stood dozens of people, many younger than Kelden and plenty older. They were all talking in small groups. Hesitant, he stepped inside. The door closed, and voices stopped at the thud of the door. Everyone peered over at him for a moment, then resumed their talking.

He felt alone.

A young pale woman approached him. She had long braided blond hair, and her wide eyes searched him. She was pretty. "Who are you?"

"I'm Kelden Stoole from Warwin. Where are you from?"

"Oh, a local." She sighed unhappily. "Never mind."

"What?" She ignored him. *What an arrogant person.* Unsure what to do, he headed to a corner of the room, sat, and leaned against the wall. People congregated. Sometimes the door opened and omitted another student.

Kelden observed the room, looking at the various groups of future students—his classmates.

Nearby, a man talked to two women. "Listen, this is getting ridiculous. We've been cooped up inside this room for *days* now, and we've gotten nothing other than more and more people coming here that don't know what's going on. Let's go exploring."

"I don't think that's such a great idea," one woman said.

"I don't know," the other one said. "I think it'd be

fun to see what the rest of the building looks like. It's so beautiful!"

The man said, "Let's go then. After the next student arrives, we'll slip out. It'll give us the longest amount of time before a new student shows up."

Both women agreed.

The man noticed Kelden's eyes on him. "You want to come too?"

Kelden shook his head. "No, thanks." He didn't want to get caught snooping around. He wanted the money and didn't want to lose it. Even more so, he wanted the experience of learning whatever it was they taught here.

Soon enough, the door opened, and another prospect entered. A minute later, the trio slipped out.

Two days slipped by, and Kelden didn't recognize anybody. Three times a day, delivered meals arrived for the entire gathering. The trio that had left to investigate the grounds never returned.

About three-quarters into the third day of Kelden trapped in a room full of strangers, the door opened. This time, an impressive man with a full, long black beard strode into the room, his robes flourished about his body. Above his left breast was another metallic pin —this one a quill. *The pins the Magicai wear match the items adorning the statue of Mother Avani outside the school.*

"Greetings." His booming voice silenced the room. "I am the Archmagicus of Ashmount. I would like to welcome all of you who traveled so far to get here and congratulate you on this journey we are about to begin. You will have a trying time here, but if you are resilient, smart, and, dare I say it, possess some luck, you may just find you're a suitable candidate. Now, if you'll follow me, we will join up with the other half." He clapped his hands.

They followed the Archmagicus down the hallway. He turned several times before stopping at an identical doorway—this one labeled WAITING HALL 1A.

"One moment." The Archmagicus entered the room and likely gave a similar speech. He walked out, and another group of people followed him.

Kelden strained to glimpse anyone he knew but couldn't see anything other than a rainbow of brown, black, blond, a smidgen of red, and some white and gray hair. Faces bobbed in and out among the crowd.

The Archmagicus led them down the hallway and several more turns before they exited another gigantic double door. This one led out the back of the university. They went down a cobblestone pathway toward another bridge that crossed the lava moat. Kelden gazed up at the enormous volcano, Ashmount. Black smoke drifted into the sky.

"Before you're allowed official admittance to the school," the Archmagicus said, stopping on the bridge, "we will give you a preliminary class, catching up those of you who may not understand exactly what it is we do here. We recognize Magicai are rarely located where many of you are from. For those that are educated, part of that knowledge may be less interesting to you. However, we will also disclose vital information about the Trials we will ask you to complete. The first Trial you've already completed—patience. We have no room for people with short attention spans or tempers . . . or a desire to explore when told to wait. Anybody who violates any rule or order will face expulsion from Ashmount. Expulsion has dire consequences. Our secrets are just that—secrets. After all, if we let expelled people leave, we'd have a rogue magic society."

Kelden was sure he heard somebody nearby say, "But there already is one."

The Archmagicus continued. "Obviously we strive to protect the world from any potential terrorism, which few individual rogue Magicai commit, but the Collectors dedicate their lives to finding these people. Don't become one. I leave you with two things. First, to those who may think us to be a little unorthodox or savage, you are correct. If you believe you may not belong here, I encourage you to let one of the Magicai know immediately, before tomorrow's class. You'll be allowed to leave without punishment."

He pointed at the volcano. "Second, your Trials will be to face the volcano and your peers in a series of contests. I would be remiss if I didn't disclose to you many people *die* during these Trials, so bow out now if this concerns you. Once the Trials begin, there is no leaving, and we will force you to complete them, or the Collectors will harvest you. That is all. You will join me for a welcoming banquet, and then I'll leave you to socialize and think about your final decision."

Immediate discussion began as the Archmagicus trekked back up to the school, the students following in his wake. Everyone seemed excited, scared, and surprised at the same time. Kelden saw the attractive blond girl talking with several well-dressed people.

"If we band together, we could probably eliminate the ones that are so *clearly* going to hold us back. Honestly, I can't believe they even *allow* the peasants in. This is an elite school for elite people. I wonder if we're allowed to kill. I mean, the Archmagicus *said* people die. I would hate to die because some farmhand threw me into a volcano. What do you all think?" She didn't allow anyone to answer and continued prattling on. "I think we need to do whatever it takes to complete the Trials. Obviously, we haven't come here for nothing. And did you hear what he said?" Somebody tried to answer, but she talked over him. "I wonder what he meant by harvested. My father's never mentioned harvesting. Maybe I'll write to him, see what he thinks about that. My father has a *lot* of connections, you see. He's really into politics . . ." Her voice faded as the crowd reshaped itself, people wading through other people.

Kelden wasn't sure what to do. To leave would be to admit his cowardice, and he wouldn't learn anything. Staying would risk his life. Although if he didn't die, who knew what could happen? He didn't want to die. He was much too young for that. As soon as he'd made the internal decision that he wouldn't die, because he was born for greater things, he heard a voice he recognized.

"Kelden!"

Somebody he knew had made it in.

He turned. Sungoa was making her way through the mob of people toward him.

Great. It's not like we didn't leave things in an awkward state.

SERADAL WINTLOCK

2nd Cycle of Autumn, 231st Reign of Garcovi
Cyrok

A light snow drifted into the clearing where the caravan rested. Snowflakes melted as soon as they touched her skin. Cold water ran down her neck and underneath her clothes, like tears freezing her soul. She shivered, a shaking that wouldn't stop.

So much death. *I should've listened to Fezzel's intuitions.* Now, nearly everyone she knew was dead. Her brother. Her mother. It had been an entire day since Captain Adavir had bound her and thrown her in the cart. Her father, Jaidik, and her neighbor Angazo Giresh lay nearby, the only other occupants. After she'd finished emptying her stomach upon learning she'd *eaten* a piece of her mother, she'd relayed her story to her father and Angazo.

Angazo's story was simple. "Wake up. Get stab. Pretend dead. Wound hurt. Not too much." He claimed the wound wasn't too deep, though anytime he moved, he winced and groaned. He was probably hurting more than he claimed.

Her father, however, was much worse off. He'd fought the soldiers during the attack and had sustained several serious injuries. A deep gash in his head oozed blood, and Sera was concerned it would become infected if left untreated. He secured many other cuts and nasty bruises, a cracked rib or two, and a broken leg. It stuck out at the wrong angle, and he said he couldn't feel it.

Jaidik had told her he'd jolted awake when she screamed, and upon witnessing Fezzel's death, he'd fought back. Because of the fight he'd put up and the wounds Jaidik caused to a pair of soldiers, Captain Adavir had wanted to punish him and his family. First, they'd desecrated Fezzel's body by pissing on it, then hacking it apart and tossing bits of him into a fire. Then they'd attempted to kill Golden Royce in front of Jaidik. Unfortunately for the man attempting this—Smugface— Golden Royce had flown out the cage, slashing him across the face with his talons. Golden Royce's escape had enraged Captain Adavir and his men so much that they'd stripped Yudri naked and forced Jaidik to watch as several of the men raped her. After an hour, Captain Adavir himself beheaded her, tossing her body into another fire. They'd then threatened to do similar things to the unconscious Sera.

The three of them weren't sure what was about to happen. Her father, with Angazo's agreement, predicted several days of torture before their inevitable deaths, since they knew who Captain Adavir was. Why leave witnesses?

Her father had given up. *It has to be his wounds. He's never given up before. Ever.*

Jaidik was firm in his beliefs though. "If one of us

reported what happened to the governess, the Cyroki military would hunt them down. They won't want that. They'll execute us within a few days."

Captain Blago Adavir and his men continued taunting her and Jaidik, eating the rest of the gyrfalcons her family owned. They took a particular delight in watching Sera squirm and cry. *If I ever get out of this, I'll find a way to protect myself. And my father.* Sera noticed a majority of birds were actually being cared for. The soldiers were using a few as food to aggravate some of the prisoners they disliked. The rest, it appeared, they wanted to keep alive. Most likely to sell.

Though Sera drifted in and out of sleep whenever she could catch some, her father slept little. Angazo seemed to sleep even less. Sometimes, when she woke, she heard the two men whispering. When confronted, they refused to explain. This frustrated her. They were prisoners and would die soon. There was no need to keep secrets now. She wasn't a child anymore.

Smugface, with the talon gash across his face, sauntered over holding several bowls of gruel. "Got your food here," he said, biting his lip and looking Sera up and down. She was sure he was going through various sexual fantasies in his head.

Angazo, as always, tried to redirect the soldier's attention to himself. "Drop it. Hungry."

Smugface frowned. "Don't ruin a man's fun." But he brought the food over and set it down. He stole one more look at Sera and then left.

"You need go, lass," Angazo said.

Because the bandits had bound their hands behind their backs, eating was an unpleasant task of trying to slide the bowls to their respective owners and then lying down and scooping out mouthfuls of the disgusting stuff with their tongues. Like dogs. It was just one more way for the soldiers to humiliate their prisoners.

"We all need to get out of here," she said.

It was now five days since the attack, and things were looking bleak. Her father's condition was fast deteriorating. She didn't like the way he slumped, eyes closed, breathing a raspy struggle. He was becoming weaker, and his skin turned pallid. Though devastated, she admitted to herself it was doubtful he'd survive. The prospect of being the last surviving member of her family was depressing, and she tried not to think about it.

"Your father and me work," Angazo said.

"On what?"

He nodded at Jaidik's legs. "Sit on split board. Pieces make sharp. Cut rope. Free you." He shifted his body to lie down on the cart, moving his face toward the bowl of gruel. His hands were raw and had several cuts with dried blood on them.

"But you must go with me." Sera didn't bother eating. She didn't see the point.

"No," Angazo said, food dripping from his mouth and splattering on the boards. "We slow. You go see governess. Learn what happen. If fast, they send force here. Overhear soldiers talking. They head to Vox. Sell gyrfalcons. Not far now. You slip out unnoticed. Reach governess. She send out regiment. Kill those bastards." He licked the spilled gruel on the cart and swallowed. "Eat. You need energy."

If she was able to free herself, she might be able to secure help. Determined and letting out a grunt, Sera fell to the floor of the cart. It was undignified and hurt like hell. She was sure she'd have multiple bruises covering her breasts, shoulders, and elbows because of these meals. Using her tongue, she pulled food into her mouth. When any fell onto the dirty wooden boards of the cart, she lapped that up too. It wouldn't do to waste any.

"Sera." Jaidik groaned, eyes half-closed. "Eat mine. You need it more than I do."

"What? No, you'll need it if you're to survive." She wouldn't be the reason her father died.

"I'm dying, I can feel it. I know you can see it. Angazo can see it too. Go ahead. Eat."

"No."

"Give me this one last wish, Seradal. Please. Eat it." Her father's gaze made her feel pitiful and useless. "Besides, it probably takes me more energy to lie face-down and eat it than it would if I didn't." He moaned and shifted his weight. "I need to rest." He closed his eyes.

Alarmed, Sera made to move.

"Don't. He tired. Not die. Yet." A flash of regret panned across Angazo's face. "Sorry." He looked horrified.

She gave him a brief smile, hoping to allay his concern. Honoring her father's wishes, she lay back down and lapped up another bowl of gruel. *Besides, if I can get enough energy saved up, perhaps I can get to Vox faster and save their lives.* It was a good thought and one that distracted her from other negative, realistic ones.

<hr>

That night, Angazo shook Sera from her sleep.

"Look," he said. With muffled exertions, he

twisted his body until she saw he held a long splinter of wood in bloody hands. "Cut rope now."

Sera almost gasped. Elated, she looked over at her father to give him a smile. He was dozing.

"Lean on me. I cut rope," Angazo said. "We get you gone. You free soon."

With a deep heave, she twisted her body back and forth, using her bound legs to push herself across the cart. She collided with Angazo's back, and he gasped in pain. "I'm sorry."

"It okay. Be quiet. Don't bring guard." His hands worked the wood against the rope.

She felt the shard sliding back and forth against the thick rope, friction slowly wearing it down. Once or twice Angazo stabbed her with the piece of wood, and she muffled cries of pain. Other times he dropped the wood, and it took several minutes of coordinated searching and retrieval to get the process started again.

Sera did her best to move her hands against the wood, hoping to create double the power. This method resulted in the wood being dropped more, however, so she stopped and sat there, helpless.

The rope frayed, and Sera's hopes rose. She could escape and get help. After a long time, the rope loosened. She slipped her hands out of the weakened binding. "Mother Avani bless you, Angazo." She wasn't a pious person, but this was a near miracle.

"I know. You welcome, lass. Now get feet undone. I keep lookout. Be fast."

She loosened the rope around her ankles a little, and after removing her boots, she slipped her feet free.

While she put her boots back on, Angazo spoke. "Listen, Sera. Your father tired. No good condition. No say 'bye.' Know he love you. We root for you. Go northeast. Find Vox. I take care Jaidik. We all right. Soldier's promise."

"Thank you." Angazo wasn't a soldier, but she pretended he was.

"Get ready go," Angazo said. "You lower yourself off cart. Then make way over there." He nodded to the edge of the clearing where the forest thickened. "I know you want free us. But can't, just run."

She thought of the few dozen prisoners that remained of their town. *How many of them will survive before I can get help?*

"Get out the light as quick as can. Try be quiet. If alert, I'll scream. Loud. Means you run fast you can. You be damn sure they chasing with horseback. I won't able distract long." He watched the patrolling soldiers. "Jump on three count," he said.

She wanted to say more. She wanted to say goodbye and tell Angazo she was grateful for his help.

"One," he said.

She wanted to hug him. Sera knew she needed to be as quiet as possible. Noise would bring a curious soldier or two over to check on them. She wanted to tell her sleeping father she loved him. Probably for the better. His head wound still oozed, and he was in considerable pain whenever awake.

"Two."

She placed her hands on the side of the cart, bracing her legs.

"Three."

She looked at him, and he nodded. Then she jumped.

She didn't expect her limbs to feel like jelly, though it'd been five days of lying in the cart. Instead of a graceful landing, she collapsed in a sprawl, arms and legs splayed out beneath her. Grimacing, she wiped snow from her face and peered through the wheel spokes on the cart. Booted feet patrolled, but nobody noticed her. Two men laughed near a fire, drinking and playing cards.

She crawled a few feet, then rested. Her limbs were weak. Blood began circulating throughout her body, and she could feel the tingling of returning senses.

Sounds of movement came from the cart she'd leaped from—a grunt and then a whispered voice above her. "Get out light!"

Sera strained her muscles to cooperate and crawled faster. She left the shadow of the cart and picked up her speed. If a soldier looked over, she wouldn't escape notice. She needed to reach the forest.

She switched into a crouching position and tried moving faster, but her limbs were tingling and numb. She stumbled. After catching herself, she continued. She reached the edge of the forest and rested her back against a tree. Sera was outside the perimeter of firelight that illuminated the small glade, and she sucked in air. She'd been holding her breath to still her nerves.

Gasping in panic and shock that she made it to the forest undetected, she caught her breath and plotted out her next actions. She needed to make her way northeast, toward Vox and to the governess, hoping Stasia Falconel would, in fact, send forces to attack the vile Captain Adavir.

She slowly made her way through the forest, setting her boots down gently. She hoped every crinkled leaf, every snapping twig, every crunch of snow—fortunately the snow was hard enough that her boots didn't leave impressions—would go unnoticed by the soldiers. Any sound she made sent her heart racing, and her stomach dropped. Somehow, she went unheard.

It was much darker inside the forest. The light from the campfires stopped being useful. The moon was bright, but the trees blocked most of it. Once she felt she'd put more than enough distance between her and Adavir's men, she walked faster.

It wasn't much longer when a faint shouting came from the camp's direction. *Angazo.* They'd discovered she was missing. She ran.

VILLIC THE IMBUER

1st Cycle of Autumn, 231st Reign of Garcovi
Vessia

Villic opened his eyes. The fire had died out, and he saw by starlight only. He must've had a vision from the gods. He should see a shaman over this.

"Hello?"

Villic grabbed his head and gritted his teeth. The voice had come from inside his head. *Lurzal's Lies! A god speaks to me!*

"No, no, definitely not a deity. You have that wrong."

Villic blinked. The being inside his head could hear his thoughts.

"Don't let me alarm you." It was too late for that. *"I'm Githandus Felimar Mydenwold."*

"I'm not familiar with that god. Get out of my head!" Villic whisper-shouted. He couldn't risk being over-heard. If anybody discovered he was hearing voices, they'd report him to the shamans, who would want to talk to him. Only they were supposed to be able to commune with the gods. He avoided the shamans whenever possible, and in this instance, it would be smarter to do so.

"I told you. I'm no god. Who are you?"

It had to be Lurzal, god of deception. Villic would have to be firm but careful. Offending a god too much could be disastrous. However, Lurzal, god of deception, needed to leave. "Get out of my head, Lurzal!" he whisper-shouted again. Villic glanced around, looking to see if anyone from his clan was around. They weren't.

"I don't know who Lurzal is. I'm one of the original Imbuers."

"This is madness." Villic was no longer whisper-shouting. He was talking. Out loud. To himself. He scanned the surrounding area. *Nobody* talked to themselves, other than shamans. To do so was to invoke the will of the gods. It was a sign of losing your mind. Villic didn't want to lose his mind. If anyone overheard him, he could be in lots of trouble.

"Fear not. What is your name?"

"Villic of the Splintered Manes. Get out of my head. *Now.*"

"I cannot leave. We are one. You may call me Githandus Felimar Mydenwold."

"I'm not calling you *anything.*"

"That seems particularly rude."

Villic's eyes widened in fear. "Are you Magicai then? Get out of my head!" In his frustration, he'd shouted out loud. Luckily, those who'd heard him were too far away to make out his words and were just staring at him. He shrugged, and they went back to their duties.

"I don't know that term. Have you heard of the region known as Jedovia?"

"No. Now be silent, strange Speaker."

"Where are we, Villic of the Splintered Manes?"

Villic told him. Speaker didn't understand. Villic didn't care.

He wondered if these were the first signs of insanity. The shamans wouldn't like that. And if he wasn't going insane and the voices *were* the gods, the shamans would like that even less. He knew he needed to be careful so he didn't get removed from the clan. A lone rider in the deserts of Vessia didn't last long.

"I'm obligated to tell you how this is going to work."

"Be quiet! No more talking!" He needed to focus on the true problem at hand: Glory Blades.

"Villic, you're on second shift," somebody said.

He didn't recognize who. Too busy focusing on not focusing on the problem in his head.

Villic lay facedown on his furs. The temperature had cooled but not enough to wrap them around his body. The god in his head had Villic's temperature up anyway. He closed his eyes to sleep.

"So tomorrow then?"

Villic bashed his head against the ground once, twice. "Quiet!" he whisper-shouted. It was more a shout.

Speaker spoke no further, and Villic slipped into sleep. He dreamed about gods yelling contradicting commands in his head, demanding he follow their orders or die.

He awoke riddled with sweat and feeling as if he'd blinked rather than slept for a few hours.

"Wake up, Villic. It's your shift."

Villic's head pounded. He felt a bruise forming on his forehead where he'd smacked it on the ground.

"Are you healthy?" Sikoi asked.

"Yes." Villic stood and waited for his eyes to adjust to the darkness.

"No sign of Glory Blades yet." Villic thought he saw Sikoi's friendly smile flash in the darkness.

"Okay."

"I'm going to sleep. Be well, Villic."

"Be well, Villic."

Villic slapped his forehead. "Be well, Sikoi." He grabbed his spear and walked to the edge of the camp, meeting up with several other arrivals.

One of them, a shaman, directed them on their patrol routes and paired them up.

Villic found himself with Lis, a fierce woman he often avoided. She wore her hair in braids, and they dangled and twirled like snakes.

"Follow me, Villic," Lis said.

"Is now a good time to explain what's happening?"

"Quiet!"

Lis slapped Villic's shoulder, one of her braids whipping him on the side, then led the way along their patrol route. "You be quiet, or you'll wake the entire camp *and* all of Glory Blades. Shamans won't be too happy with you, then. Give away our position, and maybe we get attacked. I don't want to die wandering around at night like this."

Villic shrugged. The moon illuminated the desert sands, and they could navigate with little difficulty. He stepped over a scorpion once, and he heard the rattle of a snake, but Villic's concern was directed at running into warriors from Glory Blades.

"I really think we should have a discussion."

"Stay quiet, Speaker," Villic whispered. He said the words quietly enough that he strained to hear them himself.

They circled the outskirts of the camp, listening for odd noises, watching for strange shadows.

Lis placed a hand on Villic's chest. "Shh."

He listened. Heard nothing. Popped his ears, listened harder. Then a slight rustle. The shift of a boot in sand?

A plume of fire erupted in the night, framing the face of a Glory Blades man running toward them. Another sword lit afire, and a second Glory Blades man followed.

Villic, out of instinct, threw his spear at the first person and drew his scimitar. The spear pierced the man's shoulder, and he growled before pulling it free and resuming his charge.

"Attack! We're under attack!" Lis shouted to warn the others.

"Now would be a good time—"

"Speaker, not now!" A flaming sword descended toward Villic, and he parried. Fire licked his sword, singed his hand. On his right, Lis engaged the other Glory Blades man.

"You're fighting an Imbuer."

"I don't care!" The Glory Blades man slashed at him. He leaped back, dodging.

"Villic, you're an Imbuer!"

Villic was an Imbuer?

"Yes! Call upon the powers you need, and I'll grant them."

"I don't—" He deflected another attack, countered, missed, and jumped away from another arching swipe.

"How about fire?"

Sounded good to Villic. Flames climbed up Villic's scimitar. "Killiak, lord of lords," he said in awe.

The rival clan member looked surprised. Villic went on the attack, swinging his flaming blade back and forth. The Glory Blades man blocked his attacks but was now on the retreat.

Shouts from behind, sounds of more metal on metal as the Splintered Manes fought off Glory Blades.

"Try something else. Ice? Rock?"

Villic raised his sword over his shoulder and brought it down. *Rock,* he told Speaker.

The flames vanished, and his scimitar turned into an impossible weight. Villic almost lost his balance. The rock sword came crashing down on the Glory Blades man's foot, dashing it into pieces. Hollering in pain, he tried stepping back but fell over.

A third Glory Blades clan member showed up—Lis was still fighting hers—and this one stepped in front of her fallen comrade. Villic dismissed the rock power and held his sword up in both hands, ready.

"Can you do a water sword?"

"Yes, but that won't be helpful."

The Glory Blades woman lunged at Villic, sword lashing at his thigh. He danced back, but the blade tore a chunk out of his leg.

"Ack, piss on Flaytz!" Villic rarely swore at the God of Death, but sometimes there were exceptions.

He attacked, swinging his sword and aiming for his opponent's weapon. She took the bait, going to block his attack. Villic, or Speaker, turned the blade into water. Her weapon cut through the water sword and up into the open air. Villic, or Speaker, reverted his sword from water to regular, and the blade sank into the Glory Blades woman's neck.

Villic turned to his right. Lis had dispatched her foe.

The man with the pulverized foot crawled backward into darkness. Villic let him go. The man wouldn't be able to fight again.

Breathing hard, Villic used his scimitar, ignited in

flames, to locate his spear. Then he returned to Lis. She just stared at him, open-mouthed, shocked.

"What?"

"You're one of them, Villic."

He shrugged.

She bowed her head to him, a sign of respect no single person had ever given him.

"I think it's time you talk to me."

Villic didn't like it, but he agreed with Speaker.

I t took many days, but Villic learned Speaker was the spirit of an Imbuer from thousands of years ago. Back then, the Imbuer would travel through their bloodline descendants, offering advice and power. The Imbuers disappeared at one point. Speaker wasn't sure why they'd resurfaced now or how the Imbuers were selected.

When Speaker told Villic about all the possibilities he now possessed, Villic didn't believe him. There were just too many, and Villic had never had a blessing from the gods in his entire life. *Or is this a curse?* He wasn't sure and was hesitant to approach one of the shamans. After the battle, Villic retreated to his camp. Not before Lis made a big deal about his powers to everyone who would listen though. There were others who'd discovered newfound powers in the Splintered Manes, and they'd all immediately become respected members of the clan.

He could ignite his scimitar on fire. It was the most amazing and terrifying thing Villic had ever witnessed. He could now provide the clan with unlimited fire at will. Anyone with the power could. When alone, Villic practiced with the Imbuer powers. Aside from the fire, ice, rock, and water, Villic experienced lightning, vines that grew from his weapon and lashed out, and, though Villic wouldn't want to use it because it frightened him, a flickering illusion that appeared as if he were wielding three different weapons at once. Speaker said there were more, but Villic didn't want to keep learning. He'd seen enough. It was too much too fast.

Over a four-day period, several Imbuers showed themselves. Villic—never good at numbers, counting, or measurements, except for time—thought there were over ten Imbuers. Maybe a hundred. Then again, there might've only been a hundred people in the clan. Villic didn't know.

The shamans—after learning the name of the impossible gift the gods had bestowed upon them, Imbuer—introduced the title as an official position within the clan. Honorary leaders of the clan, beneath Jedkah, leader of the Splintered Manes, and the shamans, of course. Warriors chosen by gods. Villic felt like it was also possible Jedkah and the shamans didn't want the Imbuers to kill them and take over. Villic wouldn't have done that. He didn't like responsibility. He liked to keep things simple.

"Villic? Villic!"

Villic snapped back to the present. "Speaker?"

"You keep disappearing into your thoughts. It's important to remain present."

"There's nothing around here."

"You think that. And then you're eaten by a lion."

"I've never seen a lion attack a member of the clan in my entire life. Unless we were hunting them."

"Your ancestors would care much more about their lives."

"Why care? The gods will protect me until they don't favor me anymore."

"That is the most ridiculous thing I've ever heard. There are no gods."

"Quiet yourself, Speaker. I don't want to listen to blasphemy."

"You don't know the meaning of the word blasphemy." But Villic could tell by Speaker's tone that Speaker would remain quiet.

A few skirmishes occurred with Glory Blades, though whenever Villic showed up to help, they were already in full retreat. It seemed Glory Blades weren't keen on committing too much to the fight now the Splintered Manes had Imbuers as well. Villic wondered what the point was in returning several times over again to engage in a battle and retreat, repeating the pattern without a true fight.

About a week after their first engagement with Glory Blades, Jedkah called a circle. "A messenger from the Sharpclaws passed through last night. Imbuers are showing up in all the clans. Something strange is happening, and the gods have demanded a congregation. We have met and made peace with Glory Blades and will ride together." Groans from some clan members. "You'll not fight." More groans.

Villic packed up his camp, hopped on Dunecrest, and they were off, riding side by side Glory Blades to Hathoran. All the clans would be there. The Sharpclaws, Bride Warriors, the Plagued Ones, Seven Signs, Masters of the Lost. More information trickled down to the rest of the clan as they rode, and murmurings of concern took root throughout the clan.

The congregation's purpose was to determine the source of the Imbuer power. Figure out what happened. The Camel Clans invited a Magicus from the University of Arcanical Arts to examine them. The Magicus was currently staying in Remeria, a rival of all the Camel

Clans, as they'd fought in several wars against one another. Villic knew nothing about the Magicai or the university. The shamans told the clan members to stay far away from these evil misusers of unlawful power. Now they were inviting one to meet with them? It made little sense. But the shamans insisted the Magicai could solve the mystery. Villic wasn't a godspeaker, so he couldn't say what was right or not. He just followed their directions.

EDELBROCK BRENDIS

1st Cycle of Autumn, 231st Reign of Garcovi
Lochwall, Calrym

E delbrock felt as if his new normal state of being would be a permanent grief-stricken haze. His son, dead. Thrown off a balcony like a piece of garbage. His wife had betrayed him, and Edelbrock believed she was now sleeping with his captor. Everything he'd worked for, gone. No titles, no money, no family. No future.

The worst part was Edelbrock knew Scayde wouldn't get in any trouble for the murder. His son would be discreetly disposed of, and nobody would care. *He* cared but had no voice. Scayde's power was too influential. He could get away with anything, it seemed.

The journey down to his cell seemed like it took ages. A slow march to captivity.

Marshal Everic Deywin brought him down the King's Stand staircase, which brought them outside of Buzzard's Bowl. He marched Edelbrock into the arena via the main entrance, passing Gordane's unmoving body, a bundle of robes. And blood. *My poor boy.* He whimpered when the marshal shoved him forward, not even giving Edelbrock a moment to grieve.

"Sorry, Ed, forgot we need to go back outside," the marshal said.

Sadistic bastard did this on purpose. Stifling tears, Edelbrock, foggy-brained and distracted by his need to mourn, let the marshal keep pushing him in the correct direction.

The marshal brought Edelbrock back outside the arena, bringing him to one of the House buildings that formed the pentagon around Buzzard's Bowl. They descended a stone staircase, reaching a room with a guard stationed behind a table and a Magicus standing nearby. The marshal redirected him into a small side room and forced him to change clothes. He received a pair of black sheepskin boots and a well-worn set of leather breeches and jerkin. The jerkin was tight, and his fat stomach protruded out the bottom.

The marshal laughed. "It won't be too long, and you'll shrink into it." Which meant he was going to starve.

Edelbrock wasn't a stranger to hunger. There had been plenty of times in his military career he'd gone without meals for a day or two. The suggestion he'd be losing *that* much weight, however, was disconcerting.

Next, the marshal introduced him to the Magicus, a frightening-looking woman called an Examiner. She wore dark red robes and peered at him from beneath a hood, a pair of spectacles perched on her nose, her lips coated in a dark red substance. She smelled sweet. Edelbrock assumed it was a local custom he'd heard the noblewomen of Lochwall took up—crushing various berries and painting their lips different colors with their juices. He wasn't sure why, nor did he think he'd understand it if he did.

The Magicus explained what she was doing to him, but he hardly paid attention. He caught a few words. "I'm just ensuring you aren't harboring any form of the Trace." It took a minute or two, and she removed the foolish spectacles and nodded to the marshal. Her eyes narrowed at Edelbrock. It seemed Lord Haklon hired those who shared a similar disgust for the prisoners he "caught."

A stone wall beside the sitting guard had multiple scrapes and chips. A circular indentation rested in the wall nearby. Marshal Deywin placed a small device inside the indentation, and the stone raised into the ceiling, revealing a doorway. Back when he was in the military, he'd worked with a few Magicai, though they'd been Enforcers. He'd witnessed powerful offensive capabilities, though only at a distance and in the larger battles. He hadn't had one under his command. Or commanding him. He never quite figured out how the Magicai fit into the military. They often just showed up, obliterated the Vessians—who had no Magicai fighting for them—and retreated to wherever they lived.

There were other types of Magicai aside from Enforcers and Examiners—Healers, Glyphists, and Collectors—and each provided unique talents. Their services were all expensive, and he felt his energy was better spent on learning about nobility and ways he could exploit them to enrich his own life. It didn't matter what a Magicus could do if he couldn't afford one.

The marshal set the circular device on the guard's table, then they descended a stone staircase leading below the House's hypogeum. Torches lit the way, though they were spaced farther apart than Edelbrock would prefer. Shadows danced across walls, and Edelbrock felt like dead spirits haunted them on the way down. Perhaps Gordane was already there, shaming his father for failing to protect him.

The bottom of the stairs ended in pure sand or loose dirt. A huge cell with inch-wide spaces between steel bars stretching from floor to ceiling occupied most of the immediate area. The marshal opened the cell door with a key and pushed Edelbrock into the cell. The door closed, and the lock clicked in place.

Marshal Deywin ascended the stairs, leaving Edelbrock to his fate.

Inside the cell were ten beds. Bodies inhabited seven of them. He claimed an empty one. Though awake, the seven figures didn't acknowledge him. They stared with empty eyes, clutching themselves and muttering in the dim cell. They wore the same clothing Edelbrock did, though their cloths were much dirtier and tattered.

The bed was less than pleasing. Silken sheets with innumerable stains and tears were all he had. Edelbrock was certain he'd seen several bugs scatter when he slipped underneath them. He didn't care. His life was dismal. What did he have to live for now? Revenge?

His back connected with unforgiving, hard wooden slats. It was like the bedding resting on top of them didn't exist, so flattened from time and age they'd become.

The uncomfortable bed didn't matter. They could've been in a king's cell, and Edelbrock wouldn't have slept. He sobbed, thinking of his dead son. He cried over his wife's betrayal, though he knew he'd not treated her well for years. Where had everything gone wrong? *Why did I think I could get away with murder? How did my self-ishness mask my ability to reason?*

For the first time in his life, he considered praying to

Mother Avani, asking for help. But he knew he wouldn't get any. So he kept sobbing.

He woke to the sounds of jeering. Blinking several times, he sat up. One prisoner, a man, crouched in his bed, face ducked down.

Outside the cell bars, a plethora of bald people dressed in the same clothes as Edelbrock laughed and shouted insults at them. *Gladiators.* They threw scraps of food at the bars. The food exploded on contact, spraying the cell with various bits. Six of the prisoners scrambled around the cell, picking these bits up and eating them as fast as they could off of the dirt floor. Edelbrock looked at them, disgusted.

"Look at how fat the new one is!" A shirtless man outside the cell pointed at him. His bulging chest seemed to dance while he just stood there, pointing at Edelbrock. Edelbrock was glad to be inside the cage at the moment.

The cell door opened, and somebody walked in, bearing a tray. "Here," the man said. He sounded kind and laid the tray on the ground. None of the other people outside of the cell entered. The stranger stepped back out and locked the cell. A pitcher of water sat on the tray. The six savages ran over and passed the drink around, gulping from it like wild animals. Much of it splashed onto the dirt at their feet.

The crowd outside of the cell dispersed, and it was quiet again.

The other man, who had joined Edelbrock in remaining in bed, approached. "Hey," the man said.

"Who are you?" Edelbrock asked.

"They call me Finch."

"Finch?"

"On account o' me being like a little bird."

"I'm sorry, but I'm not making the connection," Edelbrock said. The man didn't look like a bird. Well, perhaps a little hawkish. The thin man was lanky, with a sharp nose, and his head was bald.

"Aye, a little bird. I hear things and see things." Finch paused. "And I take things. That's why I'm here, I s'pose."

"So you're a thief."

"Right. That be truth."

"Where are you from?" Edelbrock frowned, not recognizing the accent. It wasn't Calrite.

"Nowhere important. Just some streets in some city. Not sure o' the name, to be honest. Locked Walls, I think." *Lochwall.* Edelbrock had little experience with Lochwall's slums. He avoided them whenever possible, though he knew native speakers didn't have Finch's accent. "I was born in a small town in Remeria. Don't remember the name o' it." Edelbrock had heard of parts of Remeria having broken language. It made sense to him now.

Edelbrock frowned. The cell seemed more lit up than yesterday. He hadn't noticed how well he could see. Glancing up, he saw panes of glass across the ceiling, revealing sky and sunlight. This made little sense though. Edelbrock was sure they were much farther underground than where the ceiling was. *Magicai.*

"Aye, that'd be Magicus work," Finch said, looking up at the glass. "Shows weather."

"You seem to know a lot about this place."

"I hope so! I did plan to rob it. That's why I'm here, after all."

"Who were the people outside the cell? The gladiators?"

Finch frowned. "Them's our future House members. Makin' sure we aren't feelin' too comfortable, I s'pose. Bein' assholes, yeh? Thing is, they grind ya to dust and then you're reborn a warrior, so I's heard."

Edelbrock didn't like the sound of that. "So, what's this?" Edelbrock motioned toward the six prisoners who were crawling across the floor, looking for any spare morsels they may have missed.

"This is the Draft cell. And them. Well, they've been here longer than we, haven't they? Ya get hungry every once in o' while, so I's suspect. Anyway, the Draft— that's what this is. They wait until they have at least ten prisoners, I guess, and then they do a Draft. They base the Draft on each House's current rankings, as o' the state o' the games, I think. This happens on the regular. Gotta keep the Houses replenished, I guess. So, each House Head will pick from us. Often, they give the crowd a show and execute the last ones drafted, so let's hope that ain't us. I just hope I'm not in Lord Scayde Haklon's House. His is the worst."

"Why?" He didn't doubt Finch on this point, but he wanted to know why Scayde's House would be worst. He figured he'd end up there some way or another. He didn't imagine Lord Haklon not taking up the opportunity to toy with Edelbrock any time he desired.

"I've heard Lord Haklon often kills fighters who disappoint him. He's ruthless. He doesn't accept failure and often punishes those that disappoint. Trigg Gelbrandy's House seems nice."

"Trigg Gelbrandy is dead," Edelbrock said. What irony this would be if Edelbrock ended up in his wife's inherited House, previously owned by the man he'd murdered.

"Impossible." Finch waved his hand at Edelbrock, unconcerned. "He's one o' the richest men in the city."

"Wish I was. Killing him is why I'm here. I was hoping to inherit his share of the arena."

"Oy. Well, I wonder who's going to take o'er his House then."

"That'd be my traitorous wife. So don't wish for that one either. I'm sure she's fucking Lord Haklon."

"Then I hope it's any of the other three," Finch said.

"I have a feeling I'm going to land in Scayde's House. Who are the other three?" The more Edelbrock thought about it, he realized the less he knew about Buzzard's Bowl. He knew the basics—how many people showed up, how much money could be made. He didn't know *who* they were though. Or what even took place inside the arena when fights occurred. Edelbrock could never afford to attend.

"Well," Finch began, "there's Castede Varono. He's a hard man but not an awful one. He expects you to train hard every day. There's also Lekhan Roelk. All I know 'bout him is he's often in last place for rankings. Not much glory or anything there. And you gotta imagine the last place House will also have the most deaths, so avoid that one's, I guess. Then you have the Velvet Mother. Nobody knows her identity, and she never shows up to the games. She always sends a decoy in her place. Every decoy is a different person, and often they're no more important than a reg'lar city soldier. Lately, the Velvet Mother's House has been a constant second place. O' course Lord Haklon's is first."

"How do you know all of this?"

"When you spend your entire life assuming that you're going to die o' starvation or die thieving, you want to know what death by thieving looks like. Nobody wants to starve to death. So I's researched Buzzard's Bowl and all the workings and hoped to find an easy rob. I messed up."

"You said ten people. How long will that take?"

"I's assuming whenever these beds're filled up with whatever miscreants and other unsuitable vagabonds they scoop up and dump here. Hoping they don't wait until we're all like that." Finch waved toward the prisoners crawling on the ground, searching for food. "I know *all* recruited gladiators have a hell o' a time before their first season. Training and hazing, I's heard. No fighting. Which means no respect. Just make sure you don't piss off other prisoners. It's not unheard o' for them to a kill a recruit."

"I have a lot to think about."

"Yeah." Finch bid him farewell and returned to his bed, leaving Edelbrock to his thoughts.

KELDEN STOOLE

2nd Cycle of Autumn, 231st Reign of Garcovi
Ashmount, Qothe

It turned out nobody else had the Trace from the group that Kelden and Sungoa traveled with. He believed he was more deserving than anyone from the group. Although Sungoa had a strong case too.

Kelden liked Sungoa more now that she was older. He understood why most people married members of the opposite sex rather than those of the same—other than obvious reproductive necessities of course. However, despite his continued appreciation of Sungoa, Kelden felt as if she shouldn't be here. Her family was a group of destitute meanderers who wandered from one town to another until they leeched enough from the locals before moving on. Or at least that's how Sungoa explained it. Her family had been doing this for so long, they'd dropped their last name to conceal their reputation as selfish squatters.

Sungoa wasn't like her family, but what was so special about *her*? Did *she* deserve admittance to the

University of Arcanical Arts? Other people worked entire lives doing things that were worthwhile. Like himself. Well, he didn't work at all, but his intentions were worthwhile. He would *do* something with this opportunity.

Perhaps the fates were indeed random. It still felt *right*, however. Kelden was where he imagined himself. Somewhere important. Sungoa being there could only be a good thing. Right?

They were sitting in a huge auditorium the morning after the banquet and facing a stage with a simple podium in the center. To his left was Sungoa, her arm touching his since they were in cramped, stiff chairs fitted to fill as many people in as possible. To his right, another prospect. An older woman. Plain looking and, if Kelden's assumption was correct, a rather unimportant person in regular life. A faint musky scent wafted in the air, and people wiped their sweating foreheads and necks. The few Vessians he saw didn't seem bothered by the heat. Maybe Vessia was hotter than Qothe. Kelden didn't know.

"This is going to change our lives," Sungoa said, looking around. A small bit of her tongue stuck out between her lips, indicating she was lost in awe of the place.

"As long as we don't die." The room was lit with hundreds of candles, either mounted on the walls or hanging from gigantic chandeliers. The light reflected in her irises.

He wanted to say more, explain the awkward exchange they'd had earlier. He wasn't sure he could conjure any worthwhile words, and rather than look like a blithering idiot again, he gave her a nod accompanied with a smile, which turned out to be a grimace. To save his embarrassment, he returned his gaze to the podium.

The Archmagicus took the stage, and the room hushed as everyone focused on him.

"To all the new prospective students, I'd like to offer a sincere welcome. Each class varies in its achievements and accomplishments, so it's always an exciting moment." The Archmagicus's voice echoed throughout the chamber, even though he couldn't be talking louder than a whisper. "There is one rule most important among all others at this establishment. The Magicai are a strong and prideful community. We detest those who seek to press their will upon us. Often those who do not possess our powers look down upon us."

He cleared his throat. "They call this place the University of Arcanical Arts. Many of you do the same. We consider ourselves to be more than a simple university. A university implies you are a school that teaches many things and that receives government funding. Although we may teach, we don't at the behest of any government or the better of its citizens. We operate as independents and teach anyone that's capable in any country. Governments often pay for our upkeep in roundabout ways, but that's because they hire our services, often for personal or political gain. It's important we maintain our identities. From the moment you allow another person, group, or entity to force you into a corner, you have lost. Thus, we call this school, for lack of a better term, Ashmount, after the great and powerful volcano that we sit beside. You have, already I'm sure, seen the protective barrier placed thousands of years ago."

Kelden stared at the Archmagicus, taking all the information in. He wanted nothing more than to join them, to become the man he was meant to become. A Magicus.

The Archmagicus straightened his posture and

examined the hundreds of people watching him. "Long ago, Magicai implemented a strategy for incoming students. Instead of accepting everyone possessing the Trace, they put them through a test. Many people either leave or die. We only want students who have a wide range of useful skills, as we want our clients to be happy when they pay for our services. The first, as I explained earlier, was patience. You've all passed the first Trial. Congratulations." He did not seem impressed. "However, the next tests are going to be much more difficult than standing in line. First, I'd like to offer a further explanation about what you can expect, both as a Magicus and as somebody who will have to go through the Trials."

Kelden leaned forward in his chair. He was eager to begin but didn't want to miss any important information.

"If you pass the Trials, we will accept you as a full-fledged Magicus. There are five paths one may learn. An Examiner will identify your school at a later date. Each branch has its own individual professor, and they will work with you until you are ready to graduate. The five branches of Ashmount are Enforcers, Healers, Collectors, Glyphists, and Examiners. Each of them specializes in a unique area. Enforcers focus on combat. They use Soul Glyphs, which are inked on their bodies ahead of time. These Soul Glyphs have a large variety of uses, but every one consumed ages the body until the Enforcer dies of old age. This grouping of Soul Glyphs is often called a *Well*.

"Each Soul Glyph is different in size, but that doesn't matter. Enforcers choose how many Soul Glyphs to consume to increase the power of whatever they wish to accomplish. Enforcers are the most common Magicus and often considered the most powerful. Plenty of people assume the Magicai can do mind tricks or manipulate people with magic. This isn't true. An Enforcer can only affect the physical realm, even by altering their own appearance. This doesn't mean the other four branches are useless. They are, in fact, needed and often command a higher salary than an Enforcer."

Kelden would become an Enforcer. The ability to develop and learn under the most skilled, the most powerful Magicai? He could hardly contain his excitement. He was here. He was going to get a chance to display his intelligence, to show everyone what he could become. And when he was done learning, when he'd discovered ways to demonstrate his power, he'd return home. He'd show the citizens of Warwin anything was possible—as long as your name was Kelden Stoole.

The Archmagicus continued. "Glyphists don't use magic the same way other branches do. Their sole purpose is to inscribe Soul Glyphs on the Enforcers. By using Soulpens, they draw up a person's life and ink it onto their skin, so the Enforcer can spend it. Every time an Enforcer consumes a Soul Glyph, they become closer to dying. Enforcers have the shortest lifespans, but the most impactful power. Glyphists are the opposite and have the longest life because they aren't dying whenever they use their ability and are never in the field."

You don't have to access your life force to be a Glyphist? And who would want to be a Glyphist anyway? What a weak ability. I want to be able to at least do something with my power.

"Examiners look inside a person. They learn to identify a person's Trace and analyze it. Using spectacles, they can see how powerful you are, how much life you have left if you're an Enforcer or Healer, and what branch you belong to. Examiners are valuable as guards. No Magicus can fool them.

"Collectors harvest magic from those who can use it. They often hunt criminals. Harvested magic, they can transfer into vials and use those vials themselves, or they can give them to Enforcers, who can use them instead of tapping into their own Well. These vials are *very* expensive and rare to accumulate, unless you are a Collector of course. There aren't a lot of criminal Magicai running around. Collectors find subterfuge and disguises much easier than Enforcers. A disguise would continually sap away at an Enforcer's Well; therefore, mere minutes into the ruse could become problematic. A constant connection to one's Well can, particularly to an untrained individual, sap away far more than you'd want or need. A single vial can keep a disguise going for a long time, because the vials work differently. They only consume the amount of power *needed*."

Why can't everyone use the vials? Kelden started worrying about becoming an Examiner. *And how does a Collector even harvest the magic from somebody?*

"Healers are the last branch and also the strangest. Healers can convert their own life force into a transferable power that is used to heal the wounded. The worse the wound, the more they consume. They don't need to use a Glyphist or Collector. They can just transfer their power. Healers don't have any other capabilities. They also die rather young. I don't envy the choice a Healer must make whenever they see a wounded person. Do they use their life and help the person? Or is that person not worth it to them? It's a tricky economy to trade days, weeks, cycles, or even years of your life to heal someone, and in the end, the choice is up to the Healer. Or employer, depending on the contract."

The Archmagicus paused and observed the crowd. Kelden wanted to be an Enforcer. Although, being an Examiner sounded like it would pay a lot of money. *But*

I'd have zero power. Healers were paid a lot, but he didn't want to sacrifice *his* life for somebody else. Glyphists sounded boring. All they did was help Enforcers by *drawing* on them. Collectors were his second choice. They could replicate an Enforcer's power.

"This will be everyone's last chance to back out of the Trials," the Archmagicus said. "Understand a good half of candidates who enter the Trials die. It is a genuine possibility your neighbor kills you within the next few days, so heed my warning and leave now. A pair of Magicai are outside to assist any who wish to leave. Yes, they'll have the coin we owe you. And for those of you who believe they have an edge up by researching or talking to somebody about the tasks you'll be doing . . . forget that information. Despite what you may have heard, we change the Trials every itera-tion, so as to not have cheaters or advantages. Any advice you might've gotten will not aid you."

Several people walked out. Kelden wondered if staying would cause his death. Sungoa also stayed, but he knew she would. She had less to return to than he did.

"Your first test will start soon. There will be Magicai along your journey. They are there to observe and will not aid you during your tests. You will reach several predetermined checkpoints where there is a mandatory stop to the Trials. These are locations for you to rest. Your first task is physical. Climb Ashmount to your first checkpoint. The first seventy-five people to arrive move on. The rest disqualify and will become a jar on Ashmount's shelves, a vial for one of the willing to consume. There are about two hundred of you, so I'd be fast. Go out the door and across the bridge. A road leads up to the volcano. Good luck."

Kelden leaped from his chair and, without even a

glance at Sungoa, joined the throes of running prospects scurrying toward the door. Somebody's elbow dug into his side. Someone else pulled at his arm so they could pass him. He remained on his feet and rejoined the pack.

It's going to be like that already, is it? All right. I can play dirty.

It was life or death after all.

DEMRI SLARN

1st Cycle of Winter, 231st Reign of Garcovi
Auchester, Remeria

Demri sat at the table in his rented room, a dim lamp providing a modicum of light to read by. He perused the letter a second time.

Mr. Maynard Piccalo,

My name is Magicus Glaouse. I'm on my way to Auchester and hope to meet with you in person to discuss the following in more detail.

As I'm sure you're aware, there are rumors of rogue Magicai roaming around, uncontested by anyone of worth. One of these men is a serial killer intent on locating a man he's seeking revenge upon. I believe you fit the description of said man, and my investigations are leading me to Auchester. Beware a Magicus named Demri Slarn. He's crippled and has an obvious stutter. His face is marred by an old burn. Disappear if somebody matching this description arrives. I will be there soon.

I will have further information in three days' time and look forward to our meeting.
    —Magicus Glaouse

Demri ground his teeth, jaw clenched and lip twitching. He wanted to rip Glaouse's head off the man's shoulders. Or rather watch as Caius did. Everything Glaouse had said was a lie.

Glaouse was a Collector, and if he'd been tracking Demri, he would be prepared for a drawn-out battle. The problem was, Demri wouldn't be able to handle that. He needed a Glyphist to replenish his abilities and a Healer to fix his crippled limbs.

He sipped a mug of hot tea Porric had brought him. The guard was showing his loyalty and usefulness. Porric had remained posted across the street during the attack on Maynard Piccalo and had informed both Caius and Demri that Magicus Glaouse had returned to Piccalo's house after they'd left and snooped around for a second.

After learning about this information, Demri had made the decision to leave the next morning. It was too late to travel far unless they hiked in the dark. He didn't wish to sneak about the night like a common criminal. Maybe when he was younger. He planned to go to a larger city, somewhere containing plenty of Magicai. He hoped he'd be able to "convince" somebody to help him for free—by healing him or replenishing his Well. If not, he wasn't against threatening, blackmailing, or hurting them. At first, he'd considered Andora, Remeria's capital. However, since Drunkard's Haven, the inn he'd attacked five years ago, he didn't want to risk going there. It's not like cripples with burned faces and stutters wandered around in droves.

The mere thought of the inn brought back a crushing

wave of depression, like it was drowning him. He'd killed many innocent people, and for what? Nothing. He'd been certain he'd found Doram Quandis. A tip had led him there. A reliable tip. It wasn't reliable enough. Between himself and Caius, they'd killed dozens of people. So no, they wouldn't go to Andora. In fact, it would satisfy Demri to flee Remeria entirely. He'd murdered far too many people in the country. It was time for a change.

He'd decided upon Lochwall in Calrym. The city was a political nightmare. Nobility ran rampant, and people were often focused on Buzzard's Bowl, the gladiator arena that drew in thousands of people, making it easier to blend in and distract from his presence. And then there was the Velvet Mother. A person famous for being unknown. The real question was whether the Velvet Mother could be somebody that may help Demri. Mysterious figures often had decent armaments and deep coffers. Demri would be fine with either, but as somebody who wanted to remain hidden as well, he thought he might make a connection there.

A bang on the door rocked Demri out of his thoughts. A second knock. "Yes?"

"It's Porric, sir. You have a guest. He has . . . incapacitated Caius, sir."

Impossible. When he pushed off the table with his hands, a small groan whimpered out of his grimacing mouth. His stiff legs didn't want to work. His face ached, tight skin on his cheek always wanting to be massaged out but never seeming to get there. He could feel the arthritis in his hips. Must be from compensating for his stiff legs. *I need a damn Healer.*

He walked—shuffled?—to the door and pulled it open. In front of him stood Porric, who snorted, then sneezed. Behind Porric, Magicus Glaouse watched a bird flying in the sky. A hawk or eagle, perhaps. Demri shamed himself for even glancing up at the damn bird, like a common peasant, distracted. Caius was on the ground; sleeping, it looked like. His knife in his hands, bloody. Demri assumed Glaouse had used some sort of force to knock Caius in the head, just enough to give a minor concussion. Demri had done it before. Hitting someone in the forehead with a specific blast of energy knocked them out cold.

"It's a wonderful thing to observe animals in the wild," Magicus Glaouse said. "You can watch them run, chase, sit still in one place for unexplained minutes, kill, eat, sleep, fuck, raise young, eat their young. You can't tell what they're about to do. *But*." He emphasized this word, turning his gaze to Demri. "*But*," he repeated with the same emphasis.

Trying to be damn annoying. *That's the thing with somebody who has your balls in a vise. They like to squeeze them until they burst, maiming you.*

"You can never predict what the animals are going to do. It's a miracle, really. Humans are much more predictable. They have hidden motives, but if you know what they've done in the past, you can often figure out where they're going. Humans"—he gestured at Caius's sleeping body—"are predictable." Glaouse's eyes flicked over Caius's bloody knife.

"What d-do you—"

"Yes, what do I want." Demri swallowed back his fury that somebody dare interrupt him. "The age-old question. Funny thing about that. Do you think the rabbit asks the hawk what he wants before the hawk swoops down and strikes? Likely not, though I profess I'm no expert."

Demri closed the door behind him and hobbled over to the bench.

"And the rabbit sits still, hoping the hawk doesn't notice him," Glaouse said.

"Why are you a Magicus when you c-could be a b-b-bird-watcher?"

"Birds are uninteresting."

"You spend a hell of a lot of t-time t-t-t-t-talking about them." Demri blinked. His eyelid stuck, so he reached up and freed it.

"So I do." Glaouse approached Demri and sat next to him. He put his hands on his knees and appeared to be watching the trees. Demri knew he wasn't. "I saw you found my letter to our former associate, Maynard Piccalo."

How did he know? Perhaps he'd seen it on the counter earlier in the day and had found it missing when he snooped around after the attack. Perhaps he'd even planted it there before Demri and Caius had gone inside. He didn't know. "Mmm."

"That is regretful. I was hoping to befriend you before taking you in. You've been a fascinating study."

"Yes, I imagine I have." Demri checked Caius again. He was stiller than a corpse and wasn't waking soon.

"I don't plan on harvesting you."

No shit. That'd be too dangerous for Glaouse. "Good."

"But I *do* have to bring you in. I would prefer you alive. *Ashmount* would prefer you alive. You have much to answer for, Demri."

Demri wouldn't argue with that. After the escapade at Drunkard's Haven and the other countless innocents he'd murdered, Demri deserved whatever retribution was coming for him. He was hoping karma would hit him a bit later on in life, though. He wasn't ready for his life to end. *So much unfinished business. I doubt Ashmount will let me live. In fact, I very much doubt they would suggest anybody attempt it. Perhaps Glaouse is trying to secure a bonus or curry extra favor with the Archmagicus. With the amount of damage I've caused, I'd be surprised if there isn't a suggestion to kill me on the spot.*

"You've caused more damage than any rumored underground Magicai organization."

Glaouse referred to the Elkavich, a name any Magicus would be hesitant to voice. Ashmount denied any such faction existed. Demri believed otherwise, however. The Magicai had wronged enough people that it seemed probable there would be an organized group devoted to retaliating against them. Demri had never found them. He wouldn't have minded assistance from them while he and Caius had been on the run over the last two decades.

"I don't see any Soul Glyphs on you. I'm sure you don't have any of this either." Glaouse touched a vial hanging from his necklace. Demri dipped his head in acknowledgment. "Being on the run for so long, I can imagine it was difficult. I'm sure there were many times you dipped into your resources when you didn't want to. You must be . . . close to the end."

"P-perhaps." He looked older than he was, but he had plenty of life left to live. Or spend. Plenty of Soul Glyphs a Glyphist could inscribe on his body. No, Glaouse was just trying to summon Demri's fear and paranoia.

"I expect you can keep your two guards in check? Or will we have to do this alone?"

"I will go. I would very m-much like to visit Ashmount once m-m-more." This was true. Though Demri didn't mean to follow through with this specific goal now. Ashmount was a sore memory. A place he wanted to raze to the ground. *In time.*

"Wonderful."

Life was all about playing your cards right. That was Demri's philosophy, anyway. His Well was nearly depleted. He had four Soul Glyphs of varying power left. Perhaps he shouldn't have squandered them in various ways that, upon reflection, he could've saved. Certainly, ending Maynard Piccalo's life with a flashy bit of magic was wasteful and emotional. However, Demri had conceded long ago that, in moments of power, he could be an irrational thinker. That pure satisfaction of ultimate victory often superseded rational decision-making.

He could've started a fight with Glaouse right then. He might've even won. After examining his hand, he decided now was not the time to play a card. *Sometimes you have to bluff before going all in.*

"We leave tomorrow morning. Best get some rest." Magicus Glaouse stood and began pacing the area. Like a hawk. Circling. Watching its prey.

Demri had been prey before. He could play the part. For a while, anyway.

EDELBROCK BRENDIS

2nd Cycle of Autumn, 231st Reign of Garcovi
Lochwall, Calrym

Days, weeks, or cycles had passed. Edelbrock couldn't tell how many. For the first few days, he'd tried keeping track. The hunger overrode any desire to think. He never learned the names of the other prisoners because they never spoke. Finch succumbed to his starvation first and joined the six other prisoners in crawling on the ground, scooping food into their mouths.

Edelbrock felt his body consuming itself, becoming weaker and weaker. And then he was crawling on the floor, joining the ranks of food-searching, starving prisoners. Twice a day the group of gladiators appeared outside the cell, throwing their latest meal's scraps at them. Both times, the cell door would open, and a pitcher of water would be delivered.

Once in a while, they'd get lucky, and a few loaves of hard, dried bread would be on the water tray. Even with the food and water, his body continued to weaken and his mind dulled.

Hunger pervaded Edelbrock's thoughts. He stopped having conversations with Finch and stayed in bed. When the food appeared, he'd jump out to scrape up whatever morsels he found. In the beginning, the dirty food bothered him. Now, dirt was an expected part of his diet. He felt his humanity draining, his animalistic instincts taking charge. Though all the Draftees were weak, they fought one another sometimes for coveted scraps of food—bits of meat or fresh fruit particular favorites. Occasionally he became desperate enough to comb through his goatee with his tongue, searching for anything—a crumb, a flicker of taste, perhaps even just an illusion that he was getting some extra nutrition somehow.

Edelbrock's stomach shrank, and his body numbed and exhausted. The mere effort it took to crawl around the ground or pick up the pitcher to drink mouthfuls of warm water drained him faster every day. He craved a bath. His gray goatee became a wild beard, untamed. His fat body lightened.

Throughout the day, he'd sometimes shake. A constant ache stabbed at his stomach. Even when he slept through the night and much of the day, he felt too exhausted to do anything else but sleep some more.

Long after he'd been there, the cell door opened to emit a ninth prisoner. A strong, soldier-looking type. Edelbrock didn't care though and ignored him. He also didn't hear whatever Marshal Deywin said to him when he dropped the prisoner off.

Days turned into weeks. Or was it weeks turning into cycles? Cycles into years? He didn't know. Time spiraled by.

Until a fateful day, when a tenth prisoner entered the

cell. The man looked almost as bad as the rest of the prisoners, so he might've been a beggar.

"The Draft will be tomorrow," the marshal said. A weak chorus of cheers came from the cell's prisoners. Their only moment of clarity. The marshal promptly turned and left.

Edelbrock sunk back into empty thoughts.

In the morning, Edelbrock woke to a feast delivered. A large bird—goose?—cooked to perfection and stuffed with onions and herbs, coated in bread crumbs. A goblet of gravy, a long loaf of bread, baked chestnuts, two types of fresh cheeses, blackberry wine, and a plate of delicious strawberry pastries covered in sugar. They consumed the food with their hands, ignoring the cutlery.

After they'd ingested the food, everyone started regaining their voices, though it took a while for some of the older prisoners to begin to speak at all. For once, Edelbrock felt full and energized, though a forgotten anger, along with a dose of fear, permeated his mind. He set aside his emotions and attempted to learn more about his current situation.

He learned about the other prisoners. One was an enormous man who used to be a mercenary. He'd attacked a merchant caravan that sold goods to King Mikas Garcovi. Rather than execute him, the king had ordered him to Buzzard's Bowl as a gift for Lord Haklon. Another was a warrior woman from Vessia and a member of the Camel Clans. She didn't explain why she was there, and he didn't have the nerve to ask. There was a skinny fellow who claimed relation to Duchess Arena Hyrel, a noblewoman who served King

Mikas. A man who knew him from before arrest said he suffered an addiction to inventing lives that weren't his. The most recent prisoner informed them all he'd been taken during the Second Cycle of Autumn. Many of the prisoners went silent once again, likely shocked and considering all the time that'd passed. *Lots of wasted time.* Edelbrock's thoughts turned to his son, Gordy, and he ruminated in them for several hours.

The cell door opened, and Marshal Deywin appeared with a regiment of guards. "It's time. Follow me."

Edelbrock stood, some of his old military courage resurfacing. "You working here now? I thought you were just helping Scayde by escorting arrests you'd made to this place."

"Better pay. And it's *Lord* Haklon."

Of course. The only reason for the marshal to change workplaces would be the income. Scayde Haklon owned the law, so nothing else would change.

The prisoners followed him, free from the dreadful hovel.

Marshal Deywin brought them through a series of corridors, the last sloping up. They passed a checkpoint with several guards and a Magicus and entered a small pit where grated windows in the walls allowed them to view the vast arena. Edelbrock peeked out, the sandy floor at eye level. He noticed how high up the stands climbed, allowing thousands of spectators. A bunch of people were sitting in the stands now. Sweat formed on his forehead and dripped down his face. They continued walking and then something startled him and several of the other prisoners.

A booming voice echoed across Buzzard's Bowl. "Welcome to our next Draft!" It was Scayde Haklon, though something was enhancing his volume. "For those of you who like to gamble and prefer to take notes on what transpires, you will find parchment, quills, and ink at the ends of each row. As always, my servants—led by Tanibris, a dear friend—have dispatched his legendary refreshment service. They'll be around momentarily."

Edelbrock groaned. "We're to be auctioned off in front of an audience?"

"They do this every Draft," Finch said.

The Camel Clans woman snorted. "You know nothing of slavery. Here they feed you, they give you shelter. They allow you to compete in luxury. The Camel Clans do none of this. If you have a nice cock or cunt, they fuck you a few times, and then toss you to the dogs."

"This is better," said Edelbrock.

A guard heard him. "Quiet!"

Marshal Deywin brought them to another room. This one had no grated window. It also had several benches. In front of the group was a huge, open archway. Edelbrock could see the sands of Buzzard's Bowl on the other side, but it was through a hazy fog.

"Finch, is that mist?"

"Nah, that's a magical barrier. Appears like a wall to spectators, so they don't get distracted by who's next to fight. Allows fighters to see a little o' what's happening, but it mutes sound. Let's them prepare. Quiet solitude for those 'bout to die gives them a chance to ready themselves. At least, that's what I's heard. Sending me to death ain't going to get any better, even if I have time to prepa—"

"I said quiet!" the guard shouted, slamming the pommel of a sword into Finch's face. Finch dropped to the ground, blood spraying the wall of the room. He groaned and remained still.

The marshal pointed at the benches. "Sit."

They heeded the command. Edelbrock stole another glance at Finch. He wasn't moving. The man must have knocked him unconscious.

People in the stands were all riled up, standing and cheering. The haziness in the archway disappeared, and the roar of the crowd washed over Edelbrock.

Scayde's voice again. "Ladies and gentlemen, I know you're waiting for the Draftees, so let's bring them out."

"Up," Marshal Deywin said. "Out the archway. Go."

Edelbrock and the prisoners exited the archway. The marshal and his men stayed behind with Finch's unconscious body.

Standing in the middle of Buzzard's Bowl was Scayde Haklon. Guards accompanied him, as did what seemed to be a selection of important people. And several Magicai. To Scayde's left and right were four more groups of varying sizes. *These must be the other House Heads and their guards.* Edelbrock recognized velvet robes at the front of one of these groups. *The Velvet Mother.* He also saw Jaylena Brendis—Maccaro now—standing among a group of her own people, glaring in his direction. Edelbrock's hands turned sweaty, and he clamped them shut. There was nothing he could do that wouldn't result in his immediate death. *Would that really be so terrible at this point?*

Scayde Haklon lifted a small cylindrical tube to his mouth. "Welcome!" His voice boomed across the arena. "Line up over here." He gestured to a bunch of red lines in the sand. Edelbrock chose one, and the rest of the prisoners followed suit, lining up in a staggered formation. No hiding here.

Scayde pointed at the empty spot where Finch should've been. "I only count nine!"

The spectators laughed. Edelbrock had a bad feeling.

Then Marshal Deywin appeared, dragging Finch by the leg and depositing him on the empty line. Finch stirred and issued a moan.

"Marshal Deywin," Lord Haklon said through the voice enhancer. "You can't expect the esteemed House Heads would want *that*?" He drew a sword, and the crowd roared.

There will be blood.

The crowd began chanting. "Kill him! Kill him!"

Scayde lowered the cylindrical device from his lips and smiled at Edelbrock. "I heard you've developed a friendship. I didn't invite you here to make *friends*."

Edelbrock felt sick. Scayde raised the sword over his head.

Finch, consciousness returned, raised his hands in protest. "Wait!"

The crowd laughed. And booed. "Kill him!"

The sword came down, followed by a familiar meaty tearing. Gore streamed from Finch's stomach, and he screamed a bloodcurdling cry. The sword withdrew, and Scayde wiped it on Finch's breeches. Edelbrock grimaced, watching Finch struggle to hold his insides inside. Edelbrock was certain Scayde slashed Finch in the gut on purpose, giving the crowd a slow death.

Behind him, Edelbrock heard Marshal Deywin spitting skachi juice. It further emphasized the injustice being done—a former lawman standing there. Doing nothing.

Another archway, across from where Edelbrock had entered, opened. Six additional prisoners escorted by guards lined up at another set of lines—Qothans by the look of them.

"This Draft is special, as we've had to round out the number so each person gets an equal share. As we've lost one"—Scayde gestured at Finch's body—"we've needed to take one from a new group that just came in. Rather than only take one of them, I figured it'd be fun to have a bonus. Everyone receives an extra Draftee today." The crowd cheered.

"As is customary," Scayde said, "the Draft will proceed in the following order. Round one, I will receive the first pick, Velvet Mother second, Castede Varono third, fourth is the new House Head Jaylena Maccaro"—Edelbrock's lip twitched at her maiden name—"who is now Jaylena Haklon."

Edelbrock's heart slammed into his chest as the crowd roared its approval.

Scayde waited for them to calm down. "And last is Lekhan Roelk. In round two, we shall reverse the order. Round three, we will determine with a random draw. Everyone, please take a moment to examine your prospective recruits."

The House Heads, excluding Scayde, walked up and down the line of prisoners, discussing with their advisers. Sometimes a House Head would stop and question one of them.

Castede Varono halted in front of Edelbrock, examining him. Castede, unlike the other four House Heads, had the build of a soldier and looked uncomfortable in the silken robes he wore. The man definitely preferred armor or leathers rather than a nobleman's flowing robes. He had a short, trimmed mustache and a ring of brown hair circling his bald pate. He also wore a fresh pair of black boots.

"You were fat." It was not a question. Edelbrock wasn't sure what to do, so he stood there, hands clasped behind his back. "I hear you used to be a military hero." It also wasn't a question but had the expectation of a response lingering at the end.

"Yes."

"And you let yourself become *this* bad. No wonder your wife left you." Castede beamed, like he'd made a funny joke. Edelbrock felt his face burning like a furnace. "Don't get angry, I jest," the man said. The man was sincere, though that didn't make it all right. "You have a thirst for revenge." Again, an expectation for a response.

"I do."

"The taste of revenge often makes a great fighter."

"I'm sure." He was unaware of what Castede was trying to unearth. It was enough, or he'd become uninterested, because Castede moved on.

When Jaylena reached him, she stalked by without so much as a glance in his direction, pretending to be engaged in conversation with one of her advisers. Edelbrock grumbled and gritted his teeth. Hands in fists and eyes locked on her figure, a guard placed himself between the two of them.

Lekhan Roelk passed by with nothing more than an up-and-down look at Edelbrock. The man was sneering and had several tattoos. Soul Glyphs. A Magicus.

When the Velvet Mother approached, they appraised Edelbrock. "You have angered Scayde, haven't you?"

"I have."

"Wonderful." They smiled and proceeded down the queue.

When Scayde arrived in front of Edelbrock, he snorted and turned to his group of followers. "*This* one tried to become a House Head. Can you believe it? The gall. *Sickening.*" They laughed.

"Didn't you throw his son off of the highest stand?" one of them asked.

Smirking, Scayde answered the guard. "Indeed. Poor little Gordy."

Edelbrock trembled and balled his hands into fists. A

servant—Tanibris was the name if Edelbrock wasn't mistaken—distributed several pieces of parchment to each of the House Heads and Marshal Deywin.

"Thank you, Tanibris," Scayde said, then raised the voice enhancer back up. "To those of you in the stands that may not know, and my darling wife, Jaylena, who is also new here . . ." The crowd cheered again. Scayde took a moment to observe Edelbrock. His upper lip quivered and his fingers dug into his palms, opening skin. " . . .my servant Tanibris has handed us a dossier with the backgrounds of our Draftees. At the end of the Draft, Tanibris will have copies available to whoever wants them, so you may learn about the new gladiators and form predictions on whom to place bets upon when they return to fight in the arena."

The House Heads took a moment to read through the parchment. Every so often, one of them would glance up and look at somebody in line, asking them to state their name so they could find their information. Meanwhile, Marshal Deywin was rearranging the line of fifteen Draftees so they matched the order on the list.

"It's time to make our selections," Scayde said. "And my first pick is Anditus Roberon."

Edelbrock didn't know what to think. He was *certain* he'd be the first pick. Scayde's guards corralled a greasy haired fellow, presumably Anditus Roberon, away from the rest of the prisoners.

And the others made their selections. The first round passed, and Edelbrock was still available. The order reversed, which meant Scayde picked last. Which meant there were four chances for Edelbrock to escape Scayde. Three, really. He didn't think Jaylena would pick him. *That'd be worse, anyway.*

Lekhan's, Castede's, and Jaylena's second picks were *not* Edelbrock.

The Velvet Mother consulted the dossiers, chin in hand. They said, "I'm sorry I am going to do this, Lord Haklon. I'm going back on my word. The Velvet Mother wants first place this year. Edelbrock Brendis is my pick."

The only sign of Scayde's displeasure was a narrowing of his eyes and a tension in his cheeks. In a calm, business-like voice, he said, "You'll regret this, you conniving *shit*. The Velvet Mother exists because *I* allow her to."

The spectators must've noticed the tension because silence descended.

"I'm sorry you feel that way, Lord Haklon, but the selection stands."

"You tell the *real* Velvet Mother I'll reclaim her portion of the arena and give it to somebody who *sticks by their word!*" Scayde Haklon, red-faced, stomped his foot and turned his back on the Velvet Mother.

Guards escorted Edelbrock over to the Velvet Mother's group. The other recruited person, not from Edelbrock's cell, shook his hand. "Nauc Othepi."

"Edelbrock Brendis."

That was it. There wasn't anything else to say. They watched the rest of the Draft proceedings and listened to the crowd cheer at various picks, though it was much more subdued than before. Scayde's enthusiasm had waned, and the crowd could sense it. Edelbrock didn't care who went where. His distraction at *not* being drafted by Scayde *or* Jaylena was a high he didn't think he'd experience out here.

"And that ends the Draft!" Scayde said into the voice enhancer. The crowd hushed. Scayde stormed off, his retinue shuffling his three new gladiators after him.

"Come," the Velvet Mother said. "Our House entrance is this way."

Edelbrock couldn't help but think he'd escaped serious torture. He also worried for the Velvet Mother's decoy. He assumed the man would die soon. If that were the case, he hoped the other representatives of the Velvet Mother were like this one.

SERADAL WINTLOCK

*2nd Cycle of Autumn, 231st Reign of Garcovi
Cyrok*

Thump. Thump. Thump. Sera's heart was a dull pounding in her ears, her chest.

Leaves cracked, twigs snapped, and branches swiped at her face, scratching her cheeks. Blood dripped down her face in tiny rivulets, pattering the ground beneath her. Her legs ached, and her lungs burned from cool air because she gasped while sprinting. Running, running, running. An unseen stone or chunk of ice rolled under her shoe, and she tripped, arms splayed in the air, making circles to catch her balance. All she caught was solid ground to her face. A small branch stabbed her thigh. Moaning, she spit out a clump of debris—snow mixed with dirt and pine needles.

She took a deep breath. Pursuit wouldn't be far behind. Earlier, she'd sworn she'd heard a horse's hooves. Her right wrist throbbed in pain. A lot of pain.

She'd likely sprained it in the fall. Or if she was unlucky, she'd broken it.

She struggled to stand back up, exhaustion besting her. The sound of a snapping branch, followed by a subdued thudding echoed through the forest, following her. It sounded like a single horse heading her way. But one was enough.

The approaching danger caused an adrenaline rush, and she staggered to her feet, running again. A small beam of moonlight flickered through a branch, and then it disappeared. Darkness returned. Running, running, running. She made out the shadow of an immense tree a foot in front of her. Dodging around it, she continued. Blindly running, hoping not to hurt herself more than she'd already done. Fear spurred her forward.

Loose strands of hair wrapped themselves around her face, sticking to her mouth and nose. She'd stopped trying to spit it out many minutes ago. Hours? Time was impossible to tell. It felt like she'd been running half the night. Her calves wanted to separate from the rest of her body. The cool air threatened to suffocate her. She was wheezing. She was lucky she hadn't started coughing. It felt like the air impeded her airway, suffocating her with the frigid harshness. She recognized the feeling. Croup was on the horizon. These hours in the cold hadn't done her any favors.

She choked, took another deep breath, and coughed. *Shit.* She didn't swear. Not often, anyway. But this was one of those moments that called for it. And thoughts didn't even count, right?

The horse was gaining on her.

Sera couldn't run anymore. Gasping, she stopped and rested against the trunk of a tree. She slid to a sitting position, cradling her wrist. Sweat coated her body. Her chest heaved as she drew in quick breaths.

Her breasts were sore and chafing. Her wrist pulsed in tune with her heartbeat, and her lungs groaned like winter ice. And her thighs burned.

Horse hooves hammered the ground. Her pursuer was even closer.

Exhaustion. A small moan escaped her. Sera closed her eyes and leaned her head against the tree trunk. She was comfortable and dying wouldn't be so bad. She'd done all she could. Ran her life away. Sometimes you lost in life. In fact, Sera ventured a guess that more people in the world were losers than winners. She wasn't sure where this line of thinking came from. Pessimism wasn't her way of thinking.

She opened her eyes, then looked over her shoulder at the approaching rider. A beam of distant light bounced up and down, up and down. There was nowhere to hide. She could crawl to the other side of the tree, but it wasn't thick enough to hide her body.

The bobbing lantern danced ever closer.

Sera wondered how her father was doing. Her father. She blinked several times, clarity returning. It wasn't about her. Giving up was sacrificing her father's life. And Angazo's. And anybody else's who still lived. She had to get to the governess.

She looked around for a weapon. Anything to defend herself. A clump of ice and snow, small enough to fit in her closed hand. It was better than nothing. She grabbed it in her undamaged left hand, making a fist around it. It was unfortunate because her right hand was her primary. *I wouldn't get very far trying to throw something at somebody with a bum wrist, though. I'll just hurt myself more.*

She grimaced and waited for the horse and rider to find her.

Seconds passed, each one an eternity.

The burning yellow glow blinded her, so she looked away and watched the rider out of the corner of her eye.

The ball rested against her hand, snow cooling her skin. A numbness in her palm. *Too bad there isn't something hardier around.* But she didn't have time to look.

"Hiyah!" A man's voice, the thrash of reins against the horse's flanks.

She shielded her eyes with an arm, trying to get a glance at the approaching rider. The lantern swung back and forth, hanging from the rider's hand. The light obscured him.

The horse raced by her. For a moment, she thought they would keep going.

"Whoa!" The horse slowed, then turned around and approached Sera. "Look what we have here!" The man dismounted. He threw the reins around a nearby sapling. Truth be told, Sera figured the horse could get away if they wanted, but the man seemed unconcerned. The ring of steel being drawn reverberated around the forest.

Sera shivered. She thought of her father. She needed to get out of this alive so she could help him.

The man approached, lantern in one hand and sword hanging at his side with the other. He didn't appear like he wanted to use it yet. He bent over, setting the lantern on the ground.

"This is going to be fun." His voice dripped with an icy pleasure.

The bandit stepped in front of the light, and she recognized him. A long slash ran down his face from a gyrfalcon claw. Golden Royce's mark. Smugface.

"Oh yes, I'm going to enjoy this. Captain Adavir isn't here to save you this time."

"You're one sorry bastard." Again with the swearing. *Extenuating circumstances, Sera.*

"Yes, I know." He fumbled one-handed with the strings to his breeches. The other hand still gripped his sword, though Sera figured if the bandit had his way, he was about to have two swords in his grasp. Disgusted, she couldn't let that happen.

She groaned and stood.

"Oh, don't do that." He whimpered. "I don't want to hurt you. Get back on the ground, and we can make this nice and simple." He continued fumbling with his ties, but his eyes were locked on her, so he wasn't making much progress.

Screaming, she charged him, the ice clump raised above her head like a savage.

Smugface jumped. He dropped his sword, and it clattered to the ground. He shouted. Either in surprise or fear, she couldn't tell. She also didn't care. He bent over to grab the hilt, but his fingers only brushed it when Sera brought the ice down as hard as she could on the man's face. He yelled again, collapsing to the ground, ice and dirt plastering his eyes. Momentum carried her to the ground too. Tangled, they wrestled to get on top of one another, both focused on the sword.

The bastard ignored his sword and drew a knife. He stabbed at her leg, and she rolled away. The knife pinned in the ground, missing her by inches.

Sera grunted while pushing herself up and then grasped a fallen branch she'd missed on her earlier search for a weapon. She threw the stick at him, and he winced. The wood smacked him in the shoulder, flipped, then bounced off his forehead and rolled away into the darkness.

"You fucking bitch!" Smugface retrieved his knife, then jumped to his feet.

Sera panicked. She drove her foot out, catching him in the chin. He gurgled, falling backward. A pink mist sprayed the air, and she thought she saw a tooth flying in the lantern light.

A flash of silver caught her gaze. His sword lay in the forest detritus, just waiting for her to claim it.

She dashed. Smugface saw her destination. He lunged forward, striking her with the knife. The blade sunk deep into her forearm, and she shrieked. Agony bit into her flesh. Blood ran down her arm—what had been her good arm. He ripped the knife out, and it tore an even longer gash. She screamed louder. White flashed across her vision, followed by black. Colors blended and formed a greenish blur. She blinked tears out of her eyes, and the color turned into a greenish-yellow mash. Trees and lantern light.

The blade pierced her again. This time in her side, slipping across a rib. She shrieked louder than before. The pain was excruciating. Instincts took over, and she pulled away from the knife.

Wheezing and a barking cough escaped her throat. The croup was starting. She choked through, splattered the air with some mucus. Sera knelt and reached out, fumbling in blindness, searching. And as luck would have it, she grabbed the sword hilt. Standing and holding it up in one hand, she waved it back and forth.

Snow crunched—Smugface stepping back. *He doesn't realize it's just a charade, a distraction to let me catch my bearings.* She'd never wielded a sword before.

She hacked through another fit of coughs, cleared her throat. Spat more phlegm. Blinked more tears until she could see. Her hand was slippery on the hilt, blood making it difficult to grasp the weapon. Her arm throbbed, wrist ached, and lungs screamed at her to rest.

Smugface grinned wickedly. He stepped forward, knife held out as far as he could, plunging it toward her stomach.

A foolish decision. She stepped back and swiped the sword in the air. It caught in the man's neck, though it didn't go far. Just enough, she figured.

He stared at her, wide-eyed. Astonishment flashed in his eyes, and the knife dropped to the ground. She let go of the sword, and he tipped over, dying.

Sera gagged. Another coughing fit. More mucus sprayed the ground below her. No, that was vomit. She trembled. More acidic muck burned her throat and painted the ground in brown chunks. *Sera stew.*

The man was gasping, the sword still embedded in his neck. His death throes became weaker. In moments, he'd be dead. She glared at him.

Sera retrieved the lantern and slowly walked to the horse. She'd ridden horses before, though not often, and knew it would beat walking. She was in far too much pain. Blood stained her clothing. She patted the horse on the side. She'd watched people do this before. The stallion snorted but otherwise seemed unbothered. Sera gathered the reins, tossed them over his head, and tried to mount.

She put one foot in the stirrup and heaved herself up, then crashed to the ground. The horse stamped a few steps away. The lantern's light was extinguished. She'd dropped it in the fall.

She moaned. The effort to stand seemed excessive. But if she remained on the ground, she knew she'd die. Her father needed her.

Struggling, Sera pushed herself back off the ground and made her way in the horse's direction. Sera bumped into him. She grasped the mane in her hand, and after feeling around in the dark with her foot to find the stirrup, she hauled herself up. Pain tore through her body, and she let out a primal grunt, threw her leg over the saddle.

Somehow, she was sitting astride the horse. He took off and cantered through the forest. *Away from Captain Adavir, I hope.* She was so turned around that she wasn't sure which way the horse was going. Sera hardly cared; she was too tired. She leaned down against the beast's neck and passed out.

She slept.

She screamed when her body hit the ground. Her abdomen throbbed. Sera lay on the edge of a flat snowy plain. The horse dragged his mouth across the ground in search of vegetation. Finding some, he ripped a clump free and chewed. Sera grunted and, struggling, stood. She hunched over, finding it near unbearable to straighten. When she grabbed the stallion's side, he snorted and walked a few feet away.

Sighing, she staggered after the animal. *I need to get my father some help.* She didn't care about her own condition. Sera reached the horse again, grabbed his mane, and heaved herself up. The wounds flared and she grimaced, not wanting to spook the horse with a scream. She directed the horse, and off they went. Out of the forest. Toward Vox.

Sera wasn't sure how long she rode the stallion. Her body ached. She was thirsty. Her dry tongue kept sticking in her mouth. The dry cough persisted and, after a while, made her gag. Several times, she passed out for a few minutes, then awoke to the familiar bouncing up and down across the flat frozen tundra. Once, she woke to find the horse standing still. It sounded like he'd been eating again. She hit his rear, and he took off. Later, she woke to find the horse walking at a gentle pace. Her wounds throbbed and ached and pounded, while her muscles screamed and pulled and stiffened.

A day went by. Or was it two? Three? Maybe it was the first day, and she was hallucinating. She was in and out of consciousness. Sera fought to stay awake, to direct the horse in the right direction. She needed to save her father.

"Hey!" Sera jolted awake at the stranger's voice. "Are you all right?"

A hand on her thigh. She winced away from it. "It's okay." A man's voice. "Here, I'm going to help you off of there, all right?"

Sera tried to speak, but her lips didn't want to work. She grumbled and then gasped as she lurched off the horse, wounds shouting at her to *stop moving*. A man's face frowned down at her, and then pain rushed to her head and her vision went black. She closed her eyes and winced as a searing headache appeared.

"Avani save us, she's almost dead."

Mother Avani, save me, Sera agreed. She didn't call for help from Mother Avani, the Great Creator, often, but today she'd take all the help she could get.

He placed her on the ground. Her mouth wouldn't work. Her brain couldn't work. Her body didn't cooperate. She lay there like a brick.

Another man's voice. "Where's she from?"

"I'm not sure. Just rode in. Quick, get Magicus Ashté. She's wounded. Bad."

"Yes, cyr!" Fading footsteps.

Sera tried to open her eyes, but bright light came crashing against her head like a mallet. She groaned and slammed her eyes shut.

"Rest easy, citizen," the first man said. "Help is on the way. Here."

Water tipped down her throat, and she drank it eagerly. The man kept the waterskin there until she drained it. Thin streams of liquid trickled down her cheek, and he wiped them away.

"Hang on. You're going to be all right."

Moments passed. Once more Sera attempted to open her eyes, but the light prevented her from doing so. She stopped trying after that.

A gasp, followed by a woman's voice. "What happened to her?"

"Don't know. She rode in like this. She's in a bad way."

"I'll take care of her. Step aside."

Sera croaked. She tried to speak. "My father."

"Shh."

"Could be important," the man said.

Sera tried again. "In the woods. Governess. Bandits. Gyrloft gone."

"Nonsense." The woman's voice was soothing.

"Gyrloft destroyed?" The man sounded incredulous.

"You're going to be all right." A soft hand placed on Sera's forehead.

"The governess. Captain Adavir. Killed everyone. Gyrloft." Sentences were difficult to form. Her head hurt.

"She'll want to hear about this," the man said.

"Then go tell her. I have a patient to help." The woman's soft hand felt as if it was growing warmer.

Then Sera felt wounds closing. Skin knit back into place. A crunching sound and a violent pain in her ribs. The knife must've cracked one. Or chipped it. She wasn't sure. Wasn't able to process. The pain was almost worse than the original wound. She screamed. Things shifted, sealed themselves back up, and snapped into place. Then calm.

"Rest."

And so she did.

Sera blinked a couple of times, but she kept them closed. The light hurt. She moaned. Her lips were dry, cracked. Thirsty. Her throat screamed for water. An incoherent mumble escaped her lips. She tried to clear her throat. It didn't work very well.

"Here." A woman's voice. A kind one.

A mug pressed against Sera's chin, and she opened her mouth to receive chilled, refreshing water. She took deep gulps, some escaping and dripping down her neck. Sera was warm. Sweaty, even. Blankets wrapped around her body.

The beverage brought back her sense. Her voice. "W-where am I?" Sera opened her eyes, and a headache pulsed. The glow of a nearby lantern. "Ugh." She snapped her eyes shut again.

"One moment." The kind voice again. "There. I've dimmed the light."

Sera opened her eyes once more. The lantern was a mere flicker now. A figure stood near it, clothed in shadow.

"Half-conscious, you rode into Vox." The woman walked over to the bedside. "It's all right not to remember. You were quite injured."

Sera shifted the blankets down her body, exposing herself to air. Her old clothes were missing, and she was in a smooth, comfortable robe.

"You've been in and out of consciousness for a day

and a half. I will send for somebody to deliver some food soon. I'm sure you're half-starved."

Sera hadn't thought about it, but the mere mention of food set her stomach rumbling. Then she remembered what had happened. *Father and Angazo.* "My father! They attacked us! They razed Gyrloft to the ground!"

The woman held a hand up to stop Sera. "I know, I know. You already mentioned some of these things. I sent some men out to investigate, and it wasn't long before they stumbled upon Captain Adavir." The woman snorted. "A man I detest."

The woman was wearing leather armor. Her shoulder displayed the patch of a gyrfalcon, stitched into the perfect position to maximize visibility. "Are you the—"

"Your father is alive," the woman interrupted. "Miraculously. You shall want to thank Magicus Ashté for her work. Your father will always have health problems. But his injuries were severe enough that healing him to the point of living took great effort and strain upon Magicus Ashté. She's aged several additional years. You were healed enough to prevent death, but I'm sure you're feeling lingering effects. It's important a Healer not waste their life when it's not necessary."

"I'm sorry to be a burden." She was grateful she'd received any healing. Sera was just a peasant of zero importance, and in Cyrok, she'd never heard of a Magicus being hired. She'd doubted she'd ever meet one in her lifetime because they were so rare in Cyrok— not enough purpose for the Magicai. She supposed a Healer would be a good investment for the capital, however expensive it was. When it came to the other countries of the world, Cyrok was noticeably insignificant when it came to the population of present Magicai.

"Nonsense. It was my choice to have you restored,

and your father too. I'm sorry to have to tell you he is . . . paralyzed. Walking will be out of the question for the rest of his life, unless you find another Healer you can afford and will commit that much of their life to him. Yet he lives."

Father. Alive! Sera was certain that he would've perished by the time any help reached him. The Healer saved her. And her father. "You're the governess," Sera said. The woman spoke with enough authority and knowledge, Sera had little doubt about it.

"I am. Stasia Falconel, Governess of Vox, stand-in leader for Cyrok when the time necessitates it, Commander of the Falcon Knights, and Guardian of the People. I prefer you address me as Stasia or cyr, if you feel the need. I'm not picky, but let's not waste our lives with endless titles and fingering each other's assholes. I'll always prefer honesty and bluntness, though I've found in politics, I am one of the few."

Sera held her hand out. "My name is Seradal Wintlock. Thank you for saving my life."

"A pleasure." The governess shook her hand with a strengthened grip, causing Sera enough discomfort that she almost gave away her displeasure with a visible wince. She held it together though. "Perhaps we can talk again when you're up to it. I have other matters to attend, and your supper is on its way." The governess walked to the doorway and stopped, calling over her shoulder, "Please remain in bed. You need to recover. I will have your father visit soon. So lie back down."

Smirking, Sera relaxed and lay back down. For the governess was right. She had been about to rush out and search for her father. Her father was alive. *She* was alive. Sera was happy, but she couldn't help remembering her mother and her brother.

H er father, though paralyzed, looked well. Two Falcon Knights carried him into her room and deposited him in a chair. They surprised her with their gentleness. Sera admitted their treatment of her and her father, mere peasants from a town that no longer existed, was rather impressive.

By the time her father visited, Sera could handle the glow of the light and requested they turned it back up when her supper arrived. The room was extravagant, and materials Sera hadn't seen before were everywhere: silk blankets, some plushy chairs made of who knew what, and, hung above the fireplace mantel, a blue emblem in the shape of a falcon. She wasn't sure what it was made from, but it gleamed and shined in the light—Governess Stasia Falconel's chosen symbol.

Vox was traditional. The governor's election was a grand event where an invitation was sent out to all Cyroki citizens, though most peasants like Sera chose not to attend. It was at this congregation that the elected person chose their own color and bird, symbols of their reign. Remnants of old regimes still lingered throughout the city, older knights now serving the governess as veterans. New recruits would become Falcon Knights. Previous orders of the Falcon Knights that Sera knew of were Hawk, Grouse, and Vulture. There were many Hawk Knights still active, and a few Grouse Knights. If there were any Vultures left, they'd be old now.

A cough from Jaidik brought Sera back to the present. The two Falcon Knights were stepping outside of the room while her father was struggling to remain upright in the chair he sat in, his useless feet dangling and dragging across the floor like a wash servant's cloth. "Seradal." He choked through another cough, cleared his throat. "How are you feeling?"

"Healing is painful."

"Dying is worse, I promise." She thought of her mother, of her brother. The awful way they'd both died.

"Is Angazo . . ." She trailed off, not wanting to finish the question.

"Angazo lives. He's much better off than either of us. When the governess arrived—" He paused, another hacking cough shaking his body. He brought a handkerchief to his mouth and wiped a spare bit of spittle leaking out. "It seems I developed a sickness of some sort."

"Maybe the Healer?"

"No. Magicus Ashté has aged enough as it is, I think. It's just a cold. If I need further treatment, I won't seek a Magicus. We can't afford one anyway. But enough about my health. Governess Falconel wanted me to brief you on a few things while I visited."

"Oh?"

"Because of your bravery and heroism, after killing that man who chased you and making your way here despite your wounds, you are being recognized. You helped foil a plot that was worse than we knew. The Falcon Knights defeated Captain Blago Adavir, routing him and his men. The governess placed Cyrok's military on high alert. A few bandits ended up captured and interrogated. They corroborated that Captain Adavir was acting on Calrym's orders. It seems King Mikas has intentions of war. Captain Adavir's orders were to recruit as many men as he could and sow as much discord through destruction as possible. The governess believes another attack is imminent."

Sera's heart plummeted to her toes. Or was it rocketing up her throat? Either way was rather uncomfortable. Her father's hacking started up again. Her mind drifted. Gyrloft's destruction was just the start. What would happen if Calrym invaded and destroyed everything? She couldn't help feeling little about that prospect. She'd never been elsewhere. If Governess Stasia Falconel's forces failed and her father, Angazo, and herself were captured or killed . . . the outcome was a frightening thought. Otherwise, she wouldn't oppose leaving Cyrok.

"Sera, I tell you this only because I promised I would." He paused. "She has enacted the Avian Draft. She wants you to become a Falcon Knight."

"I—what?"

"You are to become Cyr Seradal Wintlock and serve the governess and country as a national hero. Already Governess Falconel has given two speeches about your tale." Jaidik coughed again, harder than before.

Sera thought she saw him wipe a spot of blood away, but it was difficult to tell. "Are you okay?"

He waved her concerns away, coughing once more. "I'm fine. I just need some rest soon. This isn't what I wanted for you."

"It's not what I wanted for myself." Though Sera realized life had a funny way of choosing a path for you, whether you liked it or not.

"I'm sure we could appeal the decision. The governess is friendlier than I would have guessed."

"No."

"Sera."

"I owe her my life. And yours. Angazo's too."

Her father nodded, solemn. It wasn't like there was anything else for their family to do. Perhaps he knew that too. Becoming a knighted soldier? At least she'd have a job, a purpose, a place to be, and a decent salary.

Somebody had to look after their family. It was up to her now.

"I'm going to be a Falcon Knight." And just like that, she was. Sera could tell her father wasn't happy about it.

She couldn't quite say that she was happy either.

INTERLUDE
HARLEM MACCARO

2nd Cycle of Autumn, 231st Reign of Garcovi
Anepolis, Calrym

Exquisite cheeses. Fancy olives. Fluffy fresh-baked bread. Mouthwatering slabs of butter. Gorgeous piles of juicy berries, many of them imported from Remeria. Sweet chilled red wine. And, though Harlem was not sure of it, it appeared as if the glorious leader of Calrym, King Mikas Garcovi, had splurged and purchased a gyrfalcon from the northern lands of Cyrok for consumption. In Harlem's opinion, the expense was unnecessary and not worth it, unless you considered spite for the north to be a valid reason. Which, of course, he did.

"Let the council recognize a letter from Cyrok," the king's chancellor, Bertrand, said.

Speak of the bastards.

The chancellor stood at the king's side, unrolling a piece of weathered parchment. Aside from Bertrand, everyone sat at a large table, facing one another with the king at its head. The Great Hall inside the king's palace was where the king's main advisers, all of them dukes and duchesses, gathered to argue with one another until the king became too angry and made a decision. The titles were a privilege and a courtesy offered by the king to his direct advisers, whereupon they'd earn a significant stipend and be gifted an elaborate manor.

Harlem's eyes danced over to the cheese platter again. Food didn't appeal to him, not like it did to others in the room, but cheese? Cheese was a delicacy he savored at any opportunity. Sharp, mild, squishy, soft, hard. Cheese. It didn't matter to the nobleman; he loved it all. He popped another delectable square onto his tongue, scooping it into his mouth. Harlem chewed, deliberate, letting the cheese fall apart, a slight tang exploding on his taste buds. Swallowing, he took a sip of his red wine, letting the drink swish around in his mouth as it combined with the tart cheese. Had Harlem not been attending matters of state, he'd be happier than the most pious priest standing in front of Mother Avani. His fingers ran across his thin mustache, then around the corners of his mouth, and down his beard. Best to make sure there were no stray pieces. Maintaining professionalism was important to him. Unlike most of the power-hungry rich nobles in the room.

The chancellor's voice interrupted Harlem's bliss, reading from the parchment. "My dearest friends in the south" Many guffaws and chuckles echoed in the chamber, not excluding the king's. Harlem, unlike most of the others, was more reserved. "I'm addressing the king's council"—Harlem scoffed at this. The king's council didn't exist in Calrym but in Remeria—"in Anepolis about a matter that is both frightening and concerning to the citizens of Cyrok and myself. A band of brigands attacked and destroyed one of our towns, notable for being our primary gyrfalcon source."

"What? Damn him to death!" King Mikas slammed his fist on the table, his jeweled crown wiggling atop his head. Harlem's wine almost spilled. Harlem narrowed his eyes at the king but, of course, said nothing. "We specifically told him *not* to attack the gyrfalcons!"

A nobleman, Velturo Ondakka, spoke up. The other one who enjoyed food, but in a disgusting, gluttonous sort of way. Not the refined, savory way Harlem did. "Does it matter? We needed to cause discord and distraction, and that's *exactly* what he's done, ah-hah."

One of the few noblewomen answered—Arena Hyrel. Harlem's rival. "Surely we did not want to sound the alarm *this* early, Velturo."

"Bah!" Duke Velturo angrily shook his hand, which was holding a glass of wine, his blue surcoat now stained red. Harlem sighed. The lack of decorum was preposterous. Velturo frowned and swabbed at the stain, spreading it further because he wasn't dabbing. "It's not like it matters, Arena, ah-hah." He also had the intolerable habit of ending dialogue with that same frustrating half-laugh *every damn time*.

Duchess Arena offered a shrill snort of contempt. Harlem disliked her almost as much as Velturo. "You *would* think that Velturo. Discretion is how we accomplish things without significant resistance until it is too late. Now, Adavir has squandered that. What could we expect by hiring a band of *northern* men? Like I've said before, Your Majesty"—she turned to look at King Mikas—"if you want something done correctly, send a Calrite." Her hand uncurled, one finger pointing in Harlem's direction.

They'd been over this point. Many times. The opposition to a direct invasion at the moment was high. Harlem agreed in that regard—only because Arena nominated him to lead the expeditionary force. He knew well he was the best candidate for the job and the strongest mind in the city, a prime target for Arena to want out of the way for an extended period. Fortunately, Harlem Maccaro was also the king's favorite adviser, so he was confident that the man would want to keep him close.

"Continue." King Mikas motioned to the chancellor, gemmed rings reflecting light as he waggled his thick fingers.

The chancellor read, "After a citizen reported on the attack and the abduction of its occupants, we counterattacked and routed the brigands but weren't able to capture their leader. Upon interrogation, we confirmed the identity to be one Captain Blago Adavir, a known Calrym sympathizer and Cyroki criminal." The nobles groaned in disgust, and the king slammed his fist on the table again. "We have also learned this attack is being funded by members of Calrym's government and request a full investigation to root out the cause and to prevent any further incursions from happening. If this was, in fact, a direct command of His Majesty, the King of Calrym, then we only ask for a formal declaration of war in response to this letter. If, however, this was not at the behest of His Majesty, the King of Calrym, then we welcome any inquests made on our behalf and look forward to any discovered information. Signed Governess Stasia Falconel. Cosigned by the Cyroki ambassador and diplomat. I, uh, I can't make out the name, Your Majesty."

The king waved the chancellor away. "It makes no difference. We've received their point."

"There's still the other matter to discuss," Bertrand said, and as usual, didn't understand proper protocol.

"*Damn* it, man, stop interjecting! *I* will choose when we proceed to the *next* topic. Your. Fucking. King!" The king's fist connected with the table again. A new record before the meeting was over, perhaps?

The chancellor flushed and edged back into the recesses of the Great Hall.

Busy fishing for some gyrfalcon meat he'd dropped on his pants, Duke Velturo had no noticeable reaction to the king's rage, which was surprising considering the king often directed it at Velturo's improper table manners. The king's distraction from Velturo's distracting behavior was abnormal, even during the worst of times.

Harlem sat up straighter. When he was to address an important issue, he found it more comfortable to sit as straight as possible. It exuded confidence and authority. *But to get involved . . . no more cheese.* It would be improper to salivate over a delicacy while driving a point home. Perhaps why nobody ever listened to Duke Velturo.

"It's apparent that a decision needs to be made to either pull out of the affair altogether or commit to war," Harlem said. He needed to convince the others. "My opinion is to abandon invading the northerners. The only thing they possess of value is the gyrfalcons, and even those aren't worth the investment in a military operation. Not to mention our good friend Adavir abolished any hope of remaining covert. Clearly, we'd be wasting hordes of money, men, and other resources for a snowy wasteland too far away to offer *any* tactical or strategic advantage. Sure, we have plenty of men and much more experience in actual warfare, so they wouldn't stand a chance.

"However, we'd open ourselves to potential attack from Remeria, and we all know how happy King Alondo has been with Calrym's influence over the world. That's why we hired Adavir in the first place—to avoid giving King Alondo an opportunity. If he hears that half our military is busy in Cyrok, he'll certainly attack. Of that I'm certain. I suggest we send a response denouncing Captain Adavir and vow to help hunt the man down. A small sacrifice to avoid *dangerous* ramifications if our involvement in slaughtering townsfolk is exposed. We have many other, more local matters to focus upon." Harlem noticed Duchess Arena sneering as he ended his argument. He hadn't impressed her. *You won't win this one, Arena.*

"Your Majesty," Duchess Arena started off, sneering at Harlem before returning her attention to the king. "While *some* of us are inept at recognizing various military tactics and strategies, I am not one of them. Neither are you. When we invade Cyrok, we should have three goals. All of which aid our nation. First, complete occupation and formation of vassalage. If we place officers and politicians in the *correct* roles, we could control the entire nation and prosper. Economically, we would gain large boons to our income by inflating the prices of gyrfalcons and controlling the monopolization ourselves. Second, the strategic implications of controlling Cyrok seem to fly over Duke Harlem's head."

She sneered at Harlem again, while Duke Velturo bellowed a raucous laughter. The other noblemen made varying signs and sounds of approval. Even the frightened chancellor let out a high-pitched chuckle. *He's glad he isn't the subject of everyone else's ridicule at the moment.*

Duchess Arena continued, "If war were to break out between Calrym and Remeria, we would have a significant advantage. We could attack from two fronts—the pass in the Elderspikes and the north, sending ships to wherever we desired. Third, and the most important goal, Cyrok has already caught our attempts at insurrection. As they have explained to us, they know our involvement, however minor, includes at least one at our table. If you believe they will let this go, then by all means, pull back. But if *you* were in *their* situation, Your Majesty, I cannot see you being so forgiving. In fact, *I* would be furious. And *I* do not intend on being this council's sacrifice when the Cyroki come collecting." She looked at every individual noble, pausing for a second on each person. "Will you?"

The other nobles shouted words of acceptance. *Way to hammer that point home.* Harlem ground his molars together. She'd made a perfect argument. Aside from mentioning the actual advantages, she'd brought up the king's anger if he were to be in the same situation. And he acted upon his anger. Once he believed another regent might express a similar feeling, he often decided to strike first. Because it's what he would do, no matter what a more reasonable person would.

King Mikas nodded. "Harlem? Any further argument *against* a northern campaign?"

"It's a terrible decision politically. Only two weeks ago, you advocated for peace across all five nations and planned on sending declarations to each country. Now you want to forget about that? Everyone is frightened by us enough. Aside from the University of Arcanical Arts, no other place exudes an equivalent level of power that Calrym does. Our military is unchecked. I can't see—"

"Since when did you become such a teat-suckler, Harlem?" Duke Velturo interrupted inappropriately. Because the bastard didn't have *any* table manners. Even at her most heated, Arena would never do that. The insult added further injuries to the interruption, and Harlem was sure they were intentional. "I think Arena has a point. Put him to the test. See how he fares in the

Cyroki lands. Perhaps he'd learn to coddle something other than his mother for warmth, ah-hah."

The silence in the Great Hall was deafening. A guardsman's metal boots scraped across the floor as he shifted. All eyes watched Harlem for a response. So he gave them what they needed to hear. Really, the only response he *could* give in this scenario. "If the king wants me to lead an army to conquer the north, I'll do it. I only emphasize that you be *reasonable* and denounce these ridiculous ideas, Mikas."

If Harlem thought it was quiet before, he'd been mistaken. Slack-jawed and shocked faces sat around the table. To address the king by his first name was a hangable offense. Harlem had gotten away with it during his tenure once or twice in the past when trying to drive his point home. However, never when angry at the king. He knew he'd made a grave mistake based on the king's current expression.

Again, the fist slammed into the table. "Bertrand!" The chancellor jumped to his side. "Prepare an official declaration of war. Send it *with* warships led by Duke Harlem Maccaro."

"Your Majesty." The chancellor bowed and rushed out of the Great Hall.

"Do not disrespect me, *Harlem*." The king spat his name. "This punishment is generous."

"Then it is settled. Harlem will lead the attack." Duchess Arena glowed as she said this. "Perhaps your nephew, Sir Alyst, could attend?"

The king nodded in agreement. *Great.*

"Your Majesty." Harlem half bowed from his seat. There wasn't anything he could do at this point. He'd insulted the king.

After an awkward minute of silence, one of the other

noblemen spoke up. "Onto further matters that are, perhaps, less pressing, Your Majesty?"

Another chimed in. "Lochwall."

"What about it?" King Mikas's anger dissipated as he turned his attention elsewhere. At least the man forgot his anger as often as it came.

"Duchess Urda . . . Licheva has . . . passed," Duke Sturgeon Gothal said. He whispered when he spoke. The words seemed to come out in small beats, almost like echoes of his dying heartbeat.

Everybody repeated the obligatory "what a shame" and "that's too bad" statements, though nobody believed them. Urda Licheva had been an old, moody crone.

"The fact of the matter is we need a new duke or duchess. Licheva's estate died when she did. No other family." Wheezy old Duke Sturgeon looked like a tree, so old was his skin.

"Options? And don't say that damned Velvet Mother. I don't subscribe to this mysterious bullshit." The king didn't like mystery. Harlem had to say he agreed.

He wondered how cold it was in Cyrok and if he'd need to bring his entire collection of furs or just five coats.

"There are few options, most of which are people you have already met, Your Majesty. They include Castede Varono, Lekhan Roelk, Scayde Haklon, and, Iadura Khyst." Duke Sturgeon shifted in his chair. It seemed his weakness increased twofold whenever he spoke.

Harlem hoped he wouldn't have to deal with Captain Blago Adavir. He'd never met the man, but he detested him just from various reports he'd read. He seemed competent enough, but he was Cyroki and vicious.

"Iadura's the child?" King Mikas asked.

Velturo said, "Not anymore, Your Majesty. Iadura just experienced her fourteenth birthday *and* is engaged to a minor nobleman of the same city, ah-hah."

If fortune favored Harlem, perhaps he'd be back in a year. Cyrok couldn't put up that much of a fight. They were nomads living in the snow. *Snowmads.* He gave a slight shake of his head. He would've hung a subordinate for that joke. Harlem offered another, more surprising name. "What about Khlaux Corbéo, Your Majesty?"

"Isn't he a *guardsman*, Harlem? He'd be more suited to Arena's lap than Duke of Lochwall, ah-hah!"

"His family comes from a very noble line, Velturo," Harlem said. "It's true, restoring him would expunge his family's denigration, but he'd be moldable. Easy to control."

"Absolutely not, Harlem. We are not going to promote a doorstop to a *duke*. Have you gone mad?" Arena asked.

King Mikas nodded along with Arena, ending that suggestion. Then he said, "How about . . . Lekhan?" It was clear he didn't remember the man who held a deed to one-fifth of Buzzard's Bowl. The question appeared to be more of a guess at one of the other three names he'd already forgotten.

Advising the king toward something he enjoyed yet had not noticed might gain Harlem a bit of favor. "Haklon is owner of Buzzard's Bowl. You like him." *And the new husband to my foolish daughter.* Perhaps through his daughter's stupidity, he could regain the king's favor. *At least she isn't with that Edelbrock buffoon anymore.* Harlem *hated* him. What a shit he'd been, all strutting around like he was somebody because he'd had a small ounce of success in battle.

"Ah yes. He's a worthy candidate. Let's give Haklon the position. I do so enjoy the power he exudes and the games he hosts."

Of course, nobody felt the need to contest this, so the motion passed with a unanimous vote. It was better to keep the king happy. King Mikas wasn't happy enough to retract his order to send Duke Harlem Maccaro to Cyrok. To war.

KELDEN STOOLE

2nd Cycle of Autumn, 231st Reign of Garcovi
Ashmount, Qothe

After the initial sprint out of Ashmount, most of them slowed. The more fit bastards ran ahead of everyone. Kelden knew he could keep pace with them, but smart people didn't charge into the unknown without a few disposable bodies in front of them. Clusters of people ran together down the greenery, outside of the protective bubble, across the lava bridge, and over a selection of various-sized igneous rocks. Bits of fresher lava cluttered the terrain, but Kelden, and the others, avoided them.

The path narrowed, and only two or three people could walk side by side. This created a congestion, with the more physical people shoving the weaker ones aside. Kelden, being smart, allowed the physical people to pass whenever possible. A few feet off the path was empty air. A long plummet down. By allowing people to pass him, he avoided altercations that resulted in other people falling to their deaths.

Much higher up the volcano, a Magicus stood on a teetering column of rock, observing the prospective students as they ran toward him. Kelden was certain the Magicus only balanced atop the rock by magic.

Someone screamed behind him. A woman? Someone else growled. He stole a glance and saw a big man pummeling a smaller woman. Dozens of people ran by, ignoring the woman's assault.

A different Magicus who'd been following them was observing the altercation but not intervening. Kelden agreed with that assessment. Stopping would stall his own progress, and the Archmagicus stated the first seventy-five people to reach the checkpoint would proceed forward with the Trials. Helping a girl wouldn't further that goal. That said, sometimes a person you helped could help you later on.

Kelden stopped. He chewed his lip, thinking. *Decision, decisions.*

He recognized his arrogance. He felt his destiny was succeeding at something that would grant lots of power. He knew that, despite his selfish way of thinking, he would use magic to stop an assault like this. The large man had won already and yet continued to beat the girl.

Kelden was rather smart. He recognized where his faults lay. He knew he had little chance of confronting the meaty man head-on. So he didn't.

Grasping a decent hand-sized ball of crystallized rock, he approached the man hunching over the woman in distress. Several more candidates passed by him, ignoring the girl's plight.

Letting out a cry that could stir soldiers to battle, Kelden brought the rock down, or rather up because the giant was much taller than Kelden, into the man's head. A loud *crack.* The man thumped over, a trail of blood running down his neck.

The girl, huddled in a ball with her hands over her head, stood. "Thanks." Tears reflected in her eyes, and multiple red spots flared across her skin—the beginnings of bruises. The marks of an asshole.

"We need to keep moving."

"Yeah." Sniffling, she stood and wiped her eyes, then continued up the volcano.

Kelden followed her but noticed a Magicus staring at him. He swore the Magicus shook his head in disapproval. Kelden didn't blame the man. He'd just let twenty people pass him.

Kelden often recognized where his strengths lay as well. After the journey from Warwin, he was confident in his endurance. So he jogged. And the sniffling girl jogged too.

Their calves burned. Or Kelden's did at any rate. He assumed the girl's did too. She hadn't spoken since he'd freed her from the attacker. Who, Kelden noticed, had gotten up mere minutes after being knocked out and was climbing the mountain with renewed vigor. Kelden tried not to think about what would happen if the brutish man caught up to them.

The climb steepened, and when Kelden thought it was at its steepest, the incline got even worse. Perhaps his endurance wasn't as good as he thought. Walking across flatlands differed from climbing the volcano. Though he was doing better than many of his cohorts. They'd passed dozens of resting people.

Kelden kept surveying his peers. After the earlier incident and after observing a different man push another man *off* the volcano, he'd become much more careful. The man's scream had been ear-piercing as he plummeted an inestimable drop and was still etched in his mind. *One less competitor.* He didn't want to be one of the *less.*

Kelden thought he spied a flag in the distance. Or perhaps that was a flap of a tent. With the sun beaming straight into his eyes, it was difficult to determine what was what.

A constant stream of sweat droplets permeated his clothing and ran down the creases in his body, ending up in most unfortunate places. Many times, he'd reached for a waterskin that wasn't hanging at his side. It occurred to him that passing out from dehydration was perhaps another test. Fortitude was another valued skill.

He wiped at his drenched forehead another countless time, shaking his hand off to the side. The excess water dripped onto the dry rock beneath him, which he eyed. He considered licking the rest from his hand but thought better of that. Sweat would be an acquired taste after all.

Kelden peered behind him. Sniffles was walking slower than ever. Giant was catching up to them, staring at the pair with an intentional gaze and squinted eyes. Because of the sun or anger. Kelden couldn't tell. He was an intimidating figure, lumbering up the path, bulging muscles an impending threat.

Sniffles sniffled again. It'd been at least an hour, and she was *still* crying. "We need to hurry." He'd said this at least a dozen times, but neither of them picked up the pace at any of these occasions.

She sniffed. Kelden sighed. He considered leaving her behind.

Another hour later and Giant was mere yards away. It was clear he could see them now, and he was picking up the pace, grunting. He had to be Vessian, his dark black skin many shades darker than any Qothan's, and the heat wasn't bothering him.

"He's back," Kelden said.

Sniffles made a noncommittal sound.

He wasn't sure she'd heard him. "The man that hit you. He's almost here."

She gave another sound.

"Good luck." And he started running. Some things weren't worth fighting for.

Perhaps she'd become resigned. Perhaps she'd figured she'd lost already. Perhaps she was delirious from heatstroke. Kelden would never know because, when Giant caught up to her, she was unceremoniously flung off the side of the volcano. She didn't issue a sound as she plummeted. Another victim to Ashmount's height. This just spurned Kelden on faster.

Kelden was well aware he was next.

<hr>

Heavy breathing. Lungs on fire. A desperate need for hydration. Thigh muscles peeling from bone. That was what it felt like. His jelly legs were having a tough time climbing. Lucky for him, Giant had become distracted by a pair of prospects Kelden had passed.

He saw his destination. It was only a few hundred feet away from his current position. A few hundred feet more of a steep incline, unsteady gravel to clamber over.

A loud *thwack* cracked the quiet air. Over his shoulder, Kelden saw Giant dropping two unconscious, or dead, bodies onto the ground. His gaze met Kelden's, and Giant lumbered toward him. A shiver went down Kelden's spine. There was nobody between the two men now.

Lurching forward, Kelden launched himself up the

volcano, fueled by this revelation. If Giant caught up with him, he was sure he'd be tossed off Ashmount. Or his head slammed against the ground. Or some other grim fate.

Kelden tripped on something. His face slammed into hot gravel. Small pebbles dug into his cheeks, and he dislocated his thumb. Grunting, he hauled himself up.

A force smashed into his back, pushing him back into the hostile ground. Kelden didn't have to look. He knew what was behind him.

It was painful how unfortunate this outcome was. To come so close, just to become brutalized by this monster. It wasn't fair. But life wasn't ever fair.

He'd spent his life in a poor village. A hand grasped a chunk of his shirt.

He'd been told he was going nowhere. The hand lifted him in the air. Several pebbles cascaded down his face and fell to the ground.

His father had taught him. Though he was smart, his chance at doing anything other than physical labor was unlikely. His feet dangled off the ground.

People frowned down upon Warwin for being out in the middle of nowhere and with little of substance to it. The hand twisted his body around until Giant could peer into his eyes.

Despite these thoughts, Kelden always assumed he'd be able to overcome these misperceptions. Kelden always thought he was going somewhere. Kelden *knew* something better was coming. And it had. Now Giant was grinning like a savage. *It can't end like this.*

"You involved yourself." Giant spoke in a low rumble. An expected, monotonous voice. The voice of a man who understood nothing other than brute force. But there was an unexpected glimmer of intelligence behind the large man's eyes.

"I did," Kelden said.

"That was a bad idea."

"It might've been."

"Now it's time for—"

Kelden let out a cry, interrupting Giant. A scream? He wasn't sure how it sounded to anybody else. Kelden brought his forehead down, smashing into Giant's nose as hard as he could. Blood poured from the massive man's face, and he dropped Kelden.

The fall could have gone better. For the third time in just a few minutes, Kelden was facedown in gravel. He flipped onto his back. Giant crouched on his knees, holding a bloody face and screaming a plethora of curses.

Kelden jumped to his feet and ran. He threw himself up onto a ledge, clambered over a boulder, and scampered up the last incline. Adrenaline fueled his escape. He'd forgotten thirst. His thighs continued burning, but in the grand scheme of things, this mattered little to him. His life was on the line here.

During his ascent, he caught the eyes of a Magicus hovering in the air, observing his encounter with Giant, and offering a nod. Approval, perhaps? Kelden wasn't sure and didn't have time to process the information. He continued climbing.

He heard a roar behind him and then the sound of running. Giant had recovered.

Seconds later, it didn't matter. Kelden entered the checkpoint and collapsed. He'd made it onto the narrow plateau. There were dozens of tents and several people meandering around. Some rock walls surrounded the edges, ensuring nobody fell—Magicai work, no doubt. It provided just enough room for the tents, several small courtyards to mill about in, and a couple of long tables.

A Magicus rushed over and knelt beside him. "Here."

He offered Kelden water. "Congratulations, you are the thirty-seventh arrival. You've qualified for the next—"

Giant thrashed the Magicus aside and peered down at Kelden with a penetrating gaze. "You're dead." He raised his fist, growling.

"This is a safe zone," a Magicus called. "You will step down immediately, or we will disqualify you."

Giant's face trembled. He bared his bloodstained teeth at Kelden but dropped his hand. "Tomorrow, then."

"Get some rest." The Magicus gestured toward the tents. "You'll need it for tomorrow. Food is already inside." The Magicus gave Giant a stern frown. "I'd suggest finding a place that isn't too close together, or you may find yourself in trouble."

Giant grunted and hauled himself away, heading toward a tent at the back of the group. Kelden was thankful for this, because he didn't think he could muster the energy to even hike that far.

Kelden dragged himself up, his body exhausted. He made his way to the closest unoccupied tent, opened it up, and collapsed inside. A plate of cold food sat next to a bedroll. He consumed the spread of chicken, salted potatoes, chopped carrots in a curry sauce, and another skin of cool water. This was puzzling. To have cold water in these temperatures was unheard of back in Warwin, much less in a waterskin that had been sitting around for however many hours.

He laid his head down on his arm and passed out.

<hr>

It felt like mere minutes before a loud horn blew outside of his tent, startling him awake.

The next Trial.

Kelden lifted the tent flap to a wonderful aroma of the morning meal. It was still dark, and the only light came from lit torches. The remaining seventy-five prospects gathered around a banquet table and held, by some miracle, fresh-baked bread with butter and some jam, boiled eggs, goat milk, and venison from some animal or another.

Across the table, Sungoa slathered up a piece of bread. "You made it," he said.

She looked across the table at him and frowned, accusing him of something, he was sure. "No help to you. But yes, I did."

"I probably shouldn't have disappeared in the beginning, you're right. I've since found that having friends on this journey may be more useful than not."

"I saw."

"You saw?"

"I saw you rescue that unappreciative girl."

"A mistake I don't think I'll try to repeat."

"I wish you'd given your actual friend more attention than her."

Kelden couldn't agree more. "You're right. I don't know what I was thinking. It seemed like the right move. Secure an ally and proceed together."

"You could have started out with an ally."

"Perhaps today?"

"We'll see." But Sungoa smirked, and he knew he had her. Why he ever left her side at the start of this was a mystery to him. Caught up in the excitement of the Trials perhaps.

He took a moment to survey his surroundings. People conversed with one another. Magicai whispered back and forth, preparing for the next phase. A Magicus was placing swords into a weapon rack. Nearby was another rack with shields.

Panic set in. Kelden began counting swords. Seventy-five. They were being armed for the next Trial.

Well shit. Giant was going to have a good morning.

VILLIC THE IMBUER

2nd Cycle of Autumn, 231st Reign of Garcovi
Hathoran, Vessia

Three weeks had passed since they'd invited the Magicus. Columns of round felt tents lined in endless rows, housing members of various clans. Villic couldn't see the start or end of the rows. Hathoran had few permanent residents, caregivers who ensured the tents were taken care of, the herd of camels tended to, and the watering hole maintained to prevent it from becoming contaminated. Hathoran, designed as a replenishment station for the Camel Clans, had strict rules regarding fighting. It was the gods' will, according to the shamans. No fighting at all in Hathoran. Ever. Doing so risked your entire clan's access to the haven, which meant they could no longer trade for new camels, use the tents or watering hole, or attend congregations.

Villic had heard stories of a clan that no longer existed being expelled from the area. Killiak's Brood, a clan that had prided themselves upon being the "chosen" clan of the gods, had attempted to take over

Hathoran once. They'd succeeded, as no other clans were staying there. When news had spread about the betrayal, the other seven clans had returned, uniting briefly, expelling Killiak's Brood and killing most of the clan. Two years later, Killiak's Brood had died out. *Not so chosen, after all.*

Hathoran didn't have enough tents for every member of every clan. When the Splintered Manes and Glory Blades had arrived, many of the occupied tents had emptied, allowing their clans access to an equal portion of shelter. These tents were often reserved for children, the elders, and the shamans, the rest being occupied by the higher-ranking members of the clans. Now, as an Imbuer, Villic was high-ranking enough where he had a tent. All to himself.

"And me."

Villic sighed. He didn't like the voice in his head. And he didn't know how long he could deal with hearing it.

"You'll be fine. Compare me to thoughts. You think about things, and the thoughts respond."

Villic cleared his head, tried pushing Speaker out.

"Try as hard as you want. I'll be here. It's not such a big deal, Villic. I grant you power, you benefit, and sometimes, we talk."

Dunecrest, just outside his tent, snorted. Villic decided that was the appropriate response and snorted too.

"Villic, they're starting the gathering," someone said from outside. It sounded like Sikoi, who'd not become an Imbuer and who must be following a command to retrieve Villic.

As an Imbuer, Villic's presence was required at all official clan events because he held an important title. The gods demanded those with power have extra knowledge. It was their gift. At least, that's what the shamans said. Villic thought it was to prevent the Imbuers from rebelling against the shamans. Not that he'd do that. Villic wouldn't disappoint the gods or the shamans. He wasn't stupid.

Exiting the tent, Villic made his way through the area designated to the Splintered Manes, crossed through the Masters of the Lost's section, and found the central part of Hathoran. Within the mass of tents was a clearing where clans could hold peaceful congregations.

Villic saw Jedkah and other members of the Splintered Manes and joined them. A few nodded to him or said "hello," to which Villic nodded back.

"Say something."

"No," Villic whispered.

"You appear strange. And awkward."

Villic wasn't sure what Speaker meant.

"I mean how you act around people."

Stop listening to my thoughts, Speaker.

"I don't have a choice, Villic. I'm sort of stuck here."

Villic looked around. The different clans stood, separated from one another, around the perimeter of the clearing. In the center, flanked by several shamans from each clan, was a bright man in robes.

"Pale, not bright."

He's reflecting the sun.

"That's his skin. It's white."

Villic blinked, confused.

"There are several colors of skin. Though in your time, I am unsure what . . ." Speaker droned on, but Villic didn't listen. He was too busy watching the man in robes.

He rolled his sleeves up, showing a few dark markings on his arms to the shamans. Paint, it looked like, but Villic couldn't be sure. Was it some type of disease? Or maybe he was gods-touched?

" . . .darker skins often live in warmer areas, whereas . . ."

The shamans pointed at the marks and said something. The man nodded, then pointed into the air, and a small puff of fire appeared out of his palm. Villic jumped, then noticed he was the only one to do so and felt shame.

" . . .depends on where you were born, the climate, and . . ."

Now Villic knew the odd man was the Magicus, a man with powers the Camel Clans dreamed of—until now. With the awakening of Imbuers, the Camel Clans had their own power. The Camel Clans weren't barred from traveling across the world to learn the Magicai's magic, but whenever somebody made the journey, they never returned. Some believed the gods punished the ones who left. Others thought they'd found a better life elsewhere. Even if they had returned, it was unlikely they'd be allowed to return to their old place within the clan. Leaving was considered abandoning the clan, and returning would be a difficult process.

Villic was wondering whether the shamans allowed the Magicus to know of their newfound abilities when an Imbuer started displaying them. It seemed the gods and the shamans weren't hiding them.

The Magicus examined the Imbuer as they continued their display, appearing confused and excited—though Villic wasn't an expert on foreign expressions, let alone his own people's.

After the Imbuer finished their act, the Magicus waved everyone closer. The shamans nodded, encouraging those who hesitated forward. Villic listened to the shamans and stepped closer.

"I've seen nothing like this, nor read about it, all my life," the Magicus said. Somehow, the man spoke the Vessian language perfectly.

"Are we equals now?" a shaman asked.

"I can't imagine that." The Magicus shook his head. "If this is a new power, we'd have to conduct experiments, trials, see what you're capable of. It's entirely possible this is a sixth school of magic. The Archmagicus would love to—"

"Our gift came from Killiak, lord of lords," another shaman said.

The Magicus laughed. "My dear nomad, the only god is Mother Avani, she who protects us."

Rumblings from the clans. Villic sneered. He gripped his spear tight, ready. The Magicus was blaspheming.

"You don't come to our lands and tell *us* what's true and what's not," Jedkah said, slapping the wind with an authoritative grunt. It surprised Villic the Magicus didn't appear put off by Jedkah's markings. Often people who saw Jedkah for the first time became frightened.

"Killiak, lord of lords, demands an apology," somebody else said. Villic didn't catch who.

"Apologies be damned. We have something of note to discuss here, my friends. You're the first subjects to display this newfound power!" The Magicus held his hands out in a peaceful gesture. Villic figured it was more a ploy to use his magic if the Magicus felt threatened.

"We are not subjects!"

"Killiak demands retribution for this insult!"

"Death to the Magicus!"

Villic hefted his spear in both hands, waiting for the order to strike. The Magicus needed to make a proper apology soon, or the shamans and the gods would be most upset.

"Apologize, and accept Killiak's forgiveness," Jedkah said.

"I will not go against the genuine history of Cedain. If you would like to discuss your powers more, which is the reason I've journeyed all this way, then let us sit and talk. No more of this religious foolery that you're attempting to blather on about. I don't believe in the whimsical cluster of gods you've created for every little thing. There is *one*, and she wouldn't tolerate this language. However, I will not bother explaining to *nomads* the proper way of things. There are so many areas of contention here, it'd take all day."

"This man's an intolerant asshole."

Villic growled. Speaker was right. He couldn't let the Magicus get away with such insults. Villic called to the power of lightning, surrounding the spear in an electrifying energy, took aim, and threw it. Crackling with sparks and flashes of bright white, the spear soared up, then came crashing down at the Magicus.

He'd seen what happened and raised a barrier, deflecting the electrified spear.

It didn't matter. Others grew impatient with the Magicus and his lies. They let their energized weapons loose as well. Fire-burning tips, ice-crystallized blades, poisoned arrows, and a multitude of others found their way into the Magicus.

A screech and a cry later, the man lay dead, dozens of weapons sticking out of his body.

"Ridiculous."

"Shameful."

"Disgusting."

"For the Sharpclaws!"

"For Vessia!"

"For our freedom!"

Villic wasn't sure where all these cries came from or what most of them referred to, but he joined in with his own war scream. "For Killiak, lord of lords!"

And for some reason, his neighbors took up the cry themselves. Soon thereafter, everyone chanted it.

"For Killiak, lord of lords!"

When the cries died down, the shamans from each clan met together for a moment. Then one of them raised their arm in the air and let out a bellow. "With our new powers, *we* don't deserve this treatment! For too long the Camel Clans have been forced deeper into the deserts, further away from hospitable lands. We too desire farmlands, green grasses for our animals to consume, and comfortable temperatures. For too long, we've found ourselves oppressed by the rest of the world, laughing at our beliefs, laughing at our customs. The gods have decided, and we, the shamans, have decided to take up arms, use our newfound powers, and bring death to the foreigners. It's time to reclaim kinder lands and prove the gods are with us!"

A unanimous decision to invade Remeria over Calrym was made. The feud the Camel Clans had with Remeria went longer and deeper than that of Calrym.

A resounding cheer went through all the clans. The decision made, the Camel Clans of Vessia joined and rode toward Remeria.

EDELBROCK BRENDIS

The Velvet Mother led Edelbrock, Nauc, and the third Draftee—a large, bruised man who Edelbrock figured he'd refer to as Bruise—out of Buzzard's Bowl. In their House building, they each received a fresh set of clothes that were identical to the ones they wore before and a quick but filling meal of bread and gruel.

A blank stone wall protected the Velvet Mother's hypogeum, like the one Marshal Deywin had led him to before. The Velvet Mother produced a device and inserted it into the wall.

"New recruits?" the guardsman posted at the door asked.

The Velvet Mother nodded. They, with a small contingent of armed men, led the three prisoners through a kitchen area, then a dining hall, and into one of many chambers filled with dozens of beds. Lamps hung from the walls and illuminated the room. Shock hit Edelbrock hard. The room was reminiscent of the nights he'd spent with Trigg Gelbrandy. The blankets and pillows adorning the beds looked just as expensive. Beds made of cushions not straw. Edelbrock would've assumed they'd be sleeping on the floor.

"Through here." The Velvet Mother walked through a wooden door that was half-broken, hanging by a single hinge. They pulled the door open and revealed a cell door. "I'm sorry, but in here." For what it was worth, they seemed apologetic.

"We're still prisoners?" Edelbrock asked, incredulous. They were to be fighting for this House soon yet were confined in a cell. Again.

"Yes."

"Get in." A guard pushed Nauc forward.

"Easy. Nobody's resisting here," Nauc said. He entered with his hands raised.

Not looking too happy about it, Bruise followed.

"Why?" Edelbrock's confusion must have shown on his face because the Velvet Mother looked more sympathetic.

"It's just how things are," they said.

"In," another guard said.

Seeing no other choice, Edelbrock followed the two other prisoners inside. The Velvet Mother closed the cell door behind him with a loud clang. The lock bolted, and the broken wooden door shut, cutting off most of the light. There were no beds, not even of straw. Blankets dotted with holes littered the room. It seemed they would sleep on the floor, which was a cold stone. The empty room went much deeper than Edelbrock realized. Dozens of old and used piles of rags also littered the floor. He wrinkled his nose at the stench.

"This isn't ideal." Groaning, Edelbrock sat on the

floor in despair. He didn't like the idea of rotting inside another cell for an unknown amount of time.

"Not after the last cell," Bruise said. He walked over to a corner and collapsed, pulling a tattered blanket over his head and shoulders.

"How long were you locked up?" Nauc remained standing, pacing back and forth. Vigilant. Like he was a guard.

"A cycle, I think. It's difficult to know how much time passed. It felt like years. For me, anyway." He remembered when he first encountered the Draftees. How he'd thought they were animals. Fighting each other for scraps that were tossed on the ground. They had been like animals. He'd become an animal himself after a few days. He recalled that burning pit in his stomach. That *need* for food. The funny thing was that this was only two meals ago. He imagined he looked decrepit, like a diseased vagrant decaying in view of everyone.

Edelbrock looked over at the door. He could see into the other room, where the beds were.

"I was captured a few weeks ago," Nauc said.

"Yeah? What happened?" Edelbrock asked. He couldn't say he cared all that much, but they were in a cell with nothing to do but talk.

"I'm from Qothe. Village of Warwin. Ever heard of it?"

Edelbrock shook his head.

"No? Not surprising. You've heard of the University of Arcanical Arts, though? And the Trials?"

Edelbrock nodded.

"The Magicai were holding a test. Anyone could go and see if you had the Trace. A few people in Warwin wanted to go. A friend of mine was looking for a few skilled men to accompany the group. So I agreed. Another man accompanied us with a kid in tow. Owed a favor to the kid's father. He's the one who delivered this news about the examination for payment. Anditus Roberon. He was here. Got drafted, like us. A few bandits on the road tried to rob us, which was enough to scare off Roberon. He fled. Left the kid with us, the coward."

Nauc stopped pacing and sat. "Two of us had the Trace. The rest of us, we were paid. We took our money and left. Stopped by Yordiv to spend some of our hard-earned money. We ran into Roberon again. He was being an ass. That wouldn't have bothered me, but I blamed him for the deaths that occurred. Didn't like the way he was acting. We traded words. Roberon has two rules he lives by. The first is he will do anything to stay alive. The second is, as long as his life isn't in danger, he will do anything that doesn't endanger his life to earn some extra money.

"He wasn't there to make amends. He'd distracted us long enough for the Magicai to ambush us. During his time in Yordiv, he'd racked up some debt with a Magicus. Offered to lead them to us. This Magicus is an enslaver on the side. Captures people and ships them here. Gets paid a lot to do this. The good news is Roberon got himself betrayed and captured too. Serves him right. And he's wronged this Scayde Haklon somehow, so I'm sure he's going to get punished. I spent the last few weeks on a ship and then traveling by land in a cart, tied up."

"That's quite the journey," Edelbrock said.

"I just hope I don't have to fight any of the group that arrived here with me. The Magicus executed a few of them to enforce good behavior during the journey here."

"That would be unfortunate if you had to fight any of them. And I'm sorry for your loss."

"Me too. What about you?"

Edelbrock sighed. "Well, my story is long." But he told it. In its entirety. Though he may have left out a few minor details. Like the fact that he had assassinated Trigg Gelbrandy. Or that he had cheated on his wife with a man to secure a stake in the very place they now sat. Or that Scayde Haklon had stolen his wife and murdered his son. Really, he didn't tell his story at all. But Edelbrock sold it. And Nauc believed it. And that's all that mattered.

The wooden door slammed open, and a group of half-naked men and women stood on the other side of the cell door, leering at them. Some wore their entire uniform, many others just the trousers. All were bald.

"Come." An imposing man with arms crossed brought the trio of new prisoners out of the cell. He examined them closely as they entered the larger sleeping quarters. His muscular arms bulged as he shifted, and his thick thighs almost ripped out of his worn pants. In fact, upon closer evaluation, *all* the people waiting for them had a near perfect physique. "Kneel." He had one ear, and many red scars stuck out across his body, plastering his creamy skin. He flexed his hands, each finger wearing a metal ring.

They knelt.

"Can I do it, Savakkis?" A thin man walked over, narrowed eyes sending hateful glares at them. His voice was high-pitched, and he was, like everyone else, bald. And, Mother Avani bless it, he had *tits*. They were small, barely protrusive, but they bobbed and weaved just the same as any other set. She was a shirtless woman.

Savakkis held a hand up against her, the back of it pressing against her sternum. "You will do as I tell you." He peered down at them. "A skilled warrior rises on the back of three foundations. Obedience. Training. Suffering. A true warrior follows orders, and in this place, following orders is competing. If you refuse, they will torture you. A true warrior does not waver. They train. They succeed. A failed warrior dies. Therefore, training is of the utmost importance. A trained warrior is the greatest threat, right? No. A warrior who has suffered and has something to *prove* or *fight* for is. That is the warrior you will become. Or you will die." Savakkis lowered his hand from the woman. "You may do it."

She grinned. An evil grin. Edelbrock didn't like it. She stepped toward them, but Savakkis held her back once more. "First, these." He took off his rings and handed them to her.

"Thank you." She looked at him like an idol. Like a god. Like he were Mother Avani come to save them all. She slipped the rings on her four fingers on either hand.

"You will prepare their dinner afterward."

"I understand," she said. The woman walked up to Edelbrock. "Welcome to Buzzard's Bowl."

"Thank you."

The woman slammed her fist into his cheek, the metal rings cracking against his cheekbone. He crumpled to the ground. She beat him. He tried to shield himself. It didn't work. She kicked him with her boots. He cringed, winced, and flopped around the ground trying to evade her. All this did was create other openings. She beat him until he lost consciousness.

Though he heard her begin on the next person before he faded away.

He woke to the sound of the cell door opening. Bruised, battered, and in agony, he moaned and tried stretching out his stiffness.

"Here's your food." The woman dropped a plate onto the floor. It clanged, and food spilled everywhere. "Oops." She obviously wasn't sorry. She left.

So, it was going to be like that. Again. Great.

Alongside the other prisoners, Edelbrock crawled across the floor and scooped food into his mouth. In a dignified way, of course.

DEMRI SLARN

1st Cycle of Winter, 231st Reign of Garcovi
Remeria

Caius picked at his fingernails with his knife. Blood flecked the blade, though the man seemed unphased by this. As always. Porric stood by, observing the horizon. In case an intruder might come up and abduct him. As if there wasn't already an intruder that had abducted them.

Demri rested against the back of an old tree, snuggled between two thick roots that had been torn from the ground by a storm or some other drastic event. He watched as Magicus Glaouse slept. He considered slipping away into the jungle, but that was a gamble. He also considered the various emotional mistakes he'd made while indulging desires. Killing people in fancy ways, spending magic that he shouldn't have wasted. Caius could have sliced every one of their necks open instead. There was some *satisfaction* in being the one to kill somebody in a way that many people couldn't.

Demri felt powerful letting his essence exit his hands, taking the life of someone he *hated*.

But as that hate manifested, so too did a slew of regret. Killing people who weren't Doram Quandis, killing people who had nothing to do with Demri. Sure, there were plenty of people he'd killed who were trying to harm him. He had no regrets about them. But every time he killed somebody who he believed was his quarry, and it turned out that they weren't him, he felt a fragment worse. Not worse enough to stop pursuing his goal. Doram Quandis deserved death.

Demri was becoming too indulgent. He'd enjoyed using his powers too much. He'd become exceptional at evading other Magicai. He needed to know the route Magicus Glaouse was taking him to Ashmount. There were plenty of places he *didn't* want to go—anywhere in Remeria for starters.

Demri wasn't a man that waited. So he stood. After a decent amount of straining, pulling, grunting through stabs of pain, struggling, and glaring away Porric's attempts to assist him, at last, he stood.

Shuffling to where Magicus Glaouse slept, Demri kicked him in the side. Twice.

Glaouse sat upright, looking about in alarm. "Are we under attack?"

"Why are we t-t-traveling west?"

Glaouse wiped the sleep from his eyes. "You woke me to ask me that?"

"Yes."

"I don't trust *Remerians*." He spat the word as if he was uttering a slur and not naming an entire country of people. "I have friends in Lochwall. They will secure us safe passage."

Demri let out a noncommittal grunt and returned to his tree. Moments later, Glaouse was sleeping again.

That was wonderful news. Lochwall was where Demri wanted to go anyway. Demri was certain the guards at Lochwall wouldn't allow Demri to just waltz into the city. The bounty on his head was too significant, and his description too easy to remember, but Glaouse provided that opportunity.

And the hunt for Doram Quandis would continue.

First, they had to traverse the Elderspikes, then cross a vast area of plains, then journey through a deep coniferous forest. With no town in-between. Which meant traveling on foot for several weeks, if not longer. Perhaps Demri could convince Glaouse to use a more refined means of travel.

Caius approached, eyes slitted, an unanswered question on his face, knife gripped expectantly in his hand. Demri gave a slight shake of his head. No, they would not kill Glaouse. Not yet.

KELDEN STOOLE

2nd Cycle of Autumn, 231st Reign of Garcovi
Ashmount, Qothe

One Magicus had introduced himself as Jakci Robinius, the Enforcer professor. He wore a pin of a sword. Kelden had figured out the pins. Each branch was represented by a symbol—Healer by an angel, Collector by a vial, Enforcer by a sword, Glyphist by a quill, and Examiner by spectacles. Magicus Jakci complimented all of them on their progress so far, though Kelden was certain worse news was on the way.

The older professor paced back and forth, observing them. He had a short pointed beard and a habit of reaching up to touch it, then noticing he'd been about to stroke the hair, he would put his arm back down. "Today we will test you in a way that many of you haven't ever been tested in your life. Each of you will receive a sword and a shield. What you do with these items is up to you. However, as I'm sure you've already noticed, you'll have to pay more attention to what other people are doing with these items. There are seventy-five of you. We are going to narrow this down to the top forty that reach the volcano's peak." The Magicus went to stroke his beard again, thought better of it, and itched his nose. "Alive."

As if that needed clarification. The Magicus enjoyed theater, it seemed. *Such a waste of potential, killing off so many of us.*

Kelden flicked his eyes to Sungoa. She was chewing her lip, eyeing the rack of swords. He thought he saw a flash of eagerness across her face. A quick dash of confidence. Perhaps he could borrow some.

Magicus Jakci continued pacing, arms clasped behind his back as if that would stop his overwhelming urge to tug at his beard. "It's imperative that any accepted candidate knows how to fight. The citizens of Cedain often call on the Magicai to assist in their . . . *wars*." He didn't conceal his condescension.

"There is to be no fighting until after we allow you to depart. There will be no fighting once you pass the flags at the summit." He gave a cursory glance at Giant. "Some of you have needed reminding." He paused, stood there, and watched all of them. "There will be no more reminding." A threat. Kelden hoped Giant would break the rules so they would deal with the man. "Retrieve a sword and shield now, please."

Kelden walked forward, but an elbow caught him in the side.

"Move." A woman shoved herself in front of him. Blond, pretty. She turned and glared at him. He recognized her as the snobby girl he'd first met when he'd arrived.

He ignored her and headed toward a different weapon rack. Giant was gleefully picking up a sword there. Perhaps he'd run the rude bitch through.

"Here." Sungoa appeared at his side, spare sword and shield in her hands. He could have kissed her. He might've tried if he thought she'd be receptive toward it.

"Thank you." He grabbed the wooden shield. It was heavy, and it hurt to hold because of his thumb he'd dislocated earlier. He grabbed the sword. It, too, was heavy but familiar. The training Nauc had put him through prepared him for the sword. Not so much the shield. "Good thing we worked with Nauc."

"Yes." Sungoa seemed distracted. She was staring, a concerned expression etched upon her face.

He followed the gaze and saw Giant several feet away. The sword looked tiny in his massive fist, but he gripped it so hard that his fingers were turning white. The shield looked like a plate in his other hand. Giant watched them eagerly.

"We are going to need to do something about him," Kelden said.

Magicus Jakci Robinius loudly cleared his throat. When this failed to work, he held his finger up and a loud *crack* issued, like thunder. "Now that I have your attention." He clapped his hands. "The next Trial begins!" He stepped aside.

A group ran past him, heading up the latter half of the volcano. Several people engaged in sword fights. The moody blond was one of the few able to pass unimpeded.

"Let's move." Sungoa tapped him on the side before taking off at a run.

Kelden followed. They left the plateau and reentered the path, which was wider than the lower portion and the incline wasn't as steep. He heard a large beast trampling after them. Giant was on the move.

No. Running wouldn't solve anything. By the end of the day, Giant would still be right behind him. Or he'd be on top of him, and Kelden would be dead. The threat of the man chasing him was enough to raise Kelden's paranoia to an uncomfortable level. Something needed to change.

So instead, he stopped, held his sword and shield in front of him, and watched as Giant's strides slowed. Kelden's out-of-character move seemed to confuse him.

"Why are we doing this?" Kelden wasn't sure this strategy was the correct one to employ, but the alternative was a sword fight. He'd lose that.

Giant paused a foot in front of Kelden, sword twirling in his hand as he pondered the question. Kelden was waiting for him to strike. He gripped the shield tighter. A glance in his peripheral vision showed no sign of Sungoa. She'd run off. He was alone. A lesson learned for next time: communication is key.

"Why are we doing—"

Giant brought the sword down. An undignified screech escaped Kelden's lips before he lifted his shield in time to prevent his skull from being split. The heavy contact jarred his thumb, and he growled in pain.

Another swing, this time Giant's aim was lower. Kelden jumped back. The point of the blade ripped across both his thighs. A spot of blood dripped across the volcanic rock, shining red against black.

He swung his sword at Giant, but it met steel, and a loud ringing shook the blade, violent reverberations going through his hand. The sword dropped from his grasp. The prior preparation Kelden had received during his training was not enough for the amount of force Giant possessed.

"Shit."

"Yeah. Now die!" Giant's sword came straight at him, mouth open and a fury in the dark man's eyes. Kelden lowered his shield to protect his stomach. The blade scraped against the wood, creating a deep rivet. Splinters chipped off, and his entire arm felt like it shattered.

"Wait!" Kelden's yell halted Giant. "Why are we not working together?"

Giant's laughter boomed so loud, Kelden was certain anyone at the summit of Ashmount, or at the school itself, could have heard.

"I'm serious." Kelden took a moment. Slowed his breathing. His mind raced as he thought through several tactics. Somehow, he was stalling his death. That was a start. "Obviously you're strong."

"And you're boring." The sword shifted in Giant's hand. He was moments away from striking. Kelden was sure of it.

"What I'm saying is you could help me to the top, fight off those that are in our way."

"This does not seem like a fair deal."

"I don't mean any offense by this, but I'm confident I'm smarter than you."

Giant's face contorted in anger. Perhaps this strategy wasn't the best move.

"It's not an insult! You are a skilled man." He held his empty sword arm out, open-palmed to calm the man down. Sweat rolled down Kelden's back.

The Vessian was intimidating. He knew most were members of the Camel Clans, brutal nomads who killed and raided civilians often. His father had told him about a war called the Vessian Incursion, where several clans had attacked Remeria and Calrym. Had there not been any Magicai involved, they would have caused far more damage than they did. Thinking of his father led him to a lesson Hillion had once told him, just after his mother had died: people die when their usefulness has dissipated. Of course, his father had been deep in the drink and depression at that point, but the words had stuck, and Kelden hadn't forgotten them.

"I'm sure there will be Trials later on that require wit or smarts or a certain selection of intellect that you struggle with. A puzzle or a test. Something. I can help you with that. I know I can promise that much. Or you can kill me. I like to think you're wise enough to notice an opportunity."

"What makes you sure?" His words came out slow. Vessians had their own unique dialect that relied on sounds more than words, so the common tongue was often more difficult. At least, that's what Kelden had heard.

"Well, I'm no good at fighting, so I have to be decent at something else, right? And you're not stupid. You know I could help you. If you didn't think there was a chance, I'd be dead already." Dust blew into his face, blinding him for a moment. He coughed dirt out of his mouth and wiped excess spittle off his chin. "If we're going to get through this round, we're going to have to decide now."

"You help me. I help you. Go."

Kelden breathed a sigh of relief. He retrieved his sword. The gamble paid off.

"My name is Ko-Hkar."

"Kelden. Kelden Stoole. Pleasure is mine."

"You hit my head with a rock again, and I'll kill you."

Kelden regretted doing that. It's not like that woman he'd stopped Giant from killing, Sniffles, had done anything. "I assure you that was a onetime deal."

"Screw me, I kill you."

"I won't."

A scream echoed in the distance. Somebody stabbed? But it wasn't him.

It was turning into a good day. "We have some time to make up."

Ko-Hkar ran up the mountain in great, leaping strides. Drawing in a hefty gulp of sulfurous air, Kelden choked and followed.

Sungoa hadn't waited for Kelden. *She probably thinks I'm dead.* He didn't blame her for continuing. The opportunity to join the University of Arcanical Arts would change their lives. That statement would ring true for everyone involved.

He loped after Giant's colossal figure. Running behind the man wasn't so bad; his shadow provided a rare form of shade that shielded Kelden's eyes from the blazing sun. Twice now, he watched as Giant impaled somebody who was in the way and tossed the body aside. He would walk past the dying corpse, happy he didn't have to engage either of them.

Kelden's breathing increased. It was becoming more difficult to catch his breath. Not to mention the scorching temperature. Though Kelden had grown up in Qothe and had become accustomed to the dry heat, he lived in an area close to the ocean, which often brought in cooling breezes. There was a constant supply of breathable air with moisture in it. The sun didn't feel as if it was within reaching distance.

A roar disrupted Kelden's thoughts about the climate. Wiping his brow, he noticed Giant's shadow shift to the right. The sun's piercing glare blinded Kelden again, followed by a sudden stinging in one of his eyes from a spare trail of sweat. Grunting, he rubbed his eye with his fist and tried to see what was going on. Through blurry vision, he caught sight of an ugly man with a distorted nose charging toward him with his sword raised.

Blinking to correct his vision, Kelden raised his shield to protect his face and waved his sword out in front of him, hoping to connect. His sword bounced off something hard, then his shield shifted in his grip as his opponent slammed into him. Kelden stumbled back, cartwheeling his hands to catch his balance. He didn't want to fall and die. The ugly man hadn't thought of this and went careening past Kelden, his momentum propelling him down the path they'd been hiking up. Kelden should've held out his sword and impaled the man, but he was too busy counting his blessings and catching his breath to care.

Another loud roar. Kelden shifted his attention back up the mountain. Giant was fighting two more people. One of them was a man with long brown hair spinning around his face. The other, to Kelden's surprise, was Sungoa.

"Sungoa!" She didn't hear him. He took a deep breath and gathered up the motivation needed to sprint up there to stop this nonsense.

Then Kelden heard labored breathing behind him. The ugly man with the distorted nose was back, hacking at Kelden with his sword. Kelden parried once, twice, then stabbed. The man ducked. Which may have been a smart move for somebody that knew what they were doing, but when he dipped his body down, both of his arms went to his sides in a spectacular flourish, like a diving bird. It left his entire back exposed. Kelden drove his sword down into the man's body and twisted it, just like he'd seen Giant do.

The ugly man fell to the rocks, screaming in agony amid a wash of blood, with Kelden's blade stuck in his back. The dying man's screams echoed, and his arms flailed around, searching for the hilt in his back. *Good luck.* Not wanting to play "catch the sword," Kelden retrieved the ugly man's blade he'd dropped and hurried up Ashmount toward Giant.

Giant had already downed the man he'd been fighting. Now he was dueling Sungoa, who appeared to have found a natural knack with the blade. Her lithe, dexterous body was built for an agile fighting style. She kept dipping in and out, dodging Giant's slow but deadly blows.

"Stop!" They didn't notice or didn't care. He kept climbing. Steel on steel clanged several times as the pair's swords bounced off each other. "Please stop!"

Sungoa's gaze flashed at him for a moment, but she returned her attention to Giant, sidestepping another attack. She hopped in, dashing her blade across Giant's thigh, then jumped back out of his reach.

"I'll kill you!" Giant lunged forward, swiping at Sungoa. She brought her shield up just in time. The sword nicked the top of the shield and bounced off, diverting the direction of the blade away from her forehead.

"Giant, stop!" It took Kelden a second to realize that was not the man's name. "K—" He couldn't recall the rest of his name. Ko-something. "Ko, stop! She's a friend!"

Metal screeched again as the swords connected. He was now standing, helpless, mere feet away. "Both of you *stop!*" He shouted as loud as he could. Giant stepped back, pausing.

"She attacked," Giant said.

"You're a threat," Sungoa said. "Also, it's good to see that you're alive, Kelden." She lowered her weapon but kept watching Giant, eyes narrowed and her tongue making its way out of her lips the way it always did when she concentrated on something.

"He's agreed to help us," Kelden said.

"Agree to help you. Not me."

"She's with me. She's a friend. Sungoa could help us both."

"*Ach-tuk ogu!*" Kelden couldn't tell if this was a string of words or sounds, but either way, it must have been the Vessian language. Giant looked rather frustrated. Having to prevent the man from killing *two* people in a single day seemed to be quite the trial.

"Look, we just need to reach the top." Kelden gave Sungoa a pleading look. She rolled her eyes but gave him a nod. "Thanks. Ko?"

Giant grunted. "Fine. Name's Ko-Hkar."

"Ko-Hkar. My apologies." Truthfully, Kelden didn't give a shit about his name. But he had to play nice.

"Just call him an animal," Sungoa said.

Ko-Hkar growled. A warning.

"Be nice. He's . . ." Kelden wasn't sure what to say after that. He'd been about to spit out "a good person" as a natural compliment, but he'd yet to see a single good thing Ko-Hkar had done. Aside from *not* killing Kelden or Sungoa. Not all that great. "He's a giant."

The big man snorted. "Giant. Yes." He didn't seem upset.

"Right." Sungoa continued hiking up the path, passing a dead woman, slack-jawed and wide-eyed.

The three of them remained silent the rest of the way.

S taggering through a pair of flags, Kelden collapsed on the ground, breathless. Ko-Hkar stood ahead of him, proud arms in the air. Several Magicai walked around, observant as always. Kelden realized he stopped noticing them until arriving at a checkpoint. He peered down the trail where Sungoa was struggling to finish. She'd fallen behind by a few hundred feet. The fight with Ko-Hkar must have exhausted her.

Ashmount's summit was remarkable. The air ascending from the gigantic crater in the mountain was smoky and ashen. Up here, the rock was warm, and if Kelden had energy, he would have walked up the pass to the edge of the circular pit and examined the volcano's interior. He was too tired for that. *I hope Ashmount is just as tired as I am and has no desire to erupt while we're all gathered here.*

Slow but steady, Sungoa made her way across the flags marking the end of that leg.

Magicus Jakci Robinius and a few others hurried over to her. Kelden sneered to himself. *He* didn't get any help. Neither did Ko-Hkar.

He overheard Jakci. "I apologize, but you are number forty-one. I must insist that—"

"What!" Sungoa interrupted. "I was right behind those two!" She pointed at Kelden and Ko-Hkar.

"Yes, and they were number thirty-seven and thirty-eight. Thirty-nine and forty arrived over there." Magicus Jakci Robinius pointed to a location where another pair was standing, holding each other's shoulders and gasping, clearly exhausted from the climb. They had gone off trail, or they would've arrived where Kelden and Ko-Hkar had.

"No!" Sungoa screamed, her energy restored. She hefted her sword in her hand. "I *can't* go back!"

"Nobody said anything about you going back." Magicus Jakci Robinius steepled his fingers together. "You failed."

"I *need* this!" Sungoa sounded desperate.

"You will still offer plenty of contributions," one of the other Magicai said, raising his hands.

Sungoa stabbed the Magicus in the chest. He screamed, then slid off her sword.

A bolt of lightning? Power? Something bright slammed into Sungoa, and she dropped dead. It was the same power that had been used when Kelden had stood in line and the unruly man had been silenced. There was no question now, though. She was dead. Magicus Jakci Robinius lowered the hand that killed her.

Another Magicus ran over, kneeling before her body. He pulled out a vial and did something. Kelden couldn't tell what, as the man's back was toward him. When the Magicus stood, he pocketed the vial, which was now full of liquid, and Sungoa's body started deflating.

SERADAL WINTLOCK

2nd Cycle of Autumn, 231st Reign of Garcovi
Vox, Cyrok

One week after arriving in Vox, Sera stood with her arms behind her back and her hands clasped together. She was on an erected stage. Hundreds of Vox citizens spread out in front of her, standing in the town's center. All eyes were on Governess Stasia Falconel, who stood behind a podium, delivering a speech about the state of the country, the ruination of Gyrloft, and the current threat of war with Calrym.

She explained Sera's tale of imprisonment, escape, and what occurred thereafter. She warned of the elusive Captain Blago Adavir and his group of bandits. Although she admitted to not knowing the identity of the man funding Adavir and his men, she was adamant it was a prominent Calrite noble. Qothe was too poor to fund any external military affair. Vessia didn't have any interests outside of the Camel Clans. Remeria had excellent relations with every country at the moment and was too busy worrying about the growing power of Calrym.

Calrym, however, owned enough finances needed to keep a covert military group active, scheming noblemen had plenty of motivations to do something of this magnitude for their personal financial gain, and gyrfalcons sold for the highest prices in Calrym. And the prisoner they'd interrogated had admitted it was Calrym's doing. Governess Falconel's theory was a noble from Calrym, or even the king himself, had ordered the attack in order to secure gyrfalcons and sell them to the rich for exorbitant prices. There wasn't anything else Cyrok had of value.

"And so," the governess said, "in order to fight against all of this, we *will* need a stronger military force. I have enacted the Avian Draft and drafted Seradal Wintlock, the hero who brought us this information, into the Falcon Knights."

An extensive amount of cheering and applause ensued. Sera smiled and felt her cheeks flush. It felt odd being honored in public like this.

"Together, I hope we can secure a safer future for Vox, the Gyrloft citizens, and all of Cyrok. Over the next few weeks, the Falcon Knights will recruit new members. If anybody would like to apply or suggest somebody they believe worthy, please visit any of the local barracks." Governess Falconel turned toward Sera. "And now, through the ancient rite of the Avian Draft, I induct you, Seradal Wintlock, into the Falcon Knights. Congratulations, and may you serve your country well."

A boy rushed over and bowed before Sera. "Cyr." He proffered a folded blue cape. Resting atop the material was a silver badge in the shape of a soaring falcon. Just behind the child, Angazo stood at the front of the crowd. He waved to her, proud. Her father was still recovering in his bed, though he'd demanded he be present. They'd denied his request because of his health.

"Kneel." The governess approached her, drawing a sword from its scabbard at her side.

Sera knelt and bowed her head to avoid the staring crowd, but it also felt like the natural thing to do. Steel landed on her shoulder, then her other shoulder.

"Rise, Cyr Seradal Wintlock." Sera stood, and Governess Falconel gave her what she interpreted to be a grim smile. "Your life path is about to change, Cyr Seradal. Harsh training and even harsher realities are coming. War will be upon us. I believe you will be what our country needs." The citizens cheered again, and the governess clasped Sera's hand in hers, pulling Sera into half a hug. Her other hand clapped Sera's back, and she whispered in Sera's ear, "I tell you what I tell all the new recruits. I'm sorry for doing this to you."

Sera considered Adavir's betrayal. She didn't want anyone to be in a position to harm her or her father again. By joining the Falcon Knights, she figured she'd be able to better protect both of them from monsters like Adavir. "I'm glad to be here," she said to the governess. And Sera meant it. She wasn't sure where she was heading, but at least she had a goal, a purpose. Somewhere to *be*. Something to *do*. Otherwise, she'd lose herself to grief. She couldn't bear what her father was going through, stuck in a chair or bed for the rest of his life.

The governess leaned back, studying Sera's face. "Soon you may not believe those words."

The crowd continued cheering.

"You imagine? *Cyr* Angazo Giresh?" Angazo paced back and forth in Sera's private room. Though she couldn't see him, she imagined him waving his arms in the air as he continued to splutter out a story he'd repeated five times now. It'd now been several days since the public spectacle. Soon after Governess Falconel's speech, she'd drafted many others—including Angazo—and taken a few volunteers as well.

"Congratulations, *cyr*." Sera laughed and lifted her chin. Her new page clasped her cape around her neck. He was showing her how to put everything on the correct way. She'd been lucky to receive a page so early on in her training—another prestigious token of Cyrok's gratitude that Sera had warned the governess about Captain Adavir.

"There." The young boy who'd handed Sera her cape during the ceremony, around twelve years old, offered a cheerful grin and handed her a helm. "All done."

Sera took the helm and placed it upon her head. Aside from the cape and the badge she'd received earlier in the day, a new set of armor had been waiting in her personal room. Each Falcon Knight received personal lodging in the Roost, a set of barracks dedicated to those serving as a knight.

"I never guess they want old man. I've not held sword before!" Angazo's pacing continued. The sounds of his boots thumping on the wooden floor echoed across the small room. Sera didn't tell Angazo she'd asked the governess to draft him.

"You're not old, Angazo," Sera said. The man was a decade younger than her father.

The page pulled back the curtain. "May I present to you Cyr Seradal Wintlock!"

Her father, sitting on the lone chair in the room, let

out an audible gasp. Angazo beamed and clapped, a proud gleam in his eyes.

"Oh, stop." Sera waved a hand at them, sporting a new leather glove. A large chain mail hauberk rested on her shoulders. When the page helped her into it, she'd complained about the serious weight tugging her down. After he'd placed a belt around the hauberk, fastening it across her waist, she couldn't believe the significant improvement this had at reducing the pull. The gambeson, boots, and gloves that accompanied the chain mail armor were all made of leather. A sword and shield lay on her new bed, which she hadn't bothered to strap on yet.

"You wonderful. Together, make team," Angazo said.

"Well done." Her father smiled at her, but she could tell something wasn't well.

She assumed his irritation was both her and Angazo being given honorifics while he'd become paralyzed. And his wife and son, dead. She couldn't have felt worse for her father. He didn't deserve this. She stifled her thoughts. If she kept thinking of her dead family, she might just break down. Sera had to maintain focus on the present. There'd be time to mourn some other time.

"Thanks, both of you."

The page stepped forward. "Is there anything else I can do for you, cyr?"

"I'm good, thank you."

The page bowed and exited.

Sera turned, looking at the blue cape as it flowed. "He was strange."

"He's kid. Assigned you until given own knighthood," Angazo said. Sera knew he'd been learning as much as he could ever since his recruitment.

Sera grunted. "Perhaps I should've learned his name."

"He happy you not yelled."

Her father's empty gaze collected her attention. "Father? Are you okay?"

"I'm . . . fine." He looked up at her, returning from wherever he'd been. "Sorry, Sera, I was thinking about how proud your mother would be if she were here to witness this."

Sera thought about that. Her mother wouldn't have liked the idea of either of her children going off to fight in battles and leaving home. "She'd be livid."

Both her father and Angazo laughed at that.

A knock sounded on the door.

"Yes?" Sera answered.

The page opened it and stood there, looking frightened and embarrassed.

"Is everything all right?" Then after a moment she asked, "What's your name?"

"Y-yes, cyr. Renard, cyr." The page couldn't meet her eyes.

"Are you sure you're all right?"

"This is my first official day as a page, and I didn't want to screw it up. But I have. I forgot to tell you that Cyr Ilic Strictland requires you in the training grounds. Immediately."

"Already?"

"A resting knight's a dead knight." The page said, reciting it almost in a singsong voice, then ushered her back into her room. "No time to spare, let's get your sword and shield. I must make sure that you are presentable, or the governess might have me hanged."

Sera laughed. The page shot her a look of fear. She shook her head. "You need to relax."

"Cyr Seradal!" The page sounded horrified.

"Everyone out!" He shooed his hands at Angazo and her father. "Cyr Seradal needs to prepare herself."

<hr>

The Falcon Knights were the latest order of knights branded under their avian namesakes. Before the Falcon Knights, there were of course the Hawks who wore green capes, the Grouses who wore yellow capes, and a pair of Vultures who wore gray capes. Cyr Ilic Strictland was a Vulture, and he was the second oldest knight still active in the order. Though, as Renard, the page, explained to Sera, *active* might have been too overzealous a word. Cyr Ilic Strictland had retired from tournaments and combat to train newcomers, but he otherwise enjoyed time alone inside his home.

Many other Falcon Knights were already in the vast square training grounds. Some dueled each other with wooden swords and were naked aside from undergarments. Sera shivered just looking at them. Though it wasn't freezing today, it was too cold to be without clothing. Others were practicing their stances or their sword and shield grips, a senior knight correcting errors. A few were doing physical workouts, while others were running. Senior knights patrolled the grounds, observing the activities.

Renard had been gracious enough to point out Cyr Ilic Strictland before returning to tidy up her room. He paced back and forth, barking out commands or changes a knight needed to make. Despite being retired, Strictland was fully armed and armored aside from his helm. Heavy wrinkles shaped his face, and a thick mustache as white as a snow rabbit's pelt drew Sera's eyes.

As Sera approached, Cyr Ilic Strictland noticed her.

"Ah, you must be the new one. What's your name, soldier?"

"Seradal Wintlock."

"Were you not *knighted*?"

"*Cyr* Seradal Wintlock."

He winked. "Better. It's important to give off confidence. What better way to give off confidence than flaunting one's accolades? And never be ashamed to admit that you've a better station than others, or they might try to take it from you." The old man stroked his bushy mustache. "Hey, Cyr Kingston! Pay attention to your duelists, eh?"

"Yes, cyr!" a woman's voice called back.

Cyr Ilic shook his head. "Cyr Kingston has a habit of getting distracted. It's her biggest flaw. Every *person*, every single *thing* has a flaw. Even a flaw has a flaw. You know what that is?"

Sera didn't, and she crinkled her face in thought. She wanted to answer the man but didn't know what to say.

"A flaw's flaw is being a flaw through no fault of its own. It is what it is, and the flaw will have to adapt. Like you will as a woman. Being a knight is no simple task for the hardiest of man. Being a knight is even more difficult for a woman, more so in other countries. The Cyroki have customs others do not agree with. I've heard people claim our knights are weak because we name them after birds. Or because we allow women to serve.

"Gender is not a defining characteristic of a knight. One's actions define a person, and I've seen plenty of women cut down larger men in cold blood. Women can be as courageous as any man. The way of the bird brings us strength. Even so, it's important we learn to deal with ridicule. Your flaw is that you give too much away in your facial expressions, soldier. Don't let confusion show on your face, because the moment it's there, some-body knows you're at a disadvantage. Now, let us begin." He turned, holding out his hand to another man that stood nearby, carrying a pair of wooden swords. The man passed them to Strictland and then saluted. Strictland waved the man away. "Dismissed. Now go polish my spare suit of armor." The man saluted again, then hurried off.

Cyr Ilic handed Sera a sword. Suddenly, he swung his sword and tapped her chest with the tip. The wood against her chain mail made a *chink*ing sound. "Point to me. You're dead."

She blanched. "We hadn't even begun."

"There is no honor in war, Wintlock. Only killing. Do you want to live or have honor?"

She looked down at the chain mail she was wearing. "I want to live. I also have armor."

"Armor is good, but it won't stop a lot of weapons. If you want to train as a Falcon Knight, you pretend you aren't wearing armor at all times. Otherwise, you may become reliant upon it. Point to me stands. Reset this time. No tricks. After all, a resting knight's a dead knight."

She held her sword out in front of her.

"Begin." Strictland lunged at her.

She parried the sword, then took a swipe at him. Strictland sidestepped the attack. She swung again, but the blow deflected against his blade.

"Your eyes, they follow where you want to attack next. It is a behavior you don't want to become a habit. Concentrate on everything you are doing, but don't show me where you're going to attack next."

She went for a feint. Lunging to his right but altering the course of her blade to stab down at his thigh. Strict-land's block missed the blade, but he was faster than she figured he would be considering his age. He hopped to his right. Her stab slid right by him.

"Good! But you favor your right leg. When you attack, you're putting too much weight upon it. You will be slow. Practice this habit. Perhaps you—" He stopped midsentence and swiped at her unguarded left arm, connecting on her elbow. The leather gambeson absorbed much of the blow, but she still felt it. "Point to me. You get distracted by discussion. Don't. This can be a detrimental habit. Habits often lead to further regrets."

Frustrated at failing in obvious ways, Sera let out a breath, then brought her sword back up. She attacked in force this time, keeping her legs moving and swinging her blade as hard as she could. She would hit the man.

Smiling, Strictland backed up and parried each of her attacks. On her fourth swing, Strictland's sword connected with hers with much more force than any of the other parries, and she lost her grip. The wooden sword was thrust from her hand. He reached out and tapped the side of her helm.

"Point to me."

Exhausted, Sera returned to her room. Waiting outside was Renard. "Cyr Seradal, would you like me to retrieve some food and drink?"

"That would be great. But first, I think I'll need help to remove my armor." The armor was easy enough to put on and take off. Her arms, however, didn't want to work, and she didn't think she'd have the strength to pull off the hauberk or gambeson or perhaps even her boots.

Renard blanched. And blushed. "Cyr, I think I can find some women to—"

"Renard. You just helped me get *into* the armor."

"Yes, cyr, but we're taking *off* the armor now. It's much more difficult to hide . . . *things.*"

Sera, though appreciative of his modesty, was exhausted and didn't want to deal with this. Plus, he was little more than a child. If he was a grown man, she'd feel quite uncomfortable after what happened with Smugface in the forest. But Renard was not an adult, and even if he was, she wouldn't be interested. Nor would she be naked, even after removing the armor. She was too tired for this. "Renard, I need to lie down and eat some food. Before I can do this, I need to get this armor off me. Otherwise, I'll die of discomfort. I appreciate the courtesies, but, if you are to be serving me from now on, we need to get past this. This is a partnership, right?"

"My apologies, cyr. You are right."

"Good."

Renard helped her out of her armor, though he closed his eyes or turned away whenever anything delicate might come close to showing. He shouldn't have worried. After taking care of her armor and ensuring she needed nothing else, Renard left the room to retrieve her supper. Before he returned, she'd fallen asleep.

Knighting was hard work.

EDELBROCK BRENDIS

2nd Cycle of Autumn, 231st Reign of Garcovi
Lochwall, Calrym

He learned Chellie was the woman's name. And what a bitch she was.

The routine beatings continued. The humiliation never ceased. Thrice a day, the woman would return to feed them. Thrice a day, the woman would beat them. Then she'd issue what seemed to be pointless commands. Sometimes intended to embarrass, but often they just seemed random.

Time dripped by. Sometimes, Chellie would miss a meal. Which meant she'd miss a beating as well. Though rare, these became treasured moments. The woman became more and more sadistic. Somehow, the three of them avoided serious injuries the entire time. Only nasty bruises or a broken digit.

Discussion among the prisoners dissipated, much in the same way as before. Though they received food three times a day, it was poor quality and wasn't enough. He was losing weight rather fast.

Once, Chellie removed them from the cell so a quick cleaning could take place, courtesy of them of course. Although they received buckets to shit in, they had plenty of other stuff to clean. Rotted food scraps and rat droppings were common. Edelbrock had lost his sense of the stench.

E delbrock jolted awake. Sleep was difficult to come by, and it felt like every time he fell asleep, something startled him out of his stupor.

"Get up!" Chellie stood in the doorway.

Edelbrock sat up, signaling he was awake. If one was slow to obey, they received a foot in the ribs. This morning, as she so often liked to do, she splashed water on them. Then she spit into the pitcher several times and poured it into their community bowl.

"Drink up, you lazy cunts."

Parched, Edelbrock hauled himself over to the bowl and lapped it up like a dog. A foot slammed into his stomach. He elicited a grunt, but he'd expected it. He ignored the pain and drank his fill.

"Kiss my boot." Chellie extended her foot toward Nauc. He obliged.

Out of the three of them, Nauc was the worst off. He ate and drank the least. He'd lost a frightening amount of weight, to the point of looking skeletal. Dark lines circled his eyes. She'd worn him down.

"You. Big boy." Chellie gestured to Bruise. "Carry that one out." She pointed at Nauc. Bruise did just that.

Chellie approached Edelbrock, blocking his way to the door. He knew not to move. "And how are *you* on this fine day?"

He coughed. Speaking had become difficult. This

game was tricky. Either you said "terrible" and got your ass beaten bloody or you said "great" and got your ass beaten bloody. He said, "Fine."

"The only thing fine in here is me." She drew her fist back.

"True." Edelbrock croaked this out moments before her fist came flying at him. He winced and closed his eyes. The blow never connected.

"Excuse me?" Chellie asked.

"I agreed you're the only fine thing in here."

Chellie smiled. He never liked when she did. It often meant that she had something nefarious planned. "You, my friend, are correct." She extended a hand toward him. "Stand."

He took the hand, and she heaved him up. His shaky legs didn't support him, and he started face-planting toward her naked chest.

Chellie held her other hand out and steadied him. "Maybe later." *A joke? Strange.*

A sting in his cheek. She'd slapped him. Not hard though. "Stop staring. There are plenty of other women worth staring at."

He looked elsewhere.

"Come." Chellie led him out of the cell.

His cellmates were *sitting* on the beds. That certainly wasn't allowed.

"Sit," a gruff voiced commanded. Savakkis. He pointed toward another empty bed.

Edelbrock sat. He was beyond careful not to tread on any of their feet or look them in the eye. The last thing he wanted to do was insult anybody and get beaten.

"Today marks the moment you become one of us. You will learn how to survive in the arena. There is one thing you will not do—attempt escape. There isn't a way out of here. We've seen people try. All it does is anger those who matter, and we receive strict punishments. Is that clear?" Savakkis stared down at them, hands crossed in front of his muscular abdomen.

"Of course," Edelbrock said. He'd make sure they didn't misunderstand him at such an important moment.

Nauc and Bruise joined Edelbrock in agreement.

Savakkis said, "A skilled warrior rises on the back of three foundations. Obedience. Training. Suffering. A true warrior follows orders, and in this place, following orders is competing. If you refuse, they will torture you. A true warrior does not waver. They train. They succeed. A failed warrior dies. Therefore, training is of the utmost importance. A trained warrior is the greatest threat, right? No. A warrior who has suffered and has something to *prove* or *fight* for is. That is the warrior you will become. Or you will die. I apologize for your mistreatment, but we have found suffering is a vital component of keeping the peace down here. Everyone must suffer. Those who don't break, break us. Because they only think about escaping. And escape . . . is impossible. There is no way out unless you're released."

Edelbrock believed him. The magically sealed wards to the hypogeums only opened with the device the House Heads kept outside. Without it, no one could pass through the barrier.

"You have learned obedience. You have suffered. You will now train. I release you from the cage and invite you to stay among us. Any disobedience will lead to punishment in some form or another. We meet severe problems with death. Let's eat."

And that was that. Edelbrock was now freed.

To be inducted in the Velvet Mother's House, the trio had to have their heads—and Edelbrock's beard—shaved. Edelbrock learned the other Houses had their own requirements, which allowed everyone to identify the Houses' gladiators. The other Houses didn't shave hair. Instead, Scayde Haklon's gladiators were branded. Jaylena's wore shiny bronze bracelets on both wrists. Castede, military man that he was, ensured all his gladiators were outfitted with tall black boots, contrary to the dull browns everyone else wore. Lekhan's gladiators painted their bodies with various animal faces.

After shaving their heads, Savakkis led them to a feast in the dining hall. Edelbrock, Nauc, and Bruise gorged themselves on glazed duck, baked potatoes, a smattering of figs and apples, and a custard pie. The only thing to drink was water, but that suited Edelbrock just fine.

Perhaps Edelbrock had the courage and audacity to ask what he was thinking in that moment. Or perhaps it was due to his malnourishment. Upon reflection, he'd been lucky they answered him without a beating. "They give you this food? I figured we'd be on gruel for the rest of our time down here."

Savakkis nodded. "That very well may be the case in the other Houses. However, the Velvet Mother considers us an investment. The better food and training we receive, the better we perform during the events. The better we perform, the more money we earn for the House. The generosity doesn't extend to beverages. Water is the healthiest option as well as the cheapest and easiest to haul down here."

Edelbrock had a tough time thinking Scayde Haklon would treat his fighters well. It seemed Edelbrock stumbled upon a miracle by being drafted by the Velvet

Mother. He didn't envy the man who got drafted before him by Scayde. Anditus Roberon was his name, if Edelbrock wasn't mistaken. Nauc never talked about him in a positive way, and Edelbrock assumed Scayde hated the man more than Nauc did.

The rest of the afternoon was dedicated to showing the trio around the hypogeum. Savakkis introduced them to many other fighters. Edelbrock guessed they met several hundred gladiators, though he wasn't able to recall their names, except for Chellie's four brothers. The gladiators seemed to be a wide range of ages and from all parts of the world.

The other fighters referred to Chellie and her brothers as the Chell. Their mother, Chella, had birthed quintuplets and, either drunk or lazy or both, had named them all after herself. There was Chellik, Chellis, Chellin, and Chellit in addition to Chellie. When they were only twelve years old, Chella had sold them into slavery. The Chell had worked in the fields for four years. At sixteen years of age, they had been purchased by Scayde Haklon and placed in the Draft. Fortunately for the Chell, they had been drafted as a singular unit. Chellie explained Scayde had rules in place that prevented anybody under the age of eighteen from fighting. Thus, they had been an investment Draft, and nobody wanted to care for five people who wouldn't be fighting anytime soon. Now, the Chell were eighteen and going to be fighting in the next season. Edelbrock couldn't believe how young they were.

The hypogeum's layout was simple. The main staircase entered the kitchen, where there was a range of food stores. Beyond the kitchen was the dining hall, complete with two enormous tables surrounded by wooden chairs. Many sleeping quarters that were all the same came next, filled with beds adorned with expensive bedding and pillows, while lights hung from the ceiling. Then came the armory, filled with a multitude of weaponry along with several types of shields. Edelbrock spotted various pieces of armor, though not enough to comfort him. Beside the armory was a wide-open area used for training. It had dummies, targets for ranged weapons, hundreds of wooden swords, an empty pit in the center for sparring, and benches lining the edges. Almost a simulation of what it would be like to fight in the actual arena. Past this, a hallway lined with arches led to the gladiator's entrance to Buzzard's Bowl. Beyond the hallway was a preparation room, where they could arm themselves with the allocated gear, and then "the pit," a place where the next fighters waited and could see into Buzzard's Bowl—as long as vision wasn't obscured. It often was. They didn't venture that far during the tour, and Edelbrock didn't care to investigate it. He'd been there for the Draft.

Savakkis told Edelbrock that Scayde Haklon's head servant, Tanibris, made an occasional appearance to deliver news or complete an inspection. Anybody entering the hypogeum would always come from the kitchen area, unless it was a gladiator returning from a bout in Buzzard's Bowl.

Savakkis then declared they were now free to mingle and to prepare for the next day, when their first session of rigorous training would begin.

"Are you excited?" someone asked.

Edelbrock, busy examining the many types of swords stashed in the armory, turned to see one of the Chell brothers. Impossible to discern which as they were identical. "For?"

"The fights. Holding a sword in your hand. Hearing the crowd's roar of approval when you *beat* your opponent into the ground."

"Or groan as you stare at the blue sky, hurt and wounded. Waiting for your opponent to drive his sword into your chest. Waiting for the people to cheer *your* death."

The Chell brother chuckled. "Perhaps. Fate plays in mysterious ways."

"To answer your question, no. I am not excited. I've fought in an actual war before. It gets . . . messy." Flashes of his past military life came back to Edelbrock. Riding astride a horse, leading his men to death. Steel on steel, floods of red, the screams of the injured, and the moans of the dying. And the horrible screams of dying horses. He'd won a lot of praise for his role in all of that.

"I'm more interested in testing my abilities. Seeing what my brothers and I are capable of."

The Chell, Edelbrock later learned, referred to all five of themselves as brothers. Chellie explained it to him one day. "It's easier, and it's not like I'm into powdered faces or the courtship of a lord anyway. I'm more at peace with a knife in my hands and a man between my legs covered in blood. Both ways you're thinking." Then she laughed and walked away. Edelbrock wasn't sure how to take that.

"I'm certain you'll find you're capable of much more than you think," Edelbrock told the Chell brother now, "when on the brink of dying. The adrenaline will acti-vate a need to survive . . . though it'll activate in your enemy too. There is no honor among the condemned, something to remember." He remembered his time in war. He'd always remember.

The Chell brother smiled. "I *only* fight dirty." And he tripped Edelbrock with a quick swipe of his foot. Edel-brock plummeted to the stone floor of the armory, slamming his head on the ground. "Better prepare yourself better."

Bruised and his ego wounded, Edelbrock groaned and stood back up. He'd have to remain vigilant about his surroundings.

DEMRI SLARN

21 Years Ago
Ashmount, Qothe

"And so, as you can see, the relationship between Enforcers and Glyphists is necessary. There is *no* other way to access your powers, unless a Collector gives you one of their vials they collect. I wouldn't rely on that as they are rather selfish. They donate a majority of vials collected to Ashmount's stores, to prepare for emergencies, and they hoard the ones they're allowed to keep." The Enforcer professor spoke in a feeble voice. It was difficult for Demri to hear him even though he sat in the second row.

It was strange to even consider sitting in the second row. Mere weeks ago, he would have panicked at the thought of not sitting at the very front. Demri had gained a thirst for knowledge ever since his normal schooling. Now that he was learning about his ultimate powers, his intrigue was at its highest. He'd passed the

Trials. Somehow. He thanked his quick legs and intelligent brain for that.

At sixteen, Demri felt as if he were closer in skill and intellect to the adults in the classroom than to the younger people. That hadn't prevented feelings from developing toward one of those younger people, Myri Celioh. Demri found it difficult to focus on the Magicai at all whenever she was in the room. And Myri was an Enforcer. Like Demri. Which meant they saw each other all the time.

The Enforcer professor droned on in his quiet voice. So easy to tune out.

Blond hair. Eyes a dark green. Large, supple bre—

"Kid's staring at you again, Celioh." The voice came from behind Demri. A loud whisper from the sneering pale boy who tormented Demri at every potential opportunity. Doram Quandis. *Bastard.* Doram took to calling him "kid" even though Demri was *older* by several cycles.

Myri turned in her seat to look at both of them. Demri realized his mouth was open, so he closed it. His eyes wandered back to the front of the room, to the professor. He needed to focus. She smelled of lavender.

"Maybe he just thinks you're pretty." Doram again.

Demri's face flushed. He wanted to punch Doram, but he wouldn't win that fight. Doram was much bigger than he was.

"Shouldn't everyone?" *Her* voice. Beautiful. Soft. Angelic. He just wanted to press his lips against—

"*Everyone* doesn't stare," Doram said in that lazy, stupid-sounding voice. Low. Animalistic. Primal. Empty of thought.

"Go d-d-d . . ." Demri's anger didn't help with getting out his insult. It just, as he knew it would, made him look worse. "D-die." Not very inventive.

Doram laughed, though even he wasn't foolish enough to do it loud enough for the Magicus to bother interrupting his teachings. "Mother Avani couldn't fix that stutter you have."

Demri balled his hands into fists, fingernails digging into his palms. He could feel his face burning.

"Pay attention." *Myri's* voice. Calm. Tender. Wonderful. He'd follow her commands anywhere.

He displaced his anger and turned his focus on the Magicus again. *For her.*

The professor was still prattling about Collectors. "Collectors aren't selfish by nature, you see, it's more of a side effect of the economy they're forced to live within. They use these vials to power themselves when the time comes, and if they aren't, they often bring back the substance to their employers or back here to Ashmount. It's much more affordable to have a Glyphist extract your own substance for you to access. Yes, this contributes to your aging, but it's easier to manage. Collector vial prices are high because of the demand from . . . well, Enforcers and those who wish to keep a stock."

Demri's mind drifted. He knew much of the history about Magicai and the capabilities of each branch. He'd done lots of personal research during his time as a student.

Demri looked out the corner of his eye. Just to make sure she was still as beautiful as the last time. Then another glance. His heart thumped. She was wearing a silk dress. Blue. Her creamy skin poked out in various places. Her legs. Arms. Neck. Cleavage. She brushed a few strands of hair behind her ear and scooted forward on her seat, listening, intent. *Mother Avani, help me. She is gorgeous. We would make a wonderful coup—*

"It's happening *again*, damn it," Doram said.

Myri shot Demri a glance of annoyance. Disgust? He wasn't sure. He knew he didn't have a chance with her anyway. Not while people like Doram Quandis kept doing things like this.

And unfortunately, most people preferred Doram over Demri.

Most people found the stuttering to be too uncomfortable. Too different.

He'd show them.

<hr>

On days when Demri felt alone, he'd walk Ashmount's grounds. Often he'd find a tree to sit by and read. Within the protective bubble of course. That's where all the nice greenery was. The trees, flowers. The *air*. Butterflies, bugs, and birds. An aroma of . . . freshness. Outside of Ashmount was a desolate wasteland morons tried living in. It didn't seem as bad as Vessia did, based on what Demri read about, but it was second worst. Or perhaps Cyrok was. He'd never come to a consensus. It just seemed like the best was Calrym, followed by his home, Remeria.

Growing up, Demri had had a privileged life. Or he should have. His father was a wealthy merchant who peddled gems and other rare materials he scalped on the open market. His mother was a seamstress who somehow lucked into sewing for a prominent duchess. Their pay was enough to afford to send Demri to school, and they lived in a splendid manor. When the Magicai had come to Rivane, a port in Remeria, his father had insisted he take their test. Demri had possessed the Trace, and they'd shipped him off. He hadn't heard from his family again. Not that this was much of a surprise. His parents had insisted the house's caregivers punish

Demri anytime he stuttered too much. They'd believed they could force Demri to lose the stutter through beatings. Old medical logic, Demri had later found out. When that hadn't worked, they'd consulted a Magicus, who'd informed them the Magicai couldn't fix issues one was born with. His parents, though wealthy, weren't the brightest. It would've been nice to receive a letter from them once in a while.

School had always been an oasis away from his parents. Of course, that meant he had to come to terms with more bullying. But if he could escape into a crevice at the library or stay near a professor—they often invited him into their break room—he enjoyed reading about everything. History, language, geography.

Things got both worse and better once he'd arrived at Ashmount. The harsh treatment of fellow students got much cruder and more violent. He'd assumed this was because of the Trials where they'd killed half the other candidates. Thirty-five people survived the Trials. Seemed a waste to him. Like Demri, most became Enforcers. Good thing, too, because many had died recently fighting in the Vessian Incursion, the war taking place in Remeria. Or had it made its way to Calrym? Demri didn't know and didn't pay attention.

Also, a good portion of the candidates were adults. Adults, Demri'd learned from his own parents, were much worse than other children. The better part was that he'd become a Magicus. Not just any Magicus either. An Enforcer. The most powerful. Somebody who could do whatever they wanted. Nobody would push him around once he finished his lessons and learned about his power.

Three cycles had passed since he'd completed the Trials. Wind blew through his lengthy hair as he walked in the school's courtyard. No pressure to cut it since he'd left home, so he'd let it grow. The pages in his book, *A History of the Exploitation of Healers* by the Liberation of Healer Magicai Association (LHMA), ruffled.

He continued reading.

The Blind Sisters, an organization specializing in discreet selling of Healers into slavery, continued to operate throughout the entirety of Calrym. Powerful men, such as the king, and their closest subordinates wanted to prevent themselves from dying. By keeping a Blind Sister nearby, they ensured free access to healing any time they may need it. Blind Sisters, of course, had little choice in the matter. Healers have no combative capabilities, so once imprisoned, it was difficult to escape. Sure, they could refuse their orders, but they'd just end up dead anyway.

Though outlawed back in the 120th Reign of Juralna, it's suspected the practice never stopped. It's unlikely most kings will follow the laws they've signed into action, and abounding rumors suggest there's still an underground operation in practice. Experts believe that it's even possible the Blind Sisters never disbanded but disappeared from the public eye.

This made life even more difficult for imprisoned Healers. Before, prominent political figureheads would allow their slaves to walk alongside them, living in near harmony. This allowed them to receive necessities humans require to have a decent life. Now, afraid of public prosecution if caught with one of the Blind Sisters, the rich keep the Healers bound and gagged in closets, rooms, or cages. Even richer people may have secret dungeons or rooms dedicated to hiding groups of these Healers.

Studies by rogue Magicai have proven much of the information relayed above. Most Magicai prefer not to comment on the situation or to remain anonymous. Some have accused higher-ups at the University of Arcanical Arts, or

*Ashmount, of assisting in the slave trade. This, however, we
cannot confirm.*

A History of the Exploitation of Healers interested
Demri. These were other people who had shitty lives.
The book went into even further detail about how rough
the lives became of Healers sold into slavery. This was
Demri's second time reading it. Sometimes, though sad
as it may be, reading about the desperate lives of people
in situations worse than Demri's gave him a cruel sense
of happiness. Other people suffered more than he did.
The book also fascinated him—the lengths non-Magicai
would go to provide themselves with Magicai abilities.

Demri suspected the Blind Sisters were *still* operating fifty years after publication of the book. There was
a Healer he'd met who he'd not seen in many weeks,
which was unusual. When Demri had inquired, he'd
received the same rote response. "I'm sorry, Demri, but I
can't comment on other Magicai's orders." This was
false. He'd learned plenty about other people and their
jobs. But he also realized he was speculating. They could
be anywhere, doing anything.

The wind blew again. Pages crinkled and turned by
themselves. He looked up just in time to see Doram
Quandis and several of his friends walking in Demri's
direction. *Great.* Oh, and Myri Celioh was with them.
Even better. He marked his spot in the book and closed it,
setting it with his other possessions.

As the group of five moved closer to him, he noticed
how much Myri had grown since they'd first arrived.
Everything seemed curvier. And larger. If there wasn't the
possibility of immediate danger, he would have stared
unapologetically at her, for there was no secret anymore.
In fact, Demri sensed that Myri enjoyed being fawned

over, no matter who it was. She loved when anyone paid her attention. And he paid her more attention than anyone. She *was* gorgeous. He couldn't deny it, despite knowing it was a terrible idea to continue obsessing over her. She'd become a close friend of Doram's. Perhaps they'd even slept together. Demri wasn't sure, but that thought filled him with anger and disgust.

"You seem comfortable. Sitting in dirt." Doram smirked and elbowed one of his friends. "Looks like you're back where you belong, pig farmer."

"My f-f-father is a m-merchant!" Demri stood, angry. They never left him alone.

They all laughed. Even Myri. It was the first time she'd joined in laughing against Demri. Perhaps she *was* sleeping with Doram now. Either way, Demri's hurt doubled.

"Why are you even here, kid?" Doram asked. "You're too weak to be a Magicus."

"I p-p-p-passed the T-T-Trials just like anyone else!" Confrontation always enhanced his stutter. He became nervous. And Myri's presence didn't help matters.

Several of them chortled. One of Demri's sidekicks spoke up. "You mean you didn't notice the Magicai helping you along the way?" More laughter. Myri, too. In fact, she set her hand on Doram's shoulder to stop herself from doubling over.

"Stay away from Myri," Doram said, his threat real. Demri heard the change in his tone. He was serious.

"She's not your p-p-property."

"Aw, could I be?" Myri wrapped an arm around Doram.

Demri wanted to faint with embarrassment. Or anger. Or both. Doram didn't *deserve* her. A piece of shit like that with a delicate flower like Myri? Impossible.

She was foolish. Demri knew she'd regret hooking up with Doram. Nothing good would come of it.

Upon reflection, later in life, Demri would come to the ultimate conclusion: both Myri and Doram were pieces of shit, and Demri had become distracted by both lust and love. He never could decide which one was more prevalent.

She walked closer to Demri. He shivered. In anticipation? Nervousness? Was he scared?

"Come now, don't be afraid," she whispered to him like he was her lover. How he wished that were the case.

"I'm not," he said. Even he knew it didn't sound reassuring.

"We all make mistakes. Get this creep off me." She pulled her hand away from his. How'd that happen? Had *he* grabbed her fucking hand?

No. She'd taken his.

Doram and his friends rushed in. Fists beat him to the ground. He screamed. He fought, but he was much smaller than they were. As a kid, Demri had always been smaller than everyone. Ganged up against, he had no chance. He supposed he could've used his power. But he didn't want to kill anyone.

When he collapsed to the ground, feet kicked him. Slaps crossed his body. Somebody spat in his face.

He curled up in a ball, but the attack continued.

The beating was severe, but it wasn't life changing. He healed.

That time.

20 Years Ago

Ashmount's library had a restricted section. Books deemed too dangerous for students to read. Books that discussed disallowed theories. Experimentations gone wrong. Racy history. Anything that might confuse or corrupt a student.

But Demri Slarn was now an experienced Magicus. He'd completed the classes and was no longer a student. He had a decent work relationship with a Glyphist, who drew out Soul Glyphs for Demri many times. Demri wanted access to plenty of his power. Other Enforcers hesitated to have Soul Glyphs engraved on their skin. Demri considered those people stupid. Myri Celioh was one of them. Ever since that time in Ashmount's courtyard, he'd avoided the girl as much as he could. He'd had moderate success since she was in all of his classes. And as classes had progressed, he'd seen less and less of Doram Quandis. The man was a Collector. Once they'd made it through the introductory classes, he only saw Doram once in a while.

Demri kept the lighting at his library table to a minimum. He wanted to be undisturbed and hidden. He also knew what he was researching might raise a lot of eyebrows among Ashmount's leadership. Since the beginning, Demri had become interested in the possibilities of learning more than just what an Enforcer could do. The other Magicai were adamant it was impossible for anyone to be anything other than what an Examiner identified. To even attempt something like that could cause negative ramifications and immediate expulsion. Demri had perused a selection of textbooks and journals detailing various experiments that all denied it was possible. He ignored them. Demri felt a Magicus should be able to manipulate the Trace within them and to adhere to their desires, allowing somebody to select their path or learn another.

The Anecdotes and Curiosities of Enebrial Hubbart was a book published long after Enebrial's death. In it, Enebrial claimed he could be both an Enforcer *and* a Glyphist. After he had given several public speeches on the subject, Magicai had sent Collectors out to kill him. They'd succeeded. The Magicai of Ashmount, however, had failed to suppress Enebrial's teachings because the man had prepared for this possibility by sending his book to an independent person before delivering his first speech. After the Archmagicus at the time had announced Enebrial's death, his friend had published his writings.

Demri progressed through the book slowly, methodically. There was a lot of interesting information within, so he took various notes and suggested theories as he read. Some notes he stuck between the pages of the books. Other, more sensitive notes, he kept within his robes. He initialed them. Demri didn't want his research falling into the wrong hands, but if it did, he wanted the work to be his. Flawed thinking maybe.

Demri's goal was to figure out how to do this. If one could be both an Enforcer and a Glyphist, they'd never need help again. They could power themselves until they died, rendering Glyphists useless and opening them up to the four other branches of study. Collectors could harness the powers of an Enforcer, making their harvesting less necessary. There was a multitude of reasons it would make sense, and that's why his confusion at the Magicai's hesitancy to study any of it remained.

His eyes closed. Demri had been reading for hours. It was late, past midnight. His exhaustion was obvious, but he felt like he was close to discovering something.

"There he is." A voice at the door.

Demri opened his eyes, surprised there'd be anybody in the library at this time.

"Demri?" A professor walked in. "What are you doing here this late?"

"I told you, sir," Doram said. "He's trying to break the rules. He's trying to figure out how to extend his powers beyond that of an Enforcer." Doram followed the Magicus inside, a gloating look plastered on his face.

How did Doram know what Demri was doing? He'd never told a single soul. Because if anyone found out, they'd expel him. Or execute him. It was a serious crime to even consider researching the subject.

"Reading," Demri said. That wasn't a crime. He was terrible at thinking on the spot whenever Doram was around. Was it anger? Hatred? He wasn't afraid of the man. Well, maybe after the courtyard beating, he was. But only a little.

"I can see that. Give me the book." The Magicus held his hand out. Demri complied.

"He's trying to break the rules, sir. He's trying to be a Collector," Doram said. Not quite true. But accurate enough.

"*The Anecdotes and Curiosities of Enebrial Hubbart,* huh? An interesting read, I concur. I must insist you hand over your notes, Demri."

"Why?" Demri asked, panicked. His notes would expose him. True, he'd tried to write as little as possible to avoid this type of scenario. But he'd had to write a couple of complex theories, else he'd forget them in their entirety. And there was no messing around with magic.

"Policy, Demri. The Archmagicus will want to go over them. After all, serious allegations are being raised against you. If they are true, you will no longer be welcome here. You could face strong punishments." Which meant Collectors might harvest him.

Demri slid his notes across the table, toward the Magicus. He glared at Doram in disgust. Doram grinned back victoriously.

"Retire to your chambers, Demri. The Archmagicus will meet with you soon to discuss any problems." There would be problems. Any halfway-intelligent Magicus could decipher the hints in his work. Demri didn't understand how Doram knew.

Demri stood and walked out of the restricted section. Dozens of other Magicai watched him. They'd brought an army to make sure he did nothing stupid. *Good. They realize my power.* Or maybe they just knew he would use his.

He left the library. Four Magicai followed him to his room and posted themselves outside his door. He was a prisoner.

They will not keep me here.

If Ashmount and the Magicai dedicated themselves to learning, why wouldn't they care about advancing the ability of a Magicus? Wouldn't it be better to have advanced powers? The ability to rely on others less? This confused and frustrated him. And no matter what that Magicus professor had said, Demri had seen the truth in his eyes. The Archmagicus already thought Demri guilty. And that meant they were preparing to harvest him. So he had to leave or die.

Within minutes, Demri gathered his meager belongings. He locked his door, though that wouldn't prevent the Magicai from coming in if they wanted to, and slipped out the window. This caused immediate alarm because, of course, there were guards posted outside.

Doram stood in Demri's way, arms extended in front

of him, ready to fling magic. "We knew you'd try to escape, kid."

Heartbreakingly, Demri saw Myri. She looked angry. They all did.

"Let me g-go," he said.

"I don't think the Archmagicus would be too happy about that idea." The sadistic smile creeping up on Doram's face alarmed Demri.

It would seem the Archmagicus may have already given them the order to prevent me from leaving using any means possible. And of course he will try to use this as an excuse to kill me. Or they're acting as individuals. He didn't think so. The Magicai protected their laws over anything.

Most of the Magicai out here were newer, like Demri. They were all Enforcers or Collectors.

"Most of you d-d-don't even have any p-p-power," Demri said.

Doram snorted and waved to his companions. They all drank from a vial.

Well, fuck Mother Avani in the rear.

No way around it. Demri held his hand out, palm facing the ground. He consumed one of his Soul Glyphs, expelling the energy he sapped from himself. He shot a sizable amount of force at the ground, sending him skyrocketing up into the air and over the other Magicai. As he drifted closer to the ground, he did it again. Weaker, this time, so he landed softly, like he'd taken a few light steps.

"Kill him!" Doram said.

It was clear now. Doram's order was final.

Myri shouted, "No!"

Demri's heart issued a pang. Myri telling them not to kill him. She cared. At least a little. Enough to do the right thing. He saw her try and stop several of the others, but they pushed her aside. He ran.

A blast hit him in the back, and Demri stumbled facedown into the grassy courtyard. The skin on his cheek ripped open. He felt no other damage. It had just been a projected force. An attempt to capture, not kill.

"Don't listen to her," Doram said. "I'm in charge. Kill him!"

Doram had always been in charge, not Myri, so they listened.

A jet of flame shot across the courtyard at Demri. He flattened himself on the ground and felt it pass overhead, singeing the hair on his head.

Demri hopped to his feet, facing his attackers. He raised his hand in front of him, extending it upward. As he did, a wall of ice rose from the ground, blocking the other Magicai. He felt his body aging after the effort. Not much. But it was the first considerable feat he'd completed, so it was noticeable.

He turned and ran toward a bridge crossing the lava moat. *I need to jump off the volcano. It's my only chance of escape.*

Demri heard the ice wall shatter with a crack. They'd broken through. Footsteps of pursuers pounded behind.

Another jet of fire passed by him. An explosion blew clumps of dirt and grass up into the air, spraying his face. He blinked out the refuse and continued sprinting toward the bridge. A charge of lightning scorched the grass, inches from his left foot.

Something sharp pierced his shoulder. He groaned in pain but didn't falter. A quick glance at his injury revealed a shard of ice stained red with his blood. He turned and consumed a significant amount of energy. Several Soul Glyphs disappeared from his body to fuel it. Then he lobbed an enormous ball of fire at the group chasing him. It pleased Demri to see Myri was not among the pursuers.

Several of them screamed as the ball of fire engulfed them, turning them to flaming corpses. A few others encased themselves in shields that burned away and melted from the heat but prevented severe injury.

Doram fired a small, direct force into Demri's legs. He heard the *crack* of broken bones. Both of his femurs shattered. Demri tripped backward, making the bones grind together as he put more pressure on them. He gave an agonized scream, then plummeted to the ground. Tears streaked his face.

He tried to wiggle either of his legs. Neither worked. And every movement shifted the bones.

Seconds later, Doram and two others appeared in Demri's vision. They looked down at him, success written on their faces.

"I surrender," Demri said.

"He's trying to escape," Doram said, then held his hand out. A burst of flames lashed Demri across half of his face, licking his flesh away.

His skin sizzled. Demri felt it blister. His cheek bubbled and popped. The pain was excruciating. It was clear surrender wasn't an option. He couldn't stay.

He knew anything he did would further injure him. Unless he found a Healer, he'd also have permanent scars. However, if he stayed here, he'd die. They'd never let him live after he caused the deaths of fellow Magicai.

Doram held his hand out again, preparing for further torture.

Demri pressed his own hands to the ground and projected force from both palms. His legs lost the support of the ground as he launched himself into the air. For a second, he fell into unconsciousness while midair, the pain was so great. The descent, however, woke him.

He was heading straight toward the moat of lava.

Screaming in both pain and fear, he used his power several more times to keep himself afloat, using the force to push himself away. Distant shouting from the Magicai proved he was making fast progress.

He bounced himself through the air until he reached the edge of the volcano. Then he let himself fall. The Magicai hadn't pursued him. *Good.*

Falling from the volcano lasted much longer than Demri thought it should. He passed out another time or two on the way down. The pain was incredible. He gained consciousness a few dozen feet above ground. He used his power one last time, landed hard, and bounced once, aggravating his legs again and shocking his body with another wave of unbearable pain. Then he drifted off.

He came to. His legs were on fire. No, that was his face. Demri's legs had a persistent but dull ache. He knew the second he moved, the pain would intensify so much, he'd pass out again.

His mouth was dry. Damned, he was thirsty.

He rested his head atop a rock. His neck was stiffer than a wooden plank. He tried to sit up, but that didn't work. He groaned.

He tried to shift his legs. The pain flared up as expected.

He passed out.

Blinking, he woke again. It was dark. He'd slept through the day.

His face still felt afire. In his sleep, his head had

rolled off the rock, his neck stiffer than ever. He couldn't turn his head to the right.

He shivered. It was cold, freezing. Qothe wasn't cold on a normal night. Tonight, though, with the breeze and an inability to move, his body temperature was swept away. *Is this my tomb?*

Demri's stomach rumbled. He had to piss. He couldn't move too well. Demri yanked his robes up and tried to piss away from where he lay. Urine dribbled out, coating his body.

The cold intensified.

He'd light a fire, but there was nothing to light.

So instead, he resigned himself to dying. He closed his eyes and went to sleep, hoping the cold took him.

Daylight. The brightness activated a stunning headache. He moaned in despair.

"Careful," someone said.

Alarmed, Demri turned his head.

A man smiled at him. He was picking his teeth with a bloody knife. Blood dripped from his mouth, down his chin. "Wouldn't want you to hurt yourself."

"T-t-too late."

"Hit your head?"

"B-b-born with the stutter."

The man with the knife nodded. "Born with the burned face and broken legs, too?" He flicked the knife, the point digging into his gum. Droplets of blood dripped down his chin. "Looks like you could use some help."

"Looks like you want an infection in your m-mouth. What are you d-d-doing here?"

"Heard there was an invitation to get tested at

Ashmount for the Trace. Figured I'd see what it was all about. Wouldn't be too bad to be a Magicus." The man stopped picking at his teeth. He looked at the knife, sad.

"D-d-don't bother. They'll just k-k-kill you."

The man grunted. He started filing a fingernail with the blade. "What happened to you?"

"I j-j-jumped off the volcano."

The man laughed. "What *actually* happened."

Demri just stared at him.

"Oh. You're serious."

"Yes."

"Broke your legs."

"You're a student of observation."

"You need help."

"Yes."

"I'm not doing anything. Suppose I can help you. For a price."

"What d-d-do you want?"

"Interesting question, that. I'll let you know sometime. Until then, I'm Caius."

"D-Demri."

"Let's get you sitting up."

Not too much later and a caravan showed up, heading to Sultiva. Taking pity on the injured Demri, they offered them a free ride.

It took a long time for Demri's wounds to heal. Too long. But they healed. Enough, anyway.

———

Present Day
Remeria

Demri woke. Porric's snoring was the culprit. Or the dream. He wasn't sure which. He wiped sweat from his forehead. *Myri. Doram.* Both caused him to wake sweating. One of love, one of hatred. He hated himself for his younger feelings. *Caius.* Demri figured if the man was going to collect on the deal they'd made, he would've done it by now. But Caius was a mysterious man. Demri still didn't know where he came from or anything about his life before meeting Demri.

He wondered if anyone had ever found the notes that he'd hidden within the books at Ashmount's library. If anybody'd pieced together the same secrets he'd once found. Or if anyone suspected the Magicai of any wrongdoing at all. Most Magicai had unquestioning faith in the system. Probably because the Magicai were the ones who gave them their powers, and, because of that, their money and status. The Trials granted the Magicai an unlimited source of harvestable bodies. A quick note of apology and a sack of coin often deterred any suspicious families, though Demri, and all other Magicai, knew the truth—most people didn't survive the Trials.

Demri was one of the few who realized why. It wasn't because the Magicai wanted the best of the best. They just wanted their stores of Collector vials to remain stocked. Nobody knew this when they sent off their children to the school. Their husbands or wives. Brothers or sisters. And those who passed the Trials kept their mouths shut because they gained access to power. They'd survived, so it didn't matter that everyone else had perished. The ones who'd died most often came from families who needed money. That was why they'd gone to Ashmount in the first place. Receiving another payment on behalf of their death was a bonus in most cases. Sometimes, a prominent family would become investigative. Those matters, the Archmagicus handled personally, and they often resulted in a larger sack of coin being handed over.

They all need to burn.

Demri opened his eyes and looked across the fire. Magicus Glaouse was standing and staring up at the stars. Demri wasn't the only one who couldn't sleep that night.

He rolled over, trying to fix the cramps in his legs. Now he faced Caius. The man's eyes were open, knife in hand. He was watching Glaouse.

"Soon," Demri whispered.

To his friend.

KELDEN STOOLE

2nd Cycle of Autumn, 231st Reign of Garcovi
Ashmount, Qothe

The Magicai killed, or harvested, several other late arrivals. It was a revolting process, one that made him sick. The worst had been Sungoa, though not just because she was his friend. The harvesting was shocking to observe.

It's not that Kelden was emotionless. He just had severe difficulty expressing emotions most of the time. The death of Sungoa had surprised him. He knew he should be sad but felt relief. It was one step away from *him* being the one they harvested. Watching her body deflate was even more painful. *That could've been me.* Others being harvested was one of the worst things Kelden had ever witnessed. Sungoa was nothing now. An empty sack of skin. He didn't know how to describe it. Her entire body. Her black hair, blue eyes, her smile. Everything . . . gone. Except for that empty sack of skin, which seemed to just melt away after a time.

He supposed he didn't need to express his emotions.

Sungoa's family wasn't there watching him. Nor was anyone else that knew her or him. His guilt rose to the forefront of his thoughts. He recognized the need to feel sadness, even felt a twinge of the emotion, but expressing anything more was impossible. Ever since his mother had died, he'd vowed to be stronger. Perhaps he'd worked on that too much, and now it was difficult to even feel sadness.

None of this makes sense. Why do the Magicai want so many of them to fail the Trials? Why kill those who fail? It seemed strange. Even those who failed the Trials could be put to use somewhere. Something wasn't adding up, but Kelden didn't know what. It seemed so wasteful to have so many people die. People who could become Magicai. If he passed the Trials, he made a vow to find out.

Ko-Hkar laid a hand on his shoulder. "Warrior spirits live after death. Your friend was a good fighter. She'll be fine. Killiak, lord of lords, will watch over her. Come. We eat." Kelden knew Ko-Hkar referred to one of the Vessian gods, deities the rest of the world had forgotten centuries ago except for Mother Avani.

"What? Food? Now?" Kelden's opposition of this idea wasn't wholehearted. He wasn't one for brooding, even for people he loved. What was the sense? There was nobody to perform for, and she wasn't there to see it. He had his memories.

"Eat. Honor your friend."

Kelden stood. He took one last glance at where Sungoa's body had been. "Farewell."

Kelden was so lost in thought that he didn't remember eating. He focused on his guilt. Once a bit of time went by, he wouldn't feel anything anymore. Just the perpetual numbness swirling around inside him. A touch of emotion here or there, nothing more.

In a loud, enhanced voice, a female Magicus called out, "No time for rest. Gather round." She stood in the center of a circle, surrounded by small painted squares. Each was just big enough for a person to stand within.

Kelden and Ko-Hkar took their spots in adjacent squares alongside the other candidates. There were forty of them left.

"Wits and intelligence are important. Often, we're relied upon to solve problems. Wasting our power to solve everything would fast deplete the Magicai. Being clever is imperative. We will ask each of you a question. If you don't provide the correct answer, you will not move on." *Meaning they'll harvest us.*

She turned to the first student in her path, a man with dark brown hair. Words materialized in front of the man, hovering in the air. They could be read from any angle.

> *Not wet, nor dry.*
> *It won't be long, and soon I'll die.*
> *Often, I'm rank with curious odor.*
> *Sometimes enough that you won't go there.*
> *Found within forests and basement cracks.*
> *I'm never enough to provide what one lacks.*

The man read the words over several times, lip curled in confusion. "A frog?"

"Wrong. The answer you seek is 'dew,'" the Magicus said.

The ground beneath the man rumbled, and the ground under his feet turned softer. Slowly, he started being pulled down. The man reached out to the people on either side of him. "Help! Help!"

A sick crunching sound, and the man yelled in pain. It sounded like his bones were being ground up beneath the surface. He screamed louder, and then a snapping came from his ankles.

The Magicus wasted no time, and words appeared in the air in front of the next candidate.

It took an agonizing length of time for the small pit to consume the man. Although he'd died long before his body had disappeared, he'd screamed bloodcurdling cries during the next three people to be tested. Two of them failed, contributing their screams to the next people in line. Kelden was sure that was another part of the test.

The cacophony of dying screams didn't end. More people than not failed their questions.

Ko-Hkar kept eyeing Kelden. He knew Ko-Hkar would expect his help in this as he'd promised. There were no rules saying you couldn't help one another, and several had tried. Kelden knew plenty of answers others didn't but didn't want to say anything. Identifying himself as a threat might cause other candidates to want to kill him before the Trials ended.

The Magicus reached Ko-Hkar. Words appeared in front of him.

If me multiplied thrice equaled another number doubled nice,

Would six by five be exact or imprecise?

A logic puzzle.

Ko-Hkar started counting numbers on his fingers.

Kelden couldn't decide what to do. Should he help Ko-Hkar? By letting the man fail, he'd get rid of a potential problem. But helping the man could pay off in the long run. He decided he should help Ko-Hkar. If it wasn't for him, Kelden would've died already.

Six by five. Thirty. It couldn't be measurements because that wouldn't make sense. Screams of a dying woman two feet over shook him out of his thoughts.

Crunching bones and the sound of flesh tearing broke his concentration a second time.

Kelden ran through numbers in his head that equaled thirty when multiplied. *One by thirty. Fifteen by two. Ten by three. Six by five.* He snapped his fingers. Five by three would be fifteen. Fifteen doubled, thirty. They didn't equal one another, but the first line said "if." And if they did, the answer would be thirty, which meant six by five would be exact.

"Ko-Hkar. It's exact."

Ko-Hkar looked at Kelden, and his eyes narrowed. It seemed like he didn't trust him.

"It is, Ko-Hkar. I'm not breaking my promise—"

"Imprecise. I don't trust you."

Kelden's eyes bulged. "What are you doing?"

"Wrong," the Magicus said.

"Shit. I thought you'd betray me." The big man's ankles shattered as he lurched down. He didn't make any sounds other than an occasional grunt.

Kelden watched, horrified.

"Next," the Magicus said. She waved a hand, and words appeared in front of Kelden. He didn't notice them for several minutes, as he watched Ko-Hkar's body slipping farther down.

"I should've . . . believed . . . you," Ko-Hkar said, wincing in agony.

"Yes. You should have." Kelden recovered and read his own problem. He felt lucky in that moment to have a lack of emotions, because Ko-Hkar's nonbelief after Kelden committed himself to helping him felt *wrong*. Even though he'd considered betraying the man and might've done the same in Ko-Hkar's position.

> *I'm warm but not living.*
> *I am also alive.*

People often travel to me, then flee me soon
thereafter.
Hearts reside within.
What am I?

Kelden read the lines several times through. Failing this would lead to his death. His initial thought was a kitchen, but kitchens weren't alive.

The Magicus hadn't told them they had any time limit, so he took his time. Kelden's thoughts wandered. He thought of his father, Hillion, and of Warwin, the village he'd grown up in. Of Sungoa. Of Graylan and his family. He thought of home. *Home.* A house is warm not living. An occupied house is alive. People come and go in houses all the time. Home is where the heart is. *Home is the answer.*

"Home," he said.

"Wrong."

The ground opened beneath him, and he started sinking.

"Wait, what? Explain how it's *not*."

"The answer is 'volcano.'"

"Before you murder me, tell me how my answer is wrong. It's not." The ground enveloped his ankles, closing around him and sucking him farther down, and a pressure built up against his skin. It hurt. Something—felt like rocks—turned and ground against him. His toes snapped. Kelden moaned. Bones crunched. The ground kept yanking him, pulling his legs deeper. He felt skin splitting.

"Halt," Magicus Jakci Robinius said.

Kelden lost his balance and fell. A loud crack as an ankle broke and bones ripped through his skin. His vision darkened. He groaned again. The earth continued to chew him up.

"He got it wrong," the female Magicus said.

"He isn't wrong though. His answer fits. He proceeds."

Relief washed through Kelden, but agony followed. He couldn't concentrate.

Somebody knelt beside Kelden, and the ground opened back up. His feet were two bloody masses. The female Magicus touched him, and a wave of coolness entered his skin. Bones shifted and snapped again as they fit themselves back where they belonged, and his dislocated thumb clicked back into place.

"Congratulations on making it this far," Magicus Jakci Robinius addressed all of them who remained. It was two hours after the trivia test. Kelden's feet had been fixed, he'd had water, and now he was at the next Trial. "You've made the top twenty-four candidates, and now the trimmings become smaller in scale. Perhaps none of you will fail this." Magicus Jakci smiled. Kelden knew the Magicus didn't believe that. "This test will focus on spontaneity, how well you adapt, and your problem-solving skills."

The man started pacing, as he was wont to do. He stroked his beard. Stopped, likely conscious of the habit. Immediately began stroking it again. "Up ahead, you will meet a crater. This is the summit of the volcano. In the center of this crater, are twenty-four keys suspended in midair. Bring one back. Each one unlocks a dorm room back at Ashmount. This is your last Trial. Begin."

Though the candidates started out running, it became clear this wasn't smart. The pass to the summit was narrow and steep. Single file, the group trudged up the path.

The sulfurous odor of the volcano had been strong the entire ascent. But now it was becoming intolerable. Fumes swirled out the top of the bowl they hiked toward. It became difficult to see through the smog.

The group of candidates approached the large opening to the depths of the volcano. Several observing Magicai suspended themselves in midair and floated above the crater. The smoke seemed to evade them.

The keys twirled above the bubbling lava. What seemed like dozens of different pathways led out over the volcano. Knotted rope ladders twisted in the wind. Long wooden plank bridges creaked and groaned. A tall tower led to ropes that one could swing from. The most prominent path looked like a covered hallway extending itself all the way across the crater with plenty of windows and came out on the other side. Small buildings spaced at even intervals surrounded the volcano's gaping maw. Perhaps they were small cabins to rest within.

A sign nearby read, "The path not traveled is the way to proceed."

One of the candidates ran into the hallway. Kelden watched him make his way to the middle of the stretch. He reached his hand out of an opening and grabbed a key. About halfway through his return, it looked like the floor opened beneath him. Screaming, he plummeted into the crater.

For the first time, a Magicus approached them in the middle of a Trial. "We are now going to separate you. Think. Consider what you've seen. You will be isolated in separate soundproof buildings. You may watch other attempts at the keys, but you may not collaborate anymore. Each building contains a small portion of food and water, and that is all. If you die of natural causes, you have failed the test. We will not aid you unless you receive a key. One more thing. If you leave your building, we will not allow reentry."

Kelden entered his personal housing unit and examined the contents. The walls were empty of any decoration aside from the quote posted on the sign they'd seen earlier. "The path not traveled is the way to proceed" was painted on a wall. A stiff wooden chair was the only furniture. On the chair's seat rested a canteen filled with water. A bag—holding a small amount of hard bread, some dried venison, and an apple—sat behind the canteen.

It was clear to Kelden that the erectors of the building hadn't intended on preventing the day's heat from permeating it. He felt like he was boiling alive inside it. Trapped in an oven. He guessed it was a way to force people to attempt to retrieve their keys faster.

Kelden sat on the chair. He took a small sip of water and ate a sample of the meat. It would be important to ration his resources, but he didn't want to make a hasty decision and fall to his death. Or die of thirst.

Hours slipped past. Sweat coated his body. Steam covered the windows. He had to keep wiping it off to watch what happened outside. Twice, he'd seen people attempt different obstacles. Both times, they'd reached for a key. Both times, the obstacle sabotaged them, and they'd fallen to their deaths, the key floating back up to join its brethren.

Night approached. The sun went down, and the temperature dipped. He had no blankets or insulation to warm himself, but the volcano's warmth kept the building heated. Starlight was all Kelden had to see with.

When dawn came, a Magicus opened the door to Kelden's building.

"Eighteen of you remain. Nobody has claimed a key." The door closed, and the Magicus left.

Kelden spent the morning chewing on the hard bread. He knew this would dehydrate him more, but he also knew if he had bread leftover when he was out of water, he'd never be able to consume it.

The day grew hotter. The water's level lessened. Even rationing it, Kelden was sure he'd be out by the end of the day.

He huddled in the corner, trying to remain under the heat. This didn't make a noticeable difference, but whenever he stood, the temperature felt like it escalated. Either way, it was stifling. If he went outside without thinking about everything, he could end up dead. So he preferred to take his time. He kept thinking about all the needless deaths, all the people who could've become extra Magicai, even if they were grunts or expendable. *Do they not have the finances to pay them?* He realized that was a foolish question. They handed out coins to anybody who got tested, and there were a lot of people who traveled to Ashmount to secure that money. The brutality of the Trials surprised him. And that Kelden had survived for as long as he did. He'd passed every-thing, aside from this one. He even passed his riddle, by a technicality. Lucky. He was lucky that Jakci Robinius had been there to stop him from dying. He needed to proceed with caution.

Thirsty, he took a drink. He ate the apple, as it was already bruising. Growing up in Warwin, Kelden knew the threat of not getting enough water. The mind would start playing tricks. Hallucinations and dreamlike fantasies would become all too real. More than once, somebody had died getting lost in the wilderness. One time, somebody had survived. The detailed description they'd given when Kelden had inquired what they'd gone through was pretty frightening. They'd lost their grip on reality. If that happened, Kelden would fail the test and die. He didn't want to die.

He watched two more people die that day. One took a rope ladder. That woman didn't even get to a key before it tore in the middle and she fell to her death. The second person, gender indistinguishable because of their long hair and lithe form, climbed the tower and tried swinging on the rope. They were dexterous enough to catch a key. However, the rope snapped on the swing back to the tower.

Kelden suspected the Magicai had rigged all the obstacles. There was something he was missing.

Which of the obstacles was the path not traveled? If the Magicai had rigged all the obstacles, how would he get a key? He figured he'd try each obstacle, but he would check each individual rope, each wooden plank, every inch of the obstacle. If one of them stood out, perhaps that would be the way.

He would not be hasty. Another day of observation. He had plenty of food still and a third of the canteen left. His rationing was paying off.

Late that afternoon, either a bunch of the students had become very brave or they'd run out of food. He guessed the latter. Everyone who used an obstacle fell. Two of the students jumped off the side. Were they in that much despair?

That night, Kelden finished the rest of the hard bread, trying his best to conserve his remaining water supply.

The Magicus returned in the morning. "Seven of you remain." They left. No mention of the keys.

Kelden gnawed on venison and took time to consider what he should do. How many people survived the Trials and learned from the Magicai? It seemed an enormous waste for them to let so many potential students die. He supposed they were only looking for the best. Something wasn't making sense though. *Why have all the obstacles if they all lead to death? Are they distractions?* But then what was the clear path? Kelden was sure at least one person had been on each obstacle. He wasn't sure if it was the entire obstacle that was the issue or smaller parts of them. Or the way they'd been interacting with them.

He watched two more people attempt obstacles. Failures. As far as Kelden was aware, nobody had yet to return to safety after grabbing a key.

He finished the venison and downed the rest of the water. It was now early afternoon, and he'd waited long enough. Watched plenty of people fall to their deaths. There wasn't any more thinking he could do to figure it out. It was time to go look, before he became weak from dehydration.

Kelden was selfish. He valued his own life over anything. If given the opportunity to live forever, he'd take it without a second thought. If it was at the expense of somebody he loved, he wouldn't care who it was. He would find a replacement in the future. The problem was, in Kelden's opinion, there was no opportunity to live forever. So he had to be meticulous if he wanted to stay alive. Sometimes, he dropped this fear and did something stupid. Like helping Sniffles when Ko-Hkar was attacking her.

Light cascaded into his eyes when he opened the door. He blinked and walked toward the mouth of the crater. His first plan was to inspect each obstacle and see if he could find anything that hinted at being dangerous. If he could find the source of the sabotaged equipment, perhaps he'd be able to determine how to navigate them.

The first path to the floating keys he approached was the hallway that extended across the entire crater. He examined the exterior of the wood, and it all seemed perfect. Several windows set at equal points across walls. He decided not to spend much time on this construct. It was the easiest way toward the keys and therefore a death trap. Nothing came easy.

He examined the tower and discounted that as well. Though it was sturdy-looking, he didn't think swinging from the rope like a deranged person would let him continue living.

The rope ladders also appeared well-made. Everywhere he checked, on every piece of equipment, nothing looked suspicious. Which meant they were maybe being manipulated by the Magicai. Perhaps the Magicai controlled all the traps. He wasn't sure.

Nothing stood out. No rips, no breaks, no markings. A long column of dark gray smoke wafted his way. He coughed and dodged around it.

Suddenly, he realized the solution. *The path not traveled is the way to proceed.* He knew other candidates attempted each path. Maybe not every rope or step, but they'd traveled on them. Before the Magicai had set up the area, the only way to the center of the crater would have been floating, like the people observing him were doing now.

He peered into the depths of Ashmount. Down below, he saw bubbling lava, though distorted by a toxic-looking smog.

Kelden jumped.

It was the most frightening thing he would ever do. The lava beneath him gurgled and bubbled like a hungry monster waiting for him to fall into its giant maw. Then it seemed like he was slowing down. Until he was certain of it. Like he slid down a gentle slide made of smoke.

The fall, or the glide now, came to a soft, pillowy stop. Above him, the sky was blurry. The floating Magicai, fuzzy. He climbed to his feet, choking on fumes.

He stood on a translucent platform. *Ah, of course. They wouldn't let the ones that failed fall to their death and disappear in the lava. They'd want to harvest them. Like Sungoa.* Several blood smears across the clear surface added credibility to his theory.

At the center of the platform was a small box. He approached it and peered inside to find a bunch of small iron keys. A note pinned to the box read, *Congratulations, you have passed. Take one.*

So he did.

The platform Kelden jumped onto led toward a cavern dug into the side of the volcano's crater. Torches lit the narrow path, and he wondered why the volcanic fumes weren't affecting him. The Magicai must've done something. He set a fast pace, the lights disappearing in a downward trend. After what Kelden guessed to be an hour of hiking, he came to a door.

Opening it, he saw the setting sun. Shading his eyes, he walked out of the cavern. Two robed women were waiting. Magicai. He recognized one of them as the Healer who'd greeted him when he'd first arrived.

"You've passed. Welcome to Ashmount, Magicus," the one he didn't know said. The pin on her robes were of spectacles, making her an Examiner. She had pale skin and charcoal-black lips.

"Thank you," Kelden said.

"I'm the head Examiner. I'm here to analyze your

Trace and see which school of power you'll be most akin to. You are Kelden Stoole?" A pair of spectacles hung around her neck. She wore another pair on her face, which appeared aged and weathered.

Kelden collapsed to the ground, exhausted. He confirmed her question with a nod.

The Healer professor knelt next to him. She touched his arm. "Just checking to see if you have any wounds." After a moment, she said, "It appears you're just winded."

Not far away, he saw Ashmount. He'd come out the base of the volcano and was close to the moat of lava surrounding the school.

The Examiner smiled, writing something down. "Okay, you're good to go."

"What am I to train as?" It had to be an Enforcer. That's all he could see himself doing. It was also the most powerful role. Anything else would be unacceptable.

"You'll find out soon. I need to report my findings to the Archmagicus first. For now, go across the bridge, and you'll find a table we've set up with food. Join your classmates, and you'll receive more direction soon. Once again, congratulations."

Kelden crossed the bridge and counted six other people who'd passed the test. He knew there weren't many left behind him. All those people dead seemed like a colossal waste. Sungoa among them. Ko-Hkar too. Once again, Kelden was reminded how he *should* feel and how he *actually* felt. He should feel sad. Instead, he only felt relief it'd been her and not him who died.

He took a goblet of iced water and drained the entire thing. *How do they have ice? Or did they make it?* The other bridges that crossed the moat were upside down. *Are they always like that?* The parts of the horseshoe-shaped bridges that one walked over were submerged in the lava flow. He learned later this was to prevent civilians from showing up unexpected. A rogue Magicus could still flip the bridges, but often an Enforcer or a Collector was assigned to watch the bridges. They were also there to allow visiting Healers, Glyphists, and Examiners across since they couldn't flip a bridge on their own. The lava wasn't hot enough to melt the stone, so the bridge was left untouched.

Later, after another three people arrived from Ashmount, the Magicai brought them to a dorm. There were ten of them. Ten out of the hundreds who'd competed in the Trials. Kelden learned that each class was a different size, which was determined by how many candidates there were, the type of Trials in place, and the luck and skill of those competing. Some classes had only a couple of people, while others ended up with hundreds.

Each dorm room contained a small bed topped with silk sheets and pillows, a rug, a desk with a chair, and a trunk with a lock. Kelden doubted the lock would prevent anybody from getting into it if they desired, once they learned their abilities.

He retired to his room early. His exhaustion prevented him from wanting to do anything other than sleep. Before Kelden climbed into bed, a knock on the door startled him. When he opened it, two people greeted him—the head Examiner and, to Kelden's surprise, the Archmagicus.

The Archmagicus gestured inside the room. "May we trouble you with a bit of discussion before you rest for the night?"

Kelden allowed them entry.

The Examiner carried a sheet of parchment. She glanced down at it. "Kelden Stoole, correct?"

"Yes." He figured that was obvious, considering she'd just talked to him earlier.

"You are to be a Glyphist."

A Glyphist? That can't be right. "Are you sure?" He was to be an Enforcer.

"Yes. Should you not be?"

"I just felt like I would be an Enforcer."

The Archmagicus tightened his lips. A smile, perhaps. Or it was disapproval. Impossible to tell. "We rarely receive what we dream of, Kelden. Glyphists are both valuable and important. I think you'll be happy to have Enforcers paying you money to allow them access to their powers."

"But *I* won't have any power."

"Magical power? No. You are correct. You will not. You will have political power though. And economical power. People will pay a great deal to have a trained Glyphist around. Without a Glyphist, they cannot replenish their Enforcers' Wells. And without their power, Enforcers are useless. These powers are all inter-connected, Kelden. You need Examiners to identify people with the Trace and which branch they can use. Enforcers can use their powers to do innumerable things, though they must be physical. Glyphists power these Enforcers. Healers can protect everyone by healing them at the sacrifice of their own lives. And Collectors can harvest people with the Trace in order to power themselves with limited abilities. They can also give that power to Enforcers. All of them are important, Kelden."

"Yeah. You're right, Archmagicus."

"I am."

The head Examiner activated his newfound power, which she likened to uncorking a bottle. An icy chill spread across his body when she did it, and then he just felt *different.* She explained more, but whatever else they spoke of, Kelden didn't hear it. He had power now, but not the right power. The results dissatisfied him. Sure, he could make some money. And yes, he could profit. He'd never have an issue earning an income again, so that was a tremendous relief. He couldn't help but feel put off though, like he'd failed his personal destiny.

What made matters even worse? He was the only Glyphist out of the ten students. Everyone else ended up being Enforcers.

VILLIC THE IMBUER

1st Cycle of Winter, 231st Reign of Garcovi
Remeria

"Speaker, quiet yourself!" Sometimes, Villic forgot that when he spoke to Speaker, everyone heard. Speaker could hear Villic's thoughts and kept recommending they talk that way. This frightened Villic. He didn't like the idea that *anybody* could hear his thoughts. Those were private. Despite having tried to get along with Speaker, Villic just couldn't get over his suspicions that Speaker was a god or some test of loyalty to the gods. He wouldn't fail it.

Men from various clans stared in Villic's direction. *The gods know I'm going insane.*

"You are not going insane, Villic."

Villic hissed, unnerved by Speaker listening to his thoughts. They were packing camp, and Speaker wouldn't stop talking. "If you don't stop, I will find a group of lions and kill us *both*."

"There are no lions in Remeria. There is no death for me. I will find a new body at some point."

They'd been in the Remerian plains a week—after taking several more to traverse the rest of the Vessian desert—and were making slow progress across the grassy plains. Having just passed the Valkrynd Mountains, they were in the open area that connected Calrym, Remeria, and Vessia together. This stop had allowed their camels to rest and feed themselves, as the Camel Clans hadn't been past the mountain range guarding Remeria's true borders before. The clans planned on splitting up today and, riding at their own pace, raiding Remeria individually until they reconvened outside the capital.

Villic didn't understand that but didn't care. And he'd forgotten he wasn't in Vessia anymore. He spent more time thinking than observing his surroundings. The long stretches of land were familiar enough, but they were greener. Several large bushes, bush trees, dotted the land. It wasn't dry here, but it was humid.

Several others also struggled with the parasite in their head. Villic overheard a woman from Seven Signs cursing out loud, telling Scarab to stop. He wished he'd thought to call the voice Scarab. Scarab was a good name for something that needed to be killed.

"Don't you find it amusing that out of all people, I got the one afraid to even think? Communication is the only way this is going to work, Villic. I could prevent you from using your new powers."

I don't care. "I don't care."

"I can hear your thoughts, Villic. You need to trust me."

"I don't trust Lurzal, god of deception. You are a plague in my head. Go away." Villic gritted his teeth. If he could've killed Speaker, he would've then.

"I'm not the God of Deception, despite whatever you believe. And I'll pretend you didn't think that about me."

That's what Lurzal would say.

Speaker didn't answer him. Good. Hopefully, he'd stay hidden awhile.

A moment later, Speaker said, *"You are impossible."*

Villic slammed his head into a nearby bush tree. Chips of bark peppered the air, and a small smattering of blood stained the log that supported the plant. He rubbed his head, smearing blood across the gash he'd created. Speaker said nothing. *Maybe I killed him.*

"Foolish."

Villic screamed, dropped to his knees, and stared at the top of the bush tree. He'd normally ask for help from the gods, but the bush trees hid them from view. He was alone in the wilderness with nobody to guide him. The Splintered Manes leader would guide him, but Jedkah didn't understand what Villic was going through. He wasn't an Imbuer.

"Bashing your head in will only result in a much shorter life. Is that what you desire, Villic?"

"Why do you keep torturing me?" Villic looked at the plant again. He wanted to bash his head against it a second time, but the bark was much harder than he'd expected. He also didn't think it'd remove Speaker from his head, so there was no point.

"I merely seek understanding. Companionship. Otherwise, you're carrying me around for nothing. I am supposed to be the vessel to your powers. I cannot help someone who doesn't want it."

"I don't want it. I don't want it. I don't want it!"

"Let me know when you do." And Speaker was quiet. For good this time. More stares from other clan members. Villic ignored them.

Villic felt something change. Something retracting. Pulling back. He grabbed his spear from Dunecrest. Hefting the weapon in both hands, he thrust forward, igniting the end in flame. No fire appeared. No orange glow. Speaker wasn't letting him use his powers. At least he knew now. In battle, that would be a poor thing to find out. But at least Speaker was gone.

Villic replaced the spear and patted Dunecrest on the neck. The camel snorted.

Villic smiled. With Speaker gone and his powers no longer there, he was the old Villic. Villic of the Splintered Manes. Villic the Imbuer no longer. Perhaps during the invasion in Remeria, he'd feel normal again. Though he'd miss the respect he'd garnered from his fellow warriors, being a regular warrior again would be nice.

"Return to your camel, Villic!" Jedkah sounded angry.

Villic mounted Dunecrest fast. He didn't care if Jedkah was mad, though he wasn't going to disobey a command from the clan leader. *Villic was happy. When I return to Vessia, I'll be a new man.*

Villic had forgotten that the ultimate goal of the war was to secure land for the clans to move into. He'd forgotten that if they won, they wouldn't be returning to Vessia. The good fortune of Speaker's disappearance had distracted Villic. The sudden realization that he wouldn't be returning to Vessia if they did win didn't ruin his happiness.

As Villic joined the Splintered Manes's procession, the other clans split up and traveled in their respective clans. Jedkah explained they planned to meet outside Remeria's capital, Andora. Together, they would require far too much food to make the journey. So instead, each clan took a separate path in the hopes they'd stumble upon a village, or perhaps a caravan, or maybe a farm, so they could resupply.

INTERLUDE
ROYAL

1st Cycle of Winter, 231st Reign of Garcovi
Coldridge, Cyrok

S traight down the gullet. The warm, burning sensation of whiskey. Another shot absorbed. Royal smacked his lips and allowed his tongue to explore the wild goatee around his mouth, scooping up excess liquid before wiping his mouth with the sleeve of his captain's jacket. No sense in wasting it. He'd earn a solid reprimand for stained clothing, but he'd been beyond caring for several hours now.

The lively inn was annoying Royal. He preferred peace. Quiet was the first step to happiness. Or that's what he always said anyway. He tipped his chair back, leaning it against the corner of the room. His muddy boots propped up on the wooden table. Light danced across his legs, but he kept his face in darkness, away from prying eyes.

Though his actual name was Decklin, everyone called him Royal. Couldn't remember who had dubbed him Royal, but he remembered the reason well and good enough: "You act more like royalty than a king." Which he didn't think was true, but he didn't mind the name.

Royal leaned over and spat on the tavern floor. When people first met him and his friends introduced him as Royal, they'd often lift a brow or offer a confused look. Grungy was one way of describing him, and he wouldn't argue about it. It all came down to attitude, his friends would say.

"C'mere." The server didn't hear him. "C'mere!"

The server turned, saw who addressed her, and hurried over. "Royal." Her demeanor suggested distaste. Royal couldn't care less.

"More." He handed her his empty shot glass. "Three more."

She took the glass without a word and disappeared among the crowd of idiots jumping and cheering at the dancing ladies and the musicians.

Too many people got hyped up about a few women with short dresses. Who cared if you could see a knee? If his cock wasn't being serviced, Royal couldn't care less. He wasn't a man who enjoyed teases. That only led to servicing yourself, and Royal wasn't about hard work in any sense.

He reached up and rubbed his eyes. He knew there'd be massive dark circles around them. Sleep had become elusive as of late. News had come in: some ruffians had raided Gyrloft, burning it to the ground. Governess Stasia Falconel had dispatched messages to all towns in Cyrok, alerting them to danger. Stationed in Coldridge, Royal wasn't too concerned. Coldridge was a port town. They had military ships in the oceans doing reconnaissance and training exercises. If any attack came by sea, they'd know about it. With the governess's warning, they'd erected several outposts to survey surrounding lands and watch for land armies. Though not stated, the governess had hinted Calrym may be behind the attack.

Royal, and the rest of the military stationed in Coldridge, had two missions. Watch for *any* sign of Calrym and report back to her. The same of any armed forces they spotted. They were to prepare ships for fleeing refugees, though this was only a precaution.

A man hollered and flung money onto the dancers' stage. Royal sighed and rolled his eyes.

The server returned with three shots of whiskey, setting them next to his boots.

"How much?" he asked.

"We'll just put it on your tab."

Royal chuckled. She didn't understand. "Not the alcohol." He set his boots on the floor and leaned forward into the light. Flames from the nearby fireplace flickered. He gave her a look, up and down.

The disgust on her face was noticeable. He didn't care.

"More than you could afford," she said.

"I might have more than you think. If you change your mind, let me know." She stalked off, insulted perhaps. Contemplative, Royal hoped.

The side effects of too much alcohol were showing up. His hand trembling, he tipped a small portion of the whiskey on his pants. He downed the rest of it. Straight down the gullet. The back of his throat burned. Warmth descended through his body again. He smacked his lips and licked his whiskers. No sense wasting any of it. Wiped his mouth with the sleeve of his jacket. Set his feet back up on the table and leaned his chair back into shadows.

Many uneventful minutes passed. Royal was beside himself with happiness. Being left alone was his favorite pastime. But this didn't last for long. The server was back.

His mood interrupted, Royal glanced over at her, annoyed. "Yes?" The servers were to leave you alone unless you bothered them first. That was why he came here.

"I'll do it," she said.

Well, that changes everything. Royal sat up, eager, interested. His boots clomped on the floor again, and mud spattered the wall behind him. He couldn't care less about the tavern's wall. That's why they hired people—to clean up after pieces of shit like him.

"I'll do it," she repeated with a blank look on her face. Concealing her disgust for him. "For a half cycle of my pay."

Royal reckoned that was fine. He made far more than a tavern server. "Are you worth that?" He spat on the floor again. Damn, the whiskey made him salivate. The server gave him a disapproving gaze but said nothing more. He spent too much money there for anyone to get upset over a glob of mucus.

His tongue flicked through the open hole in the back of his mouth where he was missing a tooth. Rot had taken it. He examined the server, thoughtful. A cute girl, younger than he'd consider on a normal day. Clean hair, dirty hands. The type of body itching for a baby, though her father hadn't yet married her off. If there was going to be a dancer in the tavern, it should've been this server. He hadn't realized it when he'd asked her because he hadn't been serious. Turns out, he somehow asked the most attractive girl working that night. An empty hook secures the fish. A rare occurrence, but he'd seen it happen.

"Well?" She crossed her hands, one tapping a large tray against her thigh. Almost inviting. The position squished her bosom together, threatening to spill out of the low-cut bodice.

He belched. The fire returned to his throat, and the server winced in disgust. "Yeah. Fine. I'll wait here till your shift ends," Royal said.

"Wonderful." The server disappeared again. To go offer her insides to the nearest privy, most likely. Royal couldn't care less.

He downed another shot. Straight down the gullet. The back of his mouth roared in fury. Warmth descended through his body. He smacked his lips and licked his whiskers. No sense in wasting it. Wiped his mouth with his jacket sleeve. Muddy feet back on the table, chair leaned against the wall, face hidden in shadows. That was how Royal liked it.

His second favorite pastime was picking up women who needed money. He could often get them to perform his favorite things. His eyes wandered to the third shot of whiskey he hadn't tipped down his throat yet. His third favorite pastime was alcoholism. And that was it. He had nothing else to enjoy. Just tasks he had to do. Work? A requirement to survive. Eat? A necessary activity. Sleep? He didn't much like that either, but at least it was an escape from the things he didn't like, such as the groveling men flinging their money everywhere only to find themselves at home. Polishing their peckers like pathetic fools.

Soon, it was possible he'd have to do a lot of things he didn't want to. If Calrym invaded, that would mean fighting. He didn't want to fight. Fighting didn't scare him. He just knew fighting meant it would be difficult to find solitude, a woman to fuck, or alcohol to drink. *Well, alcohol will be readily available.* But drinking during a war could often end in death. Death meant he wouldn't be alone anymore, have women to fuck, or alcohol to drink.

Despite the demanding nature, Royal always promised to himself not to drink during wartime. Too often he heard of people dying while drunk. He had to keep a clear head.

The door to the inn burst open. A soldier stormed in, pulling his clothes around him. Cold air followed the man in, and Royal shivered. Cyrok was always cold, but winter was always colder.

The music stopped. Dancers paused in place. All attention turned to the loud man. He closed the door and stomped his feet on the entrance rug.

Royal's feet slid back to the floor. He stood and downed the last shot. Straight down the gullet. Flames caressed his throat. Warmth revitalized his body from the cold air. He smacked his lips. Licked his whiskers. No sense wasting any of it. Wiped his mouth with his jacket. Realized how wet his sleeve was when he went to do this and stopped. He didn't want a chapped mouth. Cyrok's weather was enough of a problem as it was.

The soldier walked into the center of the tavern. He was holding something. A piece of parchment. "I bring news." The man's voice was hushed, and Royal had to strain to hear it. Royal believed the man was from the docks but didn't identify him. He couldn't care less who it was. The news was the important part. The thing was, people didn't hand-deliver notes to the inn and read them aloud. Something crucial had happened, which meant bad news.

Royal picked up the sheathed sword that lay across the other chair at his table. He put it back on his belt. Made himself look like an officer. Or attempted to. The stains and smell of alcohol, and of body odor as well, fought this attempt. Nevertheless, he was in charge. His rank said so. Royal figured it was a good idea to intercept this news. Couldn't trust an underling not to spread panic.

He walked by townsfolk who were converging around the soldier. Shoved his way through. "Captain coming through. Move. Move!" They didn't want to listen to him. Whether that was because of their trans-fixed attention on the soldier, or they didn't respect him, he wasn't sure. He assumed the latter.

"What are you about to read?" Royal elbowed the soldier, alerting him to his presence. It also made Royal feel good. Despite the soldier's distaste for Royal, he *had* to listen to him.

The soldier swallowed nervously. He handed the parchment to Royal. "Cyr, I need a drink." The soldier headed toward the bar.

I need a drink too, kid. Royal looked down at the parchment and read it to himself first. It was a damn good thing he did. No need to induce panic.

Governess Stasia Falconel,

On behalf of advisement from the Calrym council, Calrym formally declares war on Cyrok. His Majesty, the King of Calyrm, authorizes Duke Harlem Maccaro command of Calrym's full military.

—King Mikas Garcovi

Sweat formed on Royal's forehead and trickled down his back. His hands trembled, whether from nerves or alcohol, he wasn't sure. Saliva collected in his mouth, and he swallowed it. Straight down the gullet.

The letter was a copy. It had no notarization stamp from a knight stationed at the docks. The Falcon Knights wouldn't have approved of this, which meant the soldier had copied it. Calrym had dropped it off like it was just a regular letter, knowing full well that

Coldridge was the closest port to Vox. Calrym wasn't hiding anything.

Shit's Blessing was upon them. War. The only reason they'd have this letter was if Calrym had already launched an attack. And they wouldn't have sent the letter with a bird or messenger. If the letter was here, so was the invasion.

He would get drunk and fuck the server. He would indulge in his pastimes for one more night. If he over-slept and missed part of his shift, he'd get reprimanded happily. It's not like they'd dismiss him now. Not that he'd care if they did.

Royal couldn't care less.

SERADAL WINTLOCK

1st Cycle of Winter, 231st Reign of Garcovi
Vox, Cyrok

She saw only blackness, an unending empty hollow devoid of life. Sleep. And good gracious did she need it. Her body ached from the exertions of training. Cyr Ilic Strictland kept her busy. She rolled over, pulling the blanket up to her chin. It was possible she issued a snore.

"Cyr, it's time to get up." Renard's voice.

Blinding light hit her eyes as the page ripped open a curtained window, allowing the morning sunlight to tear through her chamber.

"Cyr Seradal."

"I'm awake." She gurgled, moaned, and wasn't sure if her words were even coherent. But Renard got the gist.

"Good. I've brought you food to break your fast and warm water to wash. Do move faster, or the water will cool."

She didn't want to. Mother Avani couldn't have

motivated her to get up at that moment. *But* the water becoming room temperature was something she wanted to avoid.

"Cyr Ilic doesn't like it when any of the knights are late."

She mumbled something. Didn't know what it was, didn't care, a rebellious grunt. Sera sat up and thought of what might lay ahead for the day. More drills, more physical workouts, more swordplay, more everything. But at least she belonged to something. She had purpose. Sera was learning how to protect herself, her father, and anyone else she cared about.

"Like a bird, we rise with dawn," Renard recited. She rolled her eyes. He was a big fan of Strictland.

"Get my clothes ready, Renard." She reached over and took the plate of food. Toast with jam, some meat, and some egg. Her exhaustion was too much to care about what food she was eating. It was just important that she shoveled it down her mouth as fast as possible.

In the two weeks since she'd met Renard, he'd become more comfortable around her. And more help-ful. When he didn't attend her, he also attended her father. She appreciated that more than anything Renard did for her. Jaidik's condition was unchanged. His paralysis dampened his mood as did the deaths of his wife and son. Ashamed to admit it, Sera knew the deaths of her family members didn't affect her as much as they should've. She'd been busy, and when she had time, Sera preferred to try *not* thinking about them. It was too difficult, and it often led to tears.

Thinking of her father brought her back to their conversation the previous evening. She'd stomped out of his room like a child that didn't get her way. *Rightfully so.* Was it, though? He'd hinted he'd search for somebody suitable for marriage. Sera didn't want to marry right now. She wasn't sure if she wanted to marry at all. She didn't want to enter a relationship with a man who cared more about his personal ambitions than her. At least, that's what she assumed he'd be like. Her father would want to marry her to someone who would improve their station; it was routine. And now that she was being honored as a hero, her father had some capital to play with. He'd be able to take that information, however fleeting it may be, and try to increase their family's status. Sera could say no, of course. Her father didn't own her, but she didn't know if she'd have the heart to disappoint him.

Sera was an adult now. That was true once she'd received her gyrfalcon, Russell. She couldn't recall a time she'd even looked at a man like that. It's not that she couldn't recognize a handsome person, it's just she didn't care and had zero interest. *I don't have any interest in anyone.* Perhaps she hadn't met the correct person. She'd always preferred the company of Russell. She missed him. She wouldn't have minded having to spend the rest of her life with him.

"Cyr Seradal. Please, we need to move."

She snapped out of her thoughts. Renard helped her with the rest of the menial tasks she needed to prepare for the day, though he disappeared when her clothes came off and she bathed into lukewarm water. She should've moved faster. The bath lasted shorter than she liked, but the water didn't keep its temperature for long, and Renard's insistence they get moving urged her to hurry.

After Renard helped arm and armor her, she followed him to the training grounds. Snow fell from the sky, coating the grounds in white. A chilly breeze tore through her clothes, and she shivered. Cyr Ilic Strictland and the rest of the Falcon Knights stood at attention. No training was happening, which was odd though not unusual. Sometimes Cyr Ilic addressed them as a unit. What *was* unusual, however, was that the governess was in attendance. Cyr Ilic and the governess both carried worried looks and talked to one another in hushed voices. A messenger was running away from them.

Sera took her preallocated spot in the lineup and stood at attention—back rigid, knees bent just enough to allow blood circulation, arms to her sides. There was nothing she loathed more than the uncomfortable feeling of standing there, waiting for a dismissal, wondering if she would faint. Not to mention it was unnecessary pomp and show for nothing. Why did they have to stand at attention in such an uncomfortable way? She figured in the end it all came down to power. Those who were in command exerted it on the ones below them. It was how the world operated. You could be the king or the lowliest field-worker. Even if you were in charge of one grain farmer, you'd make them do something worse than what you had to do. Her father would refer to this behavior as *human nature*. Sera would have just said *nature*. Because both plants and animals exhibited identical behavioral traits by attempting to strangle their rivals.

Another Falcon Knight joined the lineup, filling in another absent hole. To her left, Angazo cleared his throat. She was glad he was becoming a knight with her. He was a familiar face amid strangers and changes.

Cyr Ilic stopped whispering with the governess and addressed them. "All right, I think that's everyone who isn't getting punished for being late. As you can see, we have a guest."

The governess directed a nod to the knights before speaking. "We have received pressing news." The governess paused. Another messenger ran up to her, delivering a message in a hushed tone. Sera doubted even the governess heard everything the messenger said, as they didn't seem to move their lips. "Cyr Ilic, send word to prepare."

Cyr Ilic saluted the governess. "Understood. Cyr Kingston, report!"

Cyr Kingston removed herself from formation.

"Bring the governess's regiment together. We march for Duroc in one hour."

"Yes, cyr!" Kingston gave a worried glance at the other Falcon Knights before leaving. Cyr Kingston was the longest running trainee in the Falcon Knights and often relegated to important tasks from veteran knights. She wasn't even from the era of the Falcon Knights. She joined during last generation as a Hawk. Her distraction was why she hadn't yet been in the field. She was being granted the opportunity now.

Governess Stasia Falconel took back over. "Early this morning, I received a letter."

Sera blinked. *It was already early.*

"It was from King Mikas Garcovi of Calrym. They have sent warships and a declaration of war. They mean to invade us. Early reports suggest they've split their forces. Half are bound for western shores, the other half to the eastern, according to a ship captain who arrived in Coldridge several days ago. They didn't attack Coldridge or any ships stationed there. They delivered this declaration of war to that ship captain at sea. Within a matter of days, I expect both Aleki and Duroc will be under siege if not pillaged and burned. I will lead the defense of the eastern border. Cyr Ilic Strictland offered to come out of retirement and join me. The Old Vulture will lead the defense of our western border."

Sera had heard of the Old Vulture. His actual name

was Vecchio Rizurri, and he was the oldest Falcon Knight by decades. Strictland, though a Vulture himself, was *twenty* years Rizurri's junior. Strictland was old. She hadn't seen the Old Vulture before, but she had a tough time believing he could be that much older than Strictland and be able to defend Cyrok from invasion.

The governess continued, "The rest of you will remain here, ready to defend the city at all costs. Your new command will be Cyr Ollitha Oxhorn. She is of the Grouse generation and has been in the field, outside of Vox, for almost a decade. Cyr Ollitha arrives today. Mother Avani be with you all." The governess saluted them. They returned the salute, and she turned on her heel, leaving them behind.

Cyr Ilic addressed them next. "You all have the day off. Spend it doing something you enjoy. Tomorrow, you continue training for battle. Remember, like a bird, we rise with dawn. It's been an honor. Dismissed."

War. They were being invaded. And for what? What did Cyrok have of importance?

"Sera?" Angazo asked. She ignored him, and he didn't pursue her. He was good at that.

Sera walked back to her room in a fog. At one point, Renard joined up with her, but she just waved him away. She needed to get out of her armor. Then she needed to speak to her father.

J aidik laid in bed, breaking his fast. Since he had nothing to be awake for, he had the luxury of sleeping in. It was the only thing he enjoyed anymore. He'd said several times since his paralysis he could now catch up on years of missed sleep.

"Seradal, what a pleasant surprise." He beamed at her, proud. Then took another bite.

"Father." She took a seat in the large cushioned chair the governess had installed for Jaidik's comfort.

"You look upset. Nothing happened, I hope?"

He hadn't heard the news. "We're at war. Calrym sent two ships. The governess filled us in this morning. I'm sure she's leaving soon. Along with Cyr Ilic."

Her father whitened. No doubt he was both concerned for her and his own well-being. Being paralyzed, he wouldn't be able to fight. Or run.

"We are to stay here, father. Cyr Ollitha Oxhorn is arriving tonight to lead the defense of the city."

"We're in excellent hands, then. The Oxhorns are a powerful family."

She didn't recall ever hearing about an Oxhorn before. "You know them?"

Jaidik chuckled. "No. I was trying to make us both feel better. Did it work?"

"For a moment." She smiled. It was nice spending time with him. When he was in high spirits, he brightened her day, though that was rare now.

"And Angazo?"

"The new recruits are staying here."

"Good." Aside from her, Angazo was her father's only link to the life he'd lost. And he lost them both more every day because of their commitment to the Falcon Knights.

She watched him eat, and he didn't speak. Several minutes of silence passed. It was nice, in a sad sort of way. Tomorrow, all thoughts would be of the encroaching army. How many days or weeks until they were attacked? Or would Governess Stasia Falconel and the Old Vulture be able to defend both sides of the continent? If either failed, the enemy's goal would be the capital. The thought of fighting Calrites didn't frighten her. Sera had a sword and armor now. If she fought another soldier off with a stick, she was happy to fight one with a sword in hand. What scared her was her father. Sera didn't want to lose her last remaining family member. She wished there was a way Magicus Ashté could help him. But doing so would chip away most of the Healer's life. Much as Sera knew it to be true, her father didn't *need* more healing. And without a lot of money, no Healer was going to waste their life on that. So, he'd remain paralyzed.

"Don't think about me, Sera."

Sera had been so lost in thought, she hadn't realized she'd been staring right at him. She cleared her teary eyes. "I'm sorry."

"I know what you're thinking. If we get attacked, you and Angazo need to stick together. You need to *live*. You're a person who's going to make a difference in the world. A *good* person, Sera. Don't waste your life attempting to help your father who can't even limp after you. If things get bad, you need to leave me."

The thought of abandoning her father enraged her. "I could never—"

"*If* it comes down to it, Sera. Please promise me you won't sacrifice yourself trying to save me."

That was a promise she would never abide by. But she knew he wouldn't drop it otherwise. "I promise, father." Inside, however, she promised to never leave him behind to die. Ever.

"Good. I love you, Sera. Never forget that."

"I love you too." She stood and wrapped her arms around him, savoring the closeness. He was warm and felt good. She felt safe. She wouldn't lose her father. Not to paralysis, not to the Calrites, and not because she broke a promise.

"Cyr Ollitha requests your presence in the training grounds." Sera could only see Renard's head. He seemed afraid to enter Jaidik's room. He seemed afraid to do anything other than barge right into her quarters. Not that she minded. Renard was part of her family now, a reliable presence.

"All right." She took a last look at her father, who'd fallen asleep just moments before. "Rest well."

The door closed, and Renard retreated to the hall, waiting for her.

She followed the page into the quiet corridor. On normal days, the stone echoed with voices of various soldiers, pages, employees, and citizens. This afternoon, it was silent. As if the war had taken them all. She knew it not to be true. A majority of the Falcon Knights, and many of the soldiers, went to defend Cyrok, but there should still be plenty of people.

"No need for armor. The meeting is individual." Renard led the way back toward the training grounds.

"What?" The only time she'd met with a Falcon Knight commander one-on-one was when she'd first sparred with Cyr Ilic. Even then, other people were sparring nearby.

"Cyr Ollitha is meeting with each trainee alone. I'm not sure why."

That was strange. Cyr Ollitha had arrived in the city no less than an hour ago. Now she was meeting with each candidate? The woman must not tire. Perhaps this Cyr Ollitha was worthy of the respect she'd garnered from the governess.

Cyr Ollitha Oxhorn stood alone in the center of the grounds. Her hands held each other as if she were praying, though her eyes remained open and alert. The woman's hair was short, almost shaved. Sera stifled some surprise at various piercings in Oxhorn's face. Piercings weren't something the Cyroki did. She assumed it was a display of ferocity, nothing else. A visible warning to those that may underestimate Oxhorn.

Renard disappeared like he always did. Sera never noticed when this happened until it already had.

"You are Cyr Seradal Wintlock." It wasn't a question.

"Cyr Ollitha." Sera saluted.

Oxhorn watched her, unimpressed. "Cyr Ilic said good things about you." Surprised, Sera was glad to hear that. "Wipe the smirk off your face. It was a minor bit of praise, not a medal."

"Yes, cyr."

"Don't attempt flattery, Cyr Seradal."

Sera didn't know what to do, so she stayed quiet.

"Good. Silence is often the best answer when being addressed by a superior." Oxhorn chewed on a lip ring for a moment, eyeing Sera. "Cyr Ilic mentioned you were making decent progress with your combat prowess, excelling in defensive maneuvers. Thus, you will begin rigorous training on offensive measures. A Falcon Knight who can't kill anything is of no use."

Sera nodded. Then she realized this was one of those times that you say it. "Yes, cyr."

"Cyr Ilic also left me a few words to impart upon you." Cyr Ollitha lifted a brow.

Sera assumed she'd noticed her surprise. *I need to get better at hiding my thoughts.*

"Yes, Cyr Ilic cares about his trainees and makes many personal connections. I'm sure it'll surprise you to know that I have always had difficulty . . . *connecting* with my peers."

"I like you, cyr." *Why can't I just keep my mouth closed?*

Cyr Ollitha's glare could've melted the Frosted Spires, so intense it was. She produced a small piece of parchment. "Over the upcoming days, we shall rectify that. Regardless, Cyr Ilic offers the following words to you: 'Cyr Seradal, your promise as a Falcon Knight has been obvious from the beginning. Your devotion not only to the country and the governess, but also to your hard work and your father is commendable. I can only hope I've imparted knowledge that will become useful to you in the upcoming years. Keep working on your footing—a resting knight's a dead knight. And there is no honor in war.'"

"He sure likes his sayings."

"Cyr Ilic likes many things, one of which is being addressed with his proper titles."

Sera blanched.

Cyr Ollitha turned her attention back to the parchment she held. "Oh. I had forgotten the last part because it was so obscure. 'Point to me.'"

She almost laughed. "Thank you, cyr."

The woman's face warmed. "You're welcome, Cyr Seradal. Be prepared to resume training tomorrow. We're going to need to work hard if we want to have a hope of defending the city."

"You think it's that bad, cyr?"

"I've been at this for quite some time. And I've never seen the capital city in a less defended position in my life. We do, however, have two groups of brave men and women led by two of the greatest people I've ever known. Though outnumbered and inexperienced, we have the advantage of our homeland. Prevail, we must."

But Sera could tell Cyr Ollitha was anxious. And that worried her.

EDELBROCK BRENDIS

1st Cycle of Winter, 231st Reign of Garcovi
Lochwall, Calrym

Training. That's all Edelbrock did. He learned about the various armor available, which amounted to none for most events according to the Buzzard's Bowl veterans. Spectators preferred their fighters vulnerable. Some leather gloves and boots. Jerkins and helmets, both rather flimsy. A collection of different sized shields. That was about it. But he practiced with the armor on. He practiced with it off. And varieties. Sometimes only boots. Sometimes it was only a helmet and gloves. This, according to Savakkis, was the way of Buzzard's Bowl. Sometimes they allowed these items. Other times, they didn't, so it was prudent to learn how everything felt.

Weapons. There were so many weapons, Edelbrock had difficulty, and he'd been in the military. There weren't bows or crossbows because spectators found those boring. They were also the only weapons that would have been able to reach the stands, meaning the

Magicai would've had to create barriers, magical or physical, to prevent anyone from dying. So Scayde Haklon didn't allow those weapons. They had access to javelins and throwing knives though. There were spears, halberds, scythes, quarterstaffs, double-edged great swords, war hammers, and glaives, which gave the fighter an advantage against those wielding one-handed weapons. Then there were the one-handed weapons: maces, clubs, battle-axes, flails, picks, and daggers. Several types of swords as well. Broadswords, a typical one-handed blade, which he was already familiar with. Falchions, which resembled a large cleaver. Curved blades, like the cutlass and scimitar. Rapiers too.

He learned all of them. Aside from the broadsword, he found he also enjoyed fighting with the weighty mace. He developed some skill with the great sword as well.

Edelbrock dedicated most of his time to training. He learned all he could and tried his hardest. He'd become determined to remain alive in the hopes that one day he'd be able to escape the arena. One day, he'd kill Scayde Haklon. And, more importantly, one day, he'd confront Jaylena about their son. He pushed thoughts of his previous life out of mind and focused. Edelbrock would ensure they both regret what they'd done.

During his training, he found himself partnered with different people. The season of fighting started four weeks into winter. Sometimes he'd spar with Nauc or Bruise, sometimes with one of the other trainees, of which there seemed to be no end. Every few weeks another Draft would occur, and Edelbrock learned the group he was in took an abnormal amount of time to become drafted. Depending on the number of fights each day—if there were any—they were often alone in the hypogeum with various servants or guard popping in and out. Scayde Haklon's head servant, Tanibris, enjoyed showing up to dispense information, do random inspections, or insult Edelbrock.

Wounds were commonplace, even for trainees. Often Edelbrock would nurse a sprain. Bruising became a normal state for his body. His body changed. He became tougher, and muscles resurfaced. He was fit again. Now, if only Jaylena could see him. Back to the figure she'd married. He wondered whether that would've prevented her betrayal. Or whether she'd gotten over the death of Gordy. Had she known? He couldn't imagine she'd be okay with that. Or would she? She hadn't cared what had happened to him. Had relished it, in fact. Had gained a lot of power too.

He tried to place himself in her position. Would he have done the same to her? *No*, he'd thought. Then he was honest with himself. The crude truth was yes. He would've. He wouldn't allow some stranger to murder his child though. Not for all the money in the world. He'd loved Gordane. The reason he'd put up with Trigg all that time was *for* Gordane. And maybe himself. Now, he had nothing. And she'd married Scayde Haklon. Thinking about this almost made him sick. So he tried not to.

When he sparred with Nauc, they tried analyzing each other's weaknesses and point them out to one another. Nauc often attacked in a predictable pattern. Edelbrock was too cautious. He knew that was because he hadn't fought in years.

Although Edelbrock didn't fight in Buzzard's Bowl, he saw how the participants returned. If they returned. They'd return enthusiastic and happy, probably because they hadn't died. He could see how battered they were, how injured. And yet, they continued training. They'd discuss victories and injuries. The fallen. This left a somber pall for a moment when they realized who was missing, but it didn't last long. There wasn't time to think about the dead. Not when you could die the next day. At least, that's the vibe Edelbrock got from them. He didn't want to die in the arena. He wanted to find a way *out*. But that prospect didn't seem possible.

The Chell now numbered four. Chellit had died fighting, taking a spear in the gut. Edelbrock felt bad for the quintuplets, but he found it difficult to mourn. He wouldn't have been able to point out Chellit as much alike as the brothers were.

Every day, Edelbrock's worry grew. Soon he'd be fighting. What would that be like? Would he die in his first fight? Would the crowd laugh at his pathetic performance? No. He'd fought plenty in his past. He knew he'd perform fine. But for how long? That was the real question and worry.

By his estimation, in a week's time, they'd lost ten fighters. Assuming other Houses lost that many, fifty people died so others could place bets and watch them kill one another. Knowing there were people in the stands—screaming and eating food, wanting them to die—was terrible. The worst part was, Edelbrock wanted to be one of those people. It would've meant power. Money. Happiness. Though now he wasn't so sure what would make him happy. With Jaylena's betrayal, he acknowledged the love he'd felt for her had died long ago.

In two weeks' time, he guessed the House lost a total of at least twenty-five people. When that occurred and he realized there were still another couple of weeks left, he felt he'd rather not be in the stands anymore. Yes, he still desired power and money but not at the expense of other lives. Once again, he knew he was lying to himself. Given the opportunity to join the spectators tomorrow, he'd be there, using the money he made to plot against Scayde and Jaylena.

"You keep holding the halberd too high. You're going to tire yourself before the fight even begins." Chellie stood opposite him, watching his stances.

He adjusted the halberd down, relaxing his muscles. They had wooden replicas of every single weapon. This allowed them to practice sparring and learn how to use them without harming themselves. However, it didn't compare to the actual weapon's weight. When they became competent with the weapon, it was advisable to do so with the real thing. This was his first time using the real halberd.

"Mmm, and so the chaff continues to fight, I see." Tanibris's condescending and flat voice came from the opposite side of the training grounds. He stood stiff and rigid, his voice monotone as usual. "Lord Haklon asked me to come down and remind you you'll be fighting in the arena next season. He wishes you the *very* best of luck, Ed."

Tanibris's adoption of Scayde's nickname for Edelbrock made his fingers twitch. He let out a slow, loose breath and continued focusing on his grip on the halberd. Thrust, pull back, slash once, twice, reset.

"A pig could outfight you."

Fortunately, other gladiators had taken annoyance at Tanibris's intrusions whenever he showed up to insult Edelbrock. This time it was Chellie. "Are you here for something, Tanibris?"

"I already got what I was looking for." Edelbrock couldn't see the man, but he could hear the snarky smile. The sound of retreating footfalls signaled the servant's departure.

Chellie spat on the ground. The effect wasn't as great as it may have been in the fighting grounds. Edelbrock imagined the spit slipping into the sands, dissipating into dirt and evaporating from heat. Down here, it just splattered on stone. In fact, it was rather disgusting. He said nothing though. It was better to have an ally than not. "What a cunt licker if I ever saw one."

Edelbrock agreed. He performed another couple of repetitions with the halberd.

"Here." Chellie tossed a wooden pole his way. He caught it, dropping the real halberd. The heavy handle whacked his shin on the way, and he winced.

The rest of the afternoon, he sparred with Chellie. She kicked his ass.

KELDEN STOOLE

1st Cycle of Winter, 231st Reign of Garcovi
Ashmount, Qothe

After receiving his money, Kelden wrote a short note to his father and sent the coin to him. He wouldn't need it at the school as all of his needs were taken care of, and Kelden knew his father could use it.

Kelden spent several days investigating Ashmount, the school. He'd had enough of the volcano. There was a vast library filled with an abundance of scrolls and books, two large kitchens where a full staff cooked brilliant meals three times a day, a gigantic dining hall to complement them, and a storeroom that could hold thousands of vials Collectors filled. The vial storage room was, of course, inaccessible to anybody other than Collectors and the Archmagicus, so Kelden didn't know how full it was.

The biggest surprise to Kelden was how many dorm rooms there were. Most of them were occupied with nameplates attached to the door. All Magicai had permanent rooms in Ashmount and came and went depending on their assignments. He learned it wasn't rare for somebody to be gone many years before returning. He'd learned there were roughly three thousand dorm rooms spread throughout Ashmount's building, and between the dorms and other rooms, Kelden heard the massive university spanned over 350,000 square feet. Kelden quickly measured an approximation of his own house and doubted they'd lived in more than thirty.

If there was one feeling Kelden struggled to cope with, it was depression. He'd been wrong about his destiny. He was *so* sure he'd become a powerful Magicus. Somebody who could *do* something. But he was just a Glyphist. It was much better than being a Healer. He didn't like the idea of sacrificing his own life to help somebody else.

Kelden attended classes. At first, he learned from all five professors about all five branches of magic.

Healers could heal anyone, other than themselves, at the cost of their own life. The more serious a wound, the more life they'd have to give. This made their services pricey. Kelden learned how to classify minor to serious wounds and how much one could expect to age as they healed them. He learned history about the Healers. The professor taught them about the Blind Sisters, an organization that specialized in selling Healers into slavery, though there wasn't any evidence to suggest they still operated. She admitted there were many Healers missing, but this wasn't abnormal. Many Healers died without warning, from saving somebody's life or of premature old age.

Magicus Kalixa Shivalli was Kelden's primary professor and in charge of Glyphists. She was a pale woman with lips painted black like charcoal. In fact, it might've been charcoal. Glyphists used their own magic to aid Enforcers by tattooing Soul Glyphs on their skin, creating a Well of power that they could consume. Without Glyphists, Enforcers couldn't spend their life force. Kelden learned Glyphists could use any type of hollow utensil or instrument as Soulpens to bring Soul Glyphs to life on somebody's skin. Magicus Kalixa detailed how the finest Glyphists often had pewter pens or feathers from exotic birds that they used to make this happen. But in the field, it often turned out a simple reed, bamboo, or hollowed stick could suffice. There was one simple rule: the thinner and smaller the utensil, the easier and faster a Glyphist could work. The more even the hollow was, the more effective it worked. Magicus Kalixa showed the differing styles of Soul Glyphs. Smaller ones for minimal power usage, then medium, large, and huge, each able to perform stronger feats of magic.

The Examiner professor was also the head Examiner who had discovered Kelden was a Glyphist. Examiners identified those who had the Trace. Examiners used spectacles to see levels of the Trace inside each person. They received extraordinary benefits from powerful individuals to serve as guards because they recognize a Magicus and sound the alarm. A Magicus couldn't hide from the spectacles of an Examiner. Though they may seem weak, they were the best antisubterfuge anyone could hire. The head Examiner at Ashmount also possessed a second pair of special spectacles, which allowed the Examiner to identify which school they should place the person. She explained this as seeing a different shade in the Trace "vein," and was the only Examiner who could identify and activate an individual's school.

Kelden remembered the Examiner from before the Trials and wondered whether he had lied about searching for Kelden's power as another way to prolong the wait. Another test of patience, perhaps. The head Examiner explained an Examiner could see activated power but not power that wasn't there to use. Which meant he *had* been lying. And, if the head Examiner was the *only* person who could activate somebody's power, what happened when they died? Someone needed to replace them. Was it just the second pair of spectacles? That would make more sense. Then why not have more spectacles? Why have only one person who could do this? Was it a special pair? *That seems likely*, Kelden reasoned. Something wasn't adding up, and Kelden felt uneasy when he made this discovery, but there wasn't anything he could do about it.

The Collector professor was Magicus Doram Quandis. He was a pale man, tall, and squinted his eyes at his students. Perhaps he was going blind. Collectors didn't have any natural powers, aside from being able to harvest power from those who had it, bottling it up for later usage, and unlocking the ability to become an Enforcer for a limited time. Both Collectors and Enforcers could use these vials, though the vial's effects wore off quickly. Using vials didn't consume a person's life. Kelden learned about a Collector's duty to harvest any fallen Magicus. And if any of the students were to die near a Collector, they too would end up in a vial. The resource was too important to squander. Kelden figured they were just selfish and wanted to stock up whenever they could. Magicus Doram also discussed a Collector's role as a bounty hunter. If a Magicus were to go rogue, Ashmount would issue a bounty.

Magicus Jakci Robinius, beard-stroking extraordinaire, taught them about Enforcers. This was Kelden's favorite to learn about, even if he missed out on what was being said because he kept dreaming about becoming an Enforcer. Enforcers accessed their Well, created with Soul Glyphs, to alter physical properties. Though some commoners feared Magicai because of their "mind-altering" abilities, Enforcers could *only* affect the physical. This meant they could conjure fire, shape stone, divert the wind, and walk through the ocean. The more serious a task, the more the Enforcer would age. Because of their fantastic abilities, people around the world sought them out. They often employed Enforcers as soldiers, mercenaries, or escorts. Magicus Jakci Robinius showed them various spells and effects, using vials from Collectors of course. This further elevated Kelden's desire to become an Enforcer.

He learned more about the pins. Though it wasn't required the Magicai wore one, it was considered an honor and respectful to allow others the knowledge of what you were trained in. The statue of Mother Avani in Ashmount's courtyard possessed these objects and was emblematic of bringing the five branches together to work as one.

After a few weeks, winter showed itself, though all that meant was the temperatures weren't as hot and the air wasn't as dry. He'd learned the basics and only attended classes taught by the Glyphist professor, Magicus Kalixa. The students learned based on their specialty, which meant Kelden learned alone since he was the only new Glyphist. The rest were Enforcers. This was both a blessing and a curse. He received full attention from Magicus Kalixa. But he also wasn't one of the many Enforcers. And if he screwed anything up, there was no diversion. Magicus Kalixa would notice and scold him.

Before she would teach him *anything* interesting or useful, Magicus Kalixa insisted Kelden become adept at crafting his own Soulpen. He spent week after boring week boring into boring materials with various boring tools, trying to create items that were perfectly hollow and as thin as possible.

"You've split it. Again," she said. He'd been waiting for her to notice and reprimand him.

"I can't get the damned reed to cooperate," he said. He didn't understand how anyone could hollow out a plant without it breaking.

"Practice. Start anew." Magicus Kalixa brought *another* reed over to his table.

"Why can't we just buy a quill and continue on to more interesting things?"

She pursed her black lips together. "Every Glyphist *must* be able to craft their own Soulpens. If you don't have access to anything hollow and you're in a bind, you can make one. But you won't be able to if you don't learn how." Magicus Kalixa sighed. Kelden was sure the Magicus was becoming tired with him. It wasn't like he wanted to be there either. "Imagine this, Magicus Kelden." She closed her eyes, steepling her fingers together in front of her mouth, kissing the fingertips. It was her thinking pose. Maybe her frustrated thinking pose.

A moment later, her eyes opened. "King Alondo Sedoa of Remeria has hired you. Calrym has declared war on Remeria, and an invasion has begun. King Alondo requires you to join his army in defense of the nation. It's imperative Glyphists continue powering the Remerian Magicai. So you journey with them. Then something happens. Perhaps the Remerian army is routed. You find yourself separated from them, alone with a few Enforcers. They've spent most, or all, of their power. You've lost all your possessions in the chaos that occurred during the fight. You can hear the enemy all around you. Perhaps you've found a hole to hide in—a dark cave or the end of an uprooted tree trunk. Either way, the enemy is closing in. The Enforcers inform you they don't have enough power to defend themselves. You don't have a Soulpen. What do you do?"

Kelden blinked. The idea was so farfetched that he wanted to throw up. But he knew that would earn a reprimand and that it *was* possible to find oneself in a similar situation. "I suppose I'd have no choice but to surrender. I understand your point, Magicus Kalixa. It's critical that I know how to construct a Soulpen in the wild if I must."

"You've split it again. Here, try another."

By the end of the day, he'd amassed a pile of split reeds so high, he could have had a bonfire going.

VILLIC THE IMBUER

2nd Cycle of Winter, 231st Reign of Garcovi
Remeria

I t had taken the Camel Clans six weeks to ride into Remeria, though they took a gentle pace to rest the camels at regular intervals, and the clan members exhausted faster in the humidity. Temperatures in Remeria were much different than in Vessia at first, and the nomads, unused to the humidity of Remeria, had a difficult time. Though they'd become used to the cold at night in the desert, they'd also slept next to fires or each other for warmth.

Dunecrest galloped across the grassy lands. *Grassy lands.* Carana, goddess of life, had blessed Remeria. The Vessians must have fallen out of favor with her thousands of years ago. As far as any shaman knew, their lands had *always* been a desert wasteland. Some offense nobody could remember had created a rift between the Camel Clans and Carana, goddess of life. Thus, the shamans took special care not to insult her and praised her daily, along with Killiak, lord of lords. Because you didn't forget him. Ever. Villic knew this.

The Splintered Manes reached a mountain range and slaughtered a small contingent of soldiers. Remerian soldiers, the shamans said.

Speaker didn't talk to Villic again. It seemed he'd driven Speaker away. And Villic lived his best life. He hunted, rode Dunecrest in peaceful silence, fought Remerians with his spear without calling upon Speaker's powers. *Perhaps the gods have answered my pleas for help and rid me of the disease.*

Shamans talked to him, concerned he hadn't enacted his abilities during raids. Villic told them Speaker had left, but the shamans insisted this was a gift from the gods. He liked the idea of gods blessing him but didn't enjoy the voice in his head. Or his internal thoughts being listened to.

Why would any of the gods choose *Villic*? The question surfaced in his mind every time he saw another Imbuer. The Splintered Manes had plenty of other, *better* choices within the tribe. Like the shamans. Or their leader, Jedkah. A shaman answered this by suggesting that even those of low birth held worth in the gods' eyes. Villic could tell this was half a slight but didn't rise to it. Challenging a shaman to a duel, even if you'd manifested powers, seemed a terrible idea. Villic didn't want to be stricken down by a shaman or a god. And even if Villic could defeat the shaman, that would mean inviting Speaker back into his head. He didn't want that to happen. Besides, everyone knew if a shaman killed you, it meant your soul was lost forever. The gods didn't favor anyone who went against their servants. If Villic managed to kill a shaman, the gods wouldn't favor him anyway. Without their blessings, he'd be thrown out of the Splintered Manes, unaccepted into other clans, and left for dead. Not a life Villic wanted.

Since Speaker's disappearance, the Splintered Manes destroyed three or four small villages in the Remerian countryside. They plundered food and Remerian money, killing anyone resisting them. The shamans claimed only those who resisted should die, as the gods would become displeased if they committed mass murder. They were not genocidal; they were just taking some fertile land for themselves. It'd been centuries too long since the Camel Clans had prospered. Now was that time. The High God, Killiak, lord of lords, commanded it. That's what the shamans said anyway. Villic wouldn't argue with a command from Killiak, no matter what anybody else said. To ignore an order from Killiak was to invite death upon yourself. Everyone knew it.

Villic joyfully fought in every battle. Speaker was missing. Not even a peep. It was lovely. It was the blessing of Carana, goddess of life or, as the rest of Cedain referred to her, Mother Avani. Except Cedain only believed in Mother Avani. The rest of the true gods remained forgotten by everyone outside of the Camel Clans. They'd remember them now, the shamans said.

***

Late in the second winter cycle, they rode toward a small village on the outskirts of a large forest that was spotted by scouts earlier that day. Villic's heart raced at the potential upcoming fight. Before Speaker, Villic enjoyed fighting, but it was different. Rough, brutal. Now? With Speaker's powers, it breathed fresh life into Villic. He loved it. He remembered when

Speaker first entered his life, frightening him. Villic also remembered not minding Speaker at first. But over time, he'd thought about it. Having a god speaking inside of you, or a blessing from a god, was *terrifying*, even if they chose you. It was enough to drive you crazy. The shamans already said Villic was crazy. Villic disagreed. The shamans said crazy people would disagree with that. Villic agreed. But *he* wasn't crazy.

He gripped the spear in his hand tighter, holding onto Dunecrest's mane with his other hand. Villic had seen Remerian citizens riding their own mounts a few times. Funny, that. Remerians used ropes to guide their horses and chairs to sit upon them instead of their legs or spears. What a strange land filled with strange people. Villic often forgot these lands were what they were fighting for and he'd be living here if they became victorious.

Lost in thought, Villic came back to the present when a huge bell tolled in the village as they approached, alerting its residents. Villic squeezed the haft of the spear in anticipation. This was the part when the Remerians rushed to protect their home. This was when the battle started.

Sure enough, there was lots of yelling, followed by a scrambled, disorganized flock of men and young boys setting up a lazy front, rusted swords, spears, and pitchforks their only means of defense. It would be easy again. The shamans said the Remerians had conscripted the battle-ready men into their armies, which meant they wouldn't be around to defend the village.

The Splintered Manes roared a battle cry in the name and glory of Mutaz, god of war. Villic joined them, pressing his knees into Dunecrest, spurring the camel on, raising his spearpoint in the air. Dunecrest charged forward, propelled by the battle cries, Villic's knees, or the pull of the herd.

The horde crashed through the thin line of defense, scattering citizens. Screams resounded as some of them were trampled and others stuck with spears. Villic's spear was ripped from his grip as it penetrated a boy wielding a cleaver, likely used to butcher meat. Villic drew the scimitar from his belt, hopping off Dunecrest, who now moved at a slow trot. Villic ducked another clan member, jumped over a writhing Remerian, and made his way to the fallen boy. The kid moaned in pain and let out a high-pitched scream when Villic twisted the spear and yanked it out. Feeling bad, Villic slashed the boy's throat open so he wouldn't suffer anymore. It was a waste of time in the middle of battle, but screams from the dying were haunting.

Shouts of alarm came from some of his clan members. Villic turned in their direction. A regiment of actual Remerian soldiers stormed out of a double-door barn and started slaughtering the Splintered Manes. Unarmored and unprepared, the camel riders weren't so great on foot—at least, not against an armored military. Armed townsfolk were something else. And not seeing any hint of true resistance, many of the Splintered Manes had hopped off their mounts, ready to finish the battle, reap the rewards of food and supplies, and perhaps claim a wife among the survivors, though that behavior was more typical of Bride Warriors. Villic felt disgusted knowing armed men were waiting for the clan to slaughter the citizens. They weren't true warriors in his mind.

Villic sprinted toward the battle, ignoring a couple of retreating Remerian citizens. He snapped up a second spear from the ground, this one bloodied and lying next to a corpse. He threw the spear in an arc over his allies. It came down, snapping in half when a shield deflected it.

A clan member took a sword in the gut. Then Villic saw Sikoi cleaved almost in half by an axe and imagined Sikoi's booming laughter as he collapsed. Lis was decapitated by a two-handed sword, her braided head flying through the air, snakes wiggling and twisting as it fell to the ground. Villic scrambled over a dead camel, sidestepped another clan member, and made his way to the front of the battle lines. A brutish man caught his eyes. He carried a bloodied axe—the man who'd killed Sikoi.

Villic stabbed at Axeman. The point of the spear penetrated his shoulder, but the large man just grunted and raised the axe above his head. Villic leaped back, the axe crashing to the ground a foot in front of him. He stabbed Axeman again, this time in the thigh. Again, Axeman had little reaction. He lifted the axe once more. The sharp blade came swishing through the air, and Villic dove to the ground, feeling the rush of air on his back. Axeman was bringing down the axe. Villic rolled to his side, the axe's blade ricocheting off a rock and the flat part smacking Villic's shoulder.

Pain coursed up and down his body. Villic rolled his arm to test for any broken bones. It was just a surface wound, for which Villic thanked Shymai, goddess of protection. Axeman took another swipe at Villic. He scrambled away on all fours. This beast was going to kill him.

Don't let me die, Shymai.

"There's another way to prevent that." Speaker.

"No."

The Remerian stepped forward, smiling in his unattained, yet assumed, victory.

Villic changed his mind. "Okay."

"Wonderful. Don't shut me out again." Villic wasn't about to argue with Speaker in that moment. *"Shall it be the flame?"*

Although he often chose flame, Villic didn't think that was the right call. Flames wouldn't stop the axe. And the beast seemed unconcerned with minor wounds.

He raised his spear to block the next blow. *Lightning.* When the axe connected, a fork of light spewed forth from the point of the spear, jumping over the axe's haft. Axeman roared as it electrified him, dropping the weapon. Villic stabbed at the man's chain mail. The spearpoint kept glancing off the armor, but with the lightning spilling out from the tip, it made little differ-ence. Chain mail was made of metal. The Remerian blackened like a gazelle over an open flame. Crispy and smoking, he collapsed.

Villic fell to the ground himself. His breathing labored, he rested against the smoldering corpse. A slight smell of cooking meat met his nostrils. This made Villic hungry. But the shamans advised against eating people, so Villic didn't. Instead, he pulled out some dried jerky from a pouch at his belt and chewed on that. He heard remnants of battle, but it seemed the Remerian soldiers were retreating.

"We can do great things together, Villic."

Quiet, Speaker.

"See, you're already communicating with me in your head. Soon, you'll even trust me."

Perhaps he needed to accept the menace Speaker was. Clearly, he wasn't a curse sent by the gods, and the shamans encouraged Imbuers to accept their gifts. *And Speaker just saved his life, even when Villic had banished him.* Villic figured it might actually be a blessing from Killiak, lord of lords. Because maybe Villic *was* worth something to the gods. Whatever the case, Villic decided being an Imbuer wasn't so bad.

Okay.

He wasn't sure how, but he heard Speaker smile.

DEMRI SLARN

2nd Cycle of Winter, 231st Reign of Garcovi
Lochwall, Calrym

The four of them arrived at Lochwall after traversing the Elderspikes, the plains, and the forest. They'd gone slow. Demri's limp, and the snow, had prevented them from going fast. Late winter had arrived. It'd taken five weeks for them to make a three-week journey. Fortunately, Glaouse had allowed them to rest a few days here and there so Demri could regain his strength.

Demri was, to put it simply, exhausted though glad the journey proved rather uneventful. Lochwall was one of the most secure, if not *the* most secure, cities in the entire world. Demri assumed the guardsmen would recognize him when they reached the portcullis. Without Magicus Glaouse, he was sure they would try to arrest him. There had been rumors about the presence of Elkavich in Lochwall for years—the group of underground Magicai who fought against the teachings of Ashmount. If that was true, Demri didn't know. But he knew because of this, security regarding stray Magicai was incredible. And he was a criminal who was easy to identify.

Aside from the Elkavich, Demri knew of many other factions that existed in Lochwall. The headquarters of the Painted Shiv, a criminal organization. Buzzard's Bowl, a gladiator arena owned by the richest of nobles, built just outside the city in a compound massive enough to match an entire district of Lochwall. The Velvet Mother, more a mystery than an actual person. Nobody was sure of her identity. If they even were a woman. Though Demri had never been inside the city before, he felt he knew it well enough by reputation alone.

The thick stone walls reached far above them with regular towers integrated into the walls. Centuries ago, the Calrym king had emptied the nation's treasury to build a defensive castle to guard the pass in the Valkrynd Mountains. The intent was to build a fortress that could lock itself down and defend against Remerians for years without needing to resupply. Turns out, you needed a huge population to maintain the plans of the king, which turned the castle into a city.

Buzzard's Bowl was itself an imposing fortress. Built to imitate Lochwall on a much smaller scale, the arena had its own set of soldiers and guards. If Demri were to hazard a guess, he'd figure penetrating Buzzard's Bowl would be as difficult as breaching Lochwall. The people who earned their riches from the arena wanted to protect their profits, and it wouldn't surprise Demri to see Lochwall's men abandon the city for the arena. Money could do a great deal to change a person's allegiance, and the nobles had all the money in Lochwall.

Glaouse stopped them a few feet from the guardsmen. "It's important that you remain quiet. I'll get us into the city, then we'll find passage to Ashmount. I'm assuming you know Lochwall's security measures well enough that if I order it, you'll find yourself arrested and harvested, Demri?"

"Yes, G-Glaouse."

"Good. Many of the people guarding this place are much more competent than you're likely used to. Few people wish to traipse through the wilderness looking for *you*." Demri wasn't sure if that was a compliment or an insult.

They climbed the hill, reaching more guards outside the gate than Demri assumed was necessary. Approaching from the Remerian side, Demri figured they'd be more cautious. He didn't expect them to be *this* cautious though. He was glad for Magicus Glaouse's presence at the moment.

"Magicus Glaouse," a guard said.

"Sergeant. In my charge, I bring these three men. The one that will concern you is him." He gestured at Demri. "That would be Demri Slarn, wanted outlaw. What's it been now, Demri? Twenty years a criminal?"

He just shrugged. Demri didn't consider himself a criminal. Sure, he'd done bad things, but they were for a purpose. Killing Doram Quandis was essential for the betterment of the world. It was the first step at eliminating corrupt Magicai. That's what he told himself anyway. Really, it was about revenge. Exposing the Magicai at Ashmount was second on the list.

"I'll go fetch our Magicus." The sergeant whistled to another guard at the other side of the portcullis, and they lifted the gate.

Demri raised a brow. If an Examiner were to come out, Demri would have some questions to answer. Questions he didn't need right now. He opened his mouth to speak, but Magicus Glaouse cut him off. "No need, sir.

I'm expected. You-know-who wants to meet with him herself. He's in my custody."

"Understood."

"Sergeant, why are there so many of you outside the city?"

"Orders, Magicus Glaouse. Sent half the men with Duke Harlem for the invasion."

"Invasion?"

"Attack on Cyrok. Didn't you know? Everyone knows."

Magicus Glaouse shrugged, both hands extended, open palms facing the sky. "I see. I've been traveling in the wilderness for several weeks. Haven't exactly had updated news."

"Ah." The sergeant glanced at Demri. "Well, good luck, Magicus Glaouse."

"Thank you, Sergeant. Here, for your kindness." Glaouse handed him several coins. The sergeant pocketed them, happy.

And just like that, Demri was inside Lochwall. *Now to get rid of Glaouse.*

To Demri's right, Caius walked alongside him. His knife flicked across his fingernails. Filing, filing, filing. Bloody. As usual. The man didn't know when to stop. At least he wasn't digging holes in his mouth anymore.

"Wow, sir. I've never been somewhere so *alive*," Porric said.

"Silence, P-P-P-Porric, or you won't b-b-be alive for long."

He stopped talking.

Magicus Glaouse navigated the streets of Lochwall and its crowds of citizens. The city bustled with thousands of people. Demri followed in his wake, glad the man's presence elicited a reaction from the crowd. They glided away from him as if he were a king's chariot.

Either they were afraid or they respected the man, or perhaps they felt this way about all Magicai.

"Where are we headed?" Caius asked.

Glaouse pointed . . . east? There were so many buildings and they'd turned so many times, Demri lost himself.

"To a friend of mine. She'll secure us safe passage to Ashmount," Glaouse said.

"Safe, sir?" Porric's paranoid voice rose above the chatter of those around them.

Demri shot him a withering look, and Porric shrank into himself.

"You can never be too safe," Glaouse said.

They continued down several streets, then turned off to a deserted alley. A broken door hung from the back of a building. Several discarded barrels and casks lay strewn about. *A cooper's?*

Glaouse walked into the building, the slanted door squeaking.

Inside it was indeed a cooper's. The business hadn't operated in many years. Several men and women sat at tables and were garbed in red clothing. Velvet. Glaouse was taking them to the Velvet Mother.

One man stood. "Magicus Glaouse. You're unexpected."

"I don't have a lot of spare time, Camden. I need passage to Qothe and fast."

"To Qothe? Are you mad?" Camden grinned, looking at the other men and women lounging in the building. They hooted and laughed.

Glaouse rubbed his eyes with two fingertips and elicited a sigh. "I understand you have difficulty with the trivial nature of your current occupation. I, however, am a respected associate of your boss's, and I need to meet with her. Announce me now, Camden, or I'll storm through here in a more unconventional way. And we *both* don't want that to happen."

Camden's eyes widened. "No, sir. We don't have to do that. I'll inform the Velvet Mother she has a visitor."

A few silent and awkward moments passed. The other guards Camden left behind watched Demri's group, anxious and alert. Demri took it upon himself to sit in Camden's empty chair. His exhaustion from the day's travel was catching up to him. This garnered a few stern expressions.

He counted the guards in case something happened. There were five, two women and three men plus Camden. Several others were likely near the Velvet Mother. He had four Soul Glyphs remaining. He didn't want to waste them unless he had to.

Camden returned. "The Velvet Mother will receive you now."

Magicus Glaouse waved them forward. "Let's go."

Camden brought them down a hall and into a room. It appeared as if it used to be storage for the cooper's supplies. Rusted adzes and other tools hung on walls lined with crates and barrels full of various stores. A wooden chair sat behind a squat desk. In the chair was a hooded diminutive figure writing a letter or a document with a withered-looking hand.

"Sit," a voice croaked, gesturing to a couple of crates that had been upturned.

Demri noticed a scuffle behind a stack of crates. A boot moving on the floor, it sounded like. A hidden guard or two.

"Magicus Glaouse, you were successful?" The slow, rhythmic voice of an old woman.

Glaouse bowed but said nothing.

The Velvet Mother lifted her hood. Her crinkled face

conjured more wrinkles as she squinted at Demri. "Magicus Demri Slarn."

He inclined his head.

"You killed my grandson."

Demri stiffened. "Who was your grands-s-son?"

"Elizer Corbéo."

"I b-b-believe you have me c-confused with somebody else."

"No, my dear. I don't believe I do." The Velvet Mother stood, unsteady on her feet. "Many years ago, the Corbéos were a family to fear. But times change, and so do the ones who rule. Scayde Haklon is now the voice of the people, and the Corbéos stay out of the spotlight. Is it because we are afraid or because we have few left alive? Both, I reckon. My daughter and her husband, Elizer's parents, are deceased. Have been for decades. The day I lost my only child was the day I died inside." Her gaze disappeared for a moment while she peered into the past. "I'm a rambling old lady now. Excuse me for that. I will say my piece and then allow you to return to the University of Arcanical Arts, where I'm sure they'll take great care of you."

Demri didn't think that would be the case. He watched her. He examined her posture, her every move. He reached inside himself, ready to consume a Soul Glyph if a problem developed. One wrong move and he'd blast her off her feet.

She, however, did not seem too interested in killing him. The Velvet Mother stamped the piece of parchment she'd been writing on. Then she rolled it up. "This will secure you passage on a ship on my coin." She handed the scroll to Glaouse.

He took the offering. "Thank you."

She nodded, though she had a grim look upon her face. "I had four grandchildren. Elizer was the youngest.

He wanted to travel the world. See various continents. Play songs, can you believe it? Act like a poor peasant, earning his keep. People like you and I are wandering the world, looking to escape death at every turn, pushing agendas in secretive ways, and Elizer wanted to *play music*." She chuckled. "He was a spirited person. And a fool. But both can be loveable qualities. It's too bad he ended up at the wrong place at the wrong time, eh?" She glared at Demri. "It's sad, and unforgivable, that one can take another's life without learning the name of that person, isn't it? That's what *you* did to Elizer. And countless others, I understand."

"I d-do what I need to d-d-do."

"Yes, I'm sure. Just like everyone else. If I was spryer and younger, I'd flay you alive myself. Watch you suffer. But I'm old. Almost dead. And the Corbéo line needs to remain quiet for a few more decades, else we'll resurface too early. We need to recover respect . . ." Her face changed into one of horror.

A scuffle sounded behind Demri. A scream, a blade being drawn. "Don't!" Camden said, then Demri heard a gurgling sound.

By the time Demri had adjusted his position, Caius was dragging Porric toward the Velvet Mother at knife-point. Camden lay facedown in a pool of blood, spluttering.

"C-C-Caius?" Demri asked.

"Sir, what are you doing, sir?" Porric's eyes bulged, his voice panicked.

Magicus Glaouse stepped in front of the Velvet Mother, downing the substance in the vial he wore around his neck. He tossed it aside and outstretched his hand, aiming at Caius. "Don't make me kill you."

Caius laughed. "Best of luck." He flung his knife at Glaouse.

Glaouse sprayed the air in front of him with flames. Crates caught fire. But he didn't shield himself. Caius's blade sunk into Glaouse's stomach. The Magicus sank to his knees with a grunt.

Demri restrained himself. He had four Soul Glyphs and wasn't sure what to do. He didn't think Caius was betraying him, though Porric wouldn't agree with that. But Porric meant nothing to Demri. Not enough to waste Demri's life on. He'd wait it out. Figure out what Caius was doing.

Porric writhed on the ground, flesh burned black. There were no Healers around as far as Demri knew. Porric was a goner.

It appeared as if Caius escaped a majority of the fire. He'd used Porric as a shield, and now he was taking advantage of Glaouse's injuries. Glaouse knelt, the hilt of the knife in his hands. It was clear he didn't want to pull the blade out. Probably a smart idea with nothing nearby to stifle the bleeding. Glaouse's distraction of his wound wasn't smart. Like a fool, he stared down at the knife in his gut.

"Demri, remember the price of saving your life?" Caius asked.

Ah. So, he is collecting on that. *How . . . unfortunate.* "I remember."

Caius nodded, leaped over Porric's body, and plunged another knife into Glaouse's neck. He twisted it and ripped out the man's throat. Then he turned to the Velvet Mother.

Demri hadn't noticed she'd walked back to her chair. Despite all the commotion, the fire burning near her, and the threat to her own life, she was writing again. Without looking up, she addressed him. "You aren't capable of peace, Demri, only destruction." To Caius, she said, "And *you*, young man—"

Caius gently tipped her head back and slit her throat midsentence, letting the blood drip onto the desk and floor. "I know you have little left, Demri, but could you put out the fire? I don't want *my* new organization burning down on my first day." Caius wanted to be the new Velvet Mother? *Shit.* Demri had given him his word though. And he would keep it.

So Demri consumed a Soul Glyph to conjure up a wave of water. It was the least he could do for the man who'd saved his life. A man who'd helped Demri for twenty years.

Then a cold realization hit. With Porric's death and Caius becoming the new Velvet Mother, he would be alone. Adrift.

Friendless. Again.

INTERLUDE
ALYST GARCOVI

2nd Cycle of Winter, 231st Reign of Garcovi
Cyrok

The wind up north had a *bite* to it. It froze your loose bits to the lands of the death and back. Nostrils frosted over. Earlobes threatened to fall from your head. Fingers and toes went white, and sometimes black. Cocks retreated, and balls retracted. Alyst Garcovi had spent several weeks on a cramped ship, followed by several weeks walking around this wasteland. *I'm over it.*

Exhaling, a plume of white breath ascended into the air, then dissipated. It was white *everywhere*. Snow was the landscape. Trees were snowy. The mountains were snowy. The only color was the sky when it wasn't snowing. Even then, half the time, it was various forms of gray.

His uncle, the King of Calrym, Mikas Garcovi, had sent Sir Alyst to represent the royal family. But he was also directed to watch Duke Harlem Maccaro. That was difficult, however, since Duke Harlem was on the western side of Cyrok, and Alyst was on the eastern side, both marching in the direction of Vox. The duke had been insistent Alyst take command of half the army. He didn't argue, though he knew he should've. It would upset his uncle when he learned of this development. Prestige and prowess were the things Alyst cared about, not watching over a duke's actions.

Horse hooves stomped in the snow. Men shivered, bundled in their furs. It seemed it was colder than they predicted, and the extra furs they'd brought didn't seem to be enough. They'd stood in line for twenty minutes now, exposed. Waiting.

Alyst could see the incoming forces. A parlay had arrived yesterday. Governess Stasia Falconel and Sir Ilic Strictland were leading this force and hoped they could discuss the situation peacefully. But Alyst wasn't in command of the invasion, and Duke Harlem was across the continent. Alyst's orders were explicit: take the capital or die trying. So he'd refused the parlay. And now, here they were. Alyst knew he could speak for the king. He didn't want to have traveled all the way to Cyrok and not have a single worthy battle. Duroc didn't count. He wanted to *add* accolades to his list of impressive deeds, not take away from them. "Won a war with peace talks" made him sound like a politician. He was a soldier. So war it was.

He drew his sword, wiped it with oil once more. It was important in the rough climate to do so. But Alyst had already done so three times earlier. He was becoming eager and antsy for the fight.

As the Cyroki defense grew closer, he made out individuals. Some people riding horseback led the procession. He could make out the governess and Sir Ilic Strictland, assuming they were the two figures riding next to one another at the head of the army. He saw the capes of the Falcon Knights, an order of idiots that allowed women to fight. It was embarrassing. Never had a woman beaten him in combat. Not that he'd ever fought one before of course. A sea of blue capes dotted with some green and yellow. Alyst had taken time to study up on Cyroki history pertaining to the Falcon Knights. He knew the blue capes belonged to most of the order, those of the Falcon era. Green would be the Hawks. Yellow, Grouse. And Sir Strictland would be in gray. Or "Cyr" because Cyrok wanted to be different and stick to their history or some shit.

Cyrok, before its discovery by Calrym, had been a nomadic nation of barbaric morons. Once they'd become integrated with the actual world, they grew accustomed to the language of Calrym and Remeria, adopting it as their own. They erected buildings and constructed ships. They incorporated normal ways of life. The citizens of Cyrok had trouble letting go of the whole bird thing. And *cyr* instead of *sir*, no matter what they were told. *Oh well. It's not like you can control every bitch you breed.*

"Ten minutes until they're here, sir," his second-in-command said. They were making good time.

Alyst walked a few feet toward the approaching enemy and pissed in the snow in their direction. He was certain they couldn't see it. Didn't care. It wasn't about the insult. He had to piss. And in this cold, pissing oneself amid a battle sounded like a wonderful way to end up with frostbite. Alyst shook his cock a few times, both to dry it and to stimulate some warmth. He tucked it back into his trousers.

He double-checked his armor. All was well. *Let's make this battle quick.* He didn't want it to extend into another day and wanted to make fast time to Vox. They'd already raided Duroc to the ground. Alyst assumed Duke Harlem had destroyed Aleki, as he'd planned. It was a race to the capital, and he'd be first.

He turned and addressed the men standing behind him. He held up a small cylindrical device to his lips, one his Magicus had given him. It projected his voice so everyone could hear him. "Men of Calrym, this is the battle we've been waiting for. Win it, and we will proceed to Vox unhindered. Whoever slays the knight, Sir Ilic Strictland, will receive a promotion and become a wealthy man. If you engage the governess, I would prefer her alive. The execution should be my responsibility, my honor. Better compensation awaits the person who delivers her to me. We outnumber the Cyroki birds, and, like hunters, we will bring them down. In the name of His Majesty, Mikas Garcovi, let's secure another win! A worthy one, this time!" He raised his sword, and the soldiers cheered.

"Forward," he screamed, pointing his sword at the Cyroki forces. They charged. Alyst charged. No cavalry, no tactics. Just a straight charge. They hadn't even set up an archery line. The march would leave the Cyroki exhausted. He also knew they outnumbered the Cyroki military at least two-to-one, maybe more. And Calrites possessed more skill. The Cyroki had no chance.

Steel met steel, leather, or flesh. A multitude of sounds broke the dim silence of the snowy wasteland. Screams. Battle cries. Screeches, bangs, and flesh ripping and tearing. Punctures, scrapes, and crashes.

Alyst smashed through the enemy lines, swinging his sword like a madman. He parried a blow, cut back with an underhanded swing, and severed a man's leg. Then he drove his sword into the fallen man's neck, finishing him. Blood spurted onto the snow, beginning what would soon become a field of red.

Cascades of magic blasted the opposing side. Alyst

had an incredible advantage coming from Calrym. The country was rich enough to afford Magicai. Cyrok didn't use their meager finances to hire Magicai, and other than the odd Healer, he doubted they had any Enforcers or Collectors. Ice shards rose from the snowy landscape in front of him, impaling soldiers from beneath. Another couple of men lost legs, stalagmites severing them.

His raspy breath pulled cold air into his lungs, and it burned. He gasped, stabbing another Cyroki in the chest. Blocked a blow with his shield from somebody else. A friendly. "Watch it," Alyst yelled at him. The man mouthed something and moved away. Alyst couldn't tell what.

He proceeded further into the enemy's lines, watching for any sign of the governess or Strictland. Killing soldiers was fun. It was thrilling. But that's not what earned accolades or respect. That wasn't how you won a war.

Snow hit Alyst in the face. The freezing coldness of it paralyzed him for a second. His helmet hadn't blocked it, which meant it had to have been a direct throw in front of him. He raised his shield, blinking snow out of his eyes. He was lucky because something collided with the block of wood.

Alyst shook his head, clearing most of the snow away, and saw a Falcon Knight attacking him. It was a woman. *Of course, the bitch would fight dirty.* Not that he blamed her. War was a dirty business.

Snarling, he swung his sword at her, but she dodged. He hefted his shield in his hand, regaining a better grip. Alyst lunged, thrusting the shield at her face. He connected, and he heard her grunt. Blood trickled out of her broken nose.

"Now you've got some experience." He taunted her

and gave a quick jab with his sword. The tip slid across her armor.

They circled each other. She feinted, and he fell for it. But she was too slow on the genuine attack, and he parried.

She closed the gap between them. He jabbed at her, and her shield blocked it. His blow was so strong that she dropped the shield into the snow. Her sword came in again, and he bashed it away with his.

He recognized his mistake. She stepped forward, a knife in her other hand. She'd dropped her shield on purpose. The blade plunged toward his face.

Alyst stepped back, leaning his head as far away as he could. The blade missed. She took a step forward and slashed with the knife again. The tip slid between a link in his chain shirt. Then the blade tore through his gambeson, puncturing his side. He gritted his teeth and stepped backward.

She collapsed to her knees, and another soldier was withdrawing a bloodied sword from her back. Alyst skewered her with his own sword and moved on, thanking the soldier with a nod.

He took time to catch his breath and examine his wound. It was difficult to tell how bad the damage was, and he couldn't remove his armor yet. He'd have to manage.

A Magicus ran by him, peppering retreating soldiers with blasts of lightning that forked out, striking at least a dozen Cyroki and frying them.

Alyst waded farther into the battlefield, climbing over a sea of dead bodies, missing limbs, and disemboweled insides. At one point, he slipped on a coil of intestines attached to a conscious man. One of his men. Alyst did him a favor and slit his throat.

He spotted the governess by the patch of the

gyrfalcon on her shoulder. She was in a circle of Falcon Knights, fighting back-to-back with them. The small group had become separated from the main body of Cyroki soldiers.

Two nearby Calrite soldiers stood, breathing hard. "You two, come with me." Alyst pointed with his sword toward the governess. Reinvigorated, they followed him.

A man with a gray cloak intercepted him. Sir Ilic Strictland. His sword was a deep red, and his aged and wrinkled face stared at Alyst, sizing him up.

"You've been busy, Strictland," Alyst said.

"A resting knight's a dead knight." Strictland exuded a calmness when he spoke. A resigned calm. But Alyst knew Strictland wouldn't let him get to the governess. Strictland had recognized they'd lost already, but he was one of those stubborn old honorable soldiers. Alyst didn't mind putting him down.

The ground trembled. Nearby, a section of ice raised into the air, then dropped, crushing dozens of Cyroki.

Alyst snarled and dropped his sword like a lance, charging Strictland. The knight parried the blow, as Alyst expected. But now they'd engaged one another. The battle was on.

Their blades crashed, their shields thumped, and Alyst's hand cramped from squeezing the handle. The steel sword reverberated each time the blades connected, both soldiers swinging with strength and experience.

Alyst ducked under a sweeping arc, then leaped forward. He attacked, but Strictland was more agile than Alyst had predicted. The older knight sidestepped, and the point of his blade slipped through Alyst's armor, grazing his skin.

"Point to me."

Alyst growled. Before he could do anything, another soldier rushed forward and engaged Strictland.

Strictland parried the blow, then bashed the soldier's face in with the hilt of his sword. The soldier collapsed against Strictland, screaming. The Falcon Knight pushed the soldier off his shoulder, then ran his sword into the soldier's chest. "I won't go down that easily, sir."

Alyst grimaced. The hole in his side burned, and he knew blood was leaking out, weakening him. He gripped his sword tighter, stepping closer. "I'll gut you, Cyroki trash. The blade will twist and turn deep inside your body, and I'll spit on your face before I let you succumb. Or maybe I'll take your head off like a turkey. Bet you'd enjoy dying like a bird, huh?" Alyst closed his eyes a moment, gritting his teeth. The pain increased.

Strictland ignored the taunts and raised his sword. A boulder of ice rose from the ground and slammed into Strictland's head, rattling him.

"Go, sir! Kill him!"

Alyst glanced over his shoulder and saw a Magicus raising his hand, lifting another chunk of snow and ice from the ground with his power. The ball of ice careened through the air and smashed into Strictland again. Alyst saw a spray of snow coat Strictland's face and took his opportunity. He rushed in and drove his sword into Strictland's stomach, then gave the blade a savage twist and yanked the sword free.

The old knight grunted, collapsing.

Alyst stood over him. "Point to me, Cyroki trash." Then he inserted his blade into Strictland's neck. Slow. So the man would feel every inch. Alyst spat in the man's face, fulfilling his promise. Then the Vulture gasped and died. A legend defeated. Alyst twisted the sword and pried it once, popping the Vulture's head clean off his shoulders. *One day, I'll die this way.* He groaned again, a jolt of heat weaving its way through his injury.

Alyst pushed his way through Calrite soldiers who'd surrounded the governess and her ragtag band of injured guards. "Governess. I think it's time you surrendered. You've become separated. Lay down your arms."

The governess sneered. "Never."

Fueled by anger and adrenaline, Alyst rushed toward the nearest Falcon Knight, a short squat man. Their blades slid across each other, but Alyst pressed his entire weight against the blade. Then, overpowering the shorter fellow, he pushed again. The knight fell to the ground, and Alyst drove his sword into the man's gut.

Another knight approached him, and Alyst prepared to fight. The surge of adrenaline had worn off, however, and he gasped, the wound in his side throbbing in pain. He fell to a knee.

A Calrite soldier intercepted the knight and fought him off, and several other battles broke out. The pause gave Alyst time to gather his strength, and he climbed back to his feet.

After the scuffle, the governess and two Falcon Knights remained.

"Lay down your arms," Alyst said again. She complied, which surprised him. The Falcon Knights followed her lead. His soldiers moved in and removed the weaponry. "Kill them."

"Wait," one of the Falcon Knights said, but Alyst's men killed him. Then the other one followed.

"We surrendered," the governess said. As if he cared about honor, laws, or anything chivalrous.

"Yeah, well, honor never really got the job done now, did it?" He gestured to his soldiers, and they knocked her to the ground. "Remove her armor."

"What are . . . you . . . doing?" The governess tried to

speak more, but it was clearly too difficult with his men wrangling her around on the ground, stripping her of the chain shirt, her gloves, and boots. They left the gambeson on. Direct stabs would go through easily enough. He winced, feeling the pain in his side again.

Alyst rarely acted on his emotional compulsions. He was, however, also related to the King of Calrym, who suffered from bouts of anger. This was something he'd inherited.

"What are you doing?" she asked again, shivering in the blood-covered snow.

"Taking your country." Alyst impaled her thigh with his sword, biting his lip in anger. Blood gushed out of her leg and his mouth, but he didn't notice. He stabbed her shoulder next. "Feel the pain you've caused me for having to come to this desolate shithole." He stabbed a third time.

And he stabbed. Again and again, he stabbed. She was long dead before he stopped. But he'd never felt more alive. Or happy. Another accolade for Sir Alyst Garcovi.

SERADAL WINTLOCK

2nd Cycle of Winter, 231st Reign of Garcovi
Vox, Cyrok

Six weeks after the governess led her army out of the city, a bitter, dejected calm descended upon the residents of Vox. An acceptance of defeat. An understanding that their lifespan was shortening. These feelings were further amplified once communication with the eastern front stopped. It seemed as if they'd just disappeared. This only further exasperated the fear. Paranoia that Governess Stasia Falconel and Cyr Ilic Strictland had perished in battle. Seven weeks after the governess had left, news arrived by one of the surviving soldiers who'd escaped on horseback: the governess and Cyr Ilic had lost the battle, and their fears were proven to be true. No news on whether either escaped alive. Though the city expected this outcome and remained pessimistic throughout, this didn't negate the shock the news produced. People fed off one another, and morale plummeted to an all-time low. Concerns elevated, their hopes rested on the Old Vulture becoming victorious in battle and returning to save them.

Sera knew there would be no rescue from the legendary Vulture. With the eastern army shattered, everyone's assumptions about Aleki were bleak. Refugees arrived from Timberglade a week after news of Strictland and Governess Falconel's defeat. They were retreating from the battle taking place near their town. It became well-known the *only* option of escaping was going to be Coldridge. So that was the current plan for Sera. Flee to Coldridge.

Cyr Ollitha Oxhorn's orders were to stay in place. Vox was defensible. Strong walls combined with frigid weather meant attempting a siege was going to be difficult and short-lived. If the Calrites caught them fleeing, they'd decimate the Cyroki.

Sera didn't like this approach. She could see they didn't have the forces to defend the city. She was careful not to voice her opinion outside of her father, Angazo, and Renard. The three of them agreed, and Jaidik, along with aid from Renard, was attempting to secure passage out of the city so they could flee to Coldridge and escape the invaders.

Sera supported the plan but felt guilty at the thought of running from her duties. Being a Falcon Knight meant having responsibilities. One of them was to defend their homeland. But with Governess Stasia Falconel missing, Cyr Ilic missing, and the encroaching enemy forces, Sera thought they needed to get some people out alive. Otherwise, the entire Falcon Knight order would collapse. Maybe a complete genocide of the Cyroki could happen. She had no clue what King Mikas Garcovi had ordered. Or what Duke Harlem had instructed the soldiers.

She'd broached the subject once with Cyr Ollitha,

who shut her down. "I'm not leaving the capital city in the hands of *Calrites*. We are Falcon Knights, and we fight to our last to protect Cyroki citizens," she'd said to Sera.

But fighting to the last wouldn't protect the people Sera loved. They'd all perish if the Falcon Knights lost the battle. And she couldn't lose her father. Sera returned her attention to Jaidik and Angazo, as they were discussing what to do next in her father's room. It was two days since the first refugees from Timberglade had arrived.

"Renard asked somebody about sneaking away in a wagon," her father said.

"Hope he no ask Falcon Knight." Angazo chewed on his lip, nervous. If they found out about their escape plan, they'd be expelled from the order and face criminal charges.

"No. He found a local citizen who's planning on leaving with a couple of friends. Seemed a bit of a brutish man, but nothing you two couldn't handle. His name is Vithor Bane. According to Renard, he used to be a ruffian who stole from travelers and merchants. He's since reformed and owns his own business." Her father had become more alive, more animated, ever since discussion about fleeing Cyrok had started.

He must be over this place. I don't blame him. Or perhaps he's just happy to have a project. She'd become bored too in the same situation.

"Doing what?" Sera asked. She didn't like the sound of Vithor. His description made her think of the men who journeyed with Captain Adavir.

"Building carts, wagons, carriages, that sort of

thing," Jaidik said. "Specializes in constructing secret holds in his creations, so that if somebody *else* robs you, your true valuables are safe."

Sera couldn't argue with the ingeniousness of that. "But he knows where all the hidden compartments are. So couldn't he just let somebody know this? Cut them in for a profit? It'd be easy to betray somebody."

Her father shrugged. "That's not a bad idea, but I assume he'd lose customers pretty quickly. As soon as rumors go around that you're selling people out, you're not going to have anybody else who'll buy from you."

"We need go, Sera." Angazo pointed over his shoulder, toward the door. Cyr Ollitha Oxhorn was calling an assembly and requiring every Falcon Knight to be in attendance.

"Be safe. I'll keep trying to work out how we can get out of here while you two are away."

Sera hugged her father, then left with Angazo to hear what Cyr Ollitha Oxhorn had to say. Calling it devastating news would've been an understatement.

It was Sera's, and Angazo's, first time in the Avian Hall. They'd only convened in the training grounds. This wasn't normal, but Cyr Ilic had preferred it over the confining walls of the room. Cyr Ollitha shared this belief, as she'd adopted it as soon as she arrived. Now, however, she was calling them here, which meant something important must be happening.

The Avian Hall was a colossal room filled with long tables, which were nothing more than long boards on long legs. The ancient wood was flush with cracks, dents, chips, and holes from knights long past. The chairs were magnificent in their elegance, contrasting with the table. They were not the original chairs; they were too new. Extravagant carvings lined the high backs, and the wood was darkened from stain. No cushions—armor would ruin them.

Falcon Knights rested arms, shoulders, and elbows on the table, chatting with one another. An aura of confusion and worry came out in their voices, which Sera shared with them.

Moments after Sera and Angazo sat, Cyr Ollitha rose from her seat, hammering the table with the hilt of a dagger. "Silence!" Hundreds of heads snapped to attention. Some of them frightened, some confused. Cyr Ollitha appeared tired. Her cheeks sagged, her eyelids drooped, and her shoulders slumped. The woman looked defeated. "We've received grave news." The room groaned. What could be worse than news of the governess and Cyr Ilic losing? "A runner from the western front arrived earlier today. The Old Vulture has ordered a full retreat. They've lost. We don't know if there's even a cohesive unit left, so we can't expect aid from that division either. We're on our own." The words were like a hammer smashing through the last thin sliver of glassy hope.

A Grouse stood. "What are we to do then? Die?"

Cyr Ollitha shook her head. "We fight. We'll defend Vox and our citizens. Hold out for as long as we can. I don't think they'll manage a siege for long. Calrites don't fare well in the harsh weather of Cyrok. Their blood will freeze, and their minds will shatter." It was, in Sera's opinion, an optimistic explanation of what may happen.

The Grouse's face fell. "We'll all die! We should make for Coldridge. Gather the citizens and *run*."

Cyr Ollitha rubbed her face with her hand, a pained expression flickering across her face. "We won't make it." Her voice was barely above a whisper. Uncharacteristic. Worried. *Accepting.* Cyr Ollitha was resigned to death. Sera wasn't the only one who caught it.

"What?"

"But this is madness!"

"We must try *something*!"

Exasperation. Fear. Desperation. Shock. The shouts from other Falcon Knights were full of emotion, and Sera felt all of them.

Cyr Ollitha repeated herself louder. "We won't make it. Cyr Alyst Garcovi routed our forces in the east. He's been heading this way for days. Who knows where Duke Harlem's forces are at the moment? We've had scattered information. The citizens will require horses, which we don't have enough of. We'd need hundreds of wagons to pull them. But they are large, easy to spot. Cyr Alyst could arrive at any moment, and he'd slaughter them all. It's best to remain here in a defensive stronghold. We'll at least have a fighting chance."

The door to the Avian Hall blew open with a crash. A Hawk doubled over in the doorway, regaining their breath. A nearby Falcon closed the door behind them. After regaining their breath, the Hawk limped farther into the room.

The Hawk removed their helm. Sera's eyes widened at the sight of Cyr Kingston, the knight Cyr Ilic had accused of becoming distracted.

Cyr Kingston scanned the room, eyes finding Cyr Ollitha. "Cyr, they're gone. Governess Stasia Falconel and Cyr Ilic Strictland . . . are dead. The eastern front is lost. I don't know how many survivors there are. I ran here as fast as possible. My apologies for not making it sooner; I wasn't able to reclaim a horse, and I have an injury." She gestured to the dark red stain on her thigh. "The enemy is pursuing. It's only a matter of hours before they're here. I'm sorry." Kingston fainted, weak from her journey. Two knights rushed over and dragged her off, probably to the infirmary.

Whispers and shouts, moans and dejected laughs. Many knights didn't believe that both Strictland and the governess could be dead or that the army was so close to the capital.

The Grouse who spoke earlier collapsed into their chair.

Cyr Ollitha sighed. She stabbed the blade of her dagger into the table. "It's time to prepare our defenses."

Sera glanced at Angazo. He had his head in his hand, and tears leaked from between his fingers.

She had to do something. She needed to help her father, Angazo, and Renard. The only way to do that was to find a way *out*.

It was time to meet Vithor Bane.

Vithor Bane's greasy, bald head reflected the lantern hanging on the wall behind him. It bounced off his skin, almost like a beacon of yellow. He was lucky he'd gone bald, Sera figured. If he'd had any hair on his head at all, it would be a shiny mess. He had a foul odor about himself too. Whiskers collected across his cheeks, upper lip, and chin. Nothing substantial. Proud of it? Sera couldn't see why he'd grow it out otherwise. He had a protruding stomach and wheezed when he walked, talked, or did anything remotely physical.

There's no way he does any of the physical labor here. Must be wealthy enough to create blueprints and source out the work.

Sera had met Vithor at his shop. He'd taken her to a

private room in the back. His office? Blueprinting thinking space? Shady side business? She couldn't identify the usage of the room.

"Like a sausage?" He held up a plate toward her, several sausages rolled over grease.

"No, thank you, Vithor."

"Vithor Bane. Mum gave me two names. I like to hear 'em both. Otherwise, you're just wasting one of them." *Odd man.*

"My apologies, Vithor Bane. My father says you can help us flee the city. Without being noticed."

"For a price, yes." He took an enormous breath and sat in his chair, leaning back and eliciting a cough.

"How much are you asking?"

"To be honest, knight, I wasn't looking for any more spares tagging along." He itched his head, then wiped his oily fingers on his trousers. Vithor Bane took a moment to chew a sausage, only three times, then swallowed. He licked his fingers, eyes staring up at the ceiling, lost in thought.

"I don't mean to be rude, but I need to know now. We have mere hours before Calrym's army will descend upon the city. I need to prepare my father. He's crippled."

"Yes, yes. I heard already. I want a gyrfalcon, a set of Falcon Knight armor complete with a cloak, and a medal, along with five thousand Calrym coin."

Sera blinked. "A domesticated gyrfalcon is impossible to find right now. I think I can acquire a set of armor that fits your . . . girth." Vithor Bane chuckled. "I don't have any Calrym currency. I can scrape up some Cyroki—"

Vithor Bane held up a hand to stop her. He wheezed several times, coughed again, consumed another sausage. "Darling, in two days' time, anything Cyroki is going to be completely worthless." He scratched his oily head, then stuck his fingers into his mouth, likely searching them for sausage grease. Sera shivered, wondering if he was lapping up head grease instead. The man made her sick. The smell of the fatty meat was making it even more nauseating.

"I . . ." Sera didn't know what to say.

Vithor Bane shoved a finger up his nose, swirling it around. He pulled it back out, examined the contents, and wiped it on his trousers. He reached for another sausage, realized there weren't any. So instead, he picked up the plate and began scooping the grease into his mouth, using the same finger he'd used to go on an expedition up his nostril. Sera wanted to gag.

"Mmm." He smacked his lips, grease dribbling down his chin and dripping onto his trousers. "Listen, darling, I'm leaving in an hour. Bring all the money you can, and maybe it'll cut it. If not . . ." His eyes wandered, boring holes through her clothing. "I'm sure we can come to another arrangement." His hand ran across his thigh.

An attempt to seduce her? All she saw was old crusts, crumbs, and flakes snag on his finger and plummet to the dirty floor beneath him. Sera nodded and escaped. She stopped in an alley two streets away and gagged. No vomit, but it was close.

Rule number one: never *touch his trousers.*

VILLIC THE IMBUER

2nd Cycle of Winter, 231st Reign of Garcovi
Remeria

The Splintered Manes had plunged deep into the forest, while other groups had continued to ride across the plains. Villic longed to go with them. Compared to the plains, the forest was hot. Villic heard shamans refer to the place as a jungle, and plenty of odd animal life screeched, cawed, or barked at the intruding force. A constant supply of insects harassed the group, and rain appeared and disappeared throughout the day. It wasn't long before everyone complained about the constant itching and sores. Some even developed fever, chills, diarrhea, and vomiting. A few who experienced these symptoms died. The bugs became a nightmare.

Before, Villic had felt great joy when he'd banished Speaker. He had fought without his Imbuer powers, reminding him of the good days. He had a clear mind, a mind that didn't have a voice speaking to him or listening in on his thoughts. But aside from Dunecrest,

Villic didn't have anyone he associated with daily. He hadn't realized it until Speaker returned three days ago, but he'd missed the conversation, even if half of it was blasphemous. Villic's preference was a solitary lifestyle because of his awkwardness around other people. Speaker was someone to talk to, and after becoming accustomed to thinking his responses to Speaker, Villic enjoyed the company.

"Villic, somebody approaches."

Speaker, since discovering Villic's habit of not paying attention to the present, had become helpful in alerting him to the presence of others. Which made him less awkward.

"Villic the Imbuer," Jedkah, leader of the Splintered Manes, said.

"Killiak's Favor upon you, Jedkah." Villic bowed his head in respect.

"Hold your head up, Villic. You're not a simple clan member anymore. You're important to the Splintered Manes now." Jedkah itched at a scab on his wrist, his eyes wandering.

"He's nervous."

Why?

"I don't know. I can't read his mind."

You just did.

"Forget it."

Jedkah spoke, but his gaze went back to the scab he still itched. "I'm sorry for Sikoi's death. I know you liked the man more than most."

"It's part of war," Villic said, thinking of Killiak, lord of lords. Though it was more appropriate to think of Mutaz, god of war, so Villic thought of him too. Which then led him to the *real* culprit of dead warriors—Flaytz, god of death. Villic's mind raced, thinking if there were any other gods he needed to remember to pay respect to. He found his hand itching his neck at several puffy bug bites.

Jedkah grunted. "Yes."

"The gods will favor him."

"Yes."

Villic couldn't remember a time where he'd been involved in a conversation where he spoke *more* than the other contributor. He found he didn't like it, so he shut his mouth.

"Villic the Imbuer," Jedkah said again, then looked past Villic. Up toward the bush treetops.

Villic wondered how something could get so high in the air yet remain attached to ground.

"I know you struggle with interactions with other people."

Villic nodded. There was no arguing about that.

"I hope the voice inside has helped."

"I have!"

You have. "He has."

"Then asking you to become a more active face in the clan won't be a problem?" Jedkah clasped his hands together, staring at the dirt.

"Nervous again. Maybe it's because he's afraid of your powers."

He's not afraid of me.

"Powers combined with your inability to communicate normally is frightening when they don't understand you."

I don't want to be more visible.

"Sometimes we have to do things we don't want to do."

What don't you want to do?

"I'd prefer my own body for one."

Villic couldn't argue with that. He didn't know how he'd survive in somebody else's mind. Didn't want to intrude on other thoughts. Private thoughts.

"So, Villic?" Jedkah asked. "We need the Imbuers to

take on more prominent roles within the clan. We're going to be relying on you more and more the farther into Remeria we push. The people need to know they can trust you. The shamans need to know. Killiak, lord of lords, needs to know his decisions are correct."

"Killiak didn't—"

Don't.

Speaker didn't.

"I will try to—"

"Great. I'll let the shamans know you'll participate at the next circle." Jedkah nodded and hurried off.

"See. Nervous."

Busy. He's going to the next Imbuer.

"No. Watch him. He's just passed several Imbuers without a word."

Speaker was right. Perhaps Jedkah *feared* Villic. There was no reason to though. Villic would continue to listen to the shamans and the gods, because it had worked so far. He slapped his skin, but the bug escaped. It'd be back. They always were.

The shamans called a circle the next evening, and Villic attended as required. All Imbuers attended the circle, and Villic hadn't missed one yet. What was different about this one, however, was Jedkah promised Villic's participation to the shamans. Villic never knew what to say in one-on-one conversations, let alone in front of a crowd of people.

"I can help, if you need," Speaker said for the third time.

Villic nodded his assent, then remembered Speaker couldn't see him. *Yes.*

"I still know if you're doing something physical, Villic."

Villic knew this too. *You're always watching, Speaker.*

"Can't say that I have much of a choice."

The shamans hushed the crowd, and even though they couldn't hear him, Villic stopped talking to Speaker. Distractions would only make things worse. *Not that I'm good at—*

"Pay attention."

Speaker was right.

"We've been in the forest awhile now," a shaman said, addressing the circle. "Scouts report we'll break out of the jungle in a day and a half. Back onto plains."

A quick cheer from all in attendance. Villic cheered louder than most. He wanted freedom from the oppressive bush trees.

The shaman raised their hand, silencing them. "I know we're all excited to ride hard again. According to scouts, there may be soldiers hiding."

"We kill them," an Imbuer said.

Another shaman nodded in agreement. They pounded the butt of their spear into the ground. "A good chance to secure extra food too."

Villic watched as others agreed. Nobody dissented from the decision, but nobody would be foolish enough to go against the shamans.

"And what say you, Villic the Imbuer?" Jedkah asked. He stood in the center of the circle, where the leader of the clan and its shamans always were, surrounded by the lower-ranking clan members.

Villic straightened and felt his face flush. He didn't expect Jedkah to call him out in front of everyone like that. He wasn't sure what to say. Villic agreed with the shamans. Wouldn't ever go against them.

"Speak."

Everyone's eyes landed on Villic. He struggled to get

the words out, couldn't. Didn't know what to say in front of everyone.

Jedkah crossed his arms, foot tapping against a large bush tree root. "Villic?"

"Say something."

It was hotter in Vessia, yet Villic couldn't recall a time he felt warmer. "Uh." He swallowed.

"Say you agree."

"I agree."

"You agree we should attack the village?" Jedkah asked.

Villic glanced around the circle, every person's eyes penetrating him, as if all the gods surrounded him. He felt as if he were on trial.

"Yes."

"Yes."

"Good." Jedkah's face relaxed. He appeared relieved.

Villic bit his lip, looked around the circle. Everyone's heads turned back toward the shamans. He had escaped their attention.

"You need practice talking in front of people."

Villic nodded. A few people noticed and gave him an odd look. *Back to normal.*

Villic avoided people as much as possible over the next day and a half. He rode Dunecrest, spoke with Speaker, and tried remaining invisible. Jedkah approached him once to stammer through some sort of speech about how proud he was at Villic's inclusion at the circle. Villic had just nodded through the entire thing and offered a "thank you" prompted by Speaker. Jedkah had swiftly exited the conversation. Villic didn't understand what had occurred, even after Speaker had tried explaining it. *"Jedkah is afraid of you,"* Speaker had said. Villic couldn't believe that. And how would Speaker know? He couldn't read minds. Speaker said he could read body language. Villic had never seen language coming from bodies and didn't want to.

At the edge of the forest, or jungle as the shamans kept referring to it, the shamans elected they'd rest for the night, then attack in the morning.

"There are other powers you could begin practicing to prepare for tomorrow."

What do you mean, Speaker?

"You've used some of the basic elemental properties of your weapons, but there are plenty of other opportunities. Other, more complex abilities."

It's been fine so far.

"You could do more."

What else do I need to do?

"Consider a more tactical style of fighting. You could conjure the wind from your weapon, knocking aside an opponent's weapon or weakening their stance."

I don't need to do all that to kill them. It's too easy.

"Villic, there are—"

Enough, Speaker. If the gods will it, I will learn more. Right now, I don't need more to slaughter these pathetic warriors.

"But—"

Enough!

Villic set up camp, took care of Dunecrest, and slept. In the morning, he left his camp set up. The plan was to leave their belongings and return later, in case the Remerians had another surprise waiting.

Hopping atop Dunecrest, Villic laid four spears across his thighs, balancing them with one hand, the other gripping Dunecrest's mane. He steered the camel with his knees, keeping him in line with the other riders.

In a few hours, they reached the village.

Villic noticed something wrong immediately. No bells tolled. No movement. No screams. In fact, there weren't *any* people. It became apparent the inhabitants had abandoned the village some time ago.

"The ruler of this country must've invited the citizens to the capital. Or relocated them someplace safer. Which means . . ."

A door opened at one of the nearby huts. A man in black robes appeared, shouting at them. Villic didn't speak the common language, the king's tongue, so he didn't understand.

"He is threatening the group."

Villic snarled. *He's a fool to threaten all of us.*

"He says he's a Magicus."

Villic stiffened at that. Magicai could pose a prominent threat. But there was only one, and the Splintered Manes had plenty of Imbuers. The Magicus couldn't kill all of them.

Shamans shouted at the man. The Magicus raised his hand and slashed it in a horizontal direction. A whip of flame ripped through a line of Vessians.

"Piss on Flaytz!" Villic cursed to the God of Death, hefting one of his spears and steering Dunecrest in the man's direction.

Shouts came from behind. Villic glanced over his shoulder, saw more doors opening. More people in robes. More Magicai.

"Shit," Speaker said.

Shit. "Shit."

DEMRI SLARN

2nd Cycle of Winter, 231st Reign of Garcovi
Lochwall, Calrym

Men scrambled back and forth, abiding by the Velvet Mother's—or was it Caius's?—commands. No questions were asked. Which meant they had no prior interactions with the actual Velvet Mother or they knew when not to question somebody. Either way, it impressed Demri.

"I want an immediate recall on *all* of our most important agents." The Velvet Mother crossed his arms. *On second thought, I don't think "he" works anymore. I'm the only one who notices the Velvet Mother is a man.* Nobody responded. "Now." They scurried to obey.

Demri and the Velvet Mother stood outside the burned-down frame of the cooper's. Just yesterday, they'd been inside murdering the previous Velvet Mother and watching Porric sacrifice himself valiantly to prevent Magicus Glaouse from killing Caius. But now, without Porric or Caius, Demri wasn't sure what to do. Stay here with the new Velvet Mother? That didn't line up with his current goal. However, there were plenty of resources here. He figured he could wait a few days and see what the Corbéos left behind. Take advantage of it. Exploit it. Maybe the Velvet Mother could help him accomplish his goal.

A tall man approached them. Unassuming and very . . . average. Not fat, not skinny. Not handsome, not ugly. A spot of freckles across the cheeks and a receding hairline. Stubbled facial hair filled in just enough to not be patchy.

"And who are *you*?" The Velvet Mother waved the man over. Demri couldn't help but notice the Velvet Mother had taken to filing their—her?—fingernails with a knife.

"St-Stanton Brick, sir. M-ma'am?" Stanton eyed the bloody knife and gulped.

"Stanton Brick?"

"That's right, sir. Stanton Brick." Stanton's eyes flashed over to Demri. Looking for an ally. Demri just stared back at him. He didn't know Demri was the more intimidating one of the pair.

"'Sir' will be fine," the Velvet Mother said. "Unless it's customary to refer to the position as female."

"There's no precedent for this. There's only ever been the one Velvet Mother. Well, the one *real* one. Plenty of us put on the robes and carried out orders in her name. To protect her identity. Any time she needed to do something public, she commanded one of us to go. I believe she's never left the building with velvet robes on."

"Let's not change anything then. Rumors are fine. They'll add to the allure."

"Of course, my lady."

Demri lifted a brow at this but kept silent. It was awkward. But it would also keep up the charade.

Changing gender pronouns would advertise the change in identity, which any intelligent person could sniff out. That wouldn't do any good for a person veiled in mystery.

"Stanton?"

"My lady?"

"What is it you *do*?"

Stanton smiled proudly. "I was her lady's closest confidant, aside from her immediate family of course. She placed me in charge of keeping a file on all her assets, employees, contacts, and plans. I helped her keep track of everything."

"You are a friend to the Corbéo family?"

"I am. Or was. Most of the Corbéos are dead now. I believe there is only *one* full-blooded Corbéo left alive."

"Explain to me what you know of the Corbéo family, please. It's important I understand how everyone views the family."

"Lady Elisi Corbéo was the former Velvet Mother. Her daughter died many years ago. But she had four grandchildren. One of them died before I started working here. I don't know his name."

"Grist."

Demri didn't know how the Velvet Mother had this type of information. It alarmed him.

Stanton nodded. "Yeah. Grist. Sounds right. Then there was Elizer. He was attempting to live life as a bard. Died five years ago in a tavern. Murdered."

"I'm aware of his history. Go on," the Velvet Mother said.

"The most well-known is Khlaux Corbéo. Last I knew, he'd taken on working at the palace in Anepolis, guarding King Mikas. He's a renowned swordsman."

"And the last?"

"Disappeared. No trace. Been missing since he was a boy."

"Tythus."

Stanton nodded once more.

"How d-do you know all of this?" Demri asked the Velvet Mother.

"I've done extensive research on the nobility living in Lochwall," she said.

Demri didn't believe that. Something was wrong. Caius had never mentioned the Corbéos. He'd never actually mentioned anything about his past.

"So, it seems, my lady, that if you wanted to finish the last of the Corbéos, we could send somebody to Anepolis?" Stanton asked.

The Velvet Mother narrowed her eyes. "No. I am not attempting to eradicate everybody associated with the prior hierarchy. *If* Khlaux becomes a threat, we will deal with him. Until then, I need you to gather all the information you've collected over the years. Now."

"Yes, my lady." Stanton rushed off to retrieve his files.

The Velvet Mother faced Demri. "I owe you an explanation, I'm afraid."

"Some answers would be m-m-most accommodating, C-C-Caius." Since they were now alone, Demri wouldn't abide by the ridiculous Velvet Mother shit. He'd known Caius for far too long for that.

"Long ago, Tythus Corbéo hired me. Before I met you, I was a mercenary and took on jobs for money or food. Often they involved killing. I'm sure this isn't a surprise." It wasn't. "Tythus was young. He hadn't yet reached adulthood. But he had *lots* of money and demanded I help him escape the city. I took the job and received a handsome advance. Tythus promised more. Unbeknownst to myself, and Tythus, spies watched us.

Later, I found out they were members of the Painted Shiv, the assassins. They saw coin transfer hands, but must've heard there'd be more, so they waited for us to meet up again. They ambushed me and stole the money. Hours later, I regained consciousness. Tythus lay next to me, dead. I disposed of the body and left the city. It became too dangerous for me to stay, and reporting the murder was out of the question. The guard would've brought *me* up on charges. So I fled. Before all this, I'd done reconnaissance on the Corbéo family, so I learned a lot about them."

"Why d-d-do you want to t-take over?"

"Because it's about damn time I earned some real money."

Demri couldn't argue with that.

SERADAL WINTLOCK

2nd Cycle of Winter, 231st Reign of Garcovi
Vox, Cyrok

Though Cyr Ollitha Oxhorn decided the Falcon Knights would remain within the city to protect a majority of the citizens, there was no quarantine in place. Which meant they'd allow Vithor Bane's carriage to pass through the gates, and any other citizen who wanted to leave. However, the Falcon Knights were required to stay and defend the city.

Sera couldn't find a gyrfalcon for Vithor Bane. She hadn't the money he'd requested either. She scrounged up a set of complete Falcon Knight armor though. Vithor Bane would require more. Whatever the cost, she'd be willing to pay it. Even if it meant being forced into having sex with him. She'd want to die afterward, but she'd do it. For her father. She hoped she'd be able to pay him via other avenues though. Losing her virginity to *that* man was terrifying. She'd never considered having sex with anyone. Sure, she'd seen an attractive man here, a pretty girl there, but there wasn't interest toward anyone. Not in the same way her brother had described liking a beautiful woman. Sera would avoid Vithor Bane's sexual advances if possible.

Because she was running from the war, she felt an awful lot of guilt. Betraying the Falcon Knights by abandoning them during the invasion was wrong. However, the thought of losing her father and Angazo, after losing everyone else she'd known, was heartbreaking. She considered going to Cyr Ollitha and explaining her dilemma, but pointing out she was contemplating desertion to her superior sounded like a foolhardy thing to do.

Sera had a limited timeline to return to Vithor Bane, and she didn't want to miss the opening. She'd already had Renard transporting various belongings and Vithor Bane's armor along with her own set. Sera and Angazo wouldn't wear their armor, so they could try and be more inconspicuous. Angazo was helping her father get to the carriage. And Sera wasn't helping. Instead, she was pacing back and forth in her room, wondering what else she could bring to the man in payment for transporting her to safety.

Renard entered the room. "Cyr? We need to leave."

"Very well." She pulled up the hood to her cloak, hoping it hid her face enough. It wouldn't do well if somebody noticed her fleeing.

They only passed a duo of knights, so engrossed in conversation that they didn't look up at her or Renard.

When they returned to Vithor Bane's, three horse-drawn carriages were being prepared. Neither Angazo nor her father were visible.

Vithor Bane was talking to a few of his men, pointing at various things. Among the group was Magicus Ashté, the woman who'd saved Sera's life when she first arrived at Vox. Ashté was Cyroki and had fine, pale skin and light brown hair.

"She knows who I am, Renard."

"The Healer?"

Sera nodded. "Which carriage are we taking?"

"We were told to load up our supplies in that one." Renard pointed to the carriage at the line's front. "But I don't believe we are to ride in the same one."

She frowned. She didn't like the idea of being separated from their gear. She hoped Vithor Bane and his men wouldn't rob them. Sera was nervous and didn't trust the man. And the Magicus being there alarmed her. She wondered if Magicus Ashté was there because Sera was. If the Magicus found her, Sera didn't doubt she'd give Sera up to the Falcon Knights.

After finishing his orders, Vithor Bane talked for a moment with Magicus Ashté, then came over to Sera and Renard alone.

"The page already brought my armor. It fits *beautifully*. I took it off to avoid suspicion. Don't want any of the guards to think I'm one of you running away." Vithor Bane smacked his lips, tongue sliding across them. He waggled it three times at Sera before retracting it. "But I see no gyrfalcon. Or money." He slipped his thumbs into pockets and stood, staring at her for a moment. "Your father and your friend are already aboard, waiting to depart. We'll figure something out." He winked at her, then waved his hand for Sera to follow him.

Disgusted, Sera fell in line behind him, Renard at her side.

"I'm a crafty man," Vithor Bane said, gesturing toward the carriages. "As you no doubt have already noticed, the carriages sit higher and have larger wheels than other carriages." She hadn't noticed until he pointed it out. "I explain this to curious passersby and authorities that it creates a more stable carriage. Harder to break the wheel, less likely to get stuck. All bullshit. Most people have no clue what I'm talking about, since I'm the sole manufacturer of transportation in this city, and who's going to bother researching *wheels*? But it sounds good, and they accept it. I am respected and sell a lot of them. Successful proprietors, I learned at a very young age, can spew bullshit all day long and never get questioned. But . . ." He stopped at the back of the last carriage in line, pulling back a cloth covering. "That allows me to be deceitful. Do you see it?"

Sera had no clue what the man was asking. She assessed the carriage. Various crates, barrels, and other possessions were organized against the sides of the carriage. A thick wooden floor was polished with a scented oil. She also spotted a washtub sitting in the back, which surprised but delighted her. But the journey to Coldridge wasn't long—about three days—and, in fact, now that Sera considered it, it amazed her they were wasting the space on it.

Vithor Bane placed his hand on one of the wooden boards, wiggled it once, twice, and it popped open. Behind it rested a handle, which he pulled on. The entire side opened to expose a large hollow crawl space beneath the carriage floorboards that was filled with several pillows and blankets. "This is how you'll be able to leave without being spotted. If you'd like to leave soon, deserter, I recommend you hop in and get comfortable. Your father and his friend are already in another space just like this. And if you ever need an item stored, or a secret kept, come to Vithor Bane, and he'll sort you out." After giving Sera a beaming smile, he walked away whistling a quick tune to himself.

"Best get in, cyr." Renard knelt down, holding his

hands together as if he were to boost her into the hiding hole.

"Renard. Get in. I'm not some helpless girl who needs help because I have to go *up*. And until we are outside the city gates, please refrain from calling me anything other than . . . Yudri." Her mother's name. It was the first female name that popped into her head.

"Yudri." He stumbled over the name, clearly uncomfortable calling her something that didn't involve her title.

"Just get in, Renard."

As Renard clambered into the carriage's secret compartment, Sera looked around, hoping they weren't being watched. A few citizens walked around. No Falcon Knights. They were patrolling walls and watching for the approaching army. A horn blared twice —the signal to the citizens that the gates would lock in two hours.

Vithor Bane's men were getting into the carriages, and they helped him up into the lead one. Surprised, she also witnessed the men helping Magicus Ashté into the crawl space of the same carriage Vithor Bane was riding in. *Curious.*

"Yudri, hurry," Renard said.

"Coming." Sera climbed into the hole, crawling on top of a blanket.

One of Vithor Bane's men closed the hatch. With a lurch, the carriage began its journey to Coldridge.

The Falcon Knights operating the gates to Vox paused the caravan's progress on their way out. They tapped on various parts of the carriage, verbally noted everything was all right, then allowed them to proceed. Nevertheless, Sera felt like her heart would beat a hole in her chest. An hour after leaving Vox, the carriages halted. Sera and Renard were let out of the hidden hold and given the back of the third carriage along with Angazo, her father, and Magicus Ashté.

"You need your sword, cyr," Renard said upon seeing Angazo's gear.

She agreed. They hopped out of the carriage and ran up the line, where they were allowed to don Sera's armor. Once armed and armored, they returned to the one they were meant to ride. Once settled, the procession continued.

Sera kept her helm on and stayed quiet for an hour after climbing into the carriage proper. She was frightened that Magicus Ashté would identify her, though there wasn't anything the Healer could've done. Perhaps she was more afraid of admitting she'd abandoned thousands of people. But if she hadn't, she would have died. And her father would have died. She wouldn't let that happen.

Renard also stayed silent. She wasn't talking, so she figured he thought he shouldn't either. Magicus Ashté exchanged pleasantries with Angazo and Jaidik, and she offered her greetings to Sera and Renard as well. Sera nodded in response, and Renard raised his hand.

At regular intervals, Sera pulled back the carriage's covering and examined the terrain, scanning for any sign of Duke Harlem's armies or, if luck would have it, the Old Vulture and his men. The gates to Vox were now closed, though Sera had lost sight of the city several miles ago. Once, she thought she saw a line of dark figures on the horizon, but she couldn't tell if that was men, a shadow, dark snow, or something else. And then they entered the forest, cutting her view off completely.

She became brave enough to remove her helm.

Magicus Ashté offered a sad smile when she saw Sera's face. "Couldn't stomach the thought of staying in Vox either, huh?"

Sera stole a glance at her father. He was in a deep whispered conversation with Angazo. "I didn't want him to die."

"I understand that." And the Healer looked like she did. Her face darkened, and her sad expression became sadder. "Many will die soon."

"Why did you leave?"

"Vithor Bane passed me in the streets a few days ago. Offered me free passage if I gave him my word that I would save him from death if something happened to him. I agreed. I didn't think saving people in a city who are all going to die was worth sacrificing my life. So here I am. Ashté is my name if you'd forgotten."

"I wouldn't forget the name of the person who saved my life," Sera said. That wasn't something she'd ever forget.

"It was well worth saving, I think. It gave the Cyroki people a fighting chance. It gave them the knowledge they were under attack. Unfortunately, it didn't amount to a lot. But at least they've been able to put up some resistance."

Sera thought of Cyr Ollitha Oxhorn and the other Falcon Knights she'd met. Cyr Kingston, the knight who became distracted. She grimaced, thinking about their dead bodies sprawled across the city. She thought of Governess Stasia Falconel and how the woman had changed Sera's life. Cyr Ilic Strictland and the training he'd provided. And again, she remembered her decision to abandon them. She didn't think she'd ever forgive herself for that.

"It's not your fault, Cyr Seradal," Renard said, looking at her. Admiring her.

Magicus Ashté agreed. "Listen to your page. With or without you, they were going to die. And this way, you may live. Continue the legacy of the Falcon Knights. Spend time with your father. Maybe one day, find revenge against those who attacked your town. Or don't and retreat somewhere to live out your days happy. Sparing yourself the worry of others . . ." Magicus Ashté's voice trailed off, and she stared at the carriage floor, lost in her thoughts.

The carriage bumped. The noise of crunching snow and ice filled the silence.

Sera sat there, thinking about everything again. She ran through her previous thoughts. Abandoning the city. The deaths of her comrades. Then her thoughts changed and focused on other things. Her mother. Waking up to her brother's flesh being stuck like a pig. Dead. She thought of Captain Blago Adavir, the bastard leading those men. *What an asshole. What a piece of—*

She stopped herself. Her mother wouldn't have liked her using foul language or thinking it. Sera didn't like foul language either. She wondered where Captain Adavir was though. Perhaps he was with the Calrites, fighting against the Cyroki. Sera wanted Captain Adavir dead. Her hatred for the man rose. The way he'd tricked the townspeople and what he'd done to all of them made her furious. She'd been so distracted training as a Falcon Knight and looking after her father, she hadn't any chance to think about Captain Adavir. And now, with Vox to be destroyed in mere hours or days, she thought about the remaining Falcon Knights. Would they be able to reassemble and establish order somehow? Would they bring her up on desertion charges when this happened? What if the Old Vulture survived and hunted her down?

She rode in silence. Thinking.

Until another couple of hours later when she heard the shouts from some unsettled caravan guards. Then Sera knew something was wrong.

She scrambled to the carriage covering and pulled it aside. Leaning out the carriage, she looked to her right, then her left, scanning the tree line. Her heart jumped into her throat, or it sank into her feet. Either way, it wasn't where it needed to be.

Mounted men flying the Calrym flag rode straight toward them. They'd followed the caravan. *How'd the caravan guards not notice until now? And how did they find us?* The Calrites had swords drawn and bows nocked, their horses kicking snow into the air as they charged. And Coldridge wasn't even close.

VILLIC THE IMBUER

2nd Cycle of Winter, 231st Reign of Garcovi
Remeria

A gigantic spike emerged from the ground, impaling several clan members. Crimson balls of fire rained from the sky, incinerating anyone they touched. Small darts of sharpened ice fell on them like arrows. The Magicai caused more damage in a few moments than the clan had lost since leaving Vessia.

Villic gathered himself and refocused on his current goal. He needed to kill the closest Magicus, who was lashing out at the Splintered Manes with his fire whip.

The clan members, after several moments of confusion, spread as far apart as they could.

Villic urged Dunecrest forward, galloping toward the fire-whip wielder. He raised a spear in his right hand and aimed, but the Magicus took a liquid-coated arrow in the chest and collapsed, his skin melting and burning as he screamed.

Turning Dunecrest around, Villic saw at least six

other Magicai unleashing their powers on the clan, slaughtering their members.

Killiak, lord of lords, help us.

"You don't need help, Villic. You have your powers."

And my gods.

"Sure. That too."

Quiet yourself, Speaker.

Villic steered Dunecrest through the fallen members of his clan. He recognized a shaman, eyes wide and staring at the blue sky above. Waiting for Flaytz, god of death, to claim their soul.

"Pay attention, Villic!"

He looked up from the dead shaman and saw a massive chasm forming mere feet in front of Dunecrest. Villic snapped the butt of his spear against Dunecrest's rear, too hard, and veered the camel to the left, avoiding the new chasm. Villic heard echoes of less fortunate members plummeting to their doom. He felt bad about the slap but had probably saved his and Dunecrest's lives.

"Close."

Thank you.

"Stay aware of your surroundings."

Villic gritted his teeth but decided not to respond. Speaker was right. The gods would look unfavorably at someone who lost focus while their clan members died around them.

He circled the chasm. It was eight camels long. Or maybe eighty. Villic didn't know measurements too well. When he arrived on the other side of the chasm, another Magicus lay slain, and dozens of Splintered Manes warriors lay dead or injured around him.

An enormous fiery ball fell from the sky, blinding Villic. A wave of heat washed over him. *Killiak, lord of lords!*

"It came from the Magicus hiding behind the shed."

Villic squinted, his eyes still adjusting from the blinding light. A small shack, sitting between two big houses, rested in shadows. A small man was peeking around the corner, watching the bulk of the clan fleeing from the burning grasses. "I see it. Forward, Dunecrest!" He spurred the camel on.

Then the Magicus noticed Villic. He held his hand out in front of him, creating dozens of small shards. *Ice?* They turned in the air, aiming at Villic and Dunecrest, the bright sun reflecting off their surface.

"Dismount!" Speaker roared.

The shards sped in Villic's direction.

"Jump!"

He did.

Dirt, grass, blood, and a camel's foot smacked Villic's face. He shouted, tumbled several more times, and came to a stop with something mushy at his back. He grunted, turned, and looked right into somebody's open stomach. Guts and blood covered his arm and shoulders, and he retched. Being no stranger to injuries or disemboweled bodies, Villic was used to seeing and smelling the insides of a human. Being coated in it was another matter. *Dunecrest.*

Villic looked around but couldn't see his friend. Corpses littered the area. Some clan members hid behind bodies of camels, arrows knocked in bows, waiting for the right opportunity. Some clan members fled from fire or ice or other abilities. Some clan members ran at different Magicai, though most of them died. Villic wiped himself off as best he could, then stood.

"Dunecrest," he called, knowing it wouldn't matter. Dunecrest didn't come by name, but Villic hoped his mount would recognize his voice. Nothing.

A lance of flame seared past his face, singeing his flesh as he turned. "Piss on Flaytz!" The Magicus hadn't forgotten about him.

Villic scrambled over a corpse and grabbed his spear. It had snapped in half from the fall. He didn't see the spares he had either. Drawing his scimitar from his belt, Villic charged toward the Magicus hiding behind the shack.

"This is dangerous." Speaker was always thinking. Sometimes not enough.

He killed Dunecrest.

The Magicus leaped out and yelled something, but Villic didn't know what he said. It didn't matter. The Magicus made his intent clear with his expression. He raised both his hands, drawing up two lines of fire in front of him. The flames reached taller than Villic stood and wider than he was. They began moving toward Villic, and quickly. Tabashi, god of fire, would be happy.

"Imbue your weapon with water."

Know when you're about to die. But Villic did it anyway, and his scimitar became a blade of water. When the fire reached Villic, he attacked it as if it were a rival clan member. Quick, sweeping motions cut the fire down and stopped it in its path. Surprised, he waded through the steam rising from burned grass and changed the sword back to steel.

"Know when you can live. Killiak, lord of lords, expects that much at least."

Villic's eyes bulged. *You spoke of the gods.*

"Pay attention!"

Villic shook his head and focused on the Magicus, who was getting ready to unleash another power.

The Magicus yelled something else. Speaker translated, *"He said he's going to kill you."*

Villic laughed, then ran. He would either kill the

Magicus himself or hopefully distract the man long enough for one of his fellow clan members to finish him.

As Villic closed the distance, he saw his opponent was a frightened middle-aged man, but the fear didn't paralyze him to inaction. He summoned a great column of wind that twisted its way in Villic's direction.

"Now is the time to run."

I can't outrun that. I've run enough. He hadn't realized how out of breath he was. Even if he was fresh, he'd never outrun the wind. Before he had another thought, the column reached him and lifted him into the sky. He flew like a bird. Saw longer distances than he'd thought possible. Looking down, he realized how high he was. Villic twirled with the current. Loud whistling made his ears throb. He prayed or maybe screamed to Killiak, lord of lords, to save him.

"I have a suggestion."

Anything.

"Get your scimitar ready."

Somehow, Villic was still gripping it.

Speaker explained at length but faster than it took Villic to twirl around the wind column six more times—or sixty? He never was great with numbers—various powers he could Imbue his weapon with. He'd become distracted again, though he thought he heard enough to stay alive. If not, he'd be meeting Flaytz, god of death, soon.

The wind column grew weaker, and Villic felt its grip letting up. He drifted down, like a feather from a bird at first. Then the column disappeared altogether. He dropped like trousers on a wedding night. *I need to marry.* He wasn't sure why the thought came to him at that particular moment.

"Is now the time to figure out who to betroth?"

Villic didn't know the word *betroth* but got Speaker's

point. He readied the scimitar, called to the power of wind, then raised his sword over his head. Yelling, he brought the blade back down. Villic slowed. It didn't feel like it would be enough. He closed his eyes and swung again. He couldn't stand not knowing, so he opened them a crack. Villic paused, hanging in the air for a moment, then his feet connected with solid ground, and he flopped over, landing on his back, looking at the sky. *The gods favor Villic the Imbuer today.*

"Or you're just lucky I showed up."

Because the gods wished it.

Speaker sighed. Villic grinned. He stood. Muscles ached, bone joints popped, but otherwise, he was fine.

He surveyed the area, looked for the Magicus who'd tossed him into the air. Villic was on the other side of the buildings and the shack. He was behind the Magicus, who was hunched against the shack's wall, peering around the edge, and firing off powers at Villic's clan.

Noise. There was so much noise. Camels snorting, feet thundering, the screams of the wounded and dying animals and people alike, warriors shouting, powers manifesting, fires burning, buildings creaking, and wind whistling. Plenty of cover. He tuned out the distractions and sprinted, hoping the Magicus wouldn't turn around.

Caution was unnecessary. He didn't use powers. He didn't listen to whatever Speaker shouted. Villic just wanted to kill the small man. His fist closed tighter around the hilt of the blade.

Then something smacked him in the back of the head, and his eyes blurred while he cried out. He twisted, searching for the culprit. No one. Something wet oozed down his neck, and the pain intensified. Villic found blackness.

V illic's head pulsed. His heart pounded. Opening his eyes, Villic saw stars. Hours had passed.

"You're back."

What happened?

"A house blew up. Probably from a Magicus. You were hit in the head by debris."

Villic sat up. The full moon lit up the wrecked village, revealing plenty of wood, corpses, and supplies laying around him. "My head." He felt the back of his skull with a pair of fingers, wincing when he found the spot. Dried blood caked his hair. So much for the favor of the gods.

"Luck isn't a deity."

Speaker was wrong. Cocaro, god of luck, would disagree.

Glancing around, he saw nothing moving. The dead were everywhere. No fires burned. Nothing. The shack remained where it was when Villic had lost consciousness. One of the houses next to it was near gone, destroyed by something.

"Perhaps they left you."

"No." Villic knew the Splintered Manes had planned on returning to their gear. He assumed they were making camp for the night there.

"Maybe they've all died."

Villic snorted. "We aren't Remerians."

"All people die."

He shrugged. *Perhaps someday. But not today.*

Villic collected his scimitar as well as a spare spear. He was headed back toward the forest when he heard a loud groan. He paused in his movements, straining to hear the noise again.

"That sounded like—"

Quiet, Speaker. I'm trying to listen.

Something rustled near the shack. Villic crouched and crawled toward the noise. Slowly, like he were a lion hunting to provide for her cubs.

A wooden plank shifted in a pile of debris, and a hand emerged. Villic realized how close he'd come to being buried. Another groan came from within. He stopped crawling and hurried over. The bright moonlight illuminated the pile enough so Villic could peer into the cracks and holes. Beneath the wreckage was the Magicus he'd been fighting before he'd gotten knocked out. The Magicus's face was a mess. Bruised forehead, cracked lips, a broken nose, and a splinter of wood through his cheek.

"*Halk,*" the Magicus said.

"What?"

"*He said, 'help,'*" Speaker translated.

"He just tried to kill us."

"*I didn't say you had to help.*"

Villic wouldn't help. Just at that moment, the moon's light winked out. He stood in darkness, listening to the moans of the Magicus as he pleaded with Villic to help. Villic looked up at the sky. He saw the outline of the moon struggling to penetrate the cloud that was masking its glow.

"The gods don't want me to kill him."

Speaker sighed. "*A cloud is not a sign from the gods.*"

"Why else would that happen? The gods have voiced their displeasure. I will help."

"*The gods don't exist, Villic. Clouds are in the sky. All the time. At night, during the day, even in the evening. They float in front of and behind things. They do not carry the will of the gods with them.*"

Villic shook his head. *You're clueless, Speaker.* And he

was, to blaspheme like that. *It's a good thing the gods can't hear you speak.*

"If your gods exist, you think they'd allow something like me to exist and not monitor what I say? That's ridiculous."

Speaker, however wrong he was about the gods most of the time, was correct. The gods could hear him. Which didn't mean good things for Villic if they knew he harbored such a person inside him. *You need to silence yourself, or the gods will strike both of us down.*

Speaker laughed but quieted. At least Speaker listened when Villic needed him to.

For the next few minutes, Villic sat cross-legged beneath the dark sky, waiting. The Magicus moaned and spoke the entire time, but Villic couldn't communicate with him, so he ignored the man. When the light returned, Villic stood, heard Speaker make a sarcastic noise in his head, and began removing the wooden planks from the Magicus. He was careful and intentional, as he didn't want to cause further injury.

It was clear the Magicus suffered many injuries. Aside from his battered face, his wheezing breaths suggested internal wounds, he had a pair of broken fingers on his right hand, and his left shoulder appeared to be dislocated. Villic hadn't uncovered the man's lower body yet.

The Magicus offered a different string of words Villic didn't understand, and Speaker translated again. *"He says you're kind and, if the roles were reversed, he probably wouldn't do the same for you. He appreciates what you're doing and asks if you know if there are any Healers around."*

I could bring him back to the Splintered Manes.

"You're going to carry him all the way back to camp?"

I need to find Dunecrest.

"I thought you believed he killed him?"

I never saw his body.

"Might be with the clan."

Maybe.

"It's not worth saving this man, Villic."

The gods wish it.

"Fine."

How do you know his language, Speaker?

"That's the language most of the bodies I've inhabited have used."

Why didn't you know what the Magicai were?

"Sometimes thousands of years pass before an Imbuer awakens. Civilizations can rise and disappear before I return. The Magicai must be a group who weren't around the last time I . . . existed. Or maybe they were, but they weren't important. However, I can't imagine that being the case."

Have you been inside other Camel Clans members before?

"No, this is a first."

How do you understand me?

"I just do. Perhaps the gods have given me the power to understand whomever I inhabit."

Don't make jokes about the gods.

"I'm not. I have no other explanation for how I can understand you, other than we share your brain."

Villic grimaced. He didn't like when Speaker reminded him about that. He forced himself to focus on the task at hand and finished digging out the Magicus, who also had a broken ankle, which Villic discovered upon bumping it.

How do I tell him I'm going to help?

"I think he's figured that out already."

I want to tell him.

Villic couldn't learn a language in a few minutes, but Speaker taught him how to pronounce the words he was to say in the king's tongue.

"I go get help. You wait here," Villic said.

The Magicus nodded and rested his head on a bundle of clothing scraps Villic had gathered for him.

"He will not stay here and wait for you if he can help it. He's going to assume you'll return and one of your comrades will execute him."

That won't happen.

"Are you sure? Think about that for a moment."

The Splintered Manes followed a specific hierarchy. Nobody could just execute the Magicus; he was a prisoner. They'd have to listen to the will of the gods spoken through the shamans. Villic had seen the gods' answer to killing the Magicus earlier. They didn't want the man to die at the hands of Villic anyway. He didn't believe the shamans would ignore the call of the gods. *Though maybe the gods want the shamans to torture him and then kill him.*

"Maybe you're misinterpreting a natural event and projecting your desires upon it."

Speaker *could* be right, though Villic didn't want that to be the case. He needed consultation with the shamans. Villic didn't want to decide himself.

After further help from Speaker, Villic said to the Magicus, "I return at sunrise."

Intent on making the deadline he'd set for himself, Villic jogged toward the Splintered Manes camp.

EDELBROCK BRENDIS

2nd Cycle of Winter, 231st Reign of Garcovi
Lochwall, Calrym

Nothing was more frustrating than days when the gladiators fought in the arena. Nobody was around—at least mentally, for most would nervously pace or whisper to their fighting partners about various strategies or train alone—and the trainees couldn't spectate or interrupt anyone's process, else they'd get yelled at and maybe hit. There were two reasonings given for trainees not being allowed to spectate. First, the new recruits needed to train as much as possible before their debut. Second, it would spoil the "surprise," a mandate put in place to *all* the Houses for *all* trainees. Scayde Haklon believed it was more fun for spectators to watch the first-year fighters flounder and figure out what was happening. Edelbrock wasn't sure why that was such a big deal. He supposed, in one aspect, it was good because watching people fight and die could contribute to worse nerves. He still wished he had a choice in the matter though.

All things considered, Edelbrock thought he was rather well prepared. He had plenty of combat experience, so he knew he'd be able to manage his nerves better than anyone who hadn't taken part in concentrated warfare. He felt rather confident with a significant selection of the weapons, though there were still a few he struggled with. Anytime he trained with any of the veteran gladiators, he had his ass handed to him. However, he was getting much better. Now when he sparred with anyone and didn't land at least one blow, it was an off day. Before, that would've been rare.

News of war spread throughout Buzzard's Bowl. Calrym had invaded Cyrok. The information made for interesting dinner conversation, but otherwise, Edelbrock focused more on his own life. If he'd been on the outside, he would've spent hours every day calculating how economies would change, what might increase in value, what might decrease, and how he could profit off the changes. Inside Buzzard's Bowl, however, he focused on having a future life to live.

Since the Velvet Mother had escorted Edelbrock, Nauc, and Bruise to their hypogeum in Buzzard's Bowl, they'd seen a representative a few times. Edelbrock learned this was normal for them to come and go. The veterans said the Velvet Mother sometimes arrived to inspect current trainees and other gladiators, chastise them for something they were doing wrong, or offer moral support and gifts—often in the way of fabulous food.

Three people showed up in the early morning hours the day before the last event was to take place in Buzzard's Bowl for that season. There'd been few casualties Edelbrock cared about. Chellin had lost an arm yesterday, and a man he'd just met had died a week ago.

Edelbrock regretted that. The man had been a good person, forced into the arena for defaulting on a loan he couldn't pay. Now he'd paid for it with his life.

Edelbrock watched as the Velvet Mother and two strangers toured the hypogeum. The Velvet Mother was being led around by one of the other two and asking questions about the place that Edelbrock thought they'd know if they were in charge. The animated stranger leading the trio was an average man with freckles and a receding hairline. Edelbrock overheard one of them call the man Stanton. The second stranger was odd. He remained silent, limping after the other two with his hood pulled over his head. The Velvet Mother asked probing questions the entire time and once passed Edelbrock but ignored him. It seemed they weren't down there to inspect the gladiators. At least not as individuals, which was fine by Edelbrock.

When a former officer in the military, Edelbrock had used to inspect his own men. By analyzing their rooms, their possessions, the overall condition of their clothes, their weapons, and their appearances, Edelbrock could ascertain what they were doing well, and, more important, what they were doing wrong. He expected a report from the Velvet Mother at the end of their tour. Edelbrock was correct.

When the Velvet Mother finished the guided tour, the gladiators were told to line up inside the training room. Stanton stood facing them, offering a smile and what seemed to be a nod of encouragement. The Velvet Mother and the quiet man whispered in the background, pointing at various individuals. When everyone finished lining up, the pair stopped conversing.

The Velvet Mother clasped their hands together, bloodied as they were. "According to my associate, you've been training rigorously. And doing well in the arena the past few seasons."

Edelbrock nodded with the rest of the gladiators. He crossed his arms in front of his chest, watching his House Head, and, for some reason, noticed how bulging his muscles had become. His arms were tight and veiny from wrist to shoulder, and his abdomen popped out in ways it never had before. Edelbrock had transformed his body.

The Velvet Mother didn't give a shit about the discovery of his body proportions and kept speaking. "I would see this progress continue. The money earned in Buzzard's Bowl, as you are all aware, is substantial. Fuck. I'm not good at this talking shit." They waved forward their silent companion. Edelbrock figured that was an odd decision. Stanton seemed to be the talker, not this quieter figure.

Edelbrock's surprise only escalated once the man spoke with a distinctive stutter and an air of authority that Edelbrock wouldn't dare cross. "As m-my c-c-companion was saying, the financial b-benefits of Buzzard's B-B-B-Bowl are lucrative. We're prepared to offer significant b-bonuses to everyone who performs well in the next season. With this money, you will be able to purchase your f-f-freedom."

Edelbrock's eardrums pulsated as a resounding cheer came from other gladiators. His heart soared, and for the first time since arriving at Buzzard's Bowl, he had hope. Hope that one day he'd be free of this place. That one day he'd be able to confront Jaylena. And Scayde Haklon.

Soon thereafter, the Velvet Mother, Stanton, and the stutterer bid them farewell and exited the hypogeum. Elation filled Edelbrock. From then on, he trained with a smile on his face. He was working to free himself.

Another wave of drafted gladiators arrived, but Edelbrock paid them no attention, nor was he expected to.

DEMRI SLARN

2nd Cycle of Winter, 231st Reign of Garcovi
Lochwall, Calrym

The Buzzard's Bowl deed was the most profitable asset the Corbéo family had. There were a few other businesses: a winery, a tavern, a couple of small-time gangs who worked on pickpocketing and other various forms of theft, and the cooper's, which the former Velvet Mother had dismantled because of its lack of profit. Then, for some unknown reason, she'd made it her headquarters, rather than the modest manor the Corbéos also owned. Demri assumed it was to maintain the cover of her identity.

They'd been fortunate Stanton had become such a crucial part of the operation in the last several years. Stanton explained how Elisi Corbéo's age had hampered her abilities, so she'd brought him in to assist her. He'd caught on fast, and it wasn't long before he'd known everything about the business and the Corbéo family. He was quick to mention any loyalty he'd felt for the

Corbéo family was nonexistent, but Demri wasn't so sure.

Because of the damage done to the cooper's during their battle with Magicus Glaouse, they'd moved the Velvet Mother's headquarters to a warehouse that stored much of the organization's supplies, including kegs and bottles for the winery and tavern; weapons, armor, and other tools; several crates of nonperishables, just in case the Velvet Mother needed to go into hiding; and, much to Demri's surprise, a locked hatch containing several safe boxes with a significant amount of money stashed away. They recovered the key in the Velvet Mother's desk at the cooper's.

Weeks after visiting the Velvet Mother's hypogeum, Caius handed over several hundred coins to Demri, in return for Demri fulfilling his promise by allowing Caius to become the Velvet Mother without resistance. Flush with money, Demri's first aim was to secure a Glyphist to replenish his Well. A close secondary was finding a Healer so that maybe, after twenty years, he could fix his legs. And perhaps the burn scar on his face. Stanton informed him of a local Glyphist who was in Lochwall and sold their services in a stall at the local market.

Demri made his way toward the small stand the Magicus operated out of. It was in the center of Lochwall's marketplace, a prime location of the Velvet Mother's pickpockets. Demri even recognized a pair walking among the crowd of customers. A large display table rested under a canopy, providing shade to the Magicus sitting in a chair behind the table and wearing the pin of a quill—Glyphist. On the customer side of the table, an old rickety wooden chair sat half under the canopy's shade. The only items on display were a

Soulpen and a menu listing prices for various-sized Soul Glyphs. A sign above the stand read MARK'S MARKS.

"Magicus M-Mark?"

The man, a tall thin reedy fellow, stood and shook his head. "Magicus Jintos." He waved an arm up at the sign. "Merely a business tactic."

Demri lifted a brow at that but said nothing. It wasn't his place to criticize a moron. And at the moment, he needed the moron. "I need your services."

"Splendid. Please take a seat. What type of Soul Glyph do you need?"

"Full replenishment."

Magicus Jintos didn't even bat an eye, expensive as the request was. Perhaps it was normal for Magicai in Lochwall to purchase a lot. Or perhaps he didn't believe Demri. So Demri reached into his cloak's dark interior, pulling out several small sacks of coins and setting them on the table with a distinctive clink.

The Magicus's eyes widened, and a toothy grin spread across his face. "Wonderful, wonderful. Take a seat. I'll have you all marked up in no time. Mark's guarantee." He laughed and sat, picking up the Soulpen.

Demri followed suit, and for the first time in many years, his Well was renewed. He'd forgotten that strange feeling of his life force being sucked out of his core and sculpted onto his skin. But it wasn't a feeling he disliked. It was one of rejuvenation. One of power. He just needed to remember not to waste it, despite whatever emotions or desires he felt at the time.

S tanton couldn't help much with locating a Healer. He said they weren't selling their services to the public in Lochwall. This wasn't abnormal. Healers didn't waste their life healing random citizens for exuberant amounts of coin. They'd die within weeks of graduating from Ashmount. Stanton told Demri that Lord Scayde Haklon, owner of Buzzard's Bowl, must have access to Healers, as the man was rich and often had to heal injured fighters for one reason or another.

Contacting Lord Haklon would prove difficult. Stanton explained the man was everywhere, but his closest confidant was the city's formal marshal, Everic Deywin, who, for reasons Stanton wasn't sure of, still went by the title. Lord Haklon's personal marshal maybe. Stanton offered to send a couple of men with a message to Marshal Deywin on Demri's behalf, so he wouldn't have to go looking himself. It didn't take long, and the men returned with a message of their own. Marshal Deywin was interested in meeting with Demri and would receive him the following afternoon just outside Haklon's estate. Demri accepted the invitation, hopeful he'd secure a lead to a Healer.

Late the next afternoon, Demri took a carriage outside the city to Haklon's Estate. Three of the Velvet Mother's men accompanied him because he brought a chest full of coins in case there was a Healer there and he didn't want to get robbed.

Marshal Everic Deywin, accompanied with an escort of several armed men, stood outside the compound. A thin mustache rested on an otherwise unremarkable face. He spat some juice out the side of his mouth and stood up straight when Demri exited the carriage.

"Magicus Demri Slarn in the flesh and blood, I see." The marshal's voice seemed slurred or distorted from the pile of skachi leaves he swished around his mouth.

"Marshal."

Marshal Deywin spat again, the glob landing only a

few inches away from Demri's foot. Demri gave the man a look, one that most men cowered from.

Marshal Deywin seemed unphased and nodded. "Don't worry, son, if I wanted to hit you, I would've."

Demri couldn't be sure, but he was pretty certain the last time anybody had called him "son" was over two decades ago. The marshal was one of those men difficult to intimidate.

Marshal Deywin waved his hand toward the vast arena behind him. "Shall we, Magicus?" There was a whiff of sarcasm in the way he spoke the title.

"Is Lord Haklon within?"

"Lord Haklon will present himself when, and if, needed. Until then, you deal with me." He spat again, this time discharging an entire leaf. Then the marshal reached into a pouch and replaced it with a new one.

Feeling hesitant about the situation, Demri followed Marshal Deywin and his men into the compound, waving away his own escort. They'd remain with the carriage to watch the money.

Buildings surrounded the arena, and the marshal brought them to one of the farthest. Inside was a small entry hall. A woman sitting behind a desk looked up as they entered. When she saw Demri, she put on a pair of spectacles. Demri swallowed nervously.

She cleared her throat. "Marshal. Are you aware the man you're walking with is an Enforcer?" The Examiner stared at Demri, almost gleeful at the thought of exposing his abilities. Then her expression changed. "Or . . . wait. Are you . . ." Her voice trailed off as they passed her, and Marshal Deywin ignored the woman.

That could have been bad.

The men following Marshal Deywin all veered off, entering a side passage. Marshal Deywin continued straight down the hall, bringing the pair of them into a small office. A rickety table rested in the middle of the room and was topped with various parchments, quills, and inkwells. A half-written letter, or other form of work, occupied the center of the table, ink-tipped quill still laying on the sheet. A dried pool of black ink formed around the tip of the quill, ruining the document. Two glass vials filled with a brownish liquid sat on one end of the table.

Marshal Deywin took a seat behind the desk, setting his worn boots up on the table without clearing the area. Dirt cascaded off the soles, filtering down onto the parchment. Demri could've shivered at the lack of care the man displayed toward what could be important documents. Demri sat across the desk and didn't enjoy having his back to the door they'd just entered. But it wasn't about what made Demri comfortable at the moment.

The marshal sniffed, then grabbed one of the two vials and spat into it. The brown discharge mixed with the old, swirling around in an odorous mess of slime. *Ah. So that's disgusting.*

"You're looking for a Healer." The marshal rolled the skachi leaves to the other side of his mouth. Demri didn't see the point in all this messing around.

"C-c-c-c-correct." That was more troublesome to say than usual. Was he nervous? He didn't know who this Scayde Haklon was. Marshal Deywin knew Demri's full name and that he was an Enforcer. Would he know about the bounty Ashmount had put on him? It was probable. Would he want to collect? Demri was worth a *lot* of money if brought in. What if this Healer business was a ruse? Demri had three ruffians outside who wouldn't fight for his life if it came down to it. They were loyal to the Velvet Mother and only her. Nor would they put up enough resistance even if they did.

At least Stanton knew where he was. But would Stanton care if something happened to Demri? Would Caius help him? Caius had other responsibilities now, and the man had already helped Demri enough for one lifetime.

"To heal what?" Marshal Deywin crossed his hands and leaned back further, the chair tipping precariously as he did so. But Demri knew his type. The thought that he'd fall over was laughable. Some men just didn't have the same set of issues Demri did.

"Everything." Yes. He was nervous.

"Face and legs?"

Demri nodded.

"That'll cost a lot of coin. And years for the Healer. Decades even."

"I'm aware."

Marshal Deywin sat up, boots slapping the floor, arms banging against the table as he leaned forward. "You're aware that I know about the bounty on your ass?"

"I figured you m-m-m-might know about it."

Marshal Deywin grinned, spitting again. Demri wasn't sure if he was more nervous or disgusted. "Don't worry about it, Demri. Lord Haklon knows you're a Magicus of significance. He doesn't want to waste a powerful connection by discarding you and tossing you across the sea to an establishment he knows nothing about. Let's say he heals you free of cost. What can you offer the man in return, son?"

Although he hadn't been able to play the political game before, Demri had a fair understanding of how it worked. Offering random things of value wouldn't help. There was a specific thing Lord Haklon wanted, or the man guessed Demri had something valuable. Demri guessed it was the latter. But he figured it would be safer to try the former first. Best not to overplay if possible.

"What does Lord Haklon want?"

"What does he want, indeed?"

The door behind Demri opened.

"Enough playing around, Everic," said a commanding voice.

Demri turned in his chair. Entering the doorway was a man, yellow cloak trailing behind him and a thin sword at his belt. He turned to Demri and extended a hand. Demri shook it.

"Lord Haklon," the marshal said, rising from the chair.

"You may leave us, Marshal Deywin."

"My lord." The marshal exited the office.

Lord Haklon commandeered Marshal Deywin's chair. He sneered at the skachi vials. Demri thought the nobleman whispered, "Revolting," but Demri might've just been thinking that himself and projecting it onto Lord Haklon's disgusted expression.

"Now." Lord Haklon leaned back, resting one hand on the pommel of his sword, the other hand tapping the desk in front of him. Another flash of disgust crossed the man's face when he looked at the half-written parchment and the mess on top of it. "I'm tempted to move us to a more dignified location, but there's no point until we've reached a mutual agreement. Magicus Demri, is it?"

"Yes, my lord."

"I'm told that you're a dangerous outlaw. A man that's been on the run for *twenty* years. Is that correct?"

"Yes."

"Admirable. Simply awe-inspiring. I must admit, Demri—may I call you that? We *are* friendly around these parts."

"Of course, my lord."

"Magnificent. Call me Scayde. This 'lord' stuff gets rather stifling when you meet somebody of *worth*. Titles are great and everything, but the elite need not focus on groveling over one another."

"I agree."

Scayde Haklon smiled. Demri didn't like it. It felt forced. But everything Scayde Haklon did seemed forced. An act. A play he was putting on, attempting to impress Demri. Perhaps this was just how the man operated. A show of force.

"May I tell a story?"

Confused, Demri nodded.

"Brilliant. I enjoy my stories. I *insist* you don't interrupt, however. It throws the story off. Mixes everything up in my head. You understand?"

Demri got a bad vibe from this but didn't think he could do anything about it. The man wanted to talk, so Demri would let him talk. "I won't interrupt."

Scayde Haklon beamed. That made Demri even *more* nervous.

Then Scayde recited his story. "There's a school you may be familiar with. It rests in Qothe, a rocky and desolate country. Many call it the University of Arcanical Arts. Those who attend find this insulting. They call it Ashmount, named after the fiery volcano it rests beside."

Scayde knew Demri knew this already. Demri wondered where this was going. *He's demonstrating his power over me.*

"A group of men and women learn mystical arts there. They call themselves Magicai. They're secretive, only allowing specific individuals entry. These few possess the Trace and learn a variety of abilities. Once trained, they're sold, like mercenaries or cattle, to the highest bidder around the world. Kings, dukes, generals, and others of vast wealth employ these men and women to do as they command. Fight their wars, heal their wounds. In return, they receive magnificent profits, allowing them to become wealthy almost overnight."

Bored, Demri crossed his arms and glanced around Marshal Deywin's disheveled office. He didn't see anything of note.

"Occasionally, a Magicus breaks protocol or restriction. When this occurs, the leaders of Ashmount place a bounty on that Magicus's head. Whoever brings the Magicus in receives a large reward. This process is often successful and fast. Few have been able to evade the roaming Collectors. Some speculate an underground group of Magicai, called the Elkavich, has formed and trains their own members intending to battle back against the rest of the Magicai, and these rogue Magicai find their way to the Elkavich to join in this inevitable battle. I've also heard it rumored Ashmount harbors secrets of its own, secrets most Magicai are unaware of."

Demri wondered how Scayde knew that type of information. It wasn't commonplace; even most Magicai didn't believe Ashmount harbored secrets.

"Two decades ago, there was a Magicus. He pored over books every day and throughout the night. Reading, researching, wondering. Fascinating work, this was. So fascinating, he didn't care about other people, or if he cared, he didn't bother to show it. Perhaps he was unwanted. Disliked. Forgotten. No one seems to know. He did, rumors suggest, find something incredible. Something of note. A secret of the school. When discovered, Ashmount's leaders confronted him. Not sure what to do, they confined him to his rooms, until they could figure it out. But this man was smart. He knew they would kill him. So he escaped. He fought novice

Magicai, and they wounded him, but he got away. By jumping off the mountain." Scayde stopped to clear his throat.

Demri wondered why Scayde was reciting Demri's past. Intimidation? Or was there something he wanted? Perhaps he was illustrating his knowledge or dedication to researching Demri.

"A man found the Magicus. He helped him, aided him. Together, they went on the run for twenty years. Nobody of importance or skill ever confronted them. So they lived. Alone but together. And they murdered countless citizens for no reason. Twenty years later, the pair arrive outside of Lochwall. When they enter the city, they end up burning down a known location of the Velvet Mother. We find several of her associates dead. Along with an old woman, Elisi Corbéo. The *real* Velvet Mother. The Magicus and the brigand have been together for a *long* time. One of them harbors a secret from the other one."

That was true. There was *one* thing Demri hadn't told Caius. He'd told *nobody*. He frowned, and Scayde took notice.

"Or maybe they both harbor a secret from each other." Scayde Haklon stood. "A man named Caius didn't want anyone to know it, but he's been living under an alias for decades." This wasn't a tremendous surprise to Demri. Caius never enjoyed discussing his past. "I'll heal you, but I want to know what you've found out. I want to know why the Magicai are so desperate to recover you, and I want to know why you've been killing citizens around Cedain at random. If you do this, I will have you healed. And as a token of friendship—the identity of the man you've been traveling with all along? He's a man presumed dead. A man that's been missing for *many* years. Tythus Corbéo. I assume he's the new Velvet Mother?"

And everything made sense. All Demri could do was stare at Scayde's shit-eating grin.

Fucking Caius.

KELDEN STOOLE

2nd Cycle of Winter, 231st Reign of Garcovi
Ashmount, Qothe

Kelden mastered the art of crafting Soulpens with reeds. Perhaps *mastered* was a strong word, considering it had taken five weeks before Magicus Kalixa told him he'd done it well. Even then, she'd made him continue practicing another week until he could make one with his eyes closed. Which she then tested him on. It took another two days for him to pass that test.

Because of the repetitious nature of the work, Kelden enjoyed his days off more than when he was in class. Something he never would've predicted. He couldn't shake the desire to become an Enforcer. Often during these breaks from class, Kelden spent his time in the library, reading about them. He could feel an obsession cultivating within, one he knew he wouldn't be able to stop. Despite that, he read on. There had to be a way to learn to be an Enforcer. Everything he read suggested otherwise. Although Glyphists could draw Soul Glyphs on an Enforcer, it wasn't possible on anyone else. He started reading about learning a second type of magic. This resulted in nothing, as anybody who'd tried had failed and died for treasonous actions against the school. Committing these experiments was a grave offense. But he wouldn't stop. He needed to learn or find something. He knew in his heart that his destiny was to become an Enforcer.

Kelden found out early on that asking about the prospect of becoming an Enforcer was a bad idea. Magicus Kalixa reprimanded him when he'd inquired about it. One time, he'd asked the Archmagicus for an audience to discuss the possibility. The Archmagicus turned away his request. This didn't prevent Kelden from further research. He continued looking.

Returning to his dorm after finally passing his test to create several perfect Soulpens back-to-back, Kelden found two letters on the floor. The first was from his father, Hillion.

My son, Kelden,

I hope things are working out well for you and Sungoa. Life at the bakery has been quiet. I have unfortunate news to pass on to you, as I don't think you are aware. The group who journeyed with you to the University of Arcanical Arts has not yet returned to Warwin. They're presumed dead. A traveler came through the other day and mentioned a man fitting the description of Roberon helping some enslavers, and then, because he'd lied to them, he was carted off along with the people he'd brought to them. It's sad to assume it, but I believe it was your companions you journeyed to the university with. It's a relief you were accepted to the univer-sity. I'm not sure why I'm surprised at Roberon's actions, but I'm glad you didn't leave Warwin alone with him. I shouldn't have trusted that swindler, and I regret sending you with him, though it seems to have paid off. You passed the Trials, and they accepted you! What wonderful news for our family name. I hope you can write back soon. Thank you for the money, son. I've invested it into the bakery.

Your father,

Hillion Stoole

Kelden wondered how long ago the letter had arrived. Either mail carriers didn't enjoy coming up to Ashmount or the Magicai kept them until they felt Kelden deserved them. The second letter was from his friend, Graylan.

Kelden,

I'm glad that you were accepted into the university. Not going with you and Sungoa is something I regret, but sometimes we have to do things we don't want because it's our responsibility. It has become boring here without you. Whenever I'm not helping my parents, I find myself alone, fishing or considering how things could've been. Maybe next year I'll journey over and see if I get as lucky as you and Sungoa were. I doubt it, but even the money would be worth it. If you find time, come and say hi. We miss you.

Good luck, Kelden.

Graylan

It was nice to see his father and best friend were doing all right. He wondered what happened to Nauc Othepi, and everyone else he'd traveled with to the university. If his father was correct and they were enslaved, he wondered where they'd be taken. Graylan, though he didn't know it, was probably fortunate he didn't come.

Kelden made a conscious decision not to write back to either his father or his friend. Friends and family were all right, but he couldn't become distracted. He had to focus on his training. He also wanted to spend all his free time investigating the possibility of becoming an Enforcer. Besides, how pathetic would it be to write to his father, or Graylan, and tell them he'd passed the training only to become a Glyphist? There would be no respect there. Only laughs.

***

After Soulpens, Magicus Kalixa taught Kelden about Soul Glyphs. Even though he already knew about them, she took him on a long expedition through the varying sizes and what each size could power. This upset him because they were discussing Enforcer powers. What did it matter? He wasn't using Soul Glyphs.

After a few boring, and envious, days of learning about this, Magicus Kalixa told Kelden they were proceeding forward with the drawing. This consisted of him drawing with a thin quill on a blank piece of paper. She would offer a random thing or image she wanted him to draw. His objective was to draw it with no mistakes and with as thin of a line as possible. She said she was looking for control over the Soulpen and images that looked professional. This was something Kelden struggled with. He'd drawn nothing before now. It took him weeks practicing the art, and still Magicus Kalixa found issues.

Outside of lessons, he continued spending late nights in the library. After exhaustive nights researching, he found something that furthered his cause. He'd been reading a book that offered new discussions on the possibilities of a Magicus's powers, *The Anecdotes and Curiosities of Enebrial Hubbart,* when he stumbled upon a small piece of parchment tucked between two of the pages. He unfolded it and couldn't believe what he read.

As Enebrial suggests on page 214, the Magicai of Ashmount suppress the individuality of the Magicus by assigning a school they believe to be most fitting. I'm certain there's a reason only the head Examiner of Ashmount has access to the "special" spectacles that allow them to "determine" who gets placed where. I almost have my proof.

He also noticed a pair of initials in the bottom right-hand corner of the note: DS. It was dated just over twenty years ago.

Kelden started reading page 214.

While investigating the process of the Trials, I interviewed Magicus Kohne.

First disclaimer: He was, at the time of the interview, eighty-six years old. A man with a self-admitted "foggy memory," Magicus Kohne had been involved with the recruitment process since he first graduated from his studies as an Examiner.

Second disclaimer: After the following interview, Magicus Kohne turned bright red and declined further comment on the matter, stating he said "too much" and he was "in trouble enough." Later sources urged me to redact his statements, as they were the ramblings of an old man. I believe them to be accurate. However, the Magicai's official stance is they thoroughly dispute the following transcript.

Enebrial: Magicus Kohne, the Magicai don't decide for themselves what branch of magic they study. Do you find that to be odd?

Kohne: No. It is, in fact, how nature intended. The Trace

chooses which path forward a Magicus shall take. You already know this, Magicus Enebrial.

Enebrial: If nature is indeed in charge of the choice, then why are there so few of one branch, yet so many of another? In my experience, nature prefers symmetry or patterns. There are no known patterns of the Trace or the branches it yields. Though, I confess, I have found one instance of a pattern. Whenever an inducted class of trainees start their learning here, they're often weighted in favor of whatever branch Ashmount is lacking. For example, if we are heading into a prominent war and we need more Enforcers, there are far and away more Enforcers and Healers. But in peacetime, the number of Enforcers is shockingly low. When there is a prominent bounty or an extensive amount of them, we have an abundance of Collectors. And Glyphists? They're always rare. I presume this is to keep the existing Glyphists happy. If you were to ask me, I would say there is a strong pattern here, Magicus Kohne. A pattern suggesting it's not natural.

Kohne: I'm not here to debate the conveniences of nature with you, Enebrial. Mother Avani looks over the world and protects us, as you're aware. Without her guidance, perhaps there wouldn't even be any Magicai.

Enebrial: No, perhaps not. But for the sake of argument, Magicus Kohne, can you comment on the patterns I mentioned?

Kohne: I see no patterns other than our loving Mother Avani watching over us.

Enebrial: So you, as the head Examiner, have no control over what happens when students are welcomed into the University of Arcanical Arts?

Kohne: University of . . . are you dense, Enebrial? It's Ashmount. You know how that insults the Order of the Magicai. This interview is over.

Enebrial: I apologize, Magicus Kohne. Please finish the

interview? We've gone through such lengths to conduct it since I'm no longer welcomed here.

Kohne: Very well. The Archmagicus would prefer this interview ends in mutual satisfaction and there be no conflict.

Enebrial: Good, good. When you select the candidates for the position of Healer, what sticks out to you as the obvious qualifying traits?

Kohne: Well, I like to think that a young woman is good or an old man. They often —(Magicus Kohne begins staring at me. He recognizes he's fallen into my trap.)

Enebrial: Go on.

Kohne: No, you heard me wrong. I didn't mean to suggest that I choose who becomes a Healer. I meant what I would prefer for the role.

Enebrial: Magicus Kohne, it's clear that you select individual candidates based on traits, meaning you choose who learns which branch. How do you control the power within the Magicai so they're forced to learn what you desire them to?

Kohne: I'm sorry, but that's enough for today. I've said more than enough on the topic. Too much.

Enebrial: Please, Magicus Kohne. (Magicus Kohne starts walking away. I follow, as I know he is eager to escape the troublesome questions. But I seek the truth.) Magicus Kohne, why are you not allowing the Magicai to select their own paths?

Kohne: (Now several feet away from me, he's spry for an old man). Leave me alone, Enebrial. I'm in trouble enough.

Enebrial: So you've spilled secrets, and now you fear retribution?

Unknown Magicus: Enebrial Hubbart, you need to leave the premises.

Enebrial: But I—

Another Unknown Magicus: It's not up for debate. Leave now.

Enebrial: Very well. Thank Magicus Kohne for his time. And offer my gratitude to the Archmagicus for helping this interview occur.

(End of interview.)

So, as you can see, Magicus Kohne let slip he chooses who receives which position. I attempted further interviews, but Magicus Kohne was always indisposed. Later, I found out that four and a half weeks after the interview, Magicus Kohne "passed from natural causes." I doubt that very much so. In the following decade, I conducted further research and investigations, but I have yet to find anything of note. Whether Magicus Kohne was forgetful or telling the truth, we may never confirm. However, I am of the mind that he slipped a tremendous secret.

Hope was the first emotion Kelden felt. He recalled rumors of war and his classmates all becoming Enforcers. Both signs aligned with Enebrial's theory. He had found *The Anecdotes and Curiosities of Enebrial Hubbart* in the speculative fiction section of the library, though it was a book, and he hadn't been looking for it. His next aim was to search through the roster of deceased Magicai. If Kelden could verify Magicus Kohne had existed, maybe Enebrial Hubbart's interview was true. If that was the case, Kelden could discover a way to become an Enforcer. He had never reached these levels of excitement before.

SERADAL WINTLOCK

2nd Cycle of Winter, 231st Reign of Garcovi
Cyrok

"They're coming," Sera said as several dozen soldiers rode closer to the caravan. She realized nobody panicked. No one had even noticed she'd spoken. "They're coming!" She held the canvas open wide, allowing the curious faces turning her way to view the approaching riders. She started trembling.

A volley of arrows launched into the air. They'd misjudged the distance, and only a few arrows peppered the side of the carriage. Most fell short.

The caravan lurched to a halt. Men shouted. She heard Vithor Bane ordering his men around. It seemed they were going to make a stand.

"Angazo, Renard, please help my father into the washtub." They complied.

Magicus Ashté retreated with them. "I'll watch over him." *Good.*

"I feel like a useless fool hiding in here," her father said.

"Better a fool than a corpse, father." Sera drew her sword and gripped her shield in her other hand. A line of men was already assembling out in front of her, readying a defense in the snow. They'd stopped in a small opening in the middle of the forest and were able to spread out. Once she joined them, along with Angazo, her best guess put the Calrites at a two-to-one advantage over them. *Spectacular.*

Sera hopped out of the carriage, her boots crunching on the icy trail. Vithor Bane was not defending the caravan. *I wonder how many men he has protecting his sorry rear, taking them away from the battle. A battle we may lose.* Mother Avani save them if the enemy had a Magicus.

The brigands Vithor Bane employed had a variety of rugged equipment—rusted swords and dented armor. The odds appeared to be less in their favor than she'd first calculated. Even if they won, many of them would die today.

The Calrites rode closer, bows stashed and swords drawn. Their leader, a porky man with a wisp of hair and a pink face, let out a breathy "whoop," and pulled on his horse's reins. The horse stopped about ten feet away, his men falling in line next to him.

"Ho there, refugees, escapees, and deserters. I must admit, I'm surprised to see as many armed people here as I do. We saw fresh tracks leaving Vox and figured we'd recapture a handful of citizens, but I stand corrected. Nevertheless, I'm here to offer sanctuary from the cold." The porky man gestured back toward the capital. "We have a warm bed and food waiting just within the city's limits. After Vox is captured, of course."

Sera pictured Falcon Knights readying themselves to fight, watching from the city's walls, preparing themselves for their deaths. She, once again, felt an enormous wave of guilt.

He smiled, as if making a genuine offer. "All you have to do is lay down your arms and trust that I, Sergeant Lom, will take care of you."

Vithor Bane's men looked to one another, understandably confused by Sergeant Lom's words. Sera had to admit this wasn't the type of engagement she was expecting.

She pushed her way through Vithor Bane's men. "I am Cyr Seradal Wintlock."

Sergeant Lom inclined his head, imitating respect, but she could clearly see the disdain he held for her on his face. "Well met. A Falcon Knight, eh? I just fought hundreds of your kin in the west. Retreated like the bitches they yearn for." His men cracked a laugh, and he chuckled. "Surrender to us now."

"We aren't stupid enough to follow you to an instant death trap."

Sergeant Lom's face fell. "A pity, knight. I'll send a prayer to your mother when your corpse lies at my feet."

"Your men already killed my mother." Sera gritted her teeth, took five steps forward, and, surprising herself more than Sergeant Lom, ran the man through the gut. She'd expected *some* resistance from his armor or a reaction from the man. Instead, a stroke of luck had her sword slid under his mail, penetrating the padded gambeson he wore underneath.

Gasping, he looked down at his fat paunch and the blade protruding from his body. Sergeant Lom tipped over and fell off his mount, ripping the sword out of Sera's grasp.

Then chaos erupted.

The Calrites rushed forward in defense of their fallen

superior, while Vithor Bane's men followed Sera's lead and attacked.

She planted a foot on the groaning sergeant's chest and tugged on the sword, extracting it. Blood rushed out and Sergeant Lom screamed. She quieted him by driving the point into his neck.

For a moment, all she could do was stare at the dead man's body, his insides leaking out. Just seconds ago, the man was sitting atop a horse. She felt the overwhelming urge to puke. Instead, she swallowed the saliva in her mouth and renewed her focus. Becoming distracted in the middle of a battle would see her wounded or killed.

A crossbow bolt soared past her, sinking into a nearby Calrite soldier's thigh. He stumbled, and Sera capitalized on this. She rushed forward and bashed the man in the face with the hilt of her sword. The soldier's nose snapped, red liquid spraying the air in front of him. Angazo then impaled the man from behind. Nodding to each other, they split up to find other targets.

A scream from behind made her turn around. A very tall Calrite soldier was trying to enter the carriage that her father was in. Renard was attacking the man with a broom handle, which proved rather ineffective. Two caravan guards lay dead at the soldier's feet.

Sera sprinted over. The Calrite man slashed at Renard. His sword got hung up in the canvas covering though.

She wanted to call out to him. Grab his attention. But the soldier's back was to her, and if Renard could just hold on for a moment longer, she'd surprise the Calrite.

Sera reached the soldier and stabbed at his back. The man freed his sword from the canvas and turned just in time. Her steel ricocheted off the side of his chain mail.

Surprised, the soldier faced her. He was so tall, Sera's eye level rested upon his stomach.

He sneered. "A woman, eh?"

She didn't have time for a discussion revolving around gender. Plus, the man would win a fair fight. She resolved the dispute right away, driving her sword up through his genitals and into his stomach. Cyr Ilic Strictland would've been proud. Seizing the opportunity and fighting dirty. War was much less glamorous than the stories suggested. *Point to me.*

The tall man collapsed, and Sera peeked into the carriage. Everyone was fine.

She turned back to the fight, examining their progress so far. Several of Vithor Bane's men were down. Many more of the Calrites lay dead or dying on the battlefield. The crystal whiteness of the ice and snow surrounding her reflected a ruby glow. The sickness returned, and she staggered to the side of the carriage, expelling her meal all over the wheel. A burning acrid fire lingered in her mouth and throat. She spat to get the taste out, but that didn't help.

Sera collected herself. She saw Angazo battling a man. He was gripping his side as if injured and losing the duel. She needed to get to him before he lost the duel.

A battle cry issued to her left. A wild hairy man wearing only a long fur coat charged toward her, a two-handed maul raised above his head.

She dove out of his way, crashing into the snow. Rolling, she put as much distance between them as she could. She connected with a pair of entangled corpses. She stood and realized she'd dropped her shield.

Maulman was charging toward her again. She braced herself, digging her feet in. The maul swung down at her. Summoning all her strength, Sera slammed her sword against the maul's haft. The deflected maul smashed into the ground. She stepped around Maulman, then slashed at him. A red gash appeared across his back, coat sliced open. He grunted.

Maulman swiveled around, a knife now in each hand. He threw one at her, but she was already moving. The hilt of the knife bounced off her shoulder. He growled and sprinted at her, snorting like a horse.

She braced herself a second time, holding the sword with both hands. When Maulman was close enough, she charged. Sera aimed the sword's point at the man's chest, and they collided.

A knife scraped across her chest, protected by her armor. The man groaned. She could feel her blade was stiff and stuck inside his body. Then they fell, a heap of tangled limbs. She landed beneath Maulman, his weight crushing her into the snow. He struggled and groaned, the hilt of her sword pressed against him. She wriggled, trying to shift the dying man off her.

Sera turned her hands, twisting the sword inside of Maulman. He yelled, coughed, and then his body gave a shudder. Maulman died, his full weight collapsing on top of her. Struggling to breathe, she wriggled her body back and forth, trying to free her arms. After half a minute's battle, her hands came loose, and she heaved him to the side, sliding out from under him. Then Sera retrieved her sword.

She took a moment to survey her surroundings, searching for Angazo. He lay on his back, a pool of blood coalescing around his unmoving body.

Her boots crunched on the snow. A couple of feet toward Angazo, she heard someone shout, "Loose!"

She turned. Five men were still on horseback, bows raised and arrows already soaring in her direction. Two of them sought other targets. The third arrow fell short, sinking into the snow in front of her. The fourth sank into her thigh, tearing flesh. Blood dripped out of the wound, and a flash of pain coursed through her. The fifth shot arced. It flew high in the sky. On the arrow's downward trajectory, Sera noticed she was the target of that shot as well. She tried dragging her leg backward but couldn't move. On her second attempt, she tripped and fell. The arrow plummeted, and Sera screamed.

The arrow cut her scream short, sinking into her neck and pinning her to the ground.

She coughed. The movement resulted in agony, shifting the arrow in her neck. Her vision darkened. She choked on her blood and struggled to inhale air around the shaft and fluid. She coughed, her lungs filling with blood and oxygen.

Sera spit, clearing her mouth. The jarring motion moved the arrow a second time, causing more pain. She coughed again. Time slowed. The bright sun winked at her. A cloud drifted past. She spat another mouthful of blood, worried she might die. It hurt, and she was pinned to the ground. And somehow, she was still alive.

A blurry figure appeared in her view. She blinked tears out of her eyes. A woman. Magicus Ashté. Sera coughed again, choking more.

"Calm yourself." The Healer knelt, touching Sera's forehead with her hand. "You'll live."

Sera closed her eyes, too tired to remain conscious.

INTERLUDE

ARENA HYREL

2nd Cycle of Winter, 231st Reign of Garcovi
Anepolis, Calrym

Arena Hyrel did not know where it came from, who had invented it, or how expensive it was to import. And, realistically, she did not care. You could not put a price on happiness. Not when you had all the money in the world anyway. The purplish polish reflected off her nails, and she smiled serenely. Noblewomen in Lochwall would not pay for this extravagance. A few years ago, she would not have herself. But that was when she had little money. Now, even if others looked at her like a crazed lunatic, she did not mind. It's not like she needed to save her finances. Plenty accumulated in the vault already.

Arena shifted uncomfortably in the rigid wood chair. Why the king would not let them bring their own chairs to the Great Hall was beyond her. Honestly, when you were among the wealthiest in the nation, why did you have to suffer? She crossed her legs, resting one atop her thigh, and sighed.

Everyone gave her a pointed look. The king's was most noticeable. She probably needed to be a bit more careful, truth be told. But it was just so *damned* uncomfortable. At least Duke Harlem Maccaro was not there anymore. She bit her lower lip, suppressing the smile threatening to appear. Thinking about the man stuck in Cyrok, fighting their war, was enough to get her through this council meeting. The fact that Harlem was incorrect about King Alondo and the Remerian army invading Calrym made everything even more delightful.

Duke Sturgeon's voice was enough to place her in a deep coma. The man just droned on and on. His voice was like a verbal disease, and that was on a good day. The constant pauses irritated her to no end. Honestly, when you were among the wealthiest in the nation, why did you have to suffer? They should expel the man and replace him. It just was not right to let the man fester and die here with them present. That's what servants were for. So that they could treat you while you died. And dress you in the frosty morning hours before a council meeting. For whomever else would fill the bath with warm water?

"And so . . . it seems," Duke Sturgeon wheezed, "as if the soldiers we sent to Cyrok are to be victorious with minimal casualties. The latest report suggests that Duke Harlem Maccaro . . ."

Arena craned her neck. It was stiff. Muscles should not be stiff. That was what servants were for. To relax them with their muscled hands. It made no sense the king forbade servants from entering the chamber during a council meeting. They could bring them refreshments, fill their wineglasses, and massage their aching necks. Honestly, when you were among the wealthiest in the nation, why did you have to suffer? King Mikas Garcovi needed some lessons on hospitality. Arena was wise enough not to deliver them.

She could not help but notice the poor table manners of Duke Velturo, sitting across the table from her. He was wiping grease from his chin, which was still dripping onto his new cape he had been bragging about just before the council met. *Foolish.* Now *that* was wasting money. Not that the man needed to worry. He had plenty of it, just as she did.

"Damn it," Duke Velturo mouthed to himself, but she caught it. He had dropped a leg of chicken, and it had rolled down his chest, leaving stains. Arena rolled her eyes. Disgusting. Repugnant. It would not have been worse if they had elevated a city urchin to the position of Duke. *That's not true.* The mere idea of that almost made Arena exclaim out loud.

Petrified by her own thoughts, Arena turned her attention back to Duke Sturgeon's summation of the previous report. One they had time to read before the assembly, which made all of this pointless and an enormous waste of their time. Not that it mattered. They had nothing else to do. Well, Arena did. But nothing of importance. It was just nice to spend one's time being pampered by one's servants.

"As Duke . . . Harlem Maccaro . . . reported, the port town Aleki has been taken and the forces now move forward," Duke Sturgeon said. "Of your nephew, Sir Alyst Garcovi, he's taken the town of Duroc, and the governess Stasia Falconel has fallen in battle. Both armies march toward the capital, Vox, last we knew." The dying man took a pause, regaining his breath.

Arena smiled. The death of the governess meant victory was on the horizon. The Cyroki would not manage without her. The other nobles clapped or cheered. Arena did not partake in the actions of peasantry.

King Mikas's flushed face watched Duke Sturgeon with impressive patience he only exhibited with Sturgeon for some reason. It also did not prevent him from becoming just as annoyed with the old man as any of the other dukes and duchesses. He tapped his jeweled fingers on the table. Arena noticed a particular ruby she had always coveted. She looked away to avoid staring. And to put the gem out of her mind.

"Is that all, Duke Sturgeon?" The king's question came through gritted teeth. It would be easy to set the king off today. Again. This was normal. The king's temper was rather annoying. For the wealthiest man in all of Calrym, he seemed to prefer being angry rather often. Why he did this to himself was anyone's guess. But if Arena was to guess, she would say the king would die of a heart attack within a few more years. Too angry. Perhaps he needed better trained servants. Ones with firm hands. Ones that could squeeze his muscles until he felt a tingling down—

Steel yourself, Arena. These thoughts are unbecoming of you.

Duke Sturgeon said, "Almost . . . done, Your Majesty. We've also received word from King Alondo Sedoa, ruler of Remeria, oath keeper of—"

Arena cleared her throat. "Enough." She could not do it anymore. "Dispense with the titles and get to the point. I have places to be."

"And *where* exactly do you need to be, ah-hah?" Duke Velturo asked. If anything was *more* annoying than Duke Sturgeon's slowness, it was Duke Velturo's laugh whenever he stopped talking. Every. Single. Time.

"Unlike you, Velturo, I have hobbies." She curled her fingers, examining the purple polish once again.

"Rumors say you don't have *enough* hobbies, Arena. Servants get around . . . if you know what I mean, ah-hah."

Arena clenched her jaw but did not respond. This was not the first time that someone brought up allegations referencing her and her servants. But there was no proof, no merit to the claims. And it was not an illegal act anyway, so she failed to see the issue. It was a poor attempt to try embarrassing her. But she did not fall for it. Not from a man who could not contain his chicken grease. "Please, Velturo. If you were physically able to make love to anything other than whatever food is falling out of your mouth, I think we'd all be immensely surprised and congratulatory. If you can ever offer proof of this, send us a letter. We will have a cake made, so that you can drool that out of your face as well."

Duke Velturo ignored the jab. Though whether this was in response to the insult or because he had dropped a bowl of olives on his trousers was an argument she decided not to have with herself.

Duke Sturgeon took the silence as a sign to proceed. "Remeria's king . . . continues to . . . request aid from Calrite forces. He claims multiple Camel Clans were sighted and they have been attacking and raiding all over. Our own reports suggest . . ."

The report was from the soldiers they had sent to the Elderspikes in order to keep a watch on Vessia, ensuring the Camel Clans did not catch Calrym unaware. Calrym had not committed to aiding King Alondo.

"Bertrand," the king said, motioning the chancellor over, "you read the recent report. I can't take any more of this."

"Of course, Your Majesty." The chancellor unscrolled a letter. "From the Sixteenth Calrite Calvary Unit, signed—"

"Bertrand," the king shouted.

The chancellor winced. "Of course, Your Majesty." He skipped down several lines. "Pertinent information only, yes, I—"

The king growled.

The chancellor began to read. "We journeyed to the Elderspikes with little to report. However, upon arrival, we've sent this letter to you as hastily as possible. It's clear the Camel Clans have invaded Remeria. We've seen several signs of devastation. Remeria is being fully attacked. Another note to make, Your Majesty, the clans move as one. There are far too many leftover campfires and camel turds for it to be a single clan. It is my expertise that there are multiple clans, if not all of them, traveling and working together."

"It's a feint, Your Majesty, ah-hah," Duke Velturo said.

King Mikas grumbled, confused. "A feint to do what, Velturo?"

"Draw out our forces and attack us. They must know we've launched a significant raid in the north, ah-hah."

Arena leaned forward, arms resting on her knee. "Let's assume the report is correct, and the Camel Clans are *all* attacking. Would we even care? Why not let the Remerian shits die? Or live if they beat the camel men. *And*, if they beat them, capitalize on that and take their riches for our own."

"You are a devious woman, Duchess Arena, ah-hah." Duke Velturo belched, then hiccupped. He held his stomach, looking nauseous.

"And *you* are a disgusting man, Velturo."

Duke Velturo made half a shrug and sipped iced water. No retort. He must not be feeling well.

She hammered home the matters of true importance. "If servants were allowed inside the chamber, somebody could burp you, Velturo. Perhaps monitor what you took in. Call it a measure of safety."

King Mikas gave the table a gentle slap. "We've discussed this at length, Duchess Arena. No servants in the chamber. They spread rumors. Perhaps you're far *closer* to the servants than many of us are, but I do not trust mine to keep matters of state a secret." He sniffed, and then said, "Even if they gave me a fair fondle here and there."

Arena blushed. The king did not often pay attention to the drama plaguing the dukes and duchesses. "Very well, Your Majesty," she said.

"If they're working together, we need to come to a decision," King Mikas said.

"Remeria . . . has . . . always been friendly with Calrym except in times of war," Duke Sturgeon said.

Arena rolled her eyes. What a fool he was. "Are we stating the obvious now, Duke Sturgeon? Because I can find nobody within this chamber more in need of replacement than you. Dying in front of us is unbecoming."

The old man wheezed in response. Duke Sturgeon ignored the dramatics of the younger members of nobility.

"I would await Harlem's return before moving upon Remeria if it came to it. I would prefer we discuss our immediate response instead," the king said. He favored Duke Harlem too much, even when he was angry with him.

Arena bit her lip in thought. King Mikas wanted sound advice. If they ignored King Alondo's request, they would be seen violating the terms of their alliance. With their forces split between Calrym and Cyrok, it was not a good idea. "If the entirety of the Camel Clans have united and are attacking Remeria, our allegiance with Remeria suggests we are, at the very least, obligated to send a small contingent into their lands to verify these claims."

"I agree, ah-hah," Velturo said.

"Your Majesty, Remeria has always been helpful to us in times of peace. Honoring our alliance will benefit us in the long term." Arena wasn't sure why Sturgeon was so concerned about the long term. At best, he had a year or two left.

Sighing, the king leaned back in his chair. He seemed distracted with something. Perhaps it was the war. Or the treaty of peace they had with Remeria. Or something else. Arena was not sure, but the king was not very present. Then he spoke. "All in favor of Duchess Arena's plan? We'll investigate these claims and come to a decision later. I believe biding our time until we learn more from Harlem about how the war progresses in the north could be prudent."

The motion passed. The only one who did not vote in Arena's favor was a bitchy noblewoman who *always* disagreed with Arena. Thus, no one paid any attention to her.

Finally, we're done with this insufferable mess. She planned on taking the rest of the day off to be pampered by her servants. These meetings were becoming intolerable. Honestly, when you were among the wealthiest in the nation, why did you have to suffer?

DEMRI SLARN

2nd Cycle of Winter, 231st Reign of Garcovi
Lochwall, Calrym

Following Demri's initial shock at the revelation that Caius was a member of the Corbéo family, Scayde Haklon was pleasant enough to allow Demri a few moments of recovery. Demri had presumed *Caius* was an alias for somebody else. Over the years, Caius was shy regarding his past, and now Demri knew why. It seemed rather odd that Caius had zero qualms over murdering his grandmother though.

"I hate to interrupt your thoughts, Demri, but I believe we have another matter to attend to. Finding you a Healer." Scayde opened the door to the marshal's office, gesturing down the hall. "Shall we retire to my personal quarters?"

"Of c-course." Demri followed the nobleman down the hall and back past the curious Examiner who, judging by the way she was staring at him, figured something was off. Then outside. Demri's provided escort started following him, but Demri waved them off.

"My rooms are just on the other side of Buzzard's Bowl. I suppose soon I'll be expected to enhance them."

"Any p-p-particular reason?"

"None that I can publicly state. Not until the reveal. Between you and me? The king made me the Duke of Lochwall."

"C-c-congratulations, Scayde."

"Thank you, Demri. This way." Scayde led Demri around the gladiator arena and toward a large manor. Guards patrolled the perimeter, and several were stationed at the front doors. Demri examined the two-floor building, impressed. A fresh coat of blue paint was noticeable.

Once Demri stepped through the front door, he found himself on a shining marble floor. A wide carpeted staircase wound its way to the upper level. Brass knobs, an iron banister, and a glorious silver chandelier stood out.

"I hope you can manage stairs, Demri?" Scayde surprised Demri. He wouldn't have thought Scayde capable of empathy.

"I think I can m-m-manage."

This was half a lie. Climbing the staircase was possible. Without help, however, it was painful. His joints ached from the inflammation of arthritis. Grimacing through the pain, he made it.

Scayde brought him to his own offices. Instead of sitting at the desk, Scayde opened the floor-to-ceiling glass doors. A set of chairs had been placed on the balcony overlooking the compound. Demri appreciated their strategic placement. They were angled so one could enjoy the view of the arena and keep the doors in sight.

Servants followed the pair of men out, arranging refreshments and a bowl of walnuts on the table between the chairs. Demri refused everything aside from iced water. He drank, quenching a thirst he hadn't recognized until he began.

Scayde placed a walnut on his tongue and chewed, looking out at Buzzard's Bowl. "You might be surprised to find out that I have plenty of enemies, Demri." Demri wasn't. The men with money often found themselves at odds with their subjects, according to the histories he'd read and experiences he'd had.

A woman stepped onto the balcony. She stood rigid and stiff, like she had a sword at her back. "Scayde? I thought your business would be over by now. We—" Demri thought her voice sounded whiny, even needy.

"Ah, my beautiful wife. Meet Magicus Demri Slarn." Demri inclined his head, and she smiled in return. "A last-minute meeting, Jay, I hope you understand. We won't be long. I promise."

"All right. I'll leave you be. I have to check in on my gladiators anyway. Make sure they're going to perform well against your powerhouse."

Scayde laughed. "You'll do just fine. Even the weak ones fight their asses off when they're about to die."

She smiled at Demri and left them alone.

"You wouldn't believe the story behind my wife."

"No?" Demri said.

"A tale for another day, I think. As I was saying earlier, I have many enemies. Whenever I locate one, I do my best to ensure I capture them alive. And because of my fortuitous position of owning a gladiator arena, do you want to take a guess what I do with them?"

"I'm assuming you make them f-f-fight."

"Correct, Demri. So I'll tell you the same thing I tell anyone I enter a business arrangement with: keep your promises to me, else you may find yourself an enemy."

"I thought M-M-Magicai couldn't c-c-c-compete."

Scayde gave him an annoyed look. "You're correct. But that doesn't mean I can't find a use for you down there."

"P-point taken."

"I need to know what you can offer me, Demri. Healing is not cheap. I'm sure you realize better than anyone how expensive it is."

"I do."

"I'm prepared to ignore the cost. You may keep the money you brought with you. I'm more interested in what you can offer me in place of coin. I have plenty of that. A Magicus's services or information can be much more valuable."

"I have plenty of b-both."

"Name something worthwhile, and I'll have you healed. Right now. At my expense."

Demri swallowed. He considered this. Was it worth exposing himself?

The sun was setting, casting a pinkish-orange glow over Buzzard's Bowl. He wondered what it was like for the poor fools who found themselves in the fights. After descending into the Velvet Mother's hypogeum, he preferred not to return. It was difficult watching all those people in such an unpleasant situation, one in which most would perish. The survival of the fittest. And that's what he needed to be. Fit.

"Okay." For the first time in his life, he would say it out loud. His fingers brushed the case at his belt. "I am an Enforcer."

To say Scayde was unimpressed would be an understatement. The man looked ready to kick Demri out.

Demri took a deep breath, composing himself. "I am also an Examiner."

Scayde's mouth dropped. "Impossible."

But it wasn't. Demri spoke the truth. He retrieved

the case from a pouch on his belt, opening it to display a pair of Examiner spectacles that he never used.

"Are there others with dual powers?"

"Not that I know of. If there are, they hide it w-well. I b-b-believe some of the rogues may have discovered ways to unlock additional p-p-powers."

"I'll want to know more. First, allow me to fulfill my promise." Scayde held two fingers up and beckoned, as if somebody were behind him.

Somebody must've been awaiting the signal because a servant with a stern face appeared.

"Tanibris, this man needs some healing."

Tanibris inclined his head. "Will we be heading down, or shall I bring a woman up here, my lord?"

"Fetch Jevlen."

"Mmm, my lord, we just acquired him. Don't you think it's too soon?" Tanibris glanced in Demri's direction. *What's he hiding?*

"No, no. It's time Jevlen learned his place."

Bowing, Tanibris exited the balcony. Demri's intuition flared up. He didn't like what was happening. Something sounded *off*. He wanted to reignite the conversation, perhaps pose a question, but Scayde was chewing on a couple of walnuts and contently admiring the scenery in front of them. Perhaps he should relax as well. Too much time spent on the road and on the run had created a paranoid, worried, and hard man.

Tanibris returned. Behind him trailed a near-naked man, his wrists and ankles in chains. Realization dawned on Demri: this man was a Blind Sister.

"Thank you, Tanibris," Scayde said.

Tanibris bowed. "Mmm, my lord."

Scayde stood and approached Jevlen, retrieving a key from a pouch on his belt. He unlocked the chains on Jevlen's wrists, and they clattered to the floor. "You are to heal the man sitting in the chair. Of *all* ailments."

Jevlen shook his head. "Absolutely not. You don't get to tell *me* how I use my powers." His skinny, frail body shook. Whether it was the breeze or nerves, Demri couldn't tell.

"In case you were unaware, *Magicus*, the university doesn't give one shit about your location. The Archmagicus himself assured me they wouldn't pursue you."

Jevlen continued shaking his head, almost as if he were trying to convince himself and not them. "No, no, no, no. The Archmagicus would *never* sell us." His thin arms waved around him with confidence, but his eyes bulged, and he appeared doubtful.

"Then please enlighten me about where the funds I paid for you went."

Jevlen's shoulders drooped, and his chin fell to his chest. "I don't know." The words were barely audible. Defeated. "I just don't know."

"Well, *I* happen to know."

"It's impossible. The Archmagicus is a good person. He cares about all the Magicai. A professor maybe. The Archmagicus wouldn't deal with you himself."

Demri wanted to intervene. That somebody was being forced to use their powers against their will upset him. A Magicus should be able to choose what they do and when they do it. But Demri had gone far too long with his injuries, and intervening would only cause problems. Problems that Demri could ill afford at the moment. A small sacrifice.

"You're correct, Jevlen. I did not. I believe my primary contact was the Collector professor."

Jevlen moaned. "I know the man. He's the least trustworthy of all of them."

"Nevertheless, the deal was made. Either heal him now, or I will toss you over the balcony."

"I'd rather die." And Jevlen took a small step toward the balcony's rail. Demri wondered if Jevlen even had the upper body strength to lift himself, so emaciated was his body.

A noise halfway between a snort and a sneeze emanated from Scayde. "You'll do no such thing. I correct myself. You heal him now, or I kill one of the others you share your room with."

Jevlen blanched.

"This is your last chance, Jevlen."

"Fine," Jevlen muttered through gritted teeth.

"Spectacular." Scayde took his seat once more, popping additional walnuts into his mouth.

Jevlen hobbled over to Demri, chains dragging behind his feet and scraping across the balcony. The sound was screechy and unpleasant to the ears. He laid a frail hand on Demri but didn't heal. Demri knew he was analyzing his injuries, finding all of what was wrong with him. "How in Mother Avani's name are you walking? Your legs are a mess."

"It took some getting used to."

"I'm sure of that."

Scayde swallowed another handful of walnuts. "Get on with it, Jevlen. Nobody else lingers when they're given a task."

"This is ridiculous. If I ever get out of here, I'll kill both the Archmagicus and Doram."

Doram? "Excuse m-m-me?"

Jevlen peered back at him, appearing confused. "Yes?"

"Did you say D-D-Doram?"

"The Collector professor at Ashmount? Doram Quandis? Yes, why?"

Doram Quandis. A professor . . . at Ashmount. A *professor* at Ashmount? Doram Quandis was a *professor at Ashmount*. The man had been hiding in the most obvious place, the one place Demri had never considered. Why would he remain there? Myri Celioh hadn't. Demri had figured Doram knew he was hunting him and would be in hiding. If he hadn't just found Doram's location, he might've become angry at himself. But he was too excited.

Jevlen stared at Demri, waiting for an answer but he was too busy celebrating. A fiery burning sensation illuminated within Demri's core. His heart pumped. His blood quickened. The pulse throbbed in his chest, a delightful booming. Revenge was near. A calm happiness descended upon him. For the first time, he had an objective. A true target. He'd found the man. And now, it was time to capitalize on that information.

VILLIC THE IMBUER

2nd Cycle of Winter, 231st Reign of Garcovi
Remeria

The moon's glow lit Villic's journey back to the Splintered Manes. He kept an eye and an ear out for Dunecrest but didn't see or hear any living camels. By the fortune of Cocaro, god of luck, the clan was camping at the same spot. After a tense exchange with a patrolling clan member who thought Villic was sneaking up on him, he allowed Villic entry. He returned to his camp first. Standing over the previous night's campfire coals was Dunecrest.

"Dunecrest!" Villic ran his hand across the camel's side. "I thought you died." He smiled, glad his old friend still lived.

The bull eyed Villic with a look that said, "The gods won't let me depart yet."

"Good. You'd wreak havoc on Flaytz, god of death. He'd kick you out for being moody."

"Are you aware the animal doesn't understand you?" Speaker asked.

"Of course he understands me, don't you?" Villic peered into the camel's eyes.

Dunecrest snorted and turned away from Villic, searching the ground for vegetation. Not finding any, he stomped off toward one of the larger bush trees.

"See. He gets moody when you doubt him."

"*Mhm.*"

"We need to talk to the shamans. Or Jedkah."

"*You're in control of the legs.*"

And everything else, I hope.

"*I suppose that depends on the gods.*" Speaker laughed.

Villic didn't find it humorous. What if the gods took away his legs? Or freedom of will? What if they relinquished his body to Speaker, and Villic found himself trapped inside Speaker? The thoughts frightened him, and he offered a quick prayer to Killiak, lord of lords. It didn't hurt to display some extra devotion.

"Villic the Imbuer, you're alive!" A patrolling clan member approached Villic on his way to the tents of Jedkah and the shamans. If Villic were to guess, he'd say her name was Liakka, but he wasn't sure.

He smiled, not meeting her eyes but staring over her shoulder at the dark jungle. It was different here. The plants everywhere. The smells, the sounds. It was wet. He missed the dry climate of the desert.

"You all right, Villic?" Liakka asked.

Villic swallowed nervously. He found her rather stunning. "Yes." He felt his face redden. Villic wasn't sure what to say to her because he'd never talked to her one-on-one before. He'd avoided her for various reasons.

"*You need to tell her you have urgent business with Jedkah. Or the shamans.*"

"I, uh, well, have urgent business."

"Oh?"

"With Jedkah."

"With Jedkah," Villic repeated.

"About?" she asked.

"There's a Magicus still alive."

"He let you go?"

"I saved his life."

"You what?" Liakka's nose crinkled and lips curled. Villic became afraid of her. He closed his eyes.

"Open your eyes. She's mad, not crazy. She won't attack you."

I wasn't afraid.

"I can hear all of your thoughts."

May Killiak damn you.

"I don't understand," Liakka said.

Villic opened his eyes. She watched him, a strange expression on her face. Like she was angry at herself, brow furrowed, lips pressed together, and her eyes looking away from him.

"That's confusion. Because you are acting odd."

"Why didn't you kill him, Villic?"

"He wasn't a threat anymore. He needed help."

"Help?" Liakka threw her hands in the air. "*You* need help, Villic. Killiak curse you for your ignorance. Mutaz"—*Mutaz, god of war,* Villic recited to himself to remember which god Mutaz was—"won't favor your cowardice."

Villic looked away from Liakka. This was why he didn't talk to anyone. He didn't like the tone, the increased volume, the anger.

"You've done our clan a disservice, Villic."

And once started, they never stopped. Because Villic didn't know what to say, but they never realized that.

"You saw a sign from the gods."

That's true. "The gods gave me a sign." Villic would've said Liakka's name, given his words with more confidence, but he didn't want to use the wrong name. People became angry when you forgot which one they were. "I asked what to do, and the moon covered itself. It was clear I wasn't to hurt him."

"Bah! You wouldn't know a sign from the gods if it tugged on your fruits, Villic." Liakka laughed, one of her hands mimicking the act of tugging on him.

Villic flushed.

"Tell her you need to speak to the shamans."

Right. "I need to speak with the shamans."

"Are you asking me, Villic?" Liakka laughed louder, deeper. She grabbed her stomach and motioned him by. Her full lips closed together in an expression Villic didn't recognize.

"That's a smirk. It's a good thing."

It dawned on Villic what was humorous. Liakka wasn't a shaman. She wasn't an Imbuer. *He* was above *her* in the hierarchy.

"Why do you clam up around everyone?"

Most people make me uncomfortable.

"Just say what you're thinking."

It's not that easy.

"Well, you can't keep standing around like the village fool."

I don't know what you mean, Speaker. Villic tuned him out. Focused on his walk, thought about how he wasn't going to be nervous around the shamans or Jedkah. Realized he would, because of course he would. They were godspeakers, and Jedkah was the leader of the clan.

He walked by a few tents, several fires, a bush tree or two. Something screamed in the distance, either a warning cry or a death screech. Nothing Villic hadn't heard in the desert before.

"By the grace of Flaytz"—*Flaytz, god of death*—"Villic

lives." Jedkah approached, smiling, arms held out like he was ready to hug Villic. Villic knew this to just be a gesture. Nobody would hug him on purpose.

"Jedkah," Villic said.

"Villic the Imbuer. You're alive," a shaman said, following Jedkah over.

Why don't I know anyone's name? Villic nodded. More shamans arrived. Sweat formed on his forehead. The jungle was hot. The desert was hot. Villic didn't sweat because of heat.

"Are you all right?" another shaman asked.

He swallowed. There were too many people looking at him.

"*Yes,*" Speaker said.

"Yes." Villic wiped his forehead with his forearm and looked down, avoiding their gaze.

"We appreciate the fact that you're here, Villic," a third shaman said. She laid her hand on his shoulder, and he near jumped above the bush trees. "It's not like you though. What news do you bring?"

Firelight danced across the dirt in front of Villic's feet. A shadow flickered, perhaps one of the bats that came out at night. They weren't easy to see like desert bats were. The full moon, and sometimes just bright starlight, illuminated clouds of them in the open area. Here, it was difficult to spot them. Too many leaves, not enough light. Villic hated it.

"*Answer them, Villic.*"

Villic snapped back to attention. The shamans watched him, patient but expectant. Jedkah's face contorted into a grimace. Villic swallowed. He knew that look on Jedkah. It meant the leader of the Splintered Manes was becoming frustrated.

"Uh." He cleared his throat. Didn't know what else to say.

"Tell them about the Magicus."

"There's a Magicus."

"Yes, we killed them," Jedkah said.

They never give me a chance to finish.

"You stop speaking."

I'm thinking. "He wasn't dead."

"You killed him?" a shaman asked.

"He's wounded. I saved his life. Told him we'd return before dawn."

"You saved him?" Jedkah asked through clenched teeth.

The kind shaman, the woman, said, "You could talk to him? Villic, you hardly speak to us in our language. You don't know the king's tongue, do you?"

"No. Speaker translated."

"What?"

"Who?"

"Huh?"

"Speaker," Villic said. "The voice inside."

"The one who grants you power," a shaman said.

Villic nodded. This conversation was getting out of hand. He was talking too much.

"Where is the Magicus?" Jedkah asked.

Villic pointed behind him.

"Bring us. We need to get to him before he leaves," the kind shaman said. Villic wished he remembered her name. He'd like to thank her.

Jedkah ordered everyone to gather their things and be ready to leave before the patrolling clan members changed shifts.

Villic returned to Dunecrest, prepared him to leave, and waited for the shamans and Jedkah to follow.

EDELBROCK BRENDIS

2nd Cycle of Winter, 231st Reign of Garcovi
Lochwall, Calrym

B uzzard's Bowl hosted four seasons of fighting a year, and they stretched on for what seemed like forever. The likelihood he would come out alive was small.

The next day, the day of the season's last event, the crowd was so wild and boisterous that Edelbrock could hear them cheering and screaming way down in the training grounds, which had never occurred before. A typical season could last anywhere from a few weeks to two full cycles, "depending on how much money the House Heads were making and the amount of cattle left to kill," one of the gladiators told Edelbrock when he'd asked.

When the gladiators returned exhausted, they'd lost their highest numbers yet. Edelbrock didn't ask how it went. The Velvet Mother's House lost. Savakkis returned wounded with punctures and slashes all over his body and had to be supported by two other men. Chellie sported a bloody nose, half a breast was missing, and a nasty gash crossed her upper thigh. None of this inspired Edelbrock. He only dreaded the arena more.

The thing he dreaded most, however, was looking up into the spectators stands. Seeing Scayde with Edelbrock's former wife, Jaylena. What a distraction that might provide. He made a vow to never look. Edelbrock wasn't sure he'd be able to abide by that vow, but he meant to. Otherwise, he believed he could become an easy kill. Revenge was a distraction he couldn't afford. Not out in the arena.

"Hey, E, you doing all right?" A gruff veteran walked into view and clapped him on the shoulder. Edelbrock's memory failed him; he couldn't recall the man's name. He had sparred with the man a few times. The veteran was an expert with long-handled weapons, like glaives and halberds.

"I'm just thinking about spring."

"*Everyone* is thinking about spring, my friend. But consider us both lucky that we're able to think about seasons at all. And for us who've fought, we're just glad winter's season is over."

Edelbrock agreed. He could be dead and buried in the ground. Or he could rot in a jail cell. That was the alternative to Buzzard's Bowl.

"Just keep training, E. It's what gets me through dark days. It's what gets everyone through. That or you wilt away into depression. Don't do that, no matter what. If the guards get a sense you're going to give up before you step foot into the arena, they'll take you away. I don't know what they do to those people. I'm sure it's not pleasant though. They never come back."

"I'm sure they're tortured for fun. Or just put down

like a sick dog." Either of those options sounded pretty accurate, considering what Scayde Haklon could do. The man was a monster.

Under the Velvet Mother, Edelbrock knew he could earn his freedom. So he continued to train.

SERADAL WINTLOCK

*2nd Cycle of Winter, 231st Reign of Garcovi
Cyrok*

A silence, permeated by the odd crunch of a wheel on snow or a light whisper of wind, drifted away. The blackness faded, and Sera's blurred vision returned. She lived. Her throat parched, she coughed, and an old woman's face swam into view, peering down at her.

The woman placed a cup at her lips, tipping cool water into her mouth. The sweet freshness rejuvenated her dry throat, and she felt a hundred times better.

She stretched. A dull ache ran up her thigh, another in her neck. *Why does this keep happening?*

Sera touched her neck, discovering the hole was gone. She'd expected to feel a bandage but found skin instead. The woman appeared in her vision again, and Sera realized she was a much older Magicus Ashté. She had wispy gray hair, wrinkles spiderwebbing across her face, and weathered, flappy skin. For the second time, the Healer had sacrificed her own life to heal Sera. This time she'd aged decades by doing so.

"Thank you."

The Healer smiled. Sera detected a hint of pain behind that expression. "You're welcome."

The crunching sounds returned. Sera felt the lurch of the carriage being pulled over a row of thick ice.

She heard the guards shout in her head again, saw the volley of arrows and the rush of the Calrite military. The Calrites had outnumbered them in the battle. "We won." She couldn't believe it.

"At substantial cost." Magicus Ashté slipped away, then returned with a bowl of gruel. "It might be cold, but you need to eat."

Sera took the bowl. Her stomach grumbled at the sight of food. She peered around the interior of the carriage. At the other side were several of Vithor Bane's men, whispering among themselves.

The Healer guessed what she was looking for and answered her unspoken question. "Your father is fine. He's in the next carriage. You both needed rest, which requires silence."

"Angazo?"

The grim expression that crossed the Magicus was decipherable, even before the slight shake of her head. Angazo was no longer with them.

She felt guilty. Right before the arrows struck her down, she'd seen him laying still. *He died a soldier, a Falcon Knight. He helped save my father's life.*

Magicus Ashté placed a soft, liver-spotted hand on Sera's shoulder. "I'm sorry."

"I will forever be thankful for that man." Sera meant that. She'd remember Angazo and the sacrifice he'd made. Feeling even guiltier than before, she realized no matter the loss here, her elation at knowing her father lived usurped the bad news. And then more guilt, as she connected the dots between the Healer's age and her being healed. "Now it's my time to apologize, Magicus. You lost a lot of time helping me."

"It wasn't just you, Cyr Seradal. But I'd be lying if I said most of the years displayed on me resulted from saving other people. Normally, I wouldn't have aided you. However, it was important to me to restore you to full health. We don't know where the Cyroki are going to end up now. We don't even know how many of us still live. And I believe you have a good heart, Sera. The Falcon Knights will need that. I chose to help you. Do not feel guilty about it. That's the wonderful thing about being a Healer—you're allowed to decide to sacrifice yourself for those who matter to you. And while I cannot say I've known you for long, you were the first and only person I've ever prevented from certain death. I believe you would've lived through the arrow in the neck, though I can't say for sure, so it's possible you're also the second person I've saved from dying."

So many people. Dead. Because of *her*. Or at least, she thought so. Though she wasn't responsible for the Gyrloft citizens that were murdered, nor the men and women of Vox, she still felt a responsibility for them. She *should* have noticed Captain Blago Adavir and his men committing an intolerable crime. She *should* have remained in Vox to fight with the rest of the country. She *should* have listened to her brother, Fezzel. Selfish. That's what she was.

"I think you should've let me die, Magicus." She spoke honestly. Why save someone who would abandon her entire country just so she could spend some more time with her paralyzed father?

"Even if that were the case, I make my own decisions, Cyr Seradal. But for the sake of argument, please enlighten me with your words. *Why* should I have let you die?"

"I left everyone at Vox to die."

The Healer grimaced. Her teary eyes became unfocused, looking at something that wasn't in the carriage. "We all did." She swallowed. "But there's nothing either of us could've accomplished by remaining in the city. By escaping, we can tell our story. Fuel seeds of discourse against Calrym and King Mikas. And other people will require our services. I feel this. Do not look back with regret, Cyr Seradal. Look back and discover knowledge. We will need to unite with other survivors if we want any hope of making our lives matter. Or we can follow the same route Vithor Bane intends and disappear into obscurity. With your father's condition, I wouldn't reprimand you if that was the decision you made. But I suggest discussing this with him before making your decision. You're free to go once you eat all of your food." The old woman ended the conversation by walking to the other end of the carriage and pulling over the protective canvas, masking the horizon.

Sera ate the porridge. It was cold, bland, and rather thin. But it was filling, and the best meal she remembered having since her mother cooked that large feast the day before they'd fled Gyrloft.

When Sera approached the last carriage in line, Renard greeted her. He seemed jovial, which wasn't new for Renard, but it was rather enhanced compared to normal.

"You're alive, Cyr Seradal!" He proffered his hand to her, assisting her into the carriage. It helped little. He was smaller than she was, and she almost pulled him out as she hopped in the back.

Her father sat upon a bench, legs stretched out in front of him. He laughed at the sight of her. "Seradal."

Renard tugged on her arm. "You need to see this!" This just made her father laugh even heartier.

"What?" Confused, she followed Renard. It was strange, seeing them both so elated despite Angazo's death.

Her father stood and walked over, embracing her.

The confusion became exaggerated happiness, which became crying, which resulted in her and her father falling to the floor of the carriage after a violent bump in the road.

"How? What? Why? What happened?" She couldn't form a proper question.

"Magicus Ashté fixed me up. I'm healthy!"

What a wonderful woman.

KELDEN STOOLE

2nd Cycle of Winter, 231st Reign of Garcovi
Ashmount, Qothe

Despite the slow, methodical approach Kelden took perusing Ashmount's catalogues, he couldn't find any trace of Magicus Kohne, the subject of Enebrial Hubbart's interview. Kelden figured several possibilities could be the cause: Magicus Kohne's information wasn't in the library, Magicus Kohne was an alias, or Magicus Kohne never existed, and Enebrial Hubbart was a liar. Kelden had strong doubts about the latter. So he continued researching.

He scoured the rest of the speculative fiction section, finding a single other book written by Enebrial Hubbart. This one, entitled *The Who, the What, and the How Answered: The Trace of a Theory*, detailed several theories about the Trace and how it operated. Enebrial Hubbart outlined various ways he theorized the Trace appeared. These ideas included heritage, proximity to magical locations that were said to enhance the Trace in nearby occupants, determination by random draw at birth, determination when the individual reaches adulthood, Mother Avani selecting people to grant powers to, and many other, more obscure ideas.

Kelden reread both of Enebrial Hubbart's works but couldn't find anything else of significance. It seemed strange because, in both books, Hubbart referenced other works he'd written. Kelden was certain Ashmount stocked *any* book written about Magicai. He suspected they had hidden Hubbart's other works or destroyed them.

Kelden explored various sections of the library, scanning titles and flipping through texts at random. He had little time to spend doing so because of his Glyphist classes. The renowned author Magicus Guylan Nalthier offered no advice either. He read through all Nalthier's theories of Magicai powers, and all he seemed to do was further the teachings of the Magicai: the Trace determined your power, and the head Examiner discovered what your calling was. Nalthier offered one tidbit of information that Kelden wasn't aware of though. Nalthier described what happened to an Enforcer who consumed all of their remaining powers at once. The result was terrifying.

A Magicus who desired to do something powerful and devastating to everything around them could expel this energy, causing a massive explosion. According to Nalthier, this occurred in history only once. He believed this was because it was an accident occurring in the middle of a battlefield. Kelden wondered why more people hadn't done this but chalked it up to people preferring not to blow themselves up. In another book written by Nalthier, he described the process as "combusting," and that most Enforcers never had enough Soul Glyphs prepared to even attain this phenomenon. As a Glyphist, Kelden realized he'd need to remember this information if any Enforcers approached him with a desire to unlock all of their power.

A few weeks into the second winter cycle, Kelden, against better judgement, started going to the library after classes. He'd stay up far too late, reading and comparing his notes. He slept less and less, which started to stilt his learning and his comprehension during class. Magicus Kalixa noticed and reprimanded him every day. But he didn't care. He didn't want to be a Glyphist anyway.

Kelden met Magicus Tikmo, an Enforcer who'd completed the Trials in the same group. Tikmo was a Vessian, a man who'd left the desert for a chance at a better life, only to be placed into a fighting role again. He wasn't pleased and was looking for a way to change his profession. After their classes, they met in the library every day and delved into books. They discussed their optimism that *something* could revert or change their powers. If there was a way, they vowed to find it.

"We no *agiato* get where," Tikmo said. His understanding of the common tongue wasn't the greatest, and he often threw in a Vessian word or two.

"Just keep reading, Tik," Kelden said.

The Passings of a Harvested Soul by Gemmica Meldonata didn't lead anywhere. Nor did *Ancient Spurrings of a Magical Nature* by Aggora Felzis. Kelden read *A Century of Imbuers: The History of a Lost Art* by Starlyn Velimar, which was a fascinating but useless read. Tikmo and Kelden perused every section of the library they thought could hide any small bit of insight: speculative fiction, history, memoirs, journals and diaries, preserved historical documents, autobiographies, biographies, and essays. *Fire: The Burning Desire to Live* and *The Growth of Failure* were both autobiographies by Klyntos Jaffrey, a man who failed the Trials, escaped, and spoke out about the harmful practices of Ashmount. Nothing Jaffrey wrote about was anything Kelden couldn't already figure out. He kept searching.

And then, one afternoon, everything changed. Bored, Kelden and Tikmo perused the fiction section. Tired, glassy-eyed, and unconvinced they would find anything, the pair walked down the aisles between bookshelves, scanning the titles and authors.

Names slid by Kelden: Dariol Cauhold, Shasta Caujin, Antondo Cavlic. They kept walking and reading. There were *so many* books that reading every title, every name, was going to take hours.

Higla Felthorne, Archibalt Feluvio, Bonado Fhlyk. All fiction authors. Kelden wiped sleep from his eyes. Tikmo continued, not so much reading the titles or authors as picking up random books that appealed visually to him.

Xervilis Huan, Enebrial Hubbart, Rickos Huckston. Kelden yawned. He kept reading. Liavella Hueclin, Winoa Huedel. Then he realized. He'd read Enebrial Hubbart's name in the fiction section. Enebrial Hubbart never wrote fiction. He was a Magicus who only wrote about his research, theories, and personal life.

"Tik," Kelden said.

Tikmo glanced at him, placing a book with a faded red cover back on the shelf.

"I think I found something." He pulled Hubbart's book out. The pages of the book were old and crisp. They crinkled when Kelden opened the book, but the cover appeared to be much newer. Refurbished perhaps. On the inside cover, a note was inscribed on the panel.

Enebrial Hubbart's "work" has been extensively reviewed, researched, and rejected by Ashmount's top Magicai. Our results have proven Hubbart was crazy, experienced alcohol problems, and chewed and consumed massive amounts of skachi, which we believe altered his mind. The rantings and ravings of Enebrial Hubbart are an important part of our history and show what can happen to a Magicus who doesn't receive proper guidance. Thus, his work remains as fictitious intrigue and interesting stories and shouldn't be misconstrued as anything else. Though Hubbart writes his work as "fact," it's little more than a child's fantasy. Enjoy this elaborate world, but understand Hubbart's "teachings" are not possible.

—Archmagicus Alixio Nahlbin.

Kelden knew Archmagicus Alixio Nahlbin was the previous Archmagicus, in charge before the current one. All the prior serving Archmagicai's names were recorded in Ashmount, though they never went by anything other than their title. The recorded names were to identify who served when. Which meant the book, *Enebrial's Literature and Informative Text on the Elite (ELITE): An Analysis of the Magicai at the University of Arcanical Arts*, had its cover replaced only a few years ago. The current Archmagicus had replaced Alixio eight years ago, and Alixio had held his position for fifteen years, which was during the time DS would've been writing their notes.

"What is the find, Kel?"

"I found another book written by Enebrial Hubbart."

"*Guntoa,*" Tikmo said in his native language.

Excited, Kelden brought *ELITE* back to their table and started reading, Tikmo at his shoulder.

To those of you who've graciously purchased or distributed my works, I can't ever thank you enough. There will be those who claim I'm delirious, crazy, or psychotic. I assure you that everything I've gathered, everything I've researched, I've

*verified countless times. I am an advocate for truths.
According to the Magicai of the University of Arcanical
Arts, this is a criminal act. This will also be my last work I
publish. Thanks for everything.*

   —EH

Kelden turned the page and read. They went slower than he would like because Tikmo read slower. But Kelden didn't complain. Five pages in, Kelden knew this work wasn't fictitious. This was real. Kelden wondered why the Magicai would permit Hubbart's work in their library, even under the false pretense that it was fiction. *Perhaps if somebody were to bring a copy into the school, it'd cause a rebellion. This way, they can claim it's a piece of fiction and has always been available to anybody who wants to read it.*

Enebrial Hubbart had plenty to say about the Trials.

The Trials are a scam, a ploy by the Magicai to trap civilians in a terrible situation. They lure them to the school with promises of monetary compensation to "test" if they have the Trace. This attracts hundreds of brigands who patrol the roads, watching for weary travelers they can take advantage of. Many people travel far distances aboard ships just for a small sack of coin that will last them a few cycles if they're lucky. Most of the travelers are hoping for that small amount of money—something that could improve their life. But as research suggests, the poor consume extra money faster than they would, had they earned acceptable wages. The disparity in wealth isn't the point of this article, so I apologize for digressing.

The truth is, this payment attracts many people. And if they arrive, an Examiner then examines them. If they don't have the Trace, these poor people are let loose, back into the world, with no security or promises of safety. Many of these people lose their money to the brigands. Or if they want to go back to their homes, they must spend a significant amount of it to do so. But that's not the worst part.

The people accepted must then undergo what they call the Trials of Ashmount, a set of rigorous and dangerous tasks. The "contestants"—"students" or "candidates" are laughable terms in this circumstance—are then set upon one another. They're encouraged to harm each other for the betterment of their own place at the school. All the while, Magicai observe their ruthless tactics. And what's the point in all of this? Is it to search for those who are skilled? Are the Magicai hoping to raise the best of the best? No. The contestants are only there to be harvested by Collectors. For those who may not know, Collectors harvest the essence, known as the Trace, into vials so they can utilize its benefits later. The entire purpose of the Trials is to replenish the school's storeroom of vials. A sickening process to be sure.

One further addendum. By researching the history of the Trials, one notices the varying class sizes change dramatically whenever there is a global crisis. I believe the difficulty of the Trials changes based on what's occurring within the world. A significant threat requires a larger injection of Enforcers, and if you read the rosters of accepted students, it's apparent they fluctuate with the needs of the University of Arcanical Arts or the world.

Kelden finished before Tikmo and turned in his seat, watching the man's eyes widen as he read the passage. "This is . . . enlightening."

"Keep read late today," Tikmo said.

It wasn't long before they stumbled upon another intriguing passage.

The Magicai are so afraid of experimentation that they limit it. They refuse to allow anybody to innovate. Why? We've known for centuries that other variations of magic existed long ago. The most recognizable and referenced in recorded history are the Imbuers of Vessia, who disappeared about one hundred fifty years ago. Given the powers the Imbuers possessed, it's strange to consider suppressing research of potential developments. The Magicai have always been against this, and I'm certain it's because of the power structure they've crafted.

The Archmagicus, along with the five branch professors, would lose much of their control should somebody outside of a leadership position discover something monumental. This would, in essence, nullify the importance of Ashmount as a school. Should other discoveries occur, new schools may open up. Competition is something the Magicai detest unless it's to their own gain (refer to pg. 5 regarding "The Trials of Ashmount" scam). Any competition or information leading to the discreditation of the Magicai would cause them to lose control, which would mean they'd have fewer vials, less Magicai following their command, less money coming in from the entire world.

Rumors persist of underground Magicai who work to research their own powers. I reached out to suspected individuals and received no reply. I suspect there is an iota of truth to there being a secret organization working against the teachings of the University of Arcanical Arts, but this is mere speculation. If any organization were to announce oneself, the Archmagicus would order every person under their employ to root it out and annihilate the group.

"I suppose this explains why they're so restrictive," Kelden said.

"Read more," Tikmo said.

The two of them stayed up all night, reading Enebrial Hubbart's revelations on the Magicai. Kelden needed sleep, and just as he was about to call a halt to their reading, they found the most incriminating words.

> *Examiners are the ones who get the worst deal. The head Examiner lies to all the other Examiners. And everyone else, for that matter. But the Examiners have more power than they know. An Examiner can see what branch of magic a person uses. As far as I can find out, Examiners see each branch of magic differently. But here's the real catch—an Examiner can activate other branches of power within a Magicus, not just the head Examiner. In fact, Examiners choose which branch each individual can access, although it seems as if a special type of spectacles are needed to do so.*
>
> *The needs of the University of Arcanical Arts determine how many of each branch it needs. When the living students are accepted, the Archmagicus discusses this with the head Examiner, and they allocate roles whichever way they wish. The Examiner just needs to open the drain, unstop the stopper, or whatever other metaphor one uses, to allow access to that flow of power. Anybody who possesses the Trace has access to all five forms of power. They just need to unlock them before they can use them. Theoretically, one could do this themselves if only we could figure out how.*

Kelden and Tikmo stared open-mouthed at one another for many minutes. There was a possibility that they could change their powers or add to them.

They didn't know *how* they were to go about attaining their powers, but every night, they met in the library and discussed distinct possibilities on how to convince the head Examiner.

Late one night, a week before spring, after an

exhausting class where Magicus Kalixa demanded that Kelden recreate a dozen various designs for Soul Glyphs, Kelden and Tikmo were discussing the findings in *ELITE*.

Magicus Doram, Magicus Jakci, and, to Kelden's and Tikmo's horror, the Archmagicus, interrupted them.

"I see you have all been rather busy," said the Archmagicus, his lips a thin straight line, his stern expression warning Kelden to be quiet.

The other two Magicai had more difficulty masking their displeasure. Magicus Doram's face was a dark shade of red. Magicus Jakci just looked disappointed and ashamed.

Doram's face contorted in fury. "You're trying to ruin *everything*." Frothy saliva spilled out the corners of his mouth.

Before now, Kelden hadn't realized just how much trouble he was in. Magicus Doram seethed. He'd never seen the man angry, never heard of the man getting angry. And now he was trembling and looked like he wanted to rip Kelden's head off.

Magicus Jakci took a more neutral approach. "A student, who will remain anonymous, reported you two gathering here after classes every night. You are, according to said student, researching forbidden topics. It's been said Enebrial Hubbart is the catalyst for this research?"

Kelden blanched. Tikmo said nothing. The only book they had at their table was *The Who, the What, and the How Answered: The Trace of a Theory*. An acceptable, if detested, book. After all, everything contained within was just a theory and not presented as fact.

The Archmagicus pulled a spare chair out and sat. "It is not a crime to be curious. However, there are specific branches of research we outlaw because of the dangers delving into them may lead. An untrained Magicus could create substantial risks or cause an unknown catastrophe by attempting to manipulate their power. It wouldn't be the first time a Magicus combusted, creating an explosion of epic proportions. If you're around that, you will die. Fast. It's not worth it."

Magicus Jakci picked up the book sitting on the table. He read the title of *The Who, the What, and the How Answered: The Trace of a Theory* aloud to himself. "It doesn't due to dwell on fairy tales." He let out a weak laugh. But Kelden noticed Magicus Jakci looked much more concerned, and the laugh may have been an attempt to mask that.

The Archmagicus took a moment to look both of them in the eyes before speaking. "From this moment forward, I expect both of you to concentrate on your *assigned* direction. No more dreaming about fanciful changes. It's impossible. We've already determined what you're capable of, and there's no way around it. I apologize if this upsets either of you, but there's nothing that can change this. Now please, return to your dorms and prepare for classes tomorrow."

"You cannot be *serious*, Archmagicus. These people are *criminals*," Magicus Doram said. "We refuse this line of work. On purpose. Consider what happened with the outlaw Demri Slarn." Magicus Doram's hands balled into fists, and his skin seemed to purple. "If we let them out of here, word will spread. A revolt *will* happen."

"Magicus Doram, we've spoken about this at length plenty of times before." The Archmagicus rubbed at his forehead, seeming exhausted. It appeared to be an argument they'd gone over many times. "We cannot suppress every attempt at curiosity. The preceding Archmagicus never should have allowed you to attack Demri like that. Who knows what he's up to or what his plans are. He's been missing for decades, leaving a wake of dead bodies behind him. Because we didn't deal with him in the correct way."

Magicus Doram glared at the students, though it felt like he was directing it toward Kelden. "I must hand in my resignation then, Archmagicus." He tore off the pin of the vial he wore, tossing it on the table.

Magicus Jakci gasped, then silenced himself.

The Archmagicus just waved Magicus Doram away. "Do as you wish, Doram. We are beyond finding a mutual consensus on this matter. If leaving resolves the issue, then leave. I will not beg for you to stay."

Magicus Doram stormed out the library, slamming the door on his way.

The Archmagicus stood, addressing Kelden and Tikmo one last time. "I hope you can find rest tonight. I fear I'll find my own to be quite lacking in effect. Good night." He strode out, Magicus Jakci in tow and Enebrial Hubbart's book disappearing with him.

On the way back to Kelden's room, he thought about all he'd read over his past research. There was just too much. And the reactions of the Archmagicus and the professors were telling. It seemed maybe Enebrial Hubbart was onto something, almost confirming every-thing the man wrote about. *The Magicai are corrupt. They stifle learning, they stifle our powers.* But why? Why didn't they allow everyone who has the Trace into the school? Sure, they harvested them for their power, but why not wait until they died? Was it that important to stock up on vials? The answers to these questions seemed obvious to Kelden.

Why did they stifle learning?

For control. To make us feel as if we owe them something.

Why didn't they allow everyone who has the Trace into the school?

To create an illusion of accomplishment and exclusivity. To create a need to "pay back" the University of Arcanical Arts for granting us such wonderful "gifts." To demonstrate the school has the power to make any of us disappear at any moment, eliciting a sense of fear and control before we even begin to learn from them.

Why not wait until they died to harvest them?

Because they can stockpile more power.

Was it that important to stock up on the vials?

No, but the more you have, the more powerful you become. The more influence you hold over the Enforcers and Collectors.

It was all a giant game of control, domination, and power. And the people at the top didn't want to lose any of it.

DEMRI SLARN

2nd Cycle of Winter, 231st Reign of Garcovi
Lochwall, Calrym

here was no discernible way to explain the feeling coursing through Demri's body. At first, immediate pain. His skin stretched and reshaped. Demri could *feel* the burn scar on his face . . . well, *burn away.* His legs were a much more extensive agony. Bones snapped, cracked, and shifted within his flesh. They tore at his muscles, popped back into place, and then ground together as they were reset. And then, just as quickly as the pain began, it stopped. The flesh healed, his legs fixed, the scar on his face—all were gone. And that's when the indescribable feeling took hold.

No longer was Demri a cripple. No more limping. The stares he'd endured, gone. Well, not all of them. He knew the stutter would continue to invite odd glances here and there. But nothing close to how it'd been for . . . *two whole decades. I've lived two decades of shit.*

Elated, Demri *walked* around Scayde Haklon's

balcony. His speed improved. The dull ache disappeared. *Both* eyelids closed when he blinked. He smiled. He *smiled*. The last time he'd smiled was back at Ashmount. Myri Celioh used to make him smile. Those were dire thoughts. He erased them from his mind and noticed Scayde observing him, amused.

Then Demri saw the Blind Sister, Jevlen. The man was at least a decade older, perhaps more. His skin hung in loose flaps from his bones, like an old man's, not because Jevlen had aged into senility, but due to his slight frame. Demri had never witnessed a Healer age that many years before. For a moment, he saddened, thinking he missed an opportunity to witness the aging take place in real time. Sadness, however, was not the appropriate emotion for the moment. Unless your name was Jevlen.

"Thank you," Demri said.

Jevlen bowed. It was obvious the bow wasn't for Demri, but to mask the man's teary eyes.

Scayde finished chewing a mouthful of walnuts. "You've done your companions a grand service, as I am no longer required to execute one of them. You may go now, Jevlen."

The Healer left, Tanibris waiting to escort the man back to his room. Cell? Demri wasn't sure. He was finding it difficult to sympathize at the moment either way.

"I need you to do me a favor, Demri." Scayde reclined in his chair, examining Buzzard's Bowl. His hand moved, then returned to its original position. The start of a gesture toward the chair next to him, likely retracted because of the miraculous restoration done to Demri's legs. The man was *smart* and realized Demri would prefer walking around.

Demri, however, was smarter. He took the seat, and Scayde's eyebrows rose in surprise.

"The Velvet Mother's organization is collapsing. The Corbéo family is virtually extinct. Khlaux is a guard serving the king. Tythus, your friend, is the only true-blooded Corbéo in Lochwall. Having a defunct family in possession of one of my shares to Buzzard's Bowl is not . . . lucrative. I need the man to hand back the deed, so I can bring in a family of wealth and influence."

"I don't b-b-believe he would be very agreeable."

"No. Neither do I." Scayde placed some more walnuts in his mouth, chewing. Slowly, deliberately. Mulling a decision over in his head? Or perhaps giving Demri some time to stew on the current information before delivering the juicy bit. Demri knew the game. He enjoyed playing it. He knew Scayde enjoyed it too.

Scayde swallowed. Here it came. "If he's unwilling to hand the deed over, I will require something else of you."

"M-meaning?"

"Whatever becomes necessary to acquire the deed. Theft? Sure. Murder? Perhaps. I'll send some men of mine if you need them."

Now it was Demri's time to stew it over. He reached over and plucked a couple of walnuts out of the bowl for himself. Chewing, he walked to the balcony's edge, grasped the railing, and looked out over the compound. Dozens of guards patrolled the grounds. Not surprising, given the level of rich people living here. And the number of poor ones that lived belowground, ready to fight so everyone up here could live luxurious lifestyles.

In one way, Demri was jealous he couldn't take part. It'd be nice to debate people, order guards around, and consume walnuts all day. But even if Scayde offered, Demri wouldn't take it up. He had other matters to pursue—namely, Doram Quandis. And in order to do that, he needed to cross an ocean. He needed Caius. Killing him was not an option. Even if Demri didn't need the man, he wouldn't be able to murder him. Caius had once saved his own life, and he'd aided Demri countless other times. Demri felt indebted to Scayde now, but that wasn't his only reason for agreeing to help the man retrieve the deed. He wanted to ensure Caius wouldn't be harmed.

"I will not hurt Caius."

"That's noble of you. You wouldn't make a very great nobleman." Scayde chuckled to himself, clearly amused by the joke.

"I believe you are c-c-correct." If they were all reminiscent of Scayde, Demri *wouldn't* enjoy it. Stuck in the same location, forever forced to mince your words, groveling to those above you, and snarling at those below you? Well, perhaps snarling at people was something Demri enjoyed. It was nice to instill fear in people. He didn't want to play a political game every hour of his life though. Demri was too blunt for that.

"So how are we going to get this deed from Tythus, Demri?"

That was the conundrum. How to get the deed from Caius without pissing him off too much? By not taking part himself. "I will t-tell you where all of his businesses are. Send your men to them and convince his men to stand down or k-k-kill them. They will fall apart fast. Do this t-tomorrow evening. I will ensure you receive your d-d-d-deed."

"A rather peaceful plan for the man that butchered a tavern full of civilians, don't you think?"

True. But Demri wasn't hunting anymore.

After giving Scayde Haklon the rest of the information he desired regarding how Demri became an Enforcer and then an Examiner, Demri returned to Caius, eager to question the man about his true identity. Eager to put this Velvet Mother shit behind them. Demri hoped that Scayde Haklon, figuring out who Caius was and taking back the deed to Buzzard's Bowl would convince Caius to leave it all behind.

Caius, busy handing out orders as the Velvet Mother, and attending to other business, wasn't around. Another irritant. Demri preferred not to wait for *anyone*, let alone somebody he'd never waited for before in his life until now.

It wasn't until later the next day that Caius was available. He'd been handling a crisis at the winery where hundreds of bottles of wine were found destroyed. A saboteur, not identified.

"Demri." Caius's voice was *unfamiliar*. Like he was talking to a subordinate. Dark circles encompassed his eyes. He had slept little, if at all.

Demri lifted a brow in response but said nothing.

"How did your foray into Haklon's estate go? My men tell me you never claimed the money you brought with you. And yet, your ailments seem cured."

"Not all of them. And I found out D-Doram is at Ashmount."

Caius grunted. "Figures." He pulled out a knife and started filing away. A return to form, in that moment. Caius was juggling two personas.

"I heard even more interesting information, T-T-Tythus."

The filing stopped. Caius's middle finger dribbled a droplet of blood. Caius examined it, licked his finger. Another droplet reappeared soon thereafter, and he ignored it. "So you know."

It wasn't a question, but Demri answered anyway. "Yes."

"You might be curious why I killed my grandmother."

"Morbidly c-curious."

"To be simple about it, I couldn't call her my own. The story I told you about Tythus, myself, was true. I left the Corbéo family, paid somebody to aid my escape, and haven't had contact with any of my family since. Didn't even know the Velvet Mother *was* a Corbéo until she revealed herself. I only knew the Corbéo name was respected in Lochwall. Admired. But I cared nothing for that power or of nobility. Not back then, anyway. Now I understand what I tossed away. When I saw an opportunity to claim my namesake's inheritance, I took it in the hopes I—we—could benefit from it. The name Tythus Corbéo means nothing. I am Caius."

Demri accepted that. It wasn't a betrayal. It was a man looking to escape who he'd been. Demri knew how that felt. Any time he thought of Ashmount, Doram Quandis, or Myri Celioh, the shame of his previous self washed over him. He *hated* it. It came to mind that Scayde Haklon would be on the way to retrieve his deed any moment now.

"All is f-f-f-forgiven, C-C-Caius. There is something a bit more important to discuss. Scayde knows who you are. He also knows how weak your family has b-b-b-become. He is coming for the d-deed to B-Buzzard's B-B-Bowl." Demri wouldn't surprise Caius the way Scayde wanted. Caius had been too good to Demri. He was Demri's only friend.

Caius frowned, staring at his fingernails. He'd gone back to filing while Demri spoke. "Scayde Haklon is the most powerful man in Lochwall. Rumor suggests that King Mikas is to arrive any day now to make him a duke. There's no way we have the human resources to repel him. Even if I used all the finances at my disposal, Haklon has . . . a *lot* more." Demri didn't argue. Caius was right after all.

"Ma'am!" Stanton Brick ran into the room, breathless. "Lord Haklon is here to see you." The man was in awe, impressed. If Demri felt he could spare the Soul Glyphs, he might've ended the man's life, so annoyed he was by the man's fawning. But he'd just replenished them and was old enough—thirty-eight with the appearance of a man in his early fifties. "He requested your presence *right away*." Stanton's legs were antsy, and he kept fiddling with his fingers.

They followed Stanton, who led them outside the warehouse Caius had moved his dealings as the Velvet Mother to. In the street sat several fancy carriages. In front of them, Scayde Haklon stood, yellow cape flowing in the wind behind him, framing him as a figure of importance. Circling him and extending across the length of the street were dozens of armed men. Several robed figures as well. Magicai.

Demri, obscured by the colossal form of Caius and the groveling Stanton, pulled out his spectacles and examined them. Three of them were Enforcers, two Collectors. He whisked the spectacles away. Everyone's focus wasn't on him for once, and nobody noticed. It wouldn't do well to have a group of Magicai inquiring why he was using spectacles when his skin was flush with Soul Glyphs. Aside from the Magicai, Demri also recognized Marshal Everic Deywin standing among them and chewing skachi.

"The Velvet Mother." Scayde took a step forward but didn't breach the line of guards standing in front of him. "Tythus Corbéo. The man who ran away from home. You have something I need."

"The deed to the arena. I know."

Scayde Haklon smiled. "I wasn't sure if your friend would forewarn you. I admit I'm glad he did. Makes this bit much easier. A forthcoming man is a person I can respect. I often have to work with troublesome people to *extract* what I require."

"I am no fool. You may have your deed. In fact, you can have *all* of my assets, Lord Haklon."

Scayde snapped his fingers. "And *I* am no fool, Caius. What's the catch?"

"Safe passage to Ashmount for myself. And Demri of course. I'm also taking a large portion of the Velvet Mother's coffers. Things are getting expensive."

"That's it?"

"That's it."

Scayde pointed at Caius. "Deal. I'll have a ship stocked and ready for you in Pinecrest. There will be two horses, supplied and ready, at the eastern gate in a couple of hours. They'll take you to Pinecrest."

One of Scayde's men stepped forward. "My lord, a ship will be difficult to come by. The war in Cyrok demanded most—"

Scayde rounded on the man and backhanded him. "Do I look like a commoner to you?"

"No! No, my lord!"

"Well, you look like a commoner to me, so kindly return to your station."

"My lord," the man mumbled, stepping back in line with the other guardsmen.

Scayde turned back to Caius. "It takes three days to reach Pinecrest. The ship will take more time to acquire, but it'll be there. Now, I need the deed."

Caius nodded. "The deed's in the desk." He gestured toward Stanton. "That's Stanton Brick. He knows the most about the Velvet Mother's assets and business ventures. He should be of great use."

Scayde's smile widened. Demri felt it seemed genuine now. "Thanks for the wise words, Caius. Marshal, please place Stanton under arrest."

"What? Why?" Stanton fell to his knees, like a priest praising Mother Avani.

Demri rolled his eyes at the pathetic man.

Without another word, Caius walked past Stanton, away from his short-lived enterprise. Demri followed, listening to Stanton pleading for his freedom. By the time they'd made it another street over, Stanton's cries escalated. *Perhaps in order to fix a cripple, you have to create a cripple.*

SERADAL WINTLOCK

2nd Cycle of Winter, 231st Reign of Garcovi
Cyrok

On the morning of the second day of travel, the mood changed from happiness and relief to sobered as they remembered Angazo. Her father's longtime friend. A knight Renard looked up to and aspired to become. They recalled the man's deeds, in particular his help when Captain Adavir held Sera and her father captive.

Their reminiscence shattered that afternoon, an angry yell coming from farther up the caravan.

A few moments later, the canvas covering their carriage ripped open. Vithor Bane climbed inside, two men accompanying him.

It was clear the man was furious. Balled fists, heavy breathing, a drip of drool. Of course, the drool landed on Vithor Bane's trousers. Where else?

"Which. One. Of. You. Killed. Her?" He struggled to get the words out. It seemed like he was choking to death on his own thoughts. If the subject of his words were any different, Sera might've expressed humor in how he was acting.

Nobody answered him.

"She was *supposed* to be *my* insurance policy. And she's dead!"

There was only one person he could be referring to: Magicus Ashté.

Vithor Bane continued fuming, pacing around the carriage, eyeing each of them. "I blame you." He snarled, pointing one of his fat, stubby fingers at Sera. "She healed you and your father. Who knows if you wouldn't have lived without her?"

"I didn't ask her to heal me." Sera rose from her seat. She had a feeling this was about to take a turn for the worse.

"The Healer collapsed, dead. Of a heart attack! Healing *you* caused her to age to a point in which she died. From old age! The woman was *twenty-fucking-six*. Do you have *any* idea how much that incredible amount of healing had to have been, to *kill* her? Do you have *any* idea how *much* that costs? No. No, you couldn't! How do you intend to pay me back?"

Sera got to her feet, balling her own fists in anger. The last thing she wanted to do was deal with this man. "I don't know how I'm to pay you for the journey, let alone the healing. But I will counter you with this, Vithor Bane: Magicus Ashté *chose* to save my life. I didn't ask her to. She wanted to. She told me so. So, you can be angry at her all you want, but it's not my fault nor my debt to pay. Period."

"I want you out! Out of my carriage! You can walk the rest of the way!" Spittle dribbled down his chin, looping down to his neck. It flung around like a stray hair, waving in the wind.

"We'll die out there!" Renard, panicked, knelt at Vithor Bane's feet. "Please, cyr, don't do this."

"Get. Out. *Now!*"

And so they did. Sera, Renard, and her father gathered their belongings and exited the carriage. Their gear they'd stored in the front carriage was laying in the snow, waiting for them. They put on as many articles of clothing as they had and left the rest behind. Vithor Bane kept Angazo's though. "Have to have *something* to make this worth it," he'd said.

The caravan took off, horses galloping for ten minutes or so to put Sera and the others farther away, and then resumed its normal pace, putting even more distance between them. Coldridge was about one day away, and night was coming. It was going to be a cold, dark hike through a forest. And if they were lucky, more of the Calrites weren't pursuing them. Shivering, Sera planted one foot in front of the other, thanking Mother Avani that her father's paralysis was no longer an issue.

Too soon, sunlight disappeared. Fiery feet, complaining calves, tormented thighs, busted backs, screaming shoulders, aching abdomens. They suffered the pains of unaided travel, foot traffic in the snowy expanse of an unforgiving wilderness. And as luck would have it, it began snowing. A light dusting of powder, but the warning was there: a potential blizzard threatened to freeze the travelers to death. They had to stop many times to light fires and warm themselves. Between the chill and their breaks, the caravan had long since pulled out of eyesight.

They were fortunate they at least had the luxury of being in the middle of a forest. If they found themselves stuck in one of the many wide-open areas of Cyrok, and a blizzard came through, they would perish fast. The trees offered protection. They also hindered visibility, so

Sera didn't know how much progress they were making toward Coldridge. Her father estimated Vithor Bane had forced them out of the carriage at the three-quarter mark of the journey.

Sera's fingers and toes were going numb. Her nose reddened and leaked. She shivered until her body ached, then she shivered some more. It was so cold even Renard stopped complaining about their trek. Jaidik claimed that shivering was a sign they were still okay. Sera didn't believe it. She felt like collapsing and taking a nap. Her father insisted they continue without sleep. So they did. One foot in front of the other.

The moon shined *just* enough light through the pine trees so they could continue stumbling ever onward without being blinded by darkness. Once, a pair of wolves howled in the distance. This pressed the group onward with a small dosage of adrenaline. Fear could be a powerful motivator, Sera knew.

During the third morning after fleeing Vox, their water skins emptied, so Sera consumed handfuls of snow. It was dangerous to do so, as the snow lowered her body temperature, but she needed to quench her thirst. They had no food. Winterberry shrubs were plentiful, which they consumed sparingly—just enough to take the edge off their hunger. Jaidik explained the berries could cause nausea or dizziness. Sera was already dizzy, so she didn't see a problem with that.

With the rise of the morning sun, the trio droned on. The farther south they made it, the deeper the snow became. Although the caravan passed through, the snow was up to their calves, which slowed their progress and caused them to exert unnecessary levels of energy.

They exited the tree line. Sera hadn't seen it coming, so thick was the forest.

Not far away, she saw the vast, freezing arctic waters of the ocean. And on the coastline, Coldridge. Sera fell to her knees, catching her breath and thanking Mother Avani again. The city, surrounded by walls, was still alive. Lights and smoke. A couple of ships in the harbor. They were mere hours away from safety.

"Let's get going," her father said. He hoisted her to her feet, then did the same for Renard. Somehow, her father had more stamina than either of them, and he'd been bedridden until two days ago.

They clambered through the snow, across the flat land. An hour passed, then another. The city crept closer.

Sera kept trudging through the snow, exhausted. Then Renard called out, "Look, horses! We're saved!"

True enough, when Sera raised her head, squinting against the sunlight reflecting off crystallized snow, she saw a pair of riders heading in their direction.

Exhausted, she sat and waited for them. The other two followed her example.

When she heard the horse's hooves crunching on the ground, she stood. Two chestnut geldings halted fifteen feet away.

A Falcon Knight, a Vulture to be more accurate, sat astride one of them, helm in hand. The man was *old* but had a powerful air of authority in how he carried himself—straight-backed and rigid. The second man had a weathered and stained captain's jacket on and a wild goatee. He was a man of the military, but no Falcon Knight. *The Old Vulture? Here?* The only other Vulture she knew of was Strictland, and he wasn't walking around.

The captain spoke first. His voice was deep and rough, and he cleared it several times before speaking. Sera thought she caught a whiff of whiskey. "Are they yours, cyr?" he asked the Falcon Knight.

The Old Vulture shook his head. "I don't recognize them. What are you doing here, cyr?" Though polite, she could tell he was wary. His hand drifted toward the pommel of his sword. She couldn't understand why. She was a Falcon Knight herself.

"I'm Cyr Seradal Wintlock. This is my page, Renard, and my father, Jaidik Wintlock." She considered lying about where they'd come from but knew that wouldn't end well. "We fled Vox."

The captain grunted. "Just took in a caravan from there. Said they were the last ones out of the city. That they witnessed the Calrym army surrounding it."

"They did. We were on that caravan. Vithor Bane blamed us for the death of a Healer, because she died helping me and fixing my father, and then he forced us to walk."

"We're just looking for some food and a warm bed," her father pleaded, hands raised out in front of him. "Then we'll figure out where to go in the morning."

The captain snorted at that. "You'll be screwed if you wait till morning. Ships are departing later today. Lucky you arrived when you did." The captain pulled out a small bottle from his coat, offering it out to them. "Whiskey? Warm yourself up a bit, perhaps?"

Sera had never tried whiskey, but she reached out and took it. There wasn't anything she *wouldn't* have taken at the moment. She took a sip. It burned her throat, and she coughed, spewing half of it onto the snow in front of her. Renard subsequently passed. Her father took a mouthful himself, swallowing it with a grimace and a smack of the lips.

"Well, up you get. We'll bring you back to the city." The captain held his hand out to her, and she climbed up behind him.

The Old Vulture took her father and Renard on his steed, which was much bigger than the captain's.

As they rode, Sera shivered against the man's back. His coat, though stained and smelling of alcohol, was comfortable to lean against. The horse's warmth between her legs was a godsend.

"What's your name?"

"Captain Decklin Hoarst, though most people just call me Royal. You can call me whatever you want. I couldn't care less."

"And who's the knight, Royal?" She needed confirmation. The wind whipped through her hair, stinging her face. It was *freezing*.

"Ah, him. He just arrived a few days ago. Fought against the Calrites but got routed. The Old Vulture, they call him. Cyr Vecchio Rizurri. He's a *legend* to your kind. Surprised you haven't heard of him."

I can't believe he made it. Perhaps there's a chance the Falcon Knights can continue to operate.

She quieted, pressing her nose against Royal. Tears leaked out her eyes, so she closed them. When she opened them again, they'd ridden through the open gate of Coldridge. The iron creaked shut behind them, and they were safe.

It wasn't the reception Sera had hoped for. Rather than being coddled, given a blanket and some warm food, and told to rest, Royal led them to a small rowboat, called a pinnace. Nearby, steaming horse carcasses lay to freeze, the harvested meat already loaded on a ship. Already shivering, she dreaded a trip across the cold ocean waters to where the moored ships creaked in the wind. Several soldiers joined them in the boat, and they rowed away from Coldridge. A few pinnaces tethered to the shore remained, awaiting further evacuees.

The continual up and down motion of the water stirred Sera's stomach, and she was grateful Royal *hadn't* stopped for food. Conversation was brief and muted. The soldiers focused on rowing. Royal and the Old Vulture seemed to have a pact to stare at the shrinking port town. Renard and her father were resolute in their silence, waiting to see what happened next. Instead of disturbing the peace, Sera examined the massive vessels, tall masts stretching toward the sky. Crow's nests tipped hundreds of feet back and forth above them, making Sera feel even sicker. It looked like the long wooden poles would snap in the wind, sending anybody up there falling to their deaths, either by crashing on the deck beneath them, hanging themselves on the various ropes that crisscrossed their way around the ships, or smacking into the hypothermic-inducing ocean.

When they neared the moored ships, Sera looked over them in awe. She'd never been this close to a seaworthy ship before, only seeing them in the distance whenever she took a gyrfalcon hunting. They passed by *Heirloom* and *Preservation*, two massive ships outfitted with dozens of cannons that must've been able to hold hundreds, if not thousands, of people. *A city, floating in the sea.* The soldiers rowed the pinnace toward *Mistveil*, a merchant ship that remained to help the fleeing citizenry, according to Royal.

They boarded *Mistveil*, and the soldiers hoisted the pinnace, attaching it to the ship.

Royal pulled out his flask, taking a deep sip. "Get out of here, everyone. Go find something to drink, and maybe a stiff man's daughter to plow if you're lucky." The soldiers laughed and departed in groups of twos and threes. Jaidik gave a grunt of annoyance at Royal's words.

Now to ask the questions that bothered Sera. "Where are we going to go? What are we to do?"

Royal was slipping his flask back into his captain's jacket when she'd asked her questions. He promptly returned the flask to hand, draining it in several large swallows. "I don't rightly care, cyr. I *do*, however, need to refill this." He shook the empty flask in the air.

"Royal. You don't get to walk away from a Falcon Knight," Sera said. And she was right. She was in command of him.

"I'm not sure what you mean. Shit's Blessing has been bestowed upon us, cyr. There's no law. There's no order. The Falcon Knights are dead. The Cyroki people? We have *maybe* a few hundred aboard this ship. And in order to survive, in order to preserve what we have left, the Old Vulture has decided to split up the citizens from the Falcon Knights. Hopefully, *some* of us will avoid the Calrites. Excuse me, cyr, but I'm thirsty, haven't had a drink in *hours*." Royal shook the flask once more and walked away from her.

"Only cares about his drink. Bastard," her father said.

Renard grabbed her arm. "He can't mean any of that, cyr."

Before Sera could respond, though, the Old Vulture himself entered her vision. "Don't mind him. He's a drunk, he's scared, and there's no helping a scared drunkard."

"Cyr." Under his intimidating gaze, Sera had forgotten his name. The Old Vulture was what everyone called him, but what was his name?

Renard saved the day. He knelt before the Old Vulture. "Cyr Vecchio Rizurri."

The Old Vulture spared a glance in Renard's direction. No doubt he was used to groveling pages. And used to groveling knights like Sera. She closed her open mouth but knew the Falcon Knight had noticed it.

"There may not be many of us left, but we'll make a resurgence," he said. Sera believed him. With the governess dead and most of the country gone, the Cyroki would need somebody to rally behind. And who better than the Old Vulture himself?

"I'm ready to serve our country, cyr," Sera said, hitting her chest once with her fist. "Do you know where *Mistveil* will land?"

"Remeria. Our primary mission is to ask the Remerian king for aid. They've long been at odds with Calrym. We hope to convince them to join us, though we admittedly have little to offer in return. We need a sizable force before we can approach King Alondo, otherwise we'll be ignored as Cyroki refugees. Beggars at the king's feet looking for a scrap of vengeance. The goal is to convince him that preserving Cyrok is beneficial." The Old Vulture frowned. He seemed to have difficulty believing his own words.

"You'll be able to convince him, cyr."

He shook his head. "I don't know that I will. I'm a tired old man. The last thing I want is to be in charge of leading a resistance. I've been making life-changing decisions for thousands of people since before you were born. My goal is to find the next leader, so that I can retire. Or at least not have to bother with the politicking and decision-making. Wielding a sword is still . . . acceptable."

"Cyr Seradal could lead," Renard said.

Damnation, Renard. Don't do that to me.

The Old Vulture turned to Renard. "Perhaps one day *you* might become a leader yourself."

Renard blushed. "I'll be lucky to become a knight."

"I agree." And the Old Vulture left Renard standing there embarrassed and humiliated.

Sera thought the entire thing was cruel but also amusing. She laughed, and Renard joined her.

Mistveil set sail along with another three. The two carrying most of the Cyroki citizens headed to Qothe and the two harboring the remnants of the Falcon Knights to Remeria.

VILLIC THE IMBUER

2nd Cycle of Winter, 231st Reign of Garcovi
Remeria

Villic brought Jedkah and the shamans back to the destroyed shack, where Villic had left the injured Magicus. He wasn't there. It wasn't yet dawn, so he'd followed through on his promise.

"He was here when I left," Villic said. He looked around, confused. Everything was how he'd left it. Except for the missing Magicus.

Speaker said, *"I told you he'd run. He knows he'd die otherwise. He can't be far. He has too many wounds."*

Quiet.

"We must search the area," a shaman said.

Within a few moments, Jedkah found the Magicus hiding underneath a different pile of rubble. The Magicus screamed and whimpered when Jedkah pulled him out.

"Is this him, Villic?" Jedkah asked.

"Yes."

Jedkah pushed the captive to the ground. "What did you promise him, Villic?"

"Help."

"Because the gods demanded it?"

"The moon retreated when I asked the gods."

Several of the shamans whispered among themselves. Jedkah frowned but waited for them to finish.

"Villic the Imbuer has misunderstood the gods," a shaman said.

The kind shaman nodded, smiling at Villic.

"She's mocking you in her head," Speaker said.

She smiles.

"Not with you. See how her face warps? It's a forced gesture. She's pretending."

No. But Villic believed Speaker. Interpreting his clan members' expressions, actions, or words was a struggle he faced every day. He heart sank. Another person who didn't understand him.

"I'm sorry."

Quiet, Speaker.

Villic closed his eyes. Ignored the shamans. Ignored Jedkah. And he ignored the voice in his head, Speaker. He pushed it all out. Focused on breathing, thinking about better times. *There weren't better times.* Perhaps when his parents were still alive. But that was long ago. Nothing had changed since. Everybody treated him the same. Occasionally somebody would be nice. Sikoi was. But he had died. Others had died too. With Speaker bringing out the truth about the kind shaman, Villic revisited everyone he'd thought was nice to him. Had they made similar faces? He couldn't remember. Didn't know that he wanted to remember.

"Villic. They need you to answer."

Answer what?

"Jedkah asked you a question."

Villic looked up at Jedkah.

The leader of the Splintered Manes stared at Villic, his arms crossed. "Can you hear me, Villic?"

Villic nodded.

"What do you think will happen if we let the Magicus leave here alive?"

Villic hadn't considered that before. "He'd go get help. He's injured."

"And after?"

"He'd tell them what happened here."

"And what do you think would happen when he told his allies about what happened here, Villic?"

"They'd come."

"To do what?"

To kill us. He'd made a mistake leaving the Magicus and trusting the moon. Then Villic's mouth drooped open. *Lurzal, god of deception.*

"Villic?" Jedkah asked.

"He tricked me!"

"Who tricked what?" a shaman asked.

"Lurzal!"

"Lurzal tricked you?" the kind—no, mean—shaman asked.

Villic nodded. "He covered the moon."

The shamans put their heads back together, whispering. *So many secrets.*

"And I'm sure most of it is bullshit."

Speaker!

"You're too trusting in their 'power,' Villic."

You are going to get me killed.

"If you were going to die by the gods, you already would have."

You don't know that.

"Have you committed grave atrocities that the gods wouldn't have been able to forgive at any point in your life?"

Yes.

"Then why are you alive?"

The shamans contacted the gods.

Speaker laughed.

"It's determined that you are correct, Villic," a shaman said.

Villic smiled. He didn't understand the gods most of the time. He wasn't a godspeaker. But sometimes he figured it out, always later than he should, but at least he arrived at the answer himself.

"If Lurzal tricked Villic the Imbuer," Jedkah said, drawing his scimitar, "then I suppose we should do what he originally thought."

What I originally thought I should?

"You wanted to kill the Magicus."

Right. Kill him. Villic frowned. Killing the injured man felt wrong.

The Magicus looked at Villic, eyes wide, a sparkling tear dripping down his cheek. Villic blinked, realizing the sun was coming up and reflecting in the man's tear. He hadn't noticed. The Magicus shouted something. *What did he say?*

"He says, 'Don't kill me, I'm harmless.'"

Villic laughed out loud. The shamans turned to him.

"Explain why you laughed. They are going to believe you're excited over the killing."

Villic didn't want that to happen. "Speaker says the man is asking you not to kill him. He says he's harmless."

The shamans and Jedkah laughed too.

Then Jedkah cut the man's head off with a quick swipe. Nobody had time to react, least of all the Magicus. It was over. The bloodied corpse tipped over, spewing red over the rubble.

"It's time we rejoin the other clans and take this fight

to the heart of their country," Jedkah said, wiping the sword off on the dead man's clothing.

The shamans whispered together once more, then talked with Jedkah for a moment.

"The shamans say we're early, and if we leave now, we won't meet the other clans. We rest for two weeks, and then it'll be time to rejoin the other clans outside the capital."

The Splintered Manes cheered.

INTERLUDE
VELTURO ONDAKKA

2nd Cycle of Winter, 231st Reign of Garcovi
Lochwall, Calrym

Lamb root pie was a favorite of Duke Velturo's. A tender lamb butchered at *precisely* twenty-four weeks of age, cooked to utter *perfection*, and combined with any variety of roots. Lamb root pie often contained several of the following—carrots, turnips, radishes, parsnips, beetroots, potatoes, sweet potatoes, or ginger—and was mashed together, along with some other ingredients Velturo was unaware of. Perhaps eggs? Cooking wasn't his forte. Eating, however, was very much so.

He chewed, happy and content. Nothing beat a hot lamb root pie. Well, that wasn't true. There was a vast variety of desserts that *would* beat it. But dessert was forthcoming and not something he needed to be too concerned over, unless it became cancelled. They were seated in Scayde Haklon's dining hall, and it'd been a while since Velturo had consumed such a splendid meal.

"Damn it, ah-hah," he muttered through an overfull mouth of pie, laughing at himself. Damned fool he was.

Chewed up contents spilled down his new tunic. He dabbed at the fleshy, half-chewed sweet potato, pressing it deeper into the cloth. Something for a servant to work out later. Something they were very much used to. He'd purchased the blue tunic, now stained orange, *exactly* for this event. Velturo didn't even know why he bothered. Most of the other dukes and duchesses, even King Mikas, regarded him as somewhat of a joke. This didn't matter to Velturo. He was still a duke. He still had vast wealth. And power. The same respect citizens offered to Harlem Maccaro or Arena Hyrel applied to him. Even Sturgeon, the old man who was on the brink of death, received the benefits of dukedom, and Velturo was sure the king had a replacement in mind.

Eyes closed, Velturo stuffed another forkful of pie into his mouth. He mumbled to himself, happy. Breaded pie crust spilled from his lips, cascading down his blue tunic. At least they didn't leave a smear on his tunic.

"You are revolting, Velturo," Arena hissed into his left ear. They weren't in Anepolis anymore, so they didn't have their old seating. Which meant, much to Arena's displeasure, they were sitting next to each other. Another pleasure of Velturo's. Anything that made the duchess uncomfortable. She was too prude for her own sake.

Velturo opened his eyes and offered a loud belch, wiping the corners of his mouth with a kerchief. "Wonderful meal, Lord Haklon. Marvelous and most delicious. I'll be visiting your cook often. *Often*, ah-hah."

Lord Haklon chuckled. "I'm glad you enjoyed it, Your Grace. Wait until they bring out the chocolate-glazed bread. It *melts* in your mouth."

Velturo's stomach rumbled. No matter what he did,

he could never seem to satiate it. He licked his lips in anticipation. Something new to try. Would it beat candied chestnuts? Chocolate custard? Honeycomb and cheese?

The king cleared his throat. Attention diverted his way. The king scratched at his chin, rings glimmering, tantalizing all who coveted wealth. Velturo enjoyed wealth, but mostly, it was about magnificent food for him. "Please excuse Velturo. He's . . . gluttonous at his best." He wouldn't argue with that statement.

Lord Haklon shook his head. "The matter is of no inconvenience to me. I like a man who enjoys fine food." He offered Velturo a wink, which Velturo would have returned, but he'd burped up some vomit and was gulping down a mug of Nochi, a spiced chocolate ale, to cover the acidic taste in his throat. Nochi was another of his favorites.

Lord Haklon returned his attention to the king. "It's always a pleasure to host Your Majesty here at Lochwall and in my personal estate, no less."

"We . . . do . . . need to make a stronger, more concerted effort to meet with you more often," said Duke Sturgeon, struggling through life. Velturo hated the old man. *Everyone* hated the old man.

The king agreed. "It's true. I only come down here for the games, I realize. And this year, I didn't even come for those. Too busy warring in the north." He laughed. They all laughed. They all knew, but wouldn't vocalize, that the king had little to do with anything in the north. Other than signing an order to attack.

For a second, Velturo wondered how Harlem was making out. Then he didn't care anymore. A servant brought them the anticipated dessert. Fluffy white bread covered in melting, oozing chocolate and topped with a powdery, sugary glaze. Velturo picked up a fork and impaled the dessert. He brought it to his mouth, reaching out with his tongue to draw it in faster. He moaned. It was *so* sweet. *Shit.* Velturo had drizzled a line of chocolate across his tunic. How could he be so careless? He tried to wipe it up with his kerchief. It turned his orange-stained blue tunic a dark brown. Velturo licked the kerchief and dabbed again. Nothing. He dabbed the kerchief in his mug, using water—he was drinking Nochi, not water—to spread a warm brown liquid around his tunic. *Shit.* Nothing to do about it now. *I get clumsier with age.*

Velturo tuned back into the conversation.

"Me, Your Majesty?" Lord Haklon was pointing at himself, feigning shock. The king must have informed him about his promotion, though it sounded like someone must have given him advance notice.

"And," the king continued, "as the new Duke of Lochwall, we will require you to report in at regular intervals. You will be in charge of . . . things. I'll have my advisers fill you in later. There's no reason to discuss the specifics over such a glorious meal." Meaning the king didn't have a damn clue what the Duke of Lochwall's responsibilities were. Not that Velturo blamed him. Velturo didn't know either. If he had advisers to do everything for him, he'd eat all day. Then he realized that's what he did, and that he, too, had advisers who did everything. Nobility was a wonderful concept. More people should be noble.

Lord Haklon—now Duke Scayde—stood, bowing to King Mikas. "This requires a celebration, Your Majesty. Please accept a token of my gratitude." He waved forward his head servant. "Tanibris?"

Tanibris approached the king, a small scroll in hand. He laid the parchment on the table in front of the king.

The king picked up the scroll and grinned. "A deed?"

Velturo took another bite of his sweet, sweet dessert. "Mmph. Exquisite." Nobody cared. Velturo would need to collect the recipe.

Duke Scayde offered another bow. "A deed to one-fifth of Buzzard's Bowl. You are now in possession of my personal fifth of the arena, which is stocked with some of the *best* fighters. And if you would like, Your Majesty, we could conduct a celebratory preseason fight among the five Houses with some of the new blood who've been preparing for their first season. It'll be a nice warmup for the spring season. Nothing uncommon, and you'd get to see some of your men in action."

"Duke Scayde, you've outdone yourself," King Mikas said. "But if I'm receiving *your* fifth of the arena, that would mean you don't have one, correct?"

"My wife possesses a fifth herself. And fortuitous as it may seem, I recently acquired *another* deed. The former owner, going by the moniker the Velvet Mother, has passed." Duke Scayde looked saddened at that. Velturo knew not to trust anything Scayde said or did. The man was brilliant at masking truths. Even so, it was lucky for Scayde she'd died. *Maybe it wasn't luck.*

"I think all of us could agree that remaining in Lochwall for another day or two wouldn't do us any harm," said King Mikas. "Perhaps we'll even stay long enough to watch the first day of games in the spring."

Velturo gave a wave of assent. If he could request more food from Scayde's cook, he'd be satisfied to stay as long as the king desired.

Arena gave a slight nod. She was clearly not happy about remaining. That made things even more pleasurable for Velturo.

Velturo inhaled while chewing, breathing in some

bread crumbs. He choked, spewing bread and chocolate over his tunic and the table. Coughing, he struggled to drain the rest of the Nochi. Nobody paid him any attention. His tunic, however, looked like a newborn's undergarments. He'd search for a tailor tomorrow.

EDELBROCK BRENDIS

2nd Cycle of Winter, 231st Reign of Garcovi
Lochwall, Calrym

The elation brought on by the Velvet Mother's promises of potential freedom and a better quality of life lifted their spirits. Medical supplies arrived, and they patched up Savakkis, Chellie, and the other injured. It was no Healer. Healers were expensive and would never waste their services on gladiators.

Although most of the gladiators had an even *happier* demeanor—they'd made it through the current season of the games—this stifled Edelbrock's feelings. He knew he'd soon be holding a weapon, standing among other people who wanted to live just as much as he did. From his experience, a man on the brink of death fought ten times harder than one who didn't have as much to worry about. Spring was approaching. Edelbrock felt prepared. He *was* prepared. He'd trained hard and figured out most of the weaponry. His old experience in the military surfaced. Edelbrock was as ready as he'd ever be. But even the hardiest veterans suffered from fear, or at least the smartest ones did. People who didn't experience fear were often killed first.

It had only been a few weeks since the games had ended, and new Draftees were brought in more frequently, though Edelbrock paid little attention to them. Now, everyone was gearing up for the next season in spring. That, unfortunately, was nothing compared to the soul-crushing event that transpired next.

Tanibris, reviled as he was, reported anyone to Scayde Haklon who ignored him—he was speaking on Scayde's behalf after all—which meant everyone paid attention to Tanibris for fear of upsetting Scayde. "Line up, everyone. Wonderful news, wonderful news." Edelbrock doubted any information coming from Scayde Haklon's head servant could be "wonderful."

Inside the dining hall, Edelbrock took a spot in line next to the bandaged Savakkis and traded worried looks with the man. They stood behind one of the long tables, Tanibris glowering at him from the other side.

"Developments and trades have taken place."

Edelbrock felt Savakkis tense beside him. He'd heard about trades before. Sometimes the House Heads traded their fighters. Edelbrock learned from other gladiators that trades happened occasionally, though participants entered in a season of the arena weren't allowed to be traded, only trainees were.

"The Velvet Mother has died," Tanibris said. "After searching everywhere for an heir, Lord Haklon could not find one." An icy chill ran down Edelbrock's spine. This wasn't good news. "Lord Haklon is an intelligent man and partnered with King Mikas Garcovi, who is now in possession of one-fifth of Buzzard's Bowl.

Congratulations, the king now has a vested interest in your battles."

Edelbrock breathed a sigh of relief. He was the king's man now, not Scayde's.

"Oh, and Lord Haklon offered the king his own group of fighters, meaning Lord Haklon is taking over this House. The king also made him the Duke of Lochwall, and Duke Scayde expects you to show extra reverence from now on."

Fear, anger, and confusion were the first three emotions to permeate Edelbrock. Fear because he knew Scayde would make his life miserable. Anger because *of course* Scayde Haklon discovered a loophole to regain Edelbrock as a slave. And confusion because *why* would anybody elevate Scayde Haklon to the Duke of Lochwall? Disgusting.

Footsteps echoed from the stone steps leading down to the kitchen. Heavy, booted, important steps. Dread increased with every clap of leather on stone. Edelbrock didn't even look up. He knew who it was. Scayde entered the dining hall and began walking the line of gladiators.

"There's going to be significant changes around here," Scayde Haklon said. "Marshal Deywin will see to them and ensure you're all aware of what they entail." Edelbrock detected a hint of viciousness. He braced himself. "And Ed! I hope you haven't enjoyed your time *too* much here. It's about to become less enjoyable. For starters, you're going to be joining a select few for a preseason bout. I look forward to seeing if you can survive, particularly when you're standing on the spot little Gordy landed."

Blackness flickered across Edelbrock's vision. Nauseated or angry or both, he wasn't sure. A searing pain in his mouth. Tears appeared in his eyes. He spat out a hard white chunk. He'd clenched his mouth so hard that he'd chipped a tooth.

Tanibris returned later in the day with a list, pinning it to the wall in the kitchen. Edelbrock was on it, of course, as were three other trainees—a man Edelbrock knew as Lucky, who had a penchant for winking at odd times and was a well-known gambler; his fellow Draftee, Bruise; and a man Edelbrock didn't know with a pock-covered face, who he decided to call Pock. They'd be competing in the preseason skirmish scheduled the following morning. Because the fight was unofficial and not sanctioned to provide entertainment, there would be no audience other than whomever was in the King's Stand, the observatory where Scayde had brought Edelbrock. It felt ages ago, though the horror of Jaylena's coldness and Gordane's death lingered, persistent. Edelbrock wouldn't forget either.

He practiced late into the night, and when it was time to sleep, he tossed and turned, worried about his first battle since he'd fought in the Vessian Incursion. Sweat laced his forehead as he considered Scayde's prediction that he'd freeze up when revisiting the place of Gordane's death.

When Edelbrock fell asleep, it seemed only minutes passed before somebody shook him awake.

"It's time," the stranger said.

Edelbrock followed the man, who turned out to be a guard Edelbrock had seen once or twice before.

"If you're hungry, we have eggs," he said.

"I'm not hungry." Edelbrock's hands twitched. The only hunger he felt was a need to get this over with.

"There's sausage too."

The guard escorted him through the pit. Edelbrock stole a glance through the grated windows and saw empty stands and blowing sands, and then they entered the preparation room.

Bruise and Pock were already there, eating sausage and eggs. The aroma caused bile to begin its journey up his throat. He swallowed it back down, feeling the acrid burn in his chest. When Edelbrock thought of battle, he imagined disemboweled horses, guts splayed around a grassy field, pools of coagulated blood, and the moans of the injured and dying surrounded by cries of victory. *Buzzard's Bowl will be similar.*

Through the archway, the hazy fog distorting his vision, he had a view of the King's Stand. Several figures moved about, and many sat in chairs. *Likely discussing who'll win. Placing bets on us. Scayde's hoping I get maimed. Death would be too kind, too quick a sentence.*

"Hungry?" Pock asked. He slid a plate of food in Edelbrock's direction.

"No."

"Suit yourself. Can't go into a fight with an empty stomach though." Pock swallowed a mouthful, then shoved more into his mouth.

"It's less that'll come up later," Edelbrock said.

Pock just shrugged.

A few seconds later, Lucky showed up with another guard in tow. He winked at Edelbrock.

"Good," the man who'd brought Edelbrock said. "In a bit, you'll hear a horn. When you do, enter through the archway. If you don't, they'll find and execute you."

The guards left, and the other three trainees started

socializing. Edelbrock didn't see a point in joining. Several of them might be dead soon.

He took several deep breaths in through the nose, out through the mouth. His head resting in his hands, he closed his eyes. Edelbrock cleared his mind, forgetting Gordane, Jaylena, and Scayde. The focus had to be on the battle, on getting through it alive.

He thought about when he'd been Major Brendis. Back when a battle meant commanding his men, sending them to their deaths. Now, it was just about his own survival. There was no chain of command in the arena. And he doubted anybody would listen to him.

The horn blared. Edelbrock looked up.

Bruise and Lucky were already walking through the archway.

Pock, halfway through Edelbrock's plate of food, vomited.

Edelbrock shook his head. "I told you." He went over to the sick man and clapped Pock on the back a few times. "Get it all out."

"I don't want to die." Pock threw up again.

"Doubt any of us want to." Edelbrock didn't want to. Being down in the hypogeum had stifled his thoughts of the future. He'd reminisced about Gordane every day, but he hadn't considered what would happen if he ever escaped Buzzard's Bowl. He wanted vengeance. On the deceitful barrister, Chardaine. He wanted to storm the law offices of Roachford and Singleton's for even employing the barrister. Edelbrock wanted vengeance of that bastard Marshal Deywin. Of his scheming former wife, Jaylena. But most of all, Edelbrock wanted to cut the prick off the prick himself, Scayde Haklon. The motivation to survive overwhelmed him with adrenaline. It was time. "You all right?" he asked Pock.

Pock wiped his chin. "I'm good, I guess."

"Then let's go survive."

I nside the arena, Edelbrock saw four fighters from each House walking toward the center, where Marshal Deywin and plenty of guards stood. Beside the marshal were several racks of weaponry. A pair of Magicai too.

Marshal Deywin spat some juice into the sands at his feet. "Today's fight works a bit different, which is why I'm here to explain it. We have a few prominent visitors up there." He pointed at the King's Stand. "Several dukes and duchesses from the capital and King Mikas himself, so best try your hardest." That wouldn't be an issue; it was life or death. The mere suggestion was ridiculous. "Duke Scayde has a horn. When that horn blows, you'll do your best to kill one another. When you hear that horn sound again, it means time's up. If you've survived, congratulations. You're each allowed a shield and one weapon of your choice. Make your selections."

There was only one variety of shield, a small circular one, so Edelbrock selected one that seemed wholesome and not dotted with cracks and dents. He took more time to consider the variety of weapons—broadswords, rapiers, cutlasses, maces, and battle-axes.

"Hurry, boy," Marshal Deywin said, spitting his skachi juice again. "Don't have all day."

Looking at the marshal, Edelbrock realized he was addressing him and offered the man a glare.

"Careful. Wouldn't want you to start the fight early." A couple of soldiers near the marshal laughed.

Edelbrock selected a rusted cutlass. *No, that's not rust.* It was not his favored weapon—he wanted to use the broadsword—but he knew if he performed well enough, then perhaps Scayde would assume it was. If Edelbrock was going to survive in the arena for any amount of time, he had to trick the man.

"All right, let's gather this shit up." Marshal Deywin directed several of his men to carry the weapon racks away. "Everyone back to their House entrances."

Edelbrock followed the other three back to the archway they'd entered through, though a Magicus had sealed it solid. He examined his allies. Bruise clasped a mace in hand, Lucky hefted a battle-axe, and Pock wielded a broadsword. To Edelbrock's right were the four fighters from the king's House, branded skin—twists of red and pink—obvious to all. Farther down in the same direction, Castede Varono's wearing their tall black boots he insisted they wore. To his left, Jaylena's fighters with their bronze bracelets on their wrists, then Lekhan Roelk's with faces of animals painted on their bodies. Across from where Edelbrock stood was the King's Stand. His eyes passed over the spot Gordane had landed. He pushed the thought from his mind. *I can mourn again later if I must.* He had to concentrate now.

The horn blasted, snapping him out of his inner turmoil.

Edelbrock's eyes flashed around, observing what every other participant was doing. Many of them charged at one another—Lucky and Bruise among the runners—while a few stood back, waiting, watching.

Pock, shifting his broadsword in his hand, looked at Edelbrock. "What now?"

"Follow my lead."

Pock nodded. It reminded him of being Major Edelbrock Brendis again.

A ring of fire burst up around the entire outer edge of the arena, forcing Edelbrock, Pock, and the other outliers inward. The inferno continued creeping up on them, pushing them closer to the center.

"They're going to make us all engage," Edelbrock said. He figured they would punish those who tried to escape unscathed. He didn't expect this though.

The heat on his back increased, so he took another dozen steps forward. "Everyone's . . . everywhere."

Men and women fought for their lives a few hundred feet in front of him. *Strange, they seem to have all separated. No group has stuck together. Nobody is fighting as a regiment or unit. Fools.* He swore two of the king's House were fighting one another.

"Every man for himself in the arena," Pock said.

"If you want to die, sure. Much more to be gained by working together."

A scream. Edelbrock turned his head and saw a barbaric-looking man charging at him, battle-axe raised above his head. Another man, this one wielding a rapier, followed.

"You take the one lagging. I'll handle the barbarian," Edelbrock said.

"Sure thing."

Edelbrock planted his feet, raised his shield, and tightened the grip on his cutlass.

Just to the side of Barbarian, a woman was impaled by a rapier. Then Barbarian was on Edelbrock. He deflected the first swing of the battle-axe with his sword, then blocked another with his shield.

Barbarian seethed, drool mixed with blood dripping from his mouth. Small bloody holes dotted the man's cheek, chin, and lips, and part of his lower lip was missing. The marks of a mace, Edelbrock guessed. *How is he still fighting?* A hit to the face like that would've downed most men.

The thought fled his mind as Edelbrock parried

another blow. He lashed out with his cutlass. The tip scratched Barbarian's stomach, leaving a trail of red.

Barbarian snarled, then laughed. "It'd hurt more to have your baby boy fall on my head!"

A rush of blood went to Edelbrock's head, fury coursed through his body, and his heart panged. *Scayde must've put him up to this.* He tried to keep calm. He tried to forget his son's death and the awful circumstances of it. But this man, Barbarian, had awoken a hidden beast. Edelbrock yearned for revenge. Fires of hatred distorted rational thought.

He screamed and lunged forward. Edelbrock's first swing took Barbarian by surprise. Barbarian recovered enough to deflect the fatal blow, but the blade still ripped a gash in his side. Edelbrock swung again and again and again. Each time, he let out a frustrated shout. His cutlass sank into Barbarian with every attack. The large man collapsed to a knee and Edelbrock kept shouting, stabbing Barbarian over and over. Splatters of blood sprayed the ground, and with each blow, Edelbrock felt it hitting his face and his arms.

It took a few moments for the blurry vision to return, for Edelbrock to come back to consciousness. To realize he'd been shouting, "For Gordane!" with each successive attack. Then he saw the gory mass at his feet. The mutilated body of Barbarian stabbed to pulp. He'd overdone it.

Remembering Pock, Edelbrock turned and looked around. Pock was kneeling by the body of the man with the rapier and puking, appearing unhurt.

Rushing over to him, Edelbrock asked, "You all right, Pock?"

"What?" He retched, but no more vomit came out.

Edelbrock grimaced, both at the sick and calling him

Pock. The ring of fire approached. "We need to move. Fire's almost here."

"I can't."

"Let's go."

The fire crept closer.

"I can't."

"You have to, or you're going to burn to death!" *How can somebody disregard their life like this?*

"I'm done. This isn't worth it."

"Pick your damn self up and *move*, soldier!"

Pock's eyes widened, and he stood, retrieving his broadsword from the body of the man he'd killed.

They stepped over a body or two and reached the center of Buzzard's Bowl.

About half the gladiators remained standing. Edelbrock sighed. He noticed the body of Bruise still clutching his mace. Nearby, Lucky stood, his left arm dangling uselessly at his side, a puncture in his thigh hindering his ability to walk without limping. *Not so lucky.* Or maybe he was. He wasn't dead.

A woman finished dispatching her quarry, then turned to Edelbrock. She engaged him with a flurry of slashes. Cutlass clashed against cutlass. He parried, counterattacked, got blocked, parried again. She was *fast*.

"Pock! Get over here." He walked in circles with the woman, and Pock came into view. He knelt, chest slumped forward. In front of him lay his weapon. Pock's head was elsewhere.

Mother Avani help these fools.

The woman jabbed at him. He swung his shield hard, blocking the blow, knocking her off balance. Darting forward, he sliced her shin open, then stepped back quickly.

She grunted.

Blades reverberated off one another several more times. Edelbrock pretended to lose his footing, and she lunged at him, aiming a slash across his chest. Edelbrock faked her out, sidestepping the attack. A clear opening appeared, and he brought the cutlass down onto her neck. She screamed. He hacked at her neck and head several more times. She collapsed to the sands, and he placed a foot on her, yanking the cutlass free.

Taking a deep breath, he looked around at the rest of the fighting. Most had injuries or lay dead.

Edelbrock glanced at the King's Stand. Jaylena was laughing, hand draped over Scayde's leg. *Eating fucking fruit.* The king was enraptured by the battle. A duke shoveled food into his mouth, somehow dropping more than he ate. A duchess examined her fingernails, looking bored. Another duke who looked old enough to be Edelbrock's great-great-great-grandfather appeared to be sunbathing. It made him sick. And what made him even sicker was, until that moment, he would've given anything to be up there with them.

"Ah, you must be Edelbrock," a man said. His scarred skin rippled with various brandings—one of King Mikas's House. He had long greasy brown hair and held a rapier in his hand, extended, tip pointing at Edelbrock. The man looked familiar.

"What gave it away?"

"The distant look. I was told to look for a man who might become distracted. Either up there"—his rapier pointed to the King's Stand—"or over there." The sword swiveled and pointed at the sand below the King's Stand.

"You found him."

The man bowed. "Name's Roberon, and I'm here to take your life. It's nothing personal. Duke Scayde offered me freedom if I completed this task."

Ah, he was at the Draft. Edelbrock snorted. "And you trust him?"

"No. But it's better than no chance of freedom at all."

"You got selected in the Draft before I did."

"Yeah."

"He hates you even more than he hates me."

Roberon's face fell. "I hadn't thought of it that way."

"Guess we don't have to fight."

"No, no, I suppose we don't."

The sound of metal on meat attracted Edelbrock's attention. A crazed woman was still hacking away at Pock's body. The man had still been kneeling, weapon out of reach. His death had been quick.

Snarling, Edelbrock tightened his grip on his cutlass.

The horn blared. The fight was over.

He'd made it. Edelbrock let his weapon fall to the sands and turned away from Roberon to examine the carnage. The deaths. All for some entertainment. Not even money because this was an exhibition match meant to entertain the king.

Then, pain. A sharp jab in his back, followed by a puncturing in his stomach. He looked down. The point of a bloodied rapier poked out him, twisting and turning.

Roberon's voice sounded in his ear. "Scayde Haklon sends his regards."

A hand pressed on Edelbrock's shoulder, and then the rapier retracted. He fell to the ground, groaning.

He blinked away tears and saw a glob of gore on the sands in front of his nose. When he blinked again, his vision cleared, and he realized it was skachi juice. Edelbrock rolled onto his back.

Roberon stood over him, the rapier pointed at his chest. "Sorry, fella, can't leave this job undone."

"Roberon," Marshal Deywin yelled. "Did you not hear the *fucking* horn? Put your sword down, boy!"

Roberon, face reddening, complied.

"Fucking great," Marshal Deywin said, standing over Edelbrock. "Duke Scayde's gonna love this." He spat some skachi juice. It landed in the sand, splattering Edelbrock's cheek. "Get a Healer over here," the marshal ordered someone. He knelt and laid a hand on Edelbrock's neck. "Hurry too. He's fading." He spat again. Shifted the glob in his mouth. "Fucking unbelievable."

Somebody ran over. "Marshal?"

"Yeah, illegal attack here. Full heal, please. Bill Roberon's House."

"Marshal, that's the king's House."

"Oh. Uh, don't do that." The marshal spit a third time. "Duke Scayde will take care of it. He'll be pissed, but rules are rules for a reason. Besides that, Duke Scayde won't want his favorite piss-toy to die at the hands of a cheat. Not as satisfactory. He wants Edelbrock humiliated, not sympathized. Close him up."

The Healer complied, placing his hand on Edelbrock. It felt as if his organs started tearing for a second time, and perhaps they had, as they went back to where they belonged. He winced, senses returning a moment later.

"All right, boy?" Marshal Deywin asked.

"I hope so."

"Then get back to your House. This isn't a charity event." He spit. This time, it hit Edelbrock square in the face.

Villic the Imbuer

1st Cycle of Spring, 232nd Reign of Garcovi
Remeria

The shamans said it was now spring, though how they could tell, Villic could never guess.

After their two-week rest, the Splintered Manes met up with Masters of the Lost, and the two clans rode together as one. If all went to plan, Glory Blades was now riding with the Seven Signs, while the Sharpclaws, Bride Warriors, and the Plagued Ones would be another unit. They'd reconvene as an army outside Andora—Remeria's capital and the location of King Alondo Sedoa, the man who could grant the Camel Clans their land.

"How does a group of camel riders intend on penetrating the walls of a capital?" Speaker asked. He had *zero* trust in the gods.

Killiak, lord of lords, will find a way in for us.

"The gods don't just obliterate stone walls, Villic. Even you know that."

Killiak, lord of lords, wouldn't deny them entry. This

was *for* his entire people. If the High God denied a request this important, it would put into question *everything* the Camel Clans knew. Even the shamans wouldn't be able to explain this. And the shamans know everything. Everyone knew that.

He will help.

"And if not?"

We'll find a way.

"The Imbuers can gain access if all else fails."

How?

"By using your powers. You keep focusing on gods when you need to be focusing on what you can do yourself."

Villic disagreed. The gods were much more powerful than Villic could ever be. But he didn't argue. Speaker was stuck in his ways.

It took almost a week to travel from the town they'd attacked—where Villic had momentarily lost Dunecrest —to where they were now: more open plains. Villic could see other Camel Clans.

Jedkah ordered them to ride hard. Seeing their allies appear on the horizon spurred them on. The leader of Masters of the Lost agreed, and the two clans pushed their camels to their limits, following the other clans toward the capital in the northeast.

When they arrived at Andora from the southwest, an immense wall of stone became larger and larger. Much bigger than anything they'd encountered in Remeria so far. He was in awe. The gods offered nothing this magnificent in Vessia. Vessia had tents, and if you were lucky, a small building. The Camel Clans never stayed in one place, so none of them had a building. One day, Villic wanted his own building. A river separated Andora from the eastern part of Remeria. He later learned a "drawn bridge" led into the city from that side.

A place to stay.

"*A home.*"

Speaker often thought he knew things. Villic couldn't trust *everything* Speaker said because Speaker doubted the gods. He wasn't sure about this "home" thing.

A horn sounded, and the clans halted. They'd come close enough to the city. Villic saw people from other clans already setting up camps. The plan was to surround the city, but he didn't think they had enough camels to do that. They either had enough to circle half the city or enough to circle the entire country. Villic wasn't sure which. He wasn't good with numbers.

Men with long weapons lined the stone walls. *Spears?*

"*Pikes. And they probably have crossbows up there too.*"

Villic didn't know what those were, but Speaker took the time to explain it. Villic only half listened to the explanation on Remerian weaponry. He'd become distracted by shouting. Men on the wall yelled at the Camel Clans. The shamans yelled back, but nobody seemed able to understand one another.

How do you know all of this information? Villic asked Speaker.

For once, Speaker didn't answer.

The gates opened, and a small group of men on fancy horses rode out. Villic could tell the horses were for show only. No way would they be able to match up to a battle-hardened Vessian camel. Some men were guards who had weapons ready. Others were odd-looking individuals with weird, flashy clothing, strange hats, and cloth hanging from their necks that flowed in the wind.

Babbling took place, and then, when it was apparent that neither could understand one another, the group retreated into the city.

There would be no negotiations, it seemed.

"I could translate."

Speaker knew their language, but Villic wasn't important enough for that sort of role. They needed a shaman to do that. Was any shaman an Imbuer? Villic didn't know. He didn't think so. Still, he wouldn't offer the role as translator. He could hardly talk with members of his own clan, let alone another country.

Villic was content following orders, offering nothing, and seeing how it all played out. If he didn't know something, the shamans, the gods, or Speaker would explain it. The Camel Clans set up camps surrounding the capital, ensuring nobody could enter or leave. Warriors on the eastern half must've forded the river. Upon closer inspection, Villic noticed the bend in the river moved much slower than elsewhere, and the water just touched the belly of the camels when the warriors rode them over.

The afternoon of the next day, Villic heard shouts and murmurs. Something had happened. Villic followed everyone's gazes and pointed fingers. A group of armed people looked down on them from atop a hill and not within the city's walls. Many of them wore colored cloaks. Unexpected reinforcements? Villic grasped his spear tightly, looked over at Dunecrest. The camel stared back at him. Villic could've sworn he smiled at him. So Villic smiled back. Then he turned back to the people on the hill.

Who are they?

"A snag in the plan," Speaker said.

It was true. Villic cursed Cocaro, god of luck.

SERADAL WINTLOCK

1st Cycle of Spring, 232nd Reign of Garcovi
The Silver Sea

The rocking of the ship, crashing of the waves, and the constant feeling of tipping over caused a perpetual fear of capsizing. Although Sera was afraid, she hardly had time to feel it. Most of the day, she vomited over the side of the ship, staring at frothy water. Sometimes a fin would poke up through the waves to greet her green face. She wondered if they were there to catch her expulsion, or if it was coincidence. Sera knew little about creatures of the ocean. Crewmates called out "shark" or "pod of dolphins," which meant nothing to her. And she didn't bother inquiring. On the rare occasion her stomach settled, she spent her time eating whatever she could keep down and resting.

Halfway through *Mistveil*'s journey, they encountered a nasty storm. The terrifying winds made the ship more mobile than ever, flinging Sera across her cabin for hours that night. Water splashed above decks, some of it seeping down the hallway and under the flimsy wooden door to her cabin that flapped open and closed. Shrieking, she ran out, only to collide into a drunken Royal, who assured her a bit of water was natural. He gave her his flask, and she drank herself to sleep. She woke to an ear-shattering crash.

Petrified the ship was sinking, she stumbled out of the cabin once more. There were no sounds of other people belowdecks, but there was a lot of commotion above her. She climbed the stairs, being thrown against the side of the ship several times. The wind whistled, men screamed and hollered, and *Mistveil* continued surging back and forth.

Hail the size of her fist pelted the sailors, the ship, and her. And, her terrors coming true, she saw one of the ship's tall masts missing, a few feet of wood sticking up in sharp jagged points. The ship lurched back and forth, throwing everyone like empty sacks. A swell of water swept a pair of men away, and Sera never heard them yell. They were just gone. Frantic and drunk, she bolted back down to her cabin. Like a young girl, she climbed under her covers and drifted off to sleep, dreaming of a happy family and better times.

When she awoke, she remembered the previous night, but the ship was still afloat, and sailors shouted back and forth. Her mind drifted to her mother, her brother. Dead. There would be no happy family. The better times were behind her. She found herself caught up in a mess. She was a knight in a war with no home. And she dealt with guilt for abandoning the country in favor of her father.

All that was crap. One might even say it was sh—a word she wouldn't use. Admittedly, that word crossed her mind once or twice as a passenger on the ship, and she knew it might come up again before they docked. Sailing was something she hoped to avoid in the future.

What made everything worse? Vithor Bane's presence. He'd boarded the same ship, and every time she crossed paths with him, he'd give her a dirty look. She was happy to see Vithor Bane had changed his trousers and no longer looked like the dirty store owner he'd been when she'd first met him. Now he walked around the ship in fine furs and leather boots. She wondered if he'd been disguising himself back in Vox. Or maybe he changed his identity based on where he was? She didn't know and avoided the man.

The traveling pace slowed with the loss of the biggest mast. The crew rowed giant oars to compensate. They were about three-quarters of the way through their journey, according to the Old Vulture. Since the beginning of the trip, they'd had little wind, and the ship had sailed at a snail's pace. After the storm, they'd been blown off course. A three-and-a-half-day trip had become a two-week experience.

S era was sick, puking, grabbing the balcony to steady herself. A hand patted her shoulder.

"Get it out," said a vaguely familiar voice.

She wretched, coughing up nothing because her stomach was empty. She straightened and saw Royal grimacing at the trail of chunks lining the hull.

"I've been there before. Here." He offered a waterskin.

"I need water. Not booze."

Royal laughed. "It is water. Drink it. It'll make you feel better."

She swallowed five or six mouthfuls of the cool

water. It eased the acrid burn in her throat.

"There you go. Straight down the gullet. Feel better?"

"A little. Thanks."

"Anytime." He stashed the waterskin away and leaned over the balcony. Upon seeing the trail of vomit again, he retracted his arms and clasped them behind his back, as if to protect himself from repeating his mistake. "We'll make landfall soon. The goal is to dock at Maceport, then head to Andora to inform King Alondo about the current state of Cyrok. Or lack thereof." Royal, despite his alcoholism, seemed rather capable. The captain was intelligent, and despite the drinking issue, remained competent when it mattered. At least so far.

"How long have you been a captain?" Sera asked.

"Long enough." Royal took out his personal flask and gave it a look. He put it back, ignoring temptation. She'd seen him do that at least a dozen times during their time sailing. "I work hard to avoid drinking on the job. Whenever people call me 'captain,' I feel obligated to be on my best behavior, which is why I encourage people not to call me that. 'Royal' works best." He smirked, like he'd been getting away with something for years. He probably had been.

"Why aren't you a knight?"

Royal took the flask back out and unscrewed the cap, taking a deep drink. *Oops.* "Not the calling for me." He was lying. She could tell that he realized she knew. He just winked. "I'm afraid I've got soldiers to order around, cyr."

She saluted him. "Dismissed, *Captain.*"

He grunted but lifted a corner of his cheek all the same.

They moored outside of Maceport and unloaded the pinnaces, minus one that disappeared during the storm. There wasn't enough room for everyone on the first trip—they determined it would take at least three—so Sera waited with her father and Renard. She couldn't be more excited to disembark and be away with the seasickness. She still felt guilty about abandoning her country, so she volunteered to allow other Cyroki citizens priority.

When it was her turn, she felt relieved and eager to return to solid land. Soldiers pulled the pinnace up to a dock, and Sera climbed out, marveling at the silent nature of the town. There were guards walking around but only a dozen citizens. Were all Remerian towns this quiet?

The spring air was warm, the sky blue, and the sun bright. Sera started to sweat beneath her armor. She, her father, and Renard traded in their heavier clothing for lighter garments and took a heavy loss in doing so, but they had no money to buy anything and couldn't wear their furs in Remeria. It was much too warm.

Though they were refugees, Royal and the Old Vulture had packed everything of value in Coldridge onto the ships when it became obvious the Cyroki defense was failing. With these finances, the Falcon Knights rented rooms at local Remerian taverns, citizens received a stipend to start new lives, and the rest were kept under safeguard for emergencies.

A day of recuperation later, whereupon they enjoyed a local dish called lamb root pie, the Old Vulture ordered the Falcon Knights together. Royal was in attendance as well. The remnants of the Cyroki military, except for the knights, had disbanded when they'd docked and reintegrated into civilian life. A few pledged their services to the Old Vulture and became Falcon Knights themselves, donning their armor. Royal, however, still wore his tattered captain's jacket, followed under the Old Vulture, but didn't join the order. Sera found this curious, but he wouldn't answer any questions about it.

The Old Vulture informed them they'd make for Andora the next day. He also gave them another small salary and told them to say any goodbyes that needed saying. They would have to leave civilians behind.

Leaving Jaidik would be difficult. After the trauma they'd gone through, Sera wasn't sure she could manage if she returned and her father had died, but he didn't want to join the Falcon Knights.

He tried to comfort her. "It'll be fine, Sera. *You'll* be fine. I'm going to stay here, petition the locals for aid. The last thing I want to do is take up a sword after everything that's happened. But we also need all the help we can get, and I'll do what I can. The Falcon Knights are doing a good thing here. The world needs to know what happened in Cyrok. I want to make sure Fezzel and Yudri didn't die in vain. I love you, Seradal." And he hugged her. It was both the best and worst hug she'd ever had. But he was safe now, and she knew she had to make up for past decisions.

After a tearful goodbye the next morning, Sera, with Renard in tow, left Maceport with the other Falcon Knights and Royal.

<hr>

T he march was uneventful. Green grass licked at their shins and stained their clothes—something many never experienced in Cyrok. Aside from the mountains, Cyrok was *flat*. Here, there were rolling hills, valleys, streams, and rivers. And the wildlife. The area was flush with insects, small mammals, and birds. Groups of deer or bison sometimes crossed their path. Flies smothered Sera's face, and they seemed to get worse when she sweat. Pests she learned were mosquitoes came out at night, buzzing in her ears and leaving sores that itched until they bled. Scents of various trees and flowers met her nose with a pleasantness she'd never experienced before, aside from food. They were guided by a river that would eventually pass by Andora.

They ate well, as they'd spent money on decent supplies. While walking, they'd eat smoked venison, hardtack, and fruit. At night, they'd cook up a filling meal of rice or potatoes, salted pork, and beans. Sometimes, some of the knights would venture off to hunt. After the hunters got lucky on a rainy day, Sera found she'd developed a strong liking for bison.

Renard proved to be a helpful asset, as he often was. He'd massage her calves in the morning, carry more than his fair share of supplies, and remained in an upbeat mood the entire time. She enjoyed his company and was grateful to travel with someone she considered family.

"So why don't you want to be a Falcon Knight, Renard?" She found this question often set the young man off on a tangent.

"*Because*. Haven't we gone over this enough, Cyr Seradal? I haven't had proper training."

"When do you want to begin?"

"We have more important things to do, cyr. Our priority is reaching the Remerian capital, petition King

Alondo for aid, and recruiting anybody who's willing to help the cause. The last thing we need to worry about is *me*."

She knew Renard was stalling out of concern. Although he put on a brave face, she recognized a change of heart in him ever since the attack on Vithor Bane's caravan where she'd almost died. He didn't have any desire to fight, and she wouldn't encourage him. She would, however, tease him.

On the afternoon of the third day of traveling, the Falcon Knights crested a hill and paused, muttering and whispering among one another. When Sera could see over it, she noticed the same thing they did.

Andora, a walled city, lay in the center of the valley. On the east side, the river they'd followed from Maceport almost cut up against the stone wall. Surrounding all sides were hundreds of people and camels. Sera saw erected tents, campfires, and sparring men and women. The city's gates closed, more men than ought to be patrolled the ramparts. Andora was under siege.

"Well, that's unexpected. The Old Vulture will know what to do, eh?" Renard said.

To Sera, however, it looked like they'd just stumbled into another war. And she knew they couldn't afford to fight in this one. She doubted the besiegers would allow them entry into the city uncontested. Resigned, she fell to her knees and looked to the skies, asking Mother Avani for help. Brushing her dark hair back over her shoulders, her mother—Yudri, with the same black hair —flashed through her mind, and tears started streaming down Sera's cheeks.

She didn't want to deal with more death.
But she'd have to.

DEMRI SLARN

1st Cycle of Spring, 232nd Reign of Garcovi
Pinecrest, Calrym

The temperatures rose as spring air wound its way through Pinecrest, and with the arrival of spring, the New Year began. In the past, that would've meant a great deal to Demri. The cold weather had often enhanced his arthritis, so his mood had always changed with the disappearance of winter. But now the pain vanished. So he enjoyed the cool breeze, though he still had plenty to worry about.

Demri assumed, as did Caius, that Stanton Brick no longer lived. If he was alive, Stanton would likely be a changed person. He didn't know any other individuals who knew the in-depth workings of the Velvet Mother's organization. So they'd quickened their pace and hoped Scayde Haklon kept his word. They rented a room at A Baker's Cousin, where you could pay to have sex with one of thirteen of the local baker's cousins. Demri didn't indulge.

Instead, the two of them ordered food and drink delivered to them. They paid extra to secure a room with a window facing the eastern gate. Caius kept watch, waiting for their mounts to arrive, pacing back and forth across the room. Demri supposed he could've done something other than sit in the chair. He now had access to easy mobility. After two decades of letting Caius take the lead on these types of things, though, he felt no need to change it.

They waited in the tavern for weeks, spending plenty of the money they'd brought with them, and Demri wondered how much they'd end up wasting if they kept having to wait.

"It's a shame," Caius said. "I feel sorry for not holding up our deal with the gladiators."

Demri waited for more.

Caius started filing again. Always filing. "It's a damn shame, Demri, to have to give everything back to that bastard after having it for such a small time. Fucking Scayde."

"Didn't have a choice. We'll figure out what to d-do with him after D-D-Doram d-dies."

"F-f-fucking Scayde." Demri's feelings on Scayde weren't as harsh, but he could recognize a prick when he met one.

"He arrived with far more backup than he needed."

"C-c-cautious."

"Too cautious. He owes me some money."

Probably.

"What if Stanton survived?"

Demri shrugged. He didn't think Stanton did survive, but it was always possible.

"He'd remain loyal," Caius said. "We could wait for Scayde to build the organization back up. He has the resources and power to do so. Then we can reclaim it for ourselves. Treat it right. Earn more money. Cement a block of power."

"One step at a t-time." Demri didn't think the plan would happen, but he needed to keep Caius focused on their true goal: finding Doram Quandis.

Caius grunted. "I'll kill the bastard."

Caius thinks he knows what it feels like to experience betrayal. That wasn't betrayal though. That was business. Betrayal is when an entire organization fucks you over and spreads lies to everyone in the hopes it gets you killed. Demri discarded the thoughts, refocusing on something else he wanted to know. "I have a question, C-C-Caius. Haven't had t-time to ask."

"Fire away."

"You're Tythus C-Corbéo."

Caius grunted again.

"Back when we k-k-killed those people in the tavern, you knew it was a C-Corbéo. Your brother."

"Yes. You were so adamant you'd finally found Doram Quandis, I didn't know you were wrong until we found Elizer in the closet. He was so scared, I thought I'd escape him noticing me, but he got there in the end. We hadn't seen each other in about twenty-five years, I believe. Not long before you and I met at Ashmount. Back then, we'd both been kids. I hardly recognized him myself. When I did, it didn't matter. The Corbéo family meant nothing to me as soon as I left. And he wouldn't have understood what we were doing. Would've turned us in if we let him go."

"We only have one another, C-Caius."

"That's all we need."

After four agonizing hours, full of boredom and anxiety that Scayde Haklon's men would show up and arrest them—though this was rather foolish as they'd been unhindered their entire stay—Caius waved Demri over to the window. Outside, two brown horses loaded up with gear were being led to the eastern gate. Four robed figures escorted the geldings.

"Seems unnecessary for that many people," Caius said. Demri agreed. "Go down anyway?"

"D-d-d-do we have a choice?"

"Yes. We don't have to go down there. But we both know you won't take that option."

It was true. With such a golden opportunity—free passage to Ashmount—no risk would deter Demri from confronting Doram Quandis.

"I'm a bit confused as to the necessity of the horses and gear, considering the dock's not too far of a walk away."

"Noble hospitality," Demri said.

The pair left their room at A Baker's Cousin, where they navigated around thirteen scantily clad women dancing, shaking, and patrolling the tavern floor, searching for horny and wealthy consumers. There was no shortage. Demri had to duck his head twice from a spare coin tossed at one of the women.

Exiting the tavern, they found themselves on a cobblestone street, one of many in Pinecrest. The gate was a few hundred steps away, and Demri watched the four figures looking around, searching. For him, he assumed.

"I'll have my knife ready." The statement was rather ridiculous. Caius always had the knife ready.

Walking was weird. He'd become so used to limping, he had to focus on *not* limping. Demri had become accustomed to the strange stagger and now felt as if something was off.

As he got closer, Demri reached inside, preparing to

consume Soul Glyphs if need be. The robed figures lined up between the horses and Demri and Caius.

One of them, a woman, spoke. "Magicus Demri? Caius?"

Caius sniffed, running the blade across his left thumb. Perhaps it was the situation or perhaps it was intentional, but the action was so aggressive that he sliced the length of his thumb, and many droplets of blood spattered the stone beneath him.

"Yes," Demri said. The robes bore an insignia—a small orange brand. A runic symbol, like two identical triangles facing away from one another and split by a line. Or was it one triangle that was split in half? Few would recognize the mark, but Demri knew it. Members of the Elkavich. He'd need to be careful here. *Does Scayde know who these people are?*

The woman lifted her hands, sleeves sliding back to her elbows. Soul Glyphs covered her arms, marking her as an Enforcer. He wished he could analyze the others, but that would require spectacles, and he didn't want to alert the Elkavich that he may have undiscovered powers.

"I believe those horses are for us," Caius said.

"Yes." The woman shifted. A slight movement, but one Demri caught. One he was sure Caius would notice as well. She'd moved her weight from one leg to another, while a simultaneous flick of one finger seemed to signal those behind her.

Demri thought there was something familiar about the woman. Her voice? The way she stood? That scent? It was the scent. Lavender. But plenty of people bathed with lavender. He was unsure what to do. He let go of the Soul Glyph.

"I see your cogs turning," she said. "I know what you're thinking, but we are here to help." Her hands reached up to her hood. "It's time we have a discussion, Demri." She pulled the hood down. A much older, but unmistakable, Myri Celioh stood before him. She'd joined the Elkavich. Wrinkles lined her face, and her blond hair was a much duller, whiter tone. "Yes, it's me. Come. Let's talk. We can't stay out in the open. You're supposed to be dead. And we're"—she pointed to the insignia—"not supposed to be here either."

Demri swallowed. Nothing in the world made him nervous. Nothing aside from her. She'd always been beautiful. Now, she'd spent enough of her life that she appeared to be a decade older than Demri, who looked to be in his fifties himself. But Mother Avani was she still delightful. He looked over at Caius, who had that *look* on his face. He was about to stab the woman. "No, C-C-Caius. She's a f-friend."

Caius glared at Demri. The man didn't like the idea of a mysterious group bringing them to a mysterious location. Demri didn't blame him. During normal circumstances anyway.

Caius gave him another look, and Demri shook his head. No. They wouldn't be attacking these people.

"Really, Demri?" Caius said. "You're thinking with your pecker? I didn't know that was possible for you."

Demri ignored the jest. Perhaps it was a trap. Demri didn't care if it was. If it was a trap, they'd sort it out. The risk was worth it to catch up with an old friend. His heart pounded in his chest. He knew he shouldn't have these types of feelings for her. There'd been nothing between them. In fact, she'd been downright awful to Demri. Until Doram Quandis tried to murder him. She had tried to stop that.

Myri raised an eyebrow, waiting for Demri. He nodded, and she smiled. His heart offered another palpitation.

Optimistic, he followed her. Demri wasn't sure where the road they traveled would lead, but he found himself not caring as his heart gave another thump. His quest for vengeance became forgotten in that moment.

Demri, too, smiled.

KELDEN STOOLE

1st Cycle of Spring, 232nd Reign of Garcovi
Ashmount, Qothe

At the arrival of warmer weather and a sunnier spring sun, the disappearance of Magicus Doram Quandis was the topic on everyone's mind for weeks after the events that led to his departure. Students theorized he was going to return and contest the position of Archmagicus. Others believed he'd gone overseas to establish his own school. A select few even voiced their opinion that Doram was out for revenge and would find some way to disrupt their learning until the students conducting the forbidden research were expelled or harvested. That information became well-known, so Kelden had no shortage of other Magicai asking him a constant barrage of questions.

It seemed there was a legitimate reason for concern. The Magicai marched around in paranoid groups, whispering to one another. Others seemed steadfast in maintaining the illusion nothing was wrong. Either way, the

Magicai seemed more awkward and less powerful to Kelden.

Kelden spent much of his time sitting in the grounds outside the school. Being alone suited him, and not too many students enjoyed time outside in the heat. He often watched Ashmount expel bits of lava while black plumes of smoke rose from the crater. Sometimes he could even look up at the barrier and watch as the lava splashed above him, cascading down the side and draining into the moat. He recalled the terrifying trek he'd endured climbing the volcano and the many who lost their lives doing so. Kelden remembered Ko-Hkar, Sniffles, and Sungoa.

After the exchange that took place between the Archmagicus and Doram Quandis, Kelden and Tikmo didn't want to get into trouble for doing anything wrong so soon after being caught. They talked about Demri Slarn, the criminal Doram had mentioned. Which led to Kelden researching about him. Kelden pored through the archives, attempting to locate criminals, their offenses, and what happened to them. There were many, more than he expected. Magicai who committed murder, theft, reneged on their contracts, and more. Magicai who killed the people who'd hired them—a big problem for Ashmount whenever this happened.

Then he found Demri's entry. Aside from investigating a way of discovering other powers not assigned by an Examiner, this Magicus engaged in a battle *on Ashmount's grounds*. How he ever escaped alive was a mystery to Kelden. Demri had to be DS, the initials Kelden found on the note inside of Enebrial Hubbart's book. The current status of the man read, "unknown, but alive." His threat level was the highest it could be. Mass murder was cited as the reason. In fact, the official report suggested any bounty hunters should bring the man in *dead* because of how dangerous and ruthless he was and should only approach Demri in overwhelming numbers. It mentioned a sidekick who hung around with Demri, a man who carried several knives but wasn't a Magicus, and to not underestimate him.

Despite enjoying his time alone, Kelden ended up spending more time in Tikmo's presence. Although Kelden hadn't yet finished his classes, he could now use Soulpens outside of Magicus Kalixa's tutorage.

The duo would often sit outside by a tree, as Kelden drew on Tikmo's skin with a Soulpen forged from the feather of a vulture. It was an interesting experience to place the Soulpen on somebody's skin and see their actual life spread itself like ink wherever he drew. He created designs and patterns. Animals. Words. Phrases. He drew symbols. Tikmo wasn't particular about whatever Kelden drew, so Kelden did whatever he felt. He'd even drawn the five symbols of the Magicai: a vial, a pair of spectacles, a sword, an angel, and a quill. By doing one or two or, sometimes if he was feeling ambitious, three Soul Glyphs a day, it wasn't long before Tikmo had access to all of his potential power. It also meant his body was covered head to toe in Soul Glyphs —a Well most Enforcers didn't have access to. Kelden figured it might end up helping him if a friendly Enforcer had access to all his power.

They'd discussed confronting the head Examiner, to see if they could force her to unlock other schools of power. They decided against this. After their recent reprimand, it'd just cause further trouble.

Today, for once, Kelden was outside at the tree alone. Blissful. Happy. The beginnings of spring felt like the start of a new life. *This is the year I discover the hidden power I know I have.*

The breeze ruffled his hair, and he lifted the grubstick back to his mouth. He took another bite, chewing and savoring his lunch. Grubsticks were a Qothan delicacy, another reason he was outside. Most people considered them vile, both in taste and in appearance. Apparently consuming an assortment of fried bugs on a skewer wasn't something that appealed to everyone. He enjoyed the crispness, and it was nice to enjoy something while his mind raced around differing possibilities regarding . . . well, everything.

Could he learn a different type of power? Was it possible to locate this Demri Slarn and ask him what he knew? Was Demri even alive any longer? Why were the Magicai so averse to investigating this anyway? It seemed like this would create even more powerful Magicai. Wouldn't that only benefit them? A more skillful Magicus could do more, which should translate to being more expensive to hire. *Unless that would elevate them to being unaffordable.* Even so, it seemed strange the Magicai didn't want to grow more powerful.

He watched the Enforcers outside of the protective shield practicing their abilities. Tikmo had explained to Kelden sometimes they'd be allocated a vial and taken outside to sling cones of fire and shards of ice, figuring out the different things they could create. They'd practice conjuring barriers. It was important for the Enforcers to learn the limits of their powers. They could only create physical forces, and nothing remained longer than an Enforcer used his power to keep it "alive." There were a few exceptions to this rule, such as voice enhancers. And larger, more powerful barriers, such as the one protecting the school. These devices were powered by substance Collectors sold. Kelden didn't know how much of the stuff it would take to power the shields or a voice enhancer, but he wondered how they supplied all of it. *By luring people like me to take part in the Trials.*

A loud rumbling on his left broke his thoughts. A Magicus was flipping the bridge closest to him. When it landed with a small crash, three hooded figures strode across and entered the protective bubble.

He watched them curiously. Kelden couldn't recall a time when random strangers arrived at Ashmount unannounced. Intrigued, he stood and went to investigate.

As he neared, he noticed something was off. The Magicus that had permitted their entrance stumbled, gripping their abdomen. Kelden thought he saw the sun reflect off something metallic. A flash, and one of the hooded figures raised a bloodied knife over their head, then plunged it into the Magicus. They screamed, falling to the grass. The hooded trio directed their gaze in Kelden's direction. He stumbled backward, tripping over himself. Landing on the cobblestone pathway, he saw the figures walking toward him. Slowly. Deliberately. The practicing Enforcers were too far away; they practiced on the other side of the university. He could shout to them, but they wouldn't be able to hear him. It was far away, and the shield provided a sound barrier.

Kelden worried about what the strangers would do next.

The three strangers walked slowly, methodically, boots tapping on the cobblestone path. Kelden glanced around. Nobody else was near. The grubstick hung at his side, forgotten in his left hand.

He wanted to move, but his legs were paralyzed. *Who could murder somebody in cold blood in such an open area? Why hasn't anyone sounded the alarm? Why haven't I sounded the alarm?*

They walked closer.

"H-hello?" Kelden's voice croaked. He wasn't sure anybody could've heard him if he wanted them to.

He saw their faces—two women, one man. The man held an almost concealed bloody knife at his side, but half an inch poked out of his robes, dripping blood.

When Kelden took a step backward, the trio increased their pace. It seemed they weren't even looking at him but staring past him. Toward Ashmount, the school. Toward the Mother Avani statue in the courtyard.

"Can I help you?" Kelden asked. They were mere feet away. None responded.

He noticed a strange insignia on their robes. An orange triangle split in half and tipped on its side, point facing eastward.

The man lunged forward, knife sinking into Kelden. Once, twice. Surprised, he gasped. *What did I do?*

The pain of the blade ripping through Kelden's stomach shocked him. The man retracted and pushed Kelden backward. He screamed and collapsed. Blood seeped through his fingers. Bleary-eyed, he watched the three people continue the path toward Ashmount, paying him no heed. He grimaced and moaned. He needed help and fast.

Kelden struggled to his knees, legs shaking. It felt like the wound tore his abdomen as he stood, so he crouched, holding his stomach with both hands, preventing his insides from spilling out. He staggered, falling again. The pain was too great.

He took a moment to take a deep breath. The hot spring air filtered through his lungs. A familiar taste of sulfur licked at his tongue. He swallowed and grimaced.

Kelden examined the gashes. They were both deep. He saw more than blood falling through the two punctures. He kept his right hand tight against the holes, struggling to stand once more. Kelden's body trembled.

He fell back on his butt and laid on his back. Blackness crossed his vision. He tried shouting for help. His voice caught in his throat, so he swallowed and shouted again. Nobody heard his weakened voice.

The three robed people circled the statue of Mother Avani. He wondered, for a moment, what they were going to do. Then the pain returned, and he didn't care. He shouted for a third time and saw that *finally* somebody heard him. They walked in his direction, then upon seeing his condition, started running. It was Tikmo.

Relieved, he let his head hit the ground. The sun burned in the sky, illuminating the protective barrier that shielded Ashmount from Ashmount. A bright blue sky was inviting as a cluster of birds flew past. A plume of dark black smog trailed up, coming from the mouth of the volcano.

He coughed, and the wound aggravated, pulsed. Kelden took another look at the people who'd attacked him. He raised a finger and pointed at them, but Tikmo kept running toward him and didn't bother with that. They stood in a triangle, holding hands. The hood of one of them fell off their head, revealing a young woman. Her hair bristled in the breeze.

The three robed figures ignited. Time slowed to a crawl.

A flash of blinding light, and the trio incinerated. The explosion grew. The statue crumbled. Ashmount's building disappeared in a cascading explosion, tossing mortar and stone everywhere. Tikmo continued running and opened his mouth to scream as he realized what was happening. He consumed his Well, forming a protective barrier around him. For a moment, the roaring flames avoided him. The barrier weakened, Tikmo's Well depleting at an incredible rate to protect himself. Then the growing ball of destruction engulfed Tikmo, and he was no more.

The inferno was still hungry, and Kelden sniffed. Becoming an Enforcer wasn't his destiny after all. He'd misunderstood. *I'm sorry, fa—*

His thoughts went unfinished. The fire consumed Kelden. He dissipated in the fiery ball before he felt anything and became a memory.

EDELBROCK BRENDIS

1st Cycle of Spring, 232nd Reign of Garcovi
Lochwall, Calrym

Scayde Haklon taunted Edelbrock often, so angry was he over having to pay for his healing. He'd suggested breaking one of Edelbrock's ankles before his first real battle, ensuring he'd die a humiliating death. He'd toyed with binding Edelbrock up, so Scayde could pluck his body apart, one slow pinch at a time, using whatever tool he desired in the moment, even suggesting Jaylena would take part by commanding Scayde which body part to attack next. Scayde's most penetrating insult, or threat, was to exhume the body of his son, Gordane, and allow a competitor to dress up in a helmet made of his bones. Then he'd changed it to a shield, so that "Gordane could actually be useful."

Edelbrock's depression escalated fast. In a surprise twist of fate, he was never tortured physically. He'd expected Scayde to command people to beat him bloody, break a bone or two, stab him somewhere that wasn't lethal. But the recent "Duke of Lochwall," as Scayde was fond of mentioning, had other business to attend to and never visited for longer than a few minutes.

Now that spring had arrived, another gladiator season would begin before midcycle. After his first experience in Buzzard's Bowl, Edelbrock wasn't too keen to return. He'd do whatever it took to survive, and his determination to escape and enact revenge was stronger than ever.

Edelbrock trained every day. In the morning, he'd exercise. He ran laps around the training pit for an hour. He'd stretch and practice different lunges and movements. During the afternoon, he'd spar with whoever offered, often Nauc. If nobody wanted to, he'd attack the wooden training posts. He often used weapons he was least comfortable with. Edelbrock knew Scayde would have people reporting his weaknesses. It's what he would've done in Scayde's position. So he tried eliminating all of them.

Both Savakkis and Chellie recovered from their wounds, though it was weird watching a single-breasted woman walking around shirtless, one tit bobbing around, tantalizing some of the men. She'd started cracking jokes about it. Lucky's arm healed fast, and though he couldn't take as much pressure with it, his name rang true since he could still support a shield with it.

Edelbrock, though not recovered from the trauma of his wife's betrayal or his son's death, was feeling like his old self. The self before he'd ever met Jaylena. The military captain, renowned and respected. The preseason fight had brought him back.

He noticed the muscular figure of Savakkis, a perfect sculpture aside from the nicks, bruises, and scars. The man was a legend. He knew how to work every weapon, knew how to exploit every enemy. Edelbrock couldn't believe how fast he'd recovered from the severe wounds he'd received. But he was fine now. *How many more seasons does he have in him?*

Watching Savakkis, Edelbrock remembered Trigg Gelbrandy and how Edelbrock had cheated on his wife with him. For power. A chance at a better life. And while this was true—he would've done *anything* to become rich back then—he also admitted that it was more than that. It was because he'd been unhappy with his wife. This didn't prevent the feelings of betrayal he felt every time he thought of her, but it was nice to have that realization, that closure. He'd never loved his wife the way he'd imagined he would. He'd always loved the idea of having a family and a good relationship. You couldn't force that with someone, he now knew. *Perhaps marrying for power or money is not the right move.* He regretted his life decisions. If he hadn't been so greedy, perhaps he wouldn't be here now. *I definitely wouldn't be here now.*

The day before Buzzard's Bowl opened back up for spectators, forcing the gladiators to fight once more, Tanibris showed up. He delivered the schedule for the first days of the fight, posting them on every wall in the hypogeum.

The first fight was going to be a large skirmish. All the new recruits battling it out. The last House with standing men or women wins. Edelbrock knew losing a fight didn't mean you died. Plenty of people returned with injuries. But he knew that if he failed, if he returned with terrible injuries, Scayde Haklon would be right there. Ready. And Edelbrock didn't want that. So he vowed to either finish himself off if the situation arose or just not lose a battle. He hoped for the latter.

On opening morning, Edelbrock walked with Nauc, Lucky, and the other first-season gladiators down the steps into the pit. The grated windows, which allowed them to view outside, had something covering them. His gaze passed over Lucky again, who gave Edelbrock his customary wink.

In the preparation room, a solid gate instead of hazy fog covered the archway to the arena. An assortment of standard gear lay about the room, so they each took their own set. Leather armor, a shield, a sword. And, oddly, a rope with a grappling hook at the end.

Edelbrock paced. He envisioned himself standing in the sands of the arena, the crowd leering at him, cheering for his execution. Scayde Haklon urging them on.

Edelbrock's thoughts stopped at an odd sound. He swore he heard crashing waves. He cocked his head but only heard the roar of a crowd. It was beginning.

The gate rose. Edelbrock's jaw dropped.

A dock led out of the pit and into a raging pool of water. It was like an ocean. Edelbrock and the others walked onto the wooden boards, creaking as they floated and rode the waves. The cries of the crowd. He heard some spectators yelling, "Die, die, die!"

A ship was moored at the end of the dock. A group of people stood on the deck already. One of Scayde's guards gestured them forward.

Edelbrock walked with the others. When they were closer, he saw it was Marshal Deywin.

The marshal spat some skachi juice into the water. "Here's the deal." He spat again. Some juice dribbled down his chin, which he swiped away with his fist. "You're going to be on that ship"—he pointed to the behemoth behind him as if they couldn't see it—"and join forces with King Mikas's House. There's another ship with gladiators from the other three Houses. Kill them. If you're wounded and find yourself able to retreat to this dock, the crowd *may* grant your life. If you please them. Best of luck. Oh, and don't fall in the water. It's not safe." Marshal Deywin passed them, reentering the pit they'd come from. The gate closed behind the marshal, sealing them in Buzzard's Bowl.

What Edelbrock thought would be a sand-filled, simple fight was more complicated. He remembered the other gladiators emphasizing the arena was unpredictable. He never realized how true that would be. The rough water swirled around the arena like a drain, splashing him and his comrades with water. Some landed on his tongue. It wasn't salt water, but fresh water. He wondered if the Magicai could conjure salt water, or perhaps they could only summon regular water.

Looking up at the roaring crowd, he spotted several Magicai on raised platforms that hadn't been there before. They stood behind and above the crowds, looking down at the ships and the water, their hands moving. *The water masters.* He hated them. He hated the crowd. He hated everyone out there. One day, he'd have his revenge.

Gripping his shield in one hand, the sword in the other, grappling hook slung over his shoulder, he climbed the rope ladder to board the ship. If this indicated what the battles were going to be like, he didn't look forward to the rest of them.

EPILOGUE
ALONDO SEDOA

1st Cycle of Spring, 232nd Reign of Garcovi
Andora, Remeria

The stone walls of Andora were sturdy under his booted feet. King Alondo Sedoa paced across the ramparts, analyzing the forces camped outside the walls. He was having a tough time preventing the consistent twitch of his upper lip, the annoyance of the current situation. His anger at the Vessians. However, a dignified king kept their temper. Most of the time.

"How many of those camel bastards are out there?" Alondo grunted as he awaited the answer. The grunt turned into a frustrated growl. He knew nearby soldiers were casting odd looks in his direction. He was beyond caring. Public image be damned. It seemed like *all* the Camel Clans showed up. Invading *his* country. Killing *his* people. This was something his great-grandfather, Mauriccin Sedoa, would have *never* allowed. Or so the stories told. Alondo had never met the man, but he believed him to be the greatest ruler ever recorded. The textbooks taught that anyway, and Alondo believed in history.

"Honestly, Your Majesty." The king's council, Atticus Crenshaw, seemed reluctant to answer.

"Yes, Atticus, *honestly* damn it. Spit it out!"

Atticus blinked several times. The man never became affected by any of the king's mood swings. "*All* of them, Your Majesty."

"What do you mean *all of them?*"

"All the Camel Clans banded together. *All* of them are here."

"That's *not* possible!" Alondo knew the Camel Clans had always been fractured. Until now, Vessia was never a threat. A majority of the nation was the Camel Clans. Everyone else living in that dry wasteland was too busy avoiding or pleasing various Camel Clans to bother Remeria or Calrym.

"On the contrary, counting them shall prove it. Would you like me to do it for you aloud?" The king's council pointed into the fields below them. "One," he said.

Alondo's lip twitched again. He wanted to yell at Atticus. Fume until Alondo's spittle ran down the council's face. But Atticus was just giving Alondo a helpful reminder that he was being unreasonable. So he calmed himself. It was difficult, but he wasn't King Mikas Garcovi. He could control himself. Alondo didn't need all the jewelry, the crown, or people bowing at his feet, begging to suck him off. Begging for his approval. He needed real information, honest people. People who told it like it was. Atticus was that man.

The king's council continued. "With proper rationing of the current store of food and hoping that disease doesn't immediately worm its way through the city, I believe we can hold out for several cycles. These are simple men, Your Majesty. They will become impatient and flee."

"What kind of king would I be were I to seal the city, do nothing, and wait for them to run away, damn it? The people will *hate* me!"

"You'll be alive. As will your people. Or you could be the strong, foolish type. Open the gates and send our men out there to die. We don't have the forces here for that. You've sent them all to the western border to—"

"I *know* what I've done, Atticus. Calrym is untrustworthy. I wanted to monitor them!" Realization dawned on Alondo. He screamed, "You were the one who advised this measure of defense in the first place!" He clamped his mouth shut, closed his eyes in shame. He was edging ever more into the territory of raving King Mikas Garcovi.

Atticus Crenshaw bowed. "I will be busy recording our supplies if you need me, Your Majesty." And infuriating Alondo further, Atticus left.

Alondo clenched his fists. He wanted to kick the wall, but he'd break his foot. He wanted to jump the stone wall and waltz over to the Camel Clan leaders, punching them in the jaw, but he wouldn't survive the fall. He wanted to thrash around screaming, causing absolute mayhem with his flailing limbs, but if he did that, he'd cause his people to panic. So he composed himself.

And when King Alondo Sedoa looked up, he saw hope. A sliver of light beckoning the lost spelunker. He'd gone caving once. Never again.

There, atop the hill stood a group of people. An army? It was the Cyroki Falcon Knights. The colors of their capes shimmered in the wind.

Hope.

The king laughed, his anger gone.

ACKNOWLEDGMENTS

All writers have a roster of people to thank, and I am no exception.

First off, I'd be remiss if I didn't offer my sincerest gratitude to my editor, Richelle Braswell. She's done a spectacular job and been a great help. I know *The Trials of Ashmount* has improved monumentally because of her advice and wisdom. Thanks for everything you helped me with. You are outstanding.

To my formatter, Amber Helt, who's been wonderful. Thank you for your patience and understanding.

Let's not forget Dusan Markovic, the brilliant artist behind the amazing cover art. Aside from being breathtakingly talented, he's also just a cool guy. Thank you for bringing my imagination to life!

I also want to mention Dawn Barnhart, a lovely person who leads the Facebook group *Fantasy Writers Forever!*—a fantastic place to network with other writers. The advice I found in here pushed me in the direction I needed to go to become a better writer.

And last, but maybe most important, the three people who gave their time to read the earliest stages of the novel. You gave a self-conscious writer a chance and then became three great friends. I appreciate it more than you know.

Jenni Lennse, who, upon reading half the novel, informed me I'd just made a new fan (my first ever, to be exact). You will always be my favorite Swede.

Leslie C. Cunningham, an all-around bloody nice bloke (did I say that right?), who has the strangest taste in favorite characters I've ever seen. Nobody else liked him, Leslie, you goon.

And Kayla Armstrong, a special friend, who enjoyed the book more than anyone and who continually inquires about further entries (they're coming, I promise). I apologize for making you listen to my incessant whining and thank you for tolerating it.

To all my readers, I thank you and will always love the support. You are fulfilling my dream. Please consider leaving a review! It'd be much appreciated and goes a long way.

About the Author

You've stumbled upon somebody who takes nothing seriously, not even author bios. It'd be a good guess to say John Palladino was born in 1988, lives in Avoca, New York, has a bachelor's degree in business management, and enjoys hibernating at home while writing. He might also lie and say he enjoys pets, long walks on the beach, and his hobbies include happiness and scuba diving. You'd see right through those lies, however, and notice he prefers the simpler things in life—reading, video games, and making ill-timed jokes. John also dislikes taking care of anything that excretes substances.

facebook.com/AGrimBastardAuthor

twitter.com/agrimbastard

amazon.com/author/agrimbastard

goodreads.com/agrimbastard